The

Silent

Prophet

By

Susan Davis Sandberg

SusanDavisSandberg@gmail.com

ISBN-13 (Print): 978-1-939577-10-8
ISBN-13 (Kindle): 978-1-939577-11-5
ISBN-13 (ePub): 978-1-939577-12-2

Cover design by John Sandberg
Cover image by Vladimir Gjorgiev, Shutterstock.com

To

*My gracious daughter-in-law Mayumi
who has been a singular blessing to
us all*

CHAPTER 1

Half the RV's had left their assigned parking spaces at the dog show when Stanley Praetzel walked around his large RV checking to make sure nothing had been carelessly tossed aside. Aleta was apt to do that.

When he re-entered the RV, the collection of big group rosettes reminded him that they'd had a good weekend.

Tank, their new Irish Wolfhound, a class dog, had placed twice in the group competition. Auggie their apricot fawn Pug, had placed in Group four times. Scooby, their chocolate Labrador Retriever puppy had managed to earn two more points toward his championship.

As Stanley gazed at the awards Aleta said softly, "I told you your bandaged ear wouldn't be noticed by the judges."

"They all asked me about it." Stanley commented.

"Are Grams and Claude still here?"

"Yes, but not many others." Stanley reported. "I don't want to be the last to leave."

"Are you worrying about my wearing the necklace the whole weekend?"

"It was an open invitation to be robbed."

"Nonsense. No one thought it was real."

"You told everyone it was," Stanley pointed out. "Can we go?"

"Well, I'm changed," Aleta said. "We can leave as soon as you change."

"I can drive home in these pants," Stanley declared.

"No, you can't. They aren't suitable for your next activity."

"What next activity? What are you talking about?"

"What did I say?" Aleta asked, perturbed.

"Nothing," Stanley said. "I'll change."

"Jeans," Aleta said.

"Come on, Tank. Let's change," Stanley said. "I'll introduce you to your new crate, otherwise known as our bedroom."

The two men on the outskirts of the RV area, who were seen tinkering with a seemingly disabled car, had watched Stanley disappear inside his RV. The smaller of the two men, Lennie Archer, slammed down the hood of the car. His larger companion climbed in the front seat and turned on the ignition.

They waited for the RV to move. After five minutes, the driver killed the engine.

"What's taking them so long?" Butch asked.

"How should I know," Lennie shot back.

"We gonna do the hood thing again?" Butch asked.

"Shut up! I'm cogitating," Lennie snapped.

"Don't upchuck in the car. We won't never get the stink out."

"Cogitating, Dummy! That means I'm thinking."

"Why didn't you say that then," Butch grumbled.

"Just start the car!"

Inside the Praetzel RV, which was still parked in the lot, Tank woofed and began pacing. A big rangy dog, his pacing included jumping on the bed in order to look through the slats covering the long rectangular back window of the RV.

"Relax Tank," Stanley said. "People are leaving. It's nothing to make noise about."

"I'll take a peak," Aleta said, rising.

She sucked in her stomach and snapped the waistband to her shorts closed.

"There! I did it! I can't breathe, but…"

"Neither can Martha," Stanley quipped.

Auggie began to fuss in his crate. He rarely made a peep once the crate door was closed. Now he was yapping frantically.

"Stanley, I think we have visitors," Aleta said. "Close the door and get dressed."

Stanley felt the RV shake slightly as a foot was placed on the lower step. He heard the door open and a male voice mutter something. He didn't recognize the voice, but the RV shook again as another person entered.

Stanley pulled up his jeans and reached under the mattress for his gun and deputy's badge. He checked the load and clicked it shut, releasing the safety.

He heard Aleta say, "He's in the bedroom."

He didn't know if she was referring to him or the dog.

The man grumbled something and Aleta called, "Stanley, stay there! These men are masked so I can't identify them. They want the necklace. That's all."

"Give it to them, Aleta," Stanley called out. "Remember Martha. She's counting on you."

There was a murmur of voices from the other room.

"They want your wallet." Aleta said.

"No they don't," Stanley said. "They want my money clip. It's in the drawer on the far right."

He heard two voices talking in low tones.

Stanley quickly removed his driver's license and two of his credit cards from his wallet. The others were bankcards that required pin numbers. They had limits on them. He didn't remove the money.

"They have the clip," Aleta said. "They want you to hand out your wallet."

Stanley immediately opened the door a crack and threw out his wallet. He closed the door quickly. Any move that the men considered threatening might result in Aleta being hurt.

"Get it, Lennie," he heard a deep voice say.

"Shut up, Dummy!" shouted an angry voice.

Stanley held his breath.

Then he heard Aleta cry out, "No, don't hit my head. Don't! Please. Just go."

"Leave her alone and go!" Stanley shouted. "I've got a gun!"

"He's got a gun, Lennie," came the panicky voice of his partner. "Let's go."

"Go start the car. She's coming with us," Lennie decided.

"Now you're the dumb one," Butch argued. "We got what we want. Let's go!"

From the other side of the bedroom door, Stanley roared, "If you take her, I come out shooting."

"Come on," Butch begged. "Let's go!"

"We won't get very far. He's got a gun," Lennie protested.

"Trade you," Stanley shouted. "Gun for my wife in here with me."

"Do it!" Butch cried. "For God's sake, do it!"

"No tricks!" Lennie charged. "Gun first."

"Wife first. Then you can block the door so we can't follow."

"Do it!" Butch yelled. "Don't coagulate or whatever it is you do. The guy's giving you an out. Don't you be the dummy."

Aleta opened the door. Stanley yanked her inside, threw out his gun and slammed the door shut. He pushed her down on the floor and lay down on top of her. He heard her whimpering softly.

He kissed her on the back of the head and gently whispered for her to hush.

Tank stood on the bed and barked as he heard the men moving something big in front of the door.

Aleta lay still, scarcely breathing. Stanley stayed on top of her after two pair of feet tromped down the stairs. Tank barked as the men ran alongside the RV to a car in the back. He shoved the blinds up with his nose.

"Tank, down!" Stanley yelled.

The big dog dropped.

A bullet broke the glass in the rear window and buried itself in the inside wall opposite the window.

The two heard a car's engine being revved up. Tires squealed as the car spun around and raced away.

Stanley rose slowly.

"Did I crush you?"

Aleta rolled over and taking his good ear pulled him toward her and kissed him soundly.

"Don't let Tank cut his feet on the glass," she said.

A bang on the RV door was followed by a shout and the tramp of two more pair of feet.

"Are you okay?" Claude's big voice boomed over the barking dogs, "Here let me get this crate out of the way."

"We have to get Tank out of the bedroom," Aleta shouted. "There's glass all over the bed."

"Do I hear sirens?" Stanley yelled.

"Harriet called the police," Claude thundered over Auggie's yapping and Scooby's barking. With the door opened part way, Aleta and Stanley squeezed out followed by Tank.

"Your pendant!" Harriet exclaimed. "Is that what they came for?"

Aleta nodded.

The sirens were closer. Claude and Stanley went out to meet them.

"I pretty much invited this I guess," Aleta fretted to her grandmother. "I wasn't too discreet."

"It probably wasn't a dog show person," Harriet said. "My guess is some locals thought they could rob the RV's while the owners were showing and were in for a shock when the dogs began barking whenever they walked near the row of RV's."

"So it's over?" Aleta asked.

"It's over." Her grandmother assured her.

"Grams, I asked Stanley to change clothes. Why did I do that?"

"Don't you know?"

"No."

CHAPTER 2

When they were finally released to go, Stanley asked Aleta one more time if she wanted to ride with her grandmother.

"And leave you with both pieces of Paige's chocolate cake? Never!"

"She does make great cakes," Stanley observed.

"You want to trade me in already?"

"I don't think Hawk will let go."

"And you would?"

Stanley smiled.

Aleta took the bait.

"You'd trade me in for a piece of cake?"

Stanley shook his head slowly. "Not just a cake. I'd want the whole package."

"Paige likes that tall drink of water she's got," Aleta shot back. "You're too ... too ... too short."

"Short?" Stanley gasped. "I'm not short."

"Compared to Hawk you are."

"Compared to Hawk, Lyle is a midget and Tom is a dwarf and Peets is just an ordinary man."

"That's what I said. Too short."

"I guess I'll just have to settle for her chocolate cake as our fee."

"Fee? What fee?"

"Paige was worried about our bill."

"I wasn't going to charge her," Aleta said. "Besides I made almost four hundred thousand on that custody case involving her brother and sister."

"There were expenses," Stanley said.

"We are not charging her a dime."

"I already set the fee at three chocolate cakes."

"Three?"

"I like Paige's cakes."

"Well, you are the senior partner."

"I'm so glad you remembered."

"We can go now," Aleta said. "Claude and Grams are waiting."

"Tell Tank to get his head out of my lap," Stanley said.

"It's just his head," Aleta remarked.

"His body follows his head."

"Tank, come here," Aleta cooed. "Stanley is busy."

"Maybe we should tie him up," Stanley suggested.

Aleta got up.

"Come on, Tank. I'm going to tether you. Please tell me you don't chew through leather leashes."

Before Stanley had driven a mile, Tank's head was nudging his arm, half a leather lead dangling from his collar.

Aleta grabbed the half lead and pulled the dog over to her and made him lay down.

"Aleta, do you have any cases pending?" Stanley asked after they'd ridden for a short time in silence.

"Just Stella Woodbridge," Aleta replied, referring to the ninety-year-old rape victim of her neighbor's forty-year-old son. "She says that she has an elderly friend that needs a lawyer."

"I'd forgotten about her. Is she back home yet?" Stanley asked.

"She's still living on Bessie Dobbins' farm."

"Is Bessie getting any painting done with two houseguests?"

"More than before. Stella and Eunice keep each other company." Aleta went on. "The way Stella talked, I got the impression she had more than one friend."

"Take them all," Stanley suggested. "Their cases will be safe ones. When's Stella's deposition scheduled?"

"Wednesday," Aleta replied. "Which reminds me, how come your operation is scheduled for tomorrow? It's Labor Day."

"The doctor was available," Stanley said. "I told him I couldn't go to court with one ear sticking out and the other one flat against my head."

"Is it really flat?" Aleta protested.

"I'm speaking comparatively," Stanley pointed out.

"You handled yourself well at the dog show," Aleta commented. "No one except the judges even noticed your bandaged ear."

"They noticed," Stanley said. "I must have told three dozen people that I was shot. I didn't tell them that my wife sent me into a house that had a man with a loaded gun."

"Why did you ask me about my caseload?" Aleta asked, switching subjects abruptly as usual.

"Because you're nervous."

"You don't think Grams was right--that it's just an aftermath of being robbed at gunpoint. It was pretty scary, you know. I know you were hiding in the bedroom, but ..."

"Aleta I wasn't hiding. I was trying to keep our losses to a minimum."

"They got everything!"

"They got nothing."

"They got my wonderful necklace," she cried, her voice breaking.

"They left me the neck it went around plus every other important part attached to that neck."

"And I didn't even get to show it to anyone."

"You wore it for two whole days."

"But Dad and Bertha and Jocelyn and your parents and ... everybody ..."

"How many times did you have your photo taken?"

"Five, I think," Aleta responded thoughtfully. "And one of them was me and Auggie and that one will come to our house."

"We'll frame that one," Stanley said. "I'm glad you wore it. It told me you liked it."

"One deposition of a ninety-year-old woman," Aleta responded to an earlier question as if there had been nothing spoken in between. "What kind of trouble will that bring?"

"From Stuart Fonts or his mother?" Stanley queried.

"He's left town." Aleta stated.

"Skipped?"

"No. He went to mooch off another relative."

"And his mother?" Stanley asked. "I thought he was her sole caretaker and she couldn't afford to hire one."

"She's not as poor as she let on. She liked having him wait on her hand and foot," Aleta told him, then added, "When I'm old, will you wait on me hand and foot?"

"I don't see why things should change just because we're old," Stanley responded poker-faced.

"I'm coming to the hospital with you tomorrow," she announced.

"That's not necessary. You would just have to wait in the waiting room."

"Well, that's a relief. I thought I was going to have to watch."

"It could take a while."

"I can wait," Aleta declared.

"It would be nice to have company," Stanley conceded. "But I'm a bit puzzled. This isn't typical of you. What's up?"

"I want to be sure the doctor doesn't wander from your ear to your nose."

"Would that be so horrible?"

"Yes."

"I can't give it to you as an anniversary present?" Stanley queried casually.

Aleta gasped in horror.

"Absolutely not! Don't even joke about it!"

"He said he wouldn't change it much. Just a tiny bit. To go with my new ears."

"He showed you a computer-generated image and you liked it!" she accused.

"Of course, I liked it. Plastic surgeons don't make money by making you uglier."

Suddenly, Aleta began to cry.

"Aleta, don't cry. I'm driving."

She undid her seat belt and went back to the tiny water closet and shut the door. Stanley pulled over into the first large gas station.

Claude and Harriet pulled in behind him and both left their RV and entered Stanley's.

"What's wrong?" Harriet asked.

She could hear Aleta sobbing in the tiny water closet.

"I told her I was thinking of getting my nose fixed tomorrow when the surgeon was evening up my ears," Stanley said. "She won't listen to reason."

"You scheduled a nose job?" Claude asked, shocked. "Without telling your wife?"

"I thought it would be a pleasant surprise," Stanley confessed.

"Aleta, come out of there!" Harriet demanded. "We need to know why this upsets you so."

Aleta opened the door, still crying. "I ruined him. I'm the one who got him shot this last time and now he's going to start fixing himself. I don't want him fixed—well, except for the ears because he will hate being lopsided. Stanley is neat and orderly and I understand that. But his nose goes with his eyes and chin and his forehead and his cheeks. It all goes together. The ears are behind the face. They really are only adjacent to the face. And he does have to even them up. I mean, not for me, but because he needs to … But his nose …

That's the main feature of his face. It dominates it. It defines it. It's a good, strong powerful nose. Changing it will ruin everything. If I wanted a Ken doll, I would have married Conan!"

The silence that followed Aleta's outburst was profound.

Stanley gathered Aleta into his arms and she cried on his shoulder long after he assured her he wouldn't let the surgeon touch his nose.

"I guess she hasn't been lying even a little bit," Claude observed. "She really does think you're handsome."

"She gets her scars eradicated," Stanley explained, still holding Aleta close.

Harriet nodded. "She wants to stay the woman you married."

Stanley kissed her gently on the top of her head.

"I think I'm beginning to understand," he murmured.

"You've got one piece of chocolate cake left," Claude noted. "Aren't you going to eat it?"

Aleta pushed herself out from Stanley's embrace.

"It's a big piece," she hiccupped as she tried to stifle her sobs. "We've got four forks."

As the four were digging into the piece of cake unceremoniously, Harriet asked, "Did you two talk about Auggie at all?"

"You mean about you showing him?" Stanley asked.

Aleta swallowed her mouthful of cake. "You ask me now?"

"I gather that's a no," Harriet responded.

Aleta took another forkful of cake.

Stanley snickered. "Grams, don't you know better than to come between Aleta and her chocolate especially when she's pregnant?"

"She's been pregnant since the day you married her," Harriet quipped. "How would you know what she's like when she isn't?"

"You do realize that it's her idea to have a large family," Stanley inserted.

"I know who's the true boss in your family."

"Except when Aleta wants something," Stanley countered.

Harriet chuckled. "I'll give you that."

She addressed Stanley directly.

"Stanley, I want to take Auggie with me on a circuit of shows these next two months. I'm planning to see if I can move Stoney up in the national rankings. Two Best in Shows has already moved him way up in the All-Breed stats. I want to hit a few Specialties and some major shows. He has a reputation now. He's never looked better."

"There's more to this, isn't there," Stanley surmised. "More than just that you want to take Auggie along for the ride."

Aleta swallowed her food. "Grams wants us to watch Keeper and Babe."

"We do that now," Stanley accepted. "Drop the other shoe."

Harriet's eyes twinkled. This man was nobody's fool.

"Keeper will whelp her litter while she's at your house."

"What?"

Harriet laughed. "I knew you'd love that part."

"But I've never whelped a litter," Stanley said clearly distraught.

"Aleta has helped me," Harriet assured him. "And Lauren promised to help her."

"You know that it's me that will wind up doing this," Stanley stated. "You do realize that, don't you?"

"Keeper is a good whelper. She doesn't even need you. She just needs a warm house and a whelping box."

Stanley looked at Harriet askance. "I don't believe you for a minute."

"So I guess that's a no," Harriet sighed.

"Of course, it's not a no," Stanley said. "I can feel Aleta's disapproval mounting. If her mouth wasn't full of cake, she'd be assuring me that she'll do the whelping."

Harriet answered before Aleta could swallow her cake.

"Stanley, I don't want to impose that much. It was a lot to ask."

"You'll have to take Tank too," Stanley said.

"Tank!" Harriet exclaimed, obviously distraught.

Stanley grinned. "Gotcha!"

Claude roared. "You did indeed. Come on, Harriet. Laugh. You did it to him."

"You didn't mean it?" Harriet asked tentatively.

"No," Stanley replied. "I like having Tank around."

Claude chuckled. "You know that if we did take him, you'd have to come. I need a co-pilot for the big plane."

"Then Aleta would have to whelp Keeper," Stanley mused. "You know, that sounds tempting."

Aleta swallowed her third forkful of cake. "You'd leave me?"

"Just think," Stanley smirked. "I wouldn't have to share my piece of cake."

"You didn't want it, did you?"

"I guess I'd miss not sharing my cake."

"You did want it!" Aleta accused. "Why didn't you say something?"

"I figured that little Martha is a chocoholic like her mother," he replied.

Aleta put her hand on her slightly bulging belly. Her tone softened. "She's a pig about it too."

"So, is the crisis over?" Claude asked. "We've got an hour's travel ahead of us."

Harriet studied her granddaughter's face. "You still sense danger?"

Aleta nodded. There was no sense lying. Her grandmother could read her too well.

"We'll stay on your tail until you're in your driveway," Harriet promised.

CHAPTER 3

After they were back on the road, Stanley asked Aleta why she didn't tell Claude and her grandmother to just go on at their own pace.

"We may need them," Aleta said simply.

"You aren't holding back on me, are you?"

"No. I only have a bad feeling."

"Why didn't you get a bad feeling before we were robbed?"

His tone had a hint of accusation buried in it.

Aleta picked up the vibe.

"You know I can't regulate premonitions any more than I can call up prophecies," she retorted.

Stanley was instantly remorseful.

"I'm sorry. I do forget sometimes."

"Why are you on edge?" Aleta asked. "I won't ask you to even watch us whelp Keeper. I prefer to ask Beatrice and Evelyn to help. And probably Julie and Madge. They're all experienced dog breeders."

"So many?"

"It could take sixteen or twenty hours," Aleta explained. "Or it could take only five or six. It'll happen at night, so you'll need your pajamas handy."

"Like on my body?"

"I guess that would work," Aleta snickered. "But you do know I see them as a challenge."

"How much notice will we have?"

"Keeper's temperature will drop twenty-four hours before she whelps."

"How do you know when to take it?"

"There's the rub. We don't.

"Aren't there any other signs?"

"Lots," Aleta said. "You're going to have fun. Trust me."

"I didn't have fun watching Emma at the end. And Ed was a nervous wreck."

"Emma was his child. Keeper is Grams' dog."

"I am not going to have fun."

"Well, of course you won't if you've made up your mind you won't," Aleta proclaimed.

"I haven't made up my mind. I just know."

"Think of it as an experience. You like to experience things."

"Some things. Not all things."

Aleta was quiet for a moment and then said abruptly, "Where are we?"

"Fifteen minutes from home."

"I mean, where exactly?"

"Approaching Catalpa Grove."

"Does it have a restaurant?"

"You aren't planning to stop, are you?"

"Oh yes, we're going to stop. You're about to have a new experience."

"Aleta, the bar serves only sandwiches; the barbecue joint serves ancient grease with its bones and douses the whole entree with a sauce that'll sear the roof of your mouth; and the pancake house serves pancakes and more pancakes and we had breakfast."

"Where's your spirit of adventure?"

"It's sleeping."

"Turn here."

"This leads to the alley behind the row of eating establishments and why am I getting the feeling I'm going to wish I hadn't disparaged all of them?

"Is Claude still behind us?"

"Yes, and he must think we're mad."

"Whoops!" Aleta exclaimed.

"Whoops?" Stanley queried.

"There are four dumpsters," Aleta said. "This could get really gross."

"I don't like the hints I'm getting," Stanley said. "Why do we care how many dumpsters there are?"

"Stop here. I've got to check with Grams."

Stanley pulled to the side of the alley and parked. Claude pulled in behind him. Aleta jumped out and left the door open. Tank followed her.

Stanley called to her to grab Tank and she looked around. Tank, however, attracted by the smell of rotting garbage, headed straight for the two dumpsters behind the barbecue joint.

He sniffed the first one, then lifted his leg and let go a long stream on the corner.

Stanley scampered out of his RV and hurried to grab the half-chewed lead before Tank decided to explore elsewhere.

"She left you," Stanley exclaimed as he grabbed the leash. "How could she be so sure you wouldn't leave?"

Tank nudged Stanley's arm and Stanley stroked the big, gray head and, softening his tone, said, "I'm not angry with you. I'm not angry with Aleta either. I just have this awful feeling that I'm going to be asked to dive into one of these dumpsters. You know that's what she's going to ask, don't you? Care to choose the right one for me?"

Stanley began to walk Tank down the row of dumpsters, but he never got past the next one.

"I know that one smells good," Stanley said. "It has lots of meat scraps. You wouldn't like the sauce though."

Tank walked around the dumpster and whined. He scratched the metal sides. Stanley saw Aleta emerge from the other RV with Claude and Harriet.

He shouted, "Tank says it's this one."

"He doesn't know what we're looking for," Aleta said. "He just smells the meat."

A back door opened, and a man in a soiled white apron appeared. "Hey, what the hell's going on out here?"

"We need to search these dumpsters for a woman," Aleta said.

The man kicked the nearest dumpster and yelled, "Anybody in there?"

To his surprise, Aleta banged on the next large metal container and three of the people listened for a response.

Stanley was hanging onto Tank who was still whining and scratching on the side of the container he'd chosen.

"Dog's hungry," the cook commented. "Don't you blokes feed him? He's scrawny!"

Tank woofed and pulled Stanley around the container part way and then back to his original spot.

The cook went back inside and returned with a huge bone.

"Here big fella," he said. "This ought to help them hunger pangs."

Tank took the bone and laid it down in front of his spot. He gave it a lick, and then went back to scratching the side of the container.

"She's in here!" Stanley called. "How about calling the sheriff?"

"What for?" the cook asked.

"To go into the dumpster and see if there's a body in there," Stanley said.

"He ain't gonna do it!"

"It's his job," Stanley said.

"No, it ain't. Now you folks has had your fun, so move along."

"This isn't a joke," Aleta said. "There's a woman in that dumpster. I saw her thrown in."

"Why didn't you stop whoever done it?" the cook charged.

"We weren't here," Aleta said.

"Then where'd you see it from?"

"We need to tell the sheriff."

"You're telling him and he ain't believing you."

"You're the sheriff?" Stanley asked, shocked.

"Catalpa Grove is smaller than small," the cook stated, "but we got a jail."

Aleta burst in. "Stanley, get in there. She's out of time. And you, Sheriff, call for an ambulance."

"Not until I see a body," the sheriff said.

Stanley meanwhile was handing Claude everything that was in his pockets. He removed his shoes as well.

"That a real badge or a fake one?" the sheriff asked.

"Real," Stanley said. "I'm off duty."

"If it's real, I guess then you can climb in my garbage if you want to."

"Gee, thanks," Stanley grunted as Claude boosted him over the edge.

As he dropped down into the stinking jumble of rancid grease soaked meat, fetid sauce, moldy bread and rotting vegetables, Stanley wondered briefly how anyone could have survived the stench for more than a few minutes.

He had removed his shoes so he could feel the body with his foot.

The slime crept up his pant legs as he lowered himself along the edge of the container.

"You're going to owe me big time, Aleta," he said tersely. "You have no idea how this stinks!"

"We can smell it from here," Aleta said.

"Multiply that by a factor of ten."

As he said that Stanley's foot slipped on the slimy floor of the container and he sat down hard. The garbage gave way to his falling body and then folded back over it as soon as Stanley was on the bottom. Stanley's foot hit something large and soft.

He knew at once he'd found the woman. He rolled onto his knees and crawled to her. There were numerous air pockets, each of which smelled as bad as the last.

His hands quickly searched the body. Her hands were tied together.

He put his hands under her arms and lifted her up, hoping her neck wasn't broken. He couldn't leave her down there buried under the noxious fumes the garbage had created. She had to breath fresh air again.

He hoisted her above him as he rose. Two pairs of hands grabbed her and pulled her out.

Stanley heard the sound of a siren coming closer.

"Is she alive?" he cried, as he gripped the sides of the dumpster, not daring to let go for fear of again falling into the revolting mess from which he'd just emerged.

The answer came after a few minutes.

"She's breathing!"

Stanley hung over the edge of the dumpster relieved. This was no place for a woman to die.

The paramedics arrived.

Stanley let himself be lifted from the dumpster, then he protested going to the hospital.

He lost the argument.

Dr. Wayne Cook met the ambulance at the Emergency Entrance.

"Do you live here?" Stanley quipped.

"I wouldn't if one of you two wasn't always getting shot or dumped into a dumpster. The ear hasn't even healed yet. You're worse than a child."

"Aleta made me..." Stanley began.

He was interrupted by laughter. "You sound like my twins."

"Well, she did!" Stanley insisted, somewhat abashed. "The paramedics insisted on bringing me in. It wasn't my idea."

"They have my list too."

"What list?"

"List of my patients," Dr. Cook said. "It's a short list, but, I'm to be called day or night when they pick up one."

"I didn't know I was one of your patients," Stanley said. "You've never even given me a physical."

"You want a physical?"

"Not now!" Stanley declared. "Now I just want you to send me home so I can shower and change."

"Well, I'm not working on you this dirty," Dr. Cook said. "First we'll clean you up then as long as you are in a hospital gown, I'll give you a physical. I'd hate to have you believe I wasn't thorough."

"I don't need a physical," Stanley protested. "It's just something doctors do. You know, check your weight and listen to your heart and take your blood pressure."

"Is there something wrong with your weight?"

"That's what you're supposed to tell me. That's what a person's doctor does."

"You've been in the hospital over half a dozen times this past year and I've actually made a house call or two. I'm curious as to what those encounters were in your mind."

"Emergency stuff."

"Are you looking for a doctor?"

"I don't need a doctor. I'm healthy as a horse."

"Well, I'm going to have the nurse get you cleaned up and then I want to talk to you about your operation tomorrow."

"You know about that?"

"I'm your doctor."

To Stanley's dismay, Dr. Cook gave him a thorough physical.

"Now I know why I don't have a doctor," he quipped after the proctological exam.

"I didn't want you to feel gypped," Dr. Cook smirked.

"It's not that I would want another doctor," Stanley said. "But I was told that you don't take private patients because being in charge of the Free Clinic and heading the Emergency Department takes all your time."

"You know that Aleta is my patient, right?"

"Aleta is special."

"Stanley, you are too. Now, tell me, does Aleta know you're planning to have a nose job?"

"She does now. I have to cancel that part."

"She's okay with the ears?"

"She says they're not part of my face."

"It is your face, not hers."

"You would have had to have been there. She was inconsolable. I think she still plans to stand over the doctor's shoulder tomorrow."

"As long as she's here, I have a special task for her," Dr. Cook said. "It'll keep her occupied."

"About my diet, Doc…"

"Why are you on a diet? Your weight is fine."

"Aleta is changing it because Bertha changed Robert's to lower his cholesterol."

Dr. Cook opened a draw and pulled a rubber tube and tied it around Stanley's upper arm.

"What are you doing?"

"Checking your cholesterol," Dr. Cook said.

"It's fine!" Stanley said.

"Have you had a blood test?"

"It was tested when I donated blood for Aleta."

"A lipid panel wasn't done. We were looking for compatibility factors and an absence of disease."

"How about when I had mono?"

"Make a fist," Dr. Cook said.

"Can't we just pretend I never brought this up?"

"Take a deep breath," came the order. "You know you're lucky I draw blood several times a day. I'm better than most doctors at this."

"What do you mean better?" Stanley snapped. "It still hurts."

"This isn't painless dentistry," he rejoined as he pulled off the rubber tourniquet. "But I usually find the vein on my first try."

He replaced the needle with a cotton ball.

"Didn't they draw blood as prep for tomorrow's operation?" Dr Cook asked.

"Could we have used that?" Stanley asked, disgruntled at the thought.

"If a lipid panel was ordered, we could have. It's too late now," Dr. Cook said. "I could have waited for your next emergency but this is better."

"Better? How is it better?"

"It's part of a normal physical. And you wanted a thorough one."

"Do you ever give mini-physicals, you know, special ones for healthy people?"

"That's what you're getting."

"Remind me not to ask you a question ever again."

"I can't do that," Dr. Cook grinned, "but I suggest you not demand what you don't need."

"I didn't demand this."

"You suggested I was lax in my care of you," Wayne Cook pointed out. "Now let's get back to what's really bothering you—your nose job."

"It's been decided."

"Aleta didn't see the projections, did she?"

"No."

"Well, she's wrong and you're right," Dr. Cook said. "If she wants you to look like the man she married, you need the change. It's so subtle that no one will notice the change, but, without it, you'll look different."

"Maybe I shouldn't do my ears."

"One's done."

"There is that."

"I promised."

"She's coming for you, right?"

"Maybe."

"You wait here," Dr. Cook said, and then walked out.

"As if I'm dressed to wander..." Stanley muttered.

Dr. Wayne Cook met Aleta as she entered the Emergency entrance.

"We need to talk," he said earnestly.

Suddenly apprehensive, she followed him into an empty examination room.

"What's wrong?" she burst out.

"Your decision about tomorrow," Dr. Cook declared. "You made a decision based on no research at all. You capriciously overturned a well-considered option your husband chose with regard to restoring balance to his face."

"He wants to look better!" she argued. "I don't want him changed!"

"Think about that the next time you send him unarmed into a house against an armed man."

"I said fixing his ear was okay. I know he needs not to be lopsided."

"He also needs not to be uglier."

"I'm not doing that!" Aleta declared, taken aback.

"The plastic surgeon is only changing his nose enough to balance out the change to his ears."

"How do you know?"

"I make it my business to know what's going on with my patients."

"And you approved?"

"The change will make him look more like the old Stanley than your idea. You can't change one part of the face without affecting the whole."

"That's why I don't want his nose touched."

"That's the reason he needs the nose done," Dr. Cook said, his tone softening as he realized Aleta was listening. "Stanley wasn't trying to make himself handsomer, although he will be. He was trying to keep from being less handsome. You can't ask him to suffer being less attractive."

"I would never ask that!"

"Release him from his promise."

"You do know I like his looks."

"Yes, I know. His face has character, but that comes from within."

"I'll release him," Aleta said. "It is his face, after all. And I'll love him no matter what."

"Now you can take him his clothes," Dr. Cook said. "I had the staff throw out the others."

"I just brought clean pants and a shirt."

"It'll cover him enough to go home."

"He won't be happy," Aleta mumbled.

"He's already been made more uncomfortable than lack of underwear could ever make him."

"What did you do?" Aleta asked, perturbed.

"Ask him," Dr. Cook grinned. "It comes under doctor-patient privilege."

Within seconds Aleta charged into Stanley's room, Dr. Cook trailing after her.

"What did Dr. Cook do?"

Startled, Stanley responded instantly, "Gave me a full physical."

"You asked for a full physical now?" his wife charged. "Your ear was dirty. That's what you came in for—to prevent the possibility of an infection."

"He cleaned the ear," Stanley stammered. "Then he gave me a physical."

"Now? At this time of night? On a holiday?"

"I imagine I will pay double," Stanley quipped recovering his balance.

Wayne Cook smiled. "Triple. It is a holiday weekend."

"But you're healthy," Aleta declared.

"I made the mistake of mentioning that he had never given me one."

"Why did you even mention that?"

"He said he was my ... Aleta, let's not talk about this."

"He told you he was your doctor? That was it? And you told him that he'd never given you a physical," Aleta guessed. "He's been taking care of us since we got married."

She caught the distressed look on her husband's face and ended with, "Oh, never mind. Dr. Cook took care of explaining that he is, didn't he?"

"Smiling the whole while I might add," Stanley commented.

"Well, as long as he enjoyed himself I'm sure he'll keep taking care of you, but you aren't to upset our doctor again."

"You can count on that!" Stanley exclaimed.

"Good," Aleta finished. "And tomorrow you can have the operation as originally planned."

"No objections?"

"It's your face," Aleta stated. "It's your decision. I trust you."

"Are you going to explain to your grandmother that you changed our minds?"

"You're going to make me somehow, aren't you?" Aleta questioned.

"I can't make you do anything, but you are a reasonable woman and mine is a reasonable request," Stanley said calmly.

Dr. Cook waited for the protest but it never came. Instead Aleta agreed to tell her grandmother without a word of protest.

Noting that her mood seemed agreeable, Dr. Cook mentioned that he had a patient he'd like her to visit while Stanley was in the operating theater.

"You don't have to keep me busy," Aleta commented knowingly. "I'm not a child."

"On the contrary," Dr. Cook said. "You're a valuable asset, but you keep saying that your gift of understanding those we can't is temporary, so I don't want to ask you to make a special trip, but as long as you're going to be here…"

"Wayne, I'm yours while Stanley is getting beautified."

"Aleta, I'm not having major plastic surgery," Stanley protested. "And I'm hoping no one will notice."

"We're going on our annual trek to the lodge and taking in two major dog shows and you'll have your ear and nose bandaged and you don't think anyone will notice?"

"The surgeon assured me I won't still need bandages by next weekend."

"Did he tell you that your nose would still be swollen and probably black and blue?"

"He said it would be minimal."

"And when is he removing the stitches in your ear?"

"Okay, so I'll look as if I'd been in an accident."

"Except to every woman."

"I'll stay home."

"No, you won't."

"I won't go into the ring."

"Tank won't care what you look like."

"I will."

Aleta smiled suddenly. "I'll take Tank in if you'll promise to watch."

"Deal!" Stanley said, then looked at his doctor and commented wryly, "I've been suckered into something, but I don't know what."

"Why did you agree then?"

"Because she puts it in terms I can't refuse."

CHAPTER 4

The next morning, the closer it got to the time for his surgery, the more nervous Aleta became.

Thus when Dr. Cook showed up a quarter of an hour before the scheduled time, Stanley said, "Aleta's ready to help now. She's kissed me seven times and told me she'll love me no matter what I look like and I'm beginning to let my imagination run down paths it shouldn't."

"Why are you worrying him, Aleta?" Dr. Cook asked gently.

"I'm not sure. It wasn't my intention."

"Why not let me give you a bit of background on the people you're going to visit."

"People?" Aleta questioned. "As in more than one?"

"I told Stanley's surgeon to do a few extra things so I can squeeze in all the visits I want."

"Extra?" Aleta sucked in a lungful of air.

"I thought with the parts of Stanley's old nose, he could fashion a second one. Two noses might be handy."

"You didn't!"

"No, but I did suggest a dimple might be nice."

"You're kidding, aren't you?"

"I like dimples."

"Stanley doesn't need a dimple."

"They're easy to do," Dr. Cook grinned. "I could probably do one myself. Save you some money."

Aleta flared up.

"You don't save us money. You're the most expensive doctor in the Tri-City area."

"And you're the most expensive lawyer," Dr. Cook shot back.

"Except when I'm free," Aleta put in.

"Ditto," Wayne Cook quipped. "Now I believe Stanley is relaxed enough so I can spirit you away to do my bidding."

Aleta hesitated. The arrival of the orderly sent to fetch Stanley prompted Aleta to leave.

"The first patient on my list is Vera Kvidahl. She emigrated from Latvia forty years ago. English is her second language. A stroke left her aphasic and partially crippled on her right side. She can't walk without a walker. Her right hand isn't fully functional. She's slowly recovering her ability to write. Her speech is a mix of English and Latvian and I'm not sure she says what she means."

"Why am I seeing her?"

"Something is wrong between her and her son. He's her sole caretaker."

"Do you suspect abuse?"

"Not the kind that leaves marks."

"Tell me nothing more," Aleta said. "Let's go."

Having said that, Aleta led the way to the elevator, punched the button to the third floor and headed straight toward Vera Kvidahl's room. She entered the open door and stopped abruptly when a beefy man hefted his two hundred eighty pounds from the chair in the corner of the room, his pale blue eyes angry.

"Who are you?"

"I'm a lawyer," Aleta said.

She noted a glimmer of hope in the eyes of the shriveled old woman lying in the bed.

Lukas killed the spark quickly when he said, "My ma don't need a lawyer."

Dr. Cook edged around Aleta and quickly introduced her to mother and son.

Lukas Kvidahl scowled.

"What's all this about, Doc?"

Aleta answered quickly. "I happen to be in the hospital because my husband is being operated on and Dr. Cook is taking me around to meet several of his patients. Your mother had a stroke recently. I'm a recovered stroke victim. Sometimes it helps for a stroke victim to talk with another."

"Ma don't need no help," Lukas declared.

"Don't be stupid, Mr. Kvidahl. We all need help after a stroke," Aleta stated sternly. "Why don't you go have breakfast and let me chat with your mother?"

"Come on, Lukas," Dr. Cook interjected. "You can use a break. I can use another cup of coffee myself."

"My stroke was light," Aleta began, "but I still sometimes substitute words I don't mean for words I meant to say. That's not a good trait in a trial lawyer. I keep thinking that someday instead of saying 'my client is innocent', I'm going to say 'my client is guilty.'"

Aleta saw the eyes twinkle a bit.

"I agree. I'd be in a pickle if I did that," Aleta chuckled.

Aleta knew Lukas was still listening at the door so she continued in a light vein until she heard the footsteps going away from the door. She kept up the inconsequential chatter until she heard the elevator depart.

Abruptly, Aleta said, "I'm a lawyer. You have a legal problem. Tell me what it is."

The old woman pointed to her mouth.

"So you are afraid I won't understand. God has given me a gift. Either I will understand you or I won't. Let's find out."

The old woman began to speak in garbled sentences. There was a word or two any onlooker would have understood, but the problem she presented was not a simple one. A person needed to understand every word.

When she finished, Aleta said, "I understand. Do you want me to be your lawyer?"

The woman muttered a few sentences of affirmation.

Aleta replied succinctly, "God does not want you to die. Your son's fate is in God's hands—not mine, not yours."

Tears sprang into Vera Kvidahl's eyes just as her son reentered the room. Dr. Cook came in on his heels.

"You made her cry!" he accused. "Get out of here."

"Dr. Cook, as Mrs. Kvidahl's attorney, I suggest you listen to me. Lukas Kvidahl has been misinterpreting his mother's wishes to the staff. As her attorney I am ordering her to remain in the hospital and be fed five times a day by the nurses. All soft foods, preferably ... Mrs. Kvidahl, what are your favorite foods?"

Aleta listened as she repeated the foods, which included mashed potatoes and ice cream, and then she asked, "You can work up a menu around that, can't you?"

Dr. Cook chuckled. "The dietitian will want to add fruits and vegetables to that list."

Aleta nodded almost absently. She had more orders.

"Mr. Lukas Kvidahl's visits are limited to visiting hours. No exceptions."

"You can't do that!" Lukas declared, his big voice rumbling through the room.

Aleta, seeing the fear spring into the old woman's eyes, said, "Considering how much you just frightened your mother, I am canceling your visitation privileges entirely."

"You haven't got the authority."

"Take me to court, Mr. Kvidahl. I'm a heavyweight as a litigator. If you lose, then you, not your mother, will pay court costs and my fee, which is three hundred dollars an hour. I am the highest paid attorney in my firm."

"Hah! My mother can't afford you neither. So there!"

"She's a pro bono case," Aleta said. "She gets my services for free. However, if you force me into court, you pay. So cool off, rethink your plans and back out of those you can back out of."

"What plans?"

"Don't play hardball with me," Aleta warned. "Cancel the financial deal. It's not legit. And I will sue you and the broker. I will win. HUD hates it when people are charged thousands for services they offer for free."

"What services?"

"Counseling on whether a reverse mortgage is wise and providing a list of approved lenders."

"We don't like dealing with government bureaucracy."

"Hogwash!" Aleta said. "Pull out!"

"You're bluffing!"

"I don't bluff," Aleta said. "I will blow the whistle on you and your cohorts. And you will wind up doing time."

"Ma won't let you do that to me."

"She has no choice anymore," Aleta said.

"She can fire you," Lukas blurted out.

"She won't."

"Ma, are you gonna let her railroad me?"

Vera Kvidahl murmured several words.

"She says to get the hell out!" Lukas declared.

Aleta smiled.

"She told you God sent me in answer to her prayer."

"I didn't get that!" Lukas said belligerently.

"Well, I did," Dr. Cook said evenly. "She shook her head when you were speaking and nodded when Aleta was talking."

"You two are in cahoots, I'll sue you both!" he shouted.

After he'd stormed out, Aleta told Vera she would draw up a power of attorney and be back with it that afternoon. "I need it to straighten out the insurance fraud and the unauthorized change in your will."

Dr. Cook saw Mrs. Kvidahl nod happily.

The two left the old woman shortly afterward. A nurse arrived with a dish with three scoops of different flavors of ice cream.

As they entered the elevator, Dr. Cook asked Aleta, "He was starving her, wasn't he?"

"I didn't ask. If I had, I would have had to have him arrested. She wasn't ready to take that step."

"We should have followed through on that ourselves," Dr. Cook said.

"You did. You called me in," Aleta reminded him. "Who's next?"

"An old gentleman who needs a simple codicil to his will. His recent heart attack changed his thinking."

"Is Stanley still in the operating room?" Aleta asked.

Dr. Cook stepped over to the nurse's station and had them check. He was back in a couple of minutes with an affirmative reply.

Aubrey Euston was elevated to a half-sitting position. He greeted Dr. Cook with a smile.

"You brought me a lawyer."

Aleta read the man's eyes when Dr. Cook mentioned her name. He knew her by reputation.

"I need a simple codicil to my will," he said. "I figure it will take an hour of an associate's time. I'd like a quote."

Aleta smiled.

"You're talking to the firm's highest paid lawyer. I cost three hundred dollars and hour and that's what you will pay. If any part of the codicil is simple enough for an associate to handle, you will get a reduced rate on that part. That, Mr. Euston, is my quote."

"You're too expensive." Euston declared.

"That I am," Aleta agreed. "It was nice meeting you. Have a good day."

"I guess I could handle three hundred dollars," Euston hedged. "Can you do it for that?"

Aleta smiled again.

"No, I can't. You are a very fastidious man and you won't like the first draft. As long as you're paying an hourly rate, I will make as many corrections as you want happily. You aren't calling your old lawyer because you wore out his patience. You will pay for your fastidiousness if you hire me."

"But, what if I . . ."

Aleta cut him off. "I am not wrangling with you. If you want to hire me then we start now. If you don't, I have another place to go."

"I only wanted to ask. . ."

Aleta looked at her watch. "You're on the clock unless you say goodbye."

"You're hired."

"I'll have the contract in your hands this afternoon," Aleta said.

"I don't want to wait," Euston complained.

"I won't work without one. I'll see you at two."

Dr. Cook lingered.

"I told you she'd see through you, you old skinflint."

"You didn't tell her?"

"Not a hint even."

"She's that good?"

"That's the word on the street."

As soon as Dr. Cook joined her, Aleta said, "I need to see Stanley now."

When Stanley was wheeled from the operating room, Aleta was waiting with Dr. Cook in the Recovery Room. They had it to themselves.

Aleta stared at Stanley's pale face and realized suddenly that she might have lost him. It didn't matter that it was a simple operation. There was always a risk.

She took his hand and stood so he could see her.

The surgeon joined them to assure them both that the surgery went well, but that they wouldn't see the end result for a couple of weeks.

"You are never having another operation!" Aleta declared.

Stanley smiled. He'd had five since he'd married her. This was the least invasive of all and this time she falls apart.

"The worst is over," Stanley said, hoping that his saying it would make it so.

"If you stay in the hospital, we can control the pain better," Dr. Cook commented.

"He'll stay," Aleta said before Stanley could answer.

"Don't I have a say in this?" Stanley asked.

"No!" Aleta determined. "We have a house full of dogs. I need to make arrangements to house them elsewhere for the week. We are taking no chances."

"That's a good idea," the surgeon said. "A bump could rearrange the flesh around the nose and put a lump where we don't want one."

"We didn't fuss like this over my ear," Stanley pointed out.

"We're talking about your nose," Aleta said, "which means no kissing for two weeks."

"Now where'd that come from?" Stanley charged.

"From me," Aleta proclaimed. "And I will be obeyed. Remember I saw my mother after her face lift and I know you won't be healed in a week."

"She had extensive work done," Stanley pointed out.

"Your nose doesn't care whether you had other work done or not. It was messed with. It needs time to heal."

"Where'd this new Aleta come from?" Stanley asked.

"She's been battling dragons while you've been sleeping," Dr. Cook said. "I think her adrenaline is still sky high. But as your doctor, let me advise you that she is making all the right choices."

"Oh, Stanley," Aleta said, her voice trembling slightly. "I've been handling clients when I should have put my energy into praying for you."

Stanley squeezed his wife's hand. "If you had poured all that energy into the operating room, the doctor wouldn't have been able to stop with a tiny correction."

"I did the right thing?" Aleta wavered.

"You always do the right thing," Stanley said.

"Not always."

"Okay. Except when you don't," Stanley agreed.

"Well, at least now you can grow a beard."

Stanley's eyes widened. "A beard?"

"You don't think I'm letting you shave."

"I'm very good at it. I've been shaving for fifteen years. I won't bump into my nose. I know where it's located."

"I'm not saying you're going to accidentally shave your nose, but you always touch your nose when you shave."

"No, I don't!" he declared.

"No shaving."

"I don't look good unshaven," Stanley protested.

"You look good all the time," Aleta declared.

"Next you'll tell me I can't wear tee shirts for a week because I have to pull them down over my head."

"Two weeks," Aleta said.

"Why don't you go call your grandmother and my mother and tell them my suffering has just begun?"

"Don't be ridiculous. You aren't suffering," Aleta snapped. "You did tell your mother, didn't you?"

"Did you tell your grandmother?"

"No."

"Well…"

"I can't tell your mother!" Aleta wailed. "She'll disown me."

"Are you planning to tell her I went on a vacation—alone?"

"I'm thinking about that."

"My mother will uncover that lie in ten seconds."

The surgeon lifted an eyebrow and Dr. Cook walked him out of earshot.

"Stanley's mother is a judge."

"And she's a formidable woman, I gather."

"She's just like Aleta," Wayne Cook said. "And Lydia loves Aleta."

"A Mrs. Praetzel got through on the phone in the operating room. I assumed it was his wife."

"His mother," Dr. Cook grinned. "They are two peas in a pod. Stanley is a lucky man."

"Lucky?"

"They both adore him."

"But she is ... er ... domineering."

"He's the boss in that family," Wayne Cook said. "Make no mistake about that."

"You know him better than I do, but I don't see it," the surgeon commented. "Hey, she's leaving."

The two doctors rushed over.

"Is anything the matter, Aleta?" Dr. Cook asked Aleta.

She smiled. "He's feeling pretty good. I have to go tell his mother what he did."

"Can't it wait?" the surgeon asked.

"Not according to Stanley," Aleta rejoined. "She needs to hear from me before he's out of recovery, he said."

"When will you take care of those legal matters?" Dr. Cook inquired.

"Stanley said I could stop at the office on the way back. He said I was to take my time because he was sleepy."

"That's normal," Dr. Cook assured her. "It takes a while for the body to shake off the anesthetic. And Mrs. Kvidahl needs that power of attorney executed as soon as possible."

"I'll get right on it," Aleta promised.

While Aleta was on her way to her office, Lukas Kvidahl was on his third drink at the only bar in Catalpa Grove. He was in a sour mood and the liquor wasn't helping him feel better.

Of the three men who walked into the bar, Lukas only knew one—his neighbor, Stuart Fouts. He greeted the big man with an accusation.

"Does your mother know you're here?"

Stuart shot back, "Does yours?"

"My ma's in the hospital. She had a stroke," Lukas said, not quite sure why he let that slip out.

"That's rough," Doyle Conan cut in. "Cousin Stuart, have your friend join us."

For some reason, Lukas decided to do just that. Being alone hadn't helped any. While he and Stuart weren't buddies, they didn't hate each other. Both were stuck with mothers who were widows and insisted that their boys live at home and take care of them. Both mothers had money and neither Stuart nor Lukas had a regular job.

"You don't look like cousins," Lukas said.

"I take after my mother's side," Doyle explained. "My Cousin Lennie and I look alike."

Then Stuart Fouts blurted out the question that popped into his head when he first saw Lukas Kvidahl. He suspected that his mother might be checking up on him. He'd been gone longer than usual and he hadn't told her where he was going.

"How come you're way out here if your ma is in the hospital?"

Lukas read an accusation in the query and reacted.

"It's that Aleta Praetzel's fault," he shot back. "She had no right interfering."

"Aleta Praetzel?" Stuart asked, shocked. "What did she do?"

"Turned my ma against me. That's what!"

"How'd she do that?" Stuart asked, suddenly interested.

"Dr. Cook brought Aleta Praetzel to see Ma and she said she could understand what Ma was saying. Hell, nobody can understand a word,"

"How come?" Doyle asked.

"The stroke. I was just about to get Ma to agree to give me power of attorney so that I could pay the hospital bill and do some business when Aleta Praetzel cons Ma into hiring her and giving her power of attorney just when I had her ready to give me that."

"She signed it right then and there?" Doyle Conan asked.

"Naw. She said she needed to go to the office, but then she told the doctor what kind of food Ma liked."

'She could have guessed that," Doyle ventured.

"Maybe the mashed potatoes and ice cream, but she knew Ma liked liver sausage, fried onion rings and French onion soup. And Ma was sitting there nodding her head each time that Praetzel dame said something Ma liked."

"Did she ever name anything wrong?" Doyle asked.

"No. But after that she did name the stuff she hated. Some of it was stuff I told the nurses she liked. She made me look bad."

"What did you say when she did that?" Doyle asked.

"I said I like those things, so I thought she did too because she would make them for me."

"That was a smart answer," Doyle said.

That comment sat well in Lukas' stomach.

Doyle Conan went on. "You can probably persuade your mother that she should give you her power of attorney and save the cost of a lawyer."

"Not if I can't see her no more," Lukas spat out. "Aleta Praetzel got me kicked out of my ma's hospital room and said I couldn't visit my ma no more and Dr. Cook backed her up."

"So what are you going to do?" Doyle asked.

Before Lukas could answer, two men entered the bar and hailed Doyle.

Doyle introduced another cousin.

Lukas could see the resemblance between Doyle and Lennie Archer. They looked like family. He soon found out that Butch was Lennie's buddy.

After everyone was introduced, Butch asked Lukas, "Did Doyle tell you about his plan?"

"No, Butch," Doyle answered quickly. "I only told Stu. We just met up with Lukas a couple minutes ago. His mother is sick in the hospital and that's what we were talking about."

"Is she going to get better?" Butch asked.

"She had a stroke, Butch," Doyle said. "She will be in the hospital for a long time."

"That's too bad," Butch said. "Does he want to be a partner? You said you needed five to make the plan work."

"He's got a lot of problems to deal with right now," Doyle told Butch.

"Okay," Butch said.

"You know, Doyle," Stu Fouts said. "Lukas might like your idea real well considering what just happened to him."

"I need to talk to Lennie and Butch first. If they want to be partners in our project, I will take them to Mom's farm and get started," Doyle said. "And Stu, you need to calm your mother down and tell her that you've got a part time job and you will be gone a lot. We don't want her to be calling you at the wrong time."

After they left, Lukas turned to Stu and asked him what idea Doyle had that he might like.

"We plan on going after the Praetzels," Stu started.

"I'm in," Lukas stated.

"Not killing them, although it might happen," Stu said. "But it will stop Aleta Praetzel from messing with your mother and make you a rich man."

"Now I'm in for sure," Lukas declared.

"Let me take you home."

"I can drive."

"I gotta get back," Stu said. "My ma wants the car. If you tell your ma your car broke down, she won't be mad, especially if you had to hitch a ride home."

"What'll I do for a ride?" Lukas asked, perturbed. "My car will be here."

"Borrow your ma's car. Yours is in the shop. I got to check back with Doyle a couple days. You can pick up your car then."

"Tell me the plan."

As Stuart Fouts was explaining Doyle's plan, Aleta Praetzel was ringing the doorbell to Stanley's parents' two-story Colonial-style home, which unlike their son's home, was surrounded by acres of formal landscaping. On the other end of the continuum was their son's unpretentious, one story, remodeled farm house set in the middle of eighty-six acres, most of which was dedicated to the care, feeding and training of horses. Even the orchard was seen as an apple producer for the horses.

The senior Praetzel's maid ushered Aleta to the formal garden in the back where Lydia and Hubert Praetzel were sitting reading. Stanley's father looked up from the Wall Street Journal and his mother folded up the New York Times when Aleta entered. The Chicago Tribune lay on the glass topped-table between them along with the Tri-City Register which carried the story about the rescue of a woman from a dumpster in Catalpa Grove.

In that story, the Arborville deputy who had rescued her was unnamed, but the paper did reveal enough information to be able to assure its readers that their local prophets were again working close to home. The recent series of rape-murders of elderly citizens had caused an outcry from the populace who scathingly rebuked the prophets for foreseeing the imminent deaths of two of Chicago's leading crime bosses while innocent Tri-City citizens were being murdered.

"How's his nose look?" Stanley's mother asked as Aleta approached.

"I imagine the swelling and discoloration will come later," Aleta said. "The ear was bandaged."

"I gather he is in Recovery."

"Yes," Aleta said. "I didn't know you knew."

Lydia pointed to the article in the Tri City Register. "Stanley?"

Aleta nodded. "He was ... so ... dare I say brave."

"Don't ask me," Lydia chuckled. "I'm barely able to form coherent sentences."

Aleta grinned. "Which you just did."

Her husband spoke up. "I think she's ready to go back to work. Her brain is as sharp as ever."

"I wish there were an interim step I could take," Lydia said.

"Why not help me for a week or two?" Aleta suggested. "Stanley can't work and Dr. Cook set me up with two clients while I was at the hospital and tomorrow Stella Woodbridge is going to give a deposition. We have that set up with a judge, but she's offered my services to some of her friends and I have a feeling our office is going to be overwhelmed again and I promised Stanley I would stop practicing except for whatever case God sent."

"And Stanley agreed to that?" Lydia asked, surprised.

"Well, no. Not exactly. But Jamara almost quit and ... no, that's not it either ... I think I tend to get too busy and I love being with Stanley. That's why I married him. To be with him ... I guess it's that I ... well, he ... this last week, he ... He gave me more than the sapphire necklace that was stolen. He gave me a week ... talk about stumbling all over oneself..."

"For a lawyer who spoke of sexual matters in open court—you do remember that I was there..."

"You were brilliant!" Aleta exclaimed.

"Brilliant?" Lydia gasped. "I hardly said five words."

"I would never have thought to have the convictions expunged from the records in five years," Aleta said. "I especially appreciated giving Jack Turner that chance to not have his mistake haunt him all his life."

"Did you hire Jack Turner?" Lydia asked.

"According to Hubbs he's a big fella and it'll take a heap of food to keep his furnace stoked, but he's got a good heart and his hands ain't afraid to pick up a shovel," Aleta responded. "His foster mother is going to drive him to work each morning. Dad will take him to school when he takes Jocelyn and Lettie. Jack will come back on the school bus and help Hubbs after school. Dad will take him home when he picks up Bertha and the girls."

"What is Jack going to be doing?"

"Hubbs has been wanting the horses exercised and now they will be."

"He's not going to ride them!" Lydia asked, shocked.

"Hubbs told him he's 'gotta drop forty of them pounds before he can hike a leg up over Minx's back, fifty to sit on Yudi, sixty pounds to get up on Shadow and seventy to ride any of the others.' My guess is that he'll do at least the first forty."

"Hubbs have a scale in the barn?" Lydia queried.

"He claims he can eyeball a man's weight," Aleta said. "The thing is Jack doesn't have to lose a pound. Hubbs doesn't care. But Hubbs knows that every horseman wants to ride, so he's just telling him right up front what the criteria is."

"And Hubbs didn't mind you hiring a helper?"

"I think he likes having an apprentice," Aleta said. "I told him when Jack moved on, we'd find another one for him to teach. That relaxed him."

"At his age being replaced is a big fear," Lydia observed.

Hubert interjected a note. "Does Stanley want to see us?"

"You do understand that he is not trying to change his appearance. The second bullet made some alterations to that ear necessary and then he had to alter the other ear to lie back as well, and then the surgeon showed him he needed ... that's the problem, he didn't need to have his nose touched, except that when his ears were laid back it changed his appearance and his nose appeared bigger."

Her voice trailed off as she stared at her father-in-law.

"I just realized something," she said.

"That he wants to look more like his father?" Lydia questioned. "He hasn't ever told you that?"

"Never."

"He used to say it a lot when he was young," his mother confided.

"I will miss the look of the man I married," Aleta said. "I really liked his face, you know."

"Yes," Lydia said softly. "That I do know."

"I told him he could grow a beard," Aleta said.

Hubert laughed. "You two had better get used to the fact that a metamorphosis has started and you may never get the old Stanley back."

"He likes being clean shaven," Aleta insisted.

"What is it you would have me do at your office while Stanley is lying in bed growing a beard?" Lydia asked.

"First I want you to act as amicus curiae during the deposition," Aleta said. "Stella is ninety. I want a solid testimony that will stand up in court. The accused won't be there. His attorney may do a slovenly job. Will you see that the hard questions are asked?"

"It could be hard on Stella," Lydia posed.

"Fouts raped her!" Aleta charged. "I will take care of her. Just be sure I have a tape that a judge will accept."

"The answer is yes. I will do that."

"Are you sure, Lydia?" Hubert asked.

"I asked for an interim step," Lydia responded. "This is it. And Aleta, I will help you later if you wish. I can still tell a garbage case from a good one."

"I have to get a power of attorney executed today for a woman that needs to stay in the hospital while I straighten out some business for her. When you two come over to visit Stanley, will you be witnesses for me?"

"Anyone could be a witness," Hubert said.

"She's had a stroke. She can't sign her name. She speaks in jumbled half-English, half-Latvian sentences," Aleta said. "I need you to ask the questions a judge would ask."

"You understand Latvian?" Hubert asked. "I thought it was Lithuanian."

"Evidently, today I understand Latvian," Aleta said, as if it were a commonplace occurrence.

"Just come get us," Hubert said.

CHAPTER 5

Tuesday morning Aleta arrived early with her mother-in-law and introduced each of the staff as they arrived, explaining that Judge Davis was here only as a lawyer filling in for Stanley until he was able to return to work.

Stella Woodbridge was driven over by Bessie Dobbins who chatted with Lydia in Stanley's office where Bessie pointed out each species of aquatic plant to Stella. Aleta had forgotten to tell her mother-in-law that Stanley wasn't planning to go public about the nose change, and her mother-in-law divulged why Stanley was in the hospital.

Bessie's reaction was unique. "Does Paul Locke know about this?"

"No," Aleta replied, taken aback.

"He has several unfinished pieces with Stanley in them," Bessie said. "He should have been told."

"I never even thought about that," Aleta admitted.

"I'll go over this morning and tell him," Bessie said. "You non-artists have a lot to learn."

Stella chuckled. "She's got two of us non-artists in her house. We hear that a lot."

Bessie turned to Aleta.

"You got a helper for Hubbs. He likes him. He says he's got a good feel for animals for a kid who hasn't been around any. You aren't planning on retiring Hubbs, are you?"

"No," Aleta replied simply.

"Good."

"Did he ask you to ask me?"

"No."

"Hubbs is in charge of his future. He's permanent as long as he wants to be. And the room is his room even if he retires."

"He won't want to be beholden."

"His presence alone is good for the horses," Aleta said. "I can hire hands. I can't ever find a man as good as Hubbs to watch over the horses."

"You're a good person," Bessie said. "I hope your husband is okay. I'll tell Paul to adjust. The horses in my paintings never look the same two days in a row."

Judge Dennis Clancy arrived shortly after Bessie left and greeted Lydia warmly. She explained her role to him and Stella simultaneously, as the man in charge of the videotaping started to set up.

"Do you expect the public defender to be lax?" Judge Clancy asked.

"I don't even know who he is," Lydia replied. "Aleta is simply covering that contingency. I'm here in case I can think of an alternative line of defense that would call for different questions."

Gray Zenon entered and Lydia relaxed. Gray was a quiet spoken, young man who had a keen mind and could argue a case well.

He was taken with the huge tanks of fish lining two walls in Stanley's office. The third wall was a picture window overlooking the refurbished main street of downtown Willow Glen, now home to a series of renown specialty shops that visitors flocked to each summer enjoying the beauty of the street itself with its matching brick-faced shops each with a large multi-paned window in which wares were displayed.

The shops flourished and Stanley kept the rents reasonable. The shop owners stayed.

Stanley had a list of businesses wanting to set up shop on the exclusive street. Stanley had started accumulating property on Second Street at the same time as he had been purchasing property on Main Street as one by one shops folded. The property owners were discouraged by the rapid development of superstores and giant malls within driving distance of the Tri-City area. They saw no future in the small downtown area with its woeful lack of parking. A three-tiered parking garage was finished before the first of the new stores on Main Street opened for business.

Gray Zenon had never visited the famed Willow Glen Main Street, and now as the young lawyer looked out the window, he wondered why. He turned to Aleta and said, "What a beautiful place to work!"

She smiled and asked pointedly, "Are you hinting?"

He chuckled. "Was I that obvious or are you that sharp?"

"If that's a multiple choice question, I choose 'B.'"

"I was drooling actually," Gray said. "The public defenders' office lacks all amenities."

"You were disappointed the last time we met."

"Well, first you hogged the spotlight with that computer contraption and not speaking," Gray said. "You were a circus! Then suddenly you went deaf. I now understand it was a virus, but the timing was astounding and I'm not using that term lightly. Then you prepped the young prosecutor so well to take over I was taken by surprise at every turn. That ranks as one of my worst days as a trial lawyer."

"Your client was reprehensible."

"I don't choose my clients," Gray rejoined. "So, what surprise have you cooked up for me today?"

Aleta introduced him to Judge Davis.

"You're here as amicus curiae," Gray commented. "However, Aleta needs no help and Judge Clancy is one of the sharpest men on the bench, so I'm obviously the one who could foul this deposition up, and if I do, it would get thrown out when this case comes to court. Have I got the picture right?"

"Aleta covers all bases," Lydia said.

"Well, let's see if I can surprise the surpriser," Gray said.

With the videotape rolling, Stella Woodbridge told her story. Aleta asked a few clarifying questions, but let the testimony stand pretty much unadorned.

It was a strong, lucid account, both detailed and emotion-laden. Gray knew that the DNA evidence would confirm that Stuart Fouts had ejaculated inside Stella Woodbridge. He could only see one visible defense.

"Your Honor," Gray said. "I'd like to request that Lydia Davis begin the questioning of Mrs. Woodbridge."

"This is irregular," Judge Clancy declared.

"Your Honor, rape is a delicate issue and the witness is ninety. It would be better if a woman asked the questions. If this were a trial, I would have one of the female prosecutors step in at this juncture."

"I'll allow it considering Lydia Davis's reputation."

Lydia looked at Gray Zenon quizzically. He hastily scribbled a few phrases on a piece of paper and handed it to her. After looking at them, she nodded. He had thought of the only defense she could see and he knew a man couldn't pull it off.

"Mrs. Woodbridge, how long ago did your husband die?" Lydia began.

"Twenty two years. He was ten years older than me. He was seventy-eight."

"Thank you, Mrs. Woodbridge," Lydia said. "May I suggest you don't give me more than I ask for."

Stella nodded.   Lydia asked several questions about when her son died.

"Was your son a loving man?" Lydia asked.

"He loved me."

"Was he demonstrative?   Did he hug you when you said hello or goodbye?"

"Yes."

"Did he put his arm around you to steady you when you were walking, help you in and out of the car—things like that?"

"Yes."

"Did he learn how to be demonstrative from his father?"

"I guess so."

"You were married over fifty years, weren't you?"

"Yes."

"After you lost both your husband and your son, didn't you long for the loving touch of a man?"

"Yes."

"Did you communicate this desire to anyone?"

"Yes."

"To whom?"

"Eunice and I talked about it.   We both miss our husbands."

"Before Eunice, did you tell Mr. Fouts how much you missed your husband?"

"Yes, I did. I used to tell him all the time when I asked him to do things like clean the trap under the sink, things that my husband used to do."

"Did you tell him how your husband used to kiss you?"

"No. That wouldn't have been appropriate."

"You don't wear a bra, do you?"

"No."

"Don't you think that's a bit provocative?"

"I guess, but I'm ninety years old and I'm pretty withered. I don't think I look very feminine anymore."

"Didn't you stop wearing one to be seen as just a wee bit sexy?"

"I stopped wearing one when I had surgery for breast cancer and they were uncomfortable and I just never got back in the habit. My husband liked it. He was still alive then, so I guess the answer to your question is yes. I did do it to be a wee bit sexy for my husband, but after he died, I stopped thinking about that."

"You were only sixty eight. Surely, you had some sexual fantasies."

"I had just finished radiation therapy and I was so tired all the time, I didn't think about sex at all. I was grieving the loss of my husband and it took me a couple years to get my energy back. By then I had settled into living by myself."

"Mr. Zenon," Lydia said. "You may continue."

Gray Zenon was disappointed. He'd heard that Lydia Davis was a powerful woman on a cross. He only saw one woman gently asking questions of another. It's true she'd elicited a lot of information, but she hadn't broken the witness. He'd have to do it.

"Mrs. Woodbridge, when the police knocked on the door, why did Mr. Fouts let you answer?"

"He knew I wouldn't give him away."

"He trusted you?" he queried sharply.

"Yes, he did. He knew I'd do anything to protect my dog, so when the cop said I was under arrest for disturbing the peace and then pulled me out the door and handcuffed me and marched me off to his squad car, I think Stuart was caught flat-footed."

"Didn't you protest that you weren't dressed?"

"Yes, but he said I had a dress on which I did, so he just went ahead and arrested me. I've never been arrested. I didn't know what to do. It's very scary."

"Scarier than the so-called rape?" Gray Zenon charged. "Wasn't that because the sex was consensual?"

"You don't know much about older women, do you? We are scared of different things than you might think. Being handcuffed and locked in the back seat of a car is very scary. Having someone threaten to kill one's loving dog is scarier than that. And that's what made being pulled from the house so scary. Biffy was still in there."

"Mrs. Woodbridge, I suggest..." Gray Zenon began.

"I'm not done answering your last question."

"I'm ready to move on," Gray Zenon stated.

"Well, I'm not answering anything else until I get to answer the question you asked. I said you didn't know much about older women. Well, this proves it. We will not be shut up. You asked a question. I have the right to give an answer as long as what I say is responsive and I am being responsive. The question had two parts. I chose to answer the questions in the order asked. And the answer to the first part is that the whole series of events scared me. The rape was beyond scary. It was a terrifying experience. It was painful and degrading. It robbed me of my dignity. It made me feel helpless, powerless, weak and old. Consensual? Not one bit! Stuart Fouts forcibly raped me. And that Mr. Zenon is the whole truth."

Gray Zenon could think of nothing more to say. The taping was stopped moments later.

Stella Woodbridge broke into tears and Aleta went over and put her arm around the old lady and assured her that she had been a very creditable witness.

"I can't ever do this again," she said. "Not ever."

"It's over," Aleta said. "I'm sure these gentlemen will excuse us. Lydia, get Mr. Chin and Mr. Jackson started on interviewing Stella's friends. Stella and I need to spend some time together before another minute passes."

Lydia ushered the three men out and closed the door.

"I was raped, Stella," Aleta said. "And I had to give a deposition as you just did. The rapists were arrested and pled guilty. I never had to repeat my story again. I'm hoping that's what will happen here. You did a wonderful job. You were up against two of the best lawyers in the state. I didn't expect Gray Zenon to tag-team you. It was partly my fault. If anything happened to you, I didn't want Stuart Fouts to get away."

"I didn't tell the whole truth," Stella said, starting to cry.

"What part wasn't the whole truth?"

"The part about the cop pulling me out of the house. I was scared, but not of being arrested, but of being let go. I was sure Stuart would stop Biffy from barking and then the cop would let me go and I'd have to go back."

"You didn't lie, Stella. You had mixed feelings. Your reaction to the rather bizarre rescue is understandably confusing. You were relieved and frightened both."

"And I wasn't honest about the cop. He assured me as soon as he put me in the squad that I wasn't under arrest but all I could think about was Biffy."

"He told me."

"You know him?"

"You were pretty confused at the time, but I thought you knew he was my husband."

"I wasn't cooperative at all. Here he was trying to save my life…"

"And he counted on your not being cooperative," Aleta explained. "He had to get you away fast."

"I don't want to go back to my house yet, but I suppose I'll have to, won't I?"

"Bessie rather likes having you there to keep Eunice out of her hair so she can paint. Why don't we wait for a bit before we make that decision? I need to find out where Stuart Fouts is and how soon we might go to trial. I also need to research the law on whether you need to do this again."

"I don't think I can."

"I will never force you. I won't even pressure you," Aleta said. "The choice will be yours. I am very proud of the job you did today. Give me a chance to find out what options we have."

"There could be options?" she asked, hopefully.

"I can already think of a couple," Aleta said.

"And he won't get away with it?'"

"I'm not including that as an option," Aleta said. "Are you okay? We are about to be interrupted."

"Are you psychic?" Stella asked.

CHAPTER 6

"I hear familiar voices outside the door," Aleta revealed as she flipped on the intercom and told Alice to send in whoever was waiting.

"It's most of the staff," Alice said. "We have a problem out here."

Judge Davis opened the door and walked in followed by the firm's new associates: Roland Chin, a short Chinese gentleman, and Andrew Jackson, a taller muscular black man. Behind them came the firm's only legal aide, freckle-faced Tim Jordan.

"Stella," Lydia said, looking directly at the old woman first. "Please let me apologize for being so rough. I was playing a role—a nasty one—setting you up for Mr. Zenon as I did. I wanted you to get justice."

"I understand," Stella said. "Why do victims have to be treated like criminals in courts?"

"Because sometimes they bear false testimony," Lydia explained.

"Oh," came the soft response.

"What's the problem?" Aleta interjected, looking from one worried face to another in the group.

"Stella, how many friends did you send over?" Lydia asked.

"Five."

"I have nine names," Tim Jordan reported.

"I told Eunice she could send a couple friends over and they could use my name," Stella explained.

"Take all nine," Aleta decided. "Those are Stanley's orders."

"What about the other thirty?" Tim asked.

Aleta gasped.

"Thirty?"

"That was how many at my last count," Tim said. "More are arriving all the time. Cora Jo is handing out numbers."

"Why Cora Jo?" Aleta asked.

"Because Cora Jo has the guts to turn down anyone who doesn't treat her with respect," Tim responded. "We have standards. She almost didn't let that lawyer guy, Gray Zenon, in."

"I guess he flunked his interview," Aleta quipped.

"He was here for an interview¿ Tim asked.

"No. He was here from the public defender's office for the deposition, but he hinted that he wanted to work here. Do you have any idea which aspect of Cora Jo he reacted to?"

"Take your pick—race, weight, attitude."

"How did he treat you?"

"He didn't guess that I'm gay if that's what you're asking. I think he snubbed me because I wasn't an associate."

"He's too ambitious for this firm," Aleta concluded.

"Lydia laughed.

"You're ambitious."

"I know that. But Stanley's not, and it's his firm."

"I think your associates are ambitious."

"They have a healthy normal level of ambition. It's what makes them good lawyers. But they respect people," Aleta explained. "Too bad. We could use another associate."

"I could help out for a few weeks," Lydia offered.

"I would like that very much," Aleta said, and then she turned to the group and addressed each individually.

"Tim, weed out all divorce cases unless there is a custody problem and a child advocate is needed. Those go to Robert.   Criminal cases, as usual, send to the public defender's office, only this time give them Gray Zenon's name. If it's a will or contract, send them directly to Chin or Jackson."

"Do I get Cora Jo to help me with the line?" Tim asked.

"Yes. I can see she's your type."

Tim raised an eyebrow.

"Ready to do battle with anyone lacking respect for this office but with a soft heart for people in need."

The staff scattered.

"You know," Lydia commented. "I wouldn't mind working in an office like this."

"You're welcome for as long as you care to stay, but I know that after a while that judge's chair will beckon and you'll be drawn back. You are a good judge. We need you on the bench."

The first to enter after that little speech was an old man with a large dog on the end of a leather leash.

"A smooth-coated Collie!" Aleta exclaimed. "What a beautiful dog! How old is he?"

"Six. His name's Collie."

Aleta chuckled.

"Talk about appropriate."

"He's being sued. Me too I guess. They want money and for me to put him down."

"He bit someone?"

"A girl. A spoiled brat!" the old man said heatedly. "I told her he had a sore ear and not to touch his ears. She stuck out her tongue at me. I took him the dog park and let him go. There were five dogs there. I knew all of them. Collie gets along with all of those dogs real well. I got to talking, so I didn't see this little girl and two of her friends come in. Collie is a friendly dog. He likes kids and my friends know that so when they saw the kids go up to Collie, they didn't say anything. The girl pulled his ear. My friends told her to back off because he growled, but she ignored them. Collie nipped her finger. Next thing I know she went screaming to her mother and then all hell broke loose."

"I gather he was cleared of rabies," Aleta said.

"Cost me a fortune to board him. They wouldn't let me visit. I told my vet and he wrote a letter and then I got him out. He was wearing a rabies tag and everything."

"How much is the family suing for?" Aleta asked.

"Ten thousand," he said.

"Counter sue," Lydia declared. "Thirty thousand."

"The boarding didn't cost me that much," the old man protested.

"Didn't cost them ten thousand for a band-aid either," Lydia returned.

She turned to Aleta.

"I get cases like this all the time. My hands are tied unless the defendant counter sues."

"I don't want to cause trouble," the old man said. "But I don't' want to pay what I shouldn't have to neither."

"What's their argument?"

"The mother says the dog shouldn't be running free if he couldn't be touched, but I argued back that none of the other dogs was going to pull his ear."

"There's a sign at the entrance to the dog park, isn't there?" Lydia asked. "Doesn't it say 'Dogs and owners only. No Children without supervision.'?"

"Yeh. How did you know?"

Aleta picked up the thread of Lydia's argument.

"Was the mother with the child?"

"Why am I suing them?"

"Because they caused you grief and expense by disobeying the rules which you obeyed," Lydia said. "If the mother wins, the city will close down the dog park. I'm surprised they weren't named in the suit."

"Oh, they were. I think they're going to settle."

"Aleta, let me take this one. I need to call the mayor. We can't let them settle."

"Go for it," Aleta urged.

Lydia flew out of the room. The old man looked at Aleta.

"Is she any good? Seems a bit flighty."

"She's a better attorney than anyone in this firm. She's helping us out because my husband's in the hospital. She's a judge."

"But thirty thousand is too much," he said.

"When you buy a used car, do you pay the first price quoted?"

"So we're planning to bargain?" the old man asked.

"Yes, we are. Tim will have papers for you to sign. If we don't win, you don't pay us at all. If we do, we get one third."

"I don't want that woman to close the dog park."

"Neither do I," Aleta said. "Alice will give you an appointment to go over your case in detail with Judge Davis. Tim will give you a contract to sign. Give him this slip."

"You only wrote a couple cords. Will he know what they mean?"

"The name tells him who's handling your case. 'Contingency' tells him the fee schedule. 'Immediate' tells him a case has been filed against you."

"Good system. Thanks."

Judge Davis reentered the room after Aleta had assigned the next two cases.

"We've got the city as a client as well," she announced.

"Willow Glen?"

"Contingency basis. Can Alice fax over the contract?"

"Just this case, right?"

"The firm they have now just keeps settling and charging a fee."

"We can't handle the city. We aren't big enough."

Lydia smiled.

"I told them that you would only consider representing them on a case by case basis."

"Stanley owns this street the office is on. We could have a conflict of interest."

"He owns more than this street, my dear. He's planning to develop Second Street as well."

"He didn't tell me any of that."

"He said you two have been talking a lot lately."

"We have, but I never ask him about his investments."

"I think he loves the fact that you don't. He loves the fact that you are careful about how you spend money. He loves being able to give you special things."

"I love that too. It gives him such pleasure."

"Take on a few city cases. It will work in your favor if you ever decide you want to be a judge."

After Tim introduced the next petitioner formally as Mrs. William Brockbank, he set a twenty-dollar bill on table in front of Aleta.

"What's this?" she asked.

"A bribe, I think," Tim said. "I moved her up in line."

"I tipped the boy," Mrs. Brockbank said.

"Put it in the cat fund," Aleta directed.

"We have a cat fund?" Tim asked.

"We do now," Aleta said, smiling.

She then turned to the richly dressed woman and said, "We aren't taking your case."

"Do you know who I am?"

"Yes," Aleta said crisply.

"We are willing to pay double your usual rate."

"Not interested."

"Is that because I tipped the boy?" Mrs. Brockbank inquired. "I realize now that was a mistake. I'm not used to waiting in line. I'm sorry if that offended you."

"It was a ridiculous action, Aleta commented.

"More so than having prospective clients stand in line," Mrs. Brockbank quipped.

"We all make mistakes," Aleta responded. "Don't give it another thought."

"So you'll take my case?"

"No."

"It's not exactly my case. It's about my son. He's seventeen, you see, and he's gotten himself in a spot of trouble."

"There are a number of child advocates in the area. I'm certain any of them will do a fine job of representing him."

"It's more complicated than that," Mrs. Brockbank said. "I plan to sue."

"Stop right there," Aleta ordered. "I'm not interested."

"But it's a money maker," she protested.

"If you don't leave, I will have Mr. Jordan call the police," Aleta said icily.

Grumbling, Mrs. Brockbank left.

"Tim, I assume the next prospect is waiting?"

"He is," Tim said. "Brandon Overmann."

"Show him in."

She heard Mr. Overmann say, "Thank you, Mr. Jordan."

Aleta quickly assessed the well-dressed man and asked, "Downsized?'

"Yes, Mrs. Praetzel."

"Age discrimination?"

"Blatant."

"Mr., Jackson will be your lawyer. He's got a fire in his belly. He'll eat your ex-employer for breakfast."

The man smiled as he took the slip Aleta handed him.

"Interesting code. Which fee tier am I on?"

Aleta smiled as she replied, "Contingency. No fee unless we win."

"Am I suing for money?"

"Oh, yes, Mr. Overmann. We are suing for money. You have a good case."

"How do you know?" he asked, puzzled.

"You don't want me to give away my trade secrets, so you?"

"Thank you for taking my case," Overmann said politely. "Good day, Mrs. Praetzel, Judge Davis."

After he left, Lydia leaned over and whispered, "I'm puzzled. Why him? Why contingency? Why not the woman?"

"Did you like her?"

"Not at all."

"I have thirty-nine clients wanting my services. Why waste time on a woman I don't like? Besides, she wants to sue someone for money."

"So does Mr. Overmann."

"No, he doesn't. He's looking or justice. I decided to go for money."

"He doesn't just want his job back?"

"He thinks he does, but they would make his life miserable if he succeeded in that goal. I chose a new one."

"You don't even know the facts of the case," her mother-in-law pointed out.

"I know the man. He selected me as the lawyer who had a chance to win his case, yet he accepted by assigning him to Mr. Jackson without dissent. He knows how a business is run. He allowed a woman to push in front of him and didn't complain. He thanked Tim politely without a negative word about the woman. He came prepared with documents to substantiate his case. His manner told me he was a gentleman. He did everything right. I was impressed."

"So, actually, was I. I just wondered if we were on the same page."

"Andrew has been dying for a case to sink his teeth into. This is one where he can do just that."

"Why are we waiting?"

Aleta hit the intercom.

"Tell Andrew he has five minutes,"

The tall black associate rushed in and closed the door quickly.

"It's a huge case, Mrs. Praetzel. Why me?"

"Didn't Mr. Overmann tell you why?"

"He said you said I'd do a good job."

Aleta grinned.

"That's not what he said."

Andrew sheepishly quoted the man.

"He said I would eat his ex-employer for breakfast."

"He told you he wanted us to help him get his job back, right?"

"That's why I'm confused. You took his case on a contingency basis."

"We aren't going for his old job. They would hound him right out of it. We're going for a golden parachute for him. I suggest you start by asking him to explain his case to you and then ask to see his documents. Spend the rest of the morning with him. Eat lunch with him. Get to know him. You have the same taste in suits. Don't think he hasn't noticed. Be honest with him. You will have the whole firm behind you, but I want you to be lead counsel on this one."

"Thank you!" Andrew exclaimed and hurried out.

"Why did he come in?" Lydia asked.

"To find out what direction he was supposed to go. Overmann said east; I apparently said west."

"I gather you don't take many cases on contingency."

"Hardly any," Aleta said. "But in this case I sensed blatant injustice."

"I'm surprised you didn't take it yourself."

"I told Stanley I wouldn't take any case unless I felt God wanted me to. We have two super associates who are ready to spread their wings. The smaller cases are keeping them busy and giving them experience. Chin is more ready than Jackson, but this case is one where Andrew can come into his own."

"How will Chin feel about this?"

Aleta pressed the intercom.

"Alice, ask Mr. Chin to come to my office for a few minutes."

Roland Chin walked in a minute later.

Aleta got right to the point.

"Roland, I just gave Andrew a huge case. It's a case you could have argued well, but Andrew has a passion in this area. I do, however, have a special project I want you to head. May we discuss that at one today?"

Roland Chin left smiling.

CHAPTER 7

It was just before one when Dr. Cook entered Stanley's hospital room and complained because Alfredo hadn't arrived with the food.

"The hospital has a cafeteria," Stanley quipped.

"You invited me to lunch."

"You're early," Stanley remarked. "I said one o'clock."

"You're not even supposed to be here. You were signed out at eight this morning."

"That was a mistake," Stanley said. "Aleta had the day planned and I was scheduled to stay here."

"You could have gone home."

"And disrupt Aleta's schedule?"

The hefty neurosurgeon, Dr. Michael Taekman, appeared in the doorway.

"Okay, I'm here. Where's lunch?"

"Coming," Stanley said. "Alfredo doesn't know doctors ever actually look at their watches."

"We keep track of time," Michael said jovially. "We're always late."

"Except for meals," Stanley noted. "Where are Chesney and Hughes?"

"We're here," Dr. Chesney said, entering the room. "I could use a good meal. I'm going to have a busy evening. I brought Herve with me."

Stanley brightened at the sight of his old hospital roommate.

"Not home cooking this time," Stanley explained. "Aleta ordered take-out."

"I like the company," the ancient psychiatrist, Dr. Herve Schwartzman, said. "The food is immaterial"

"Not to me," Dr. Michael Taekman said. "These pounds demand only the best and lots of it."

"Soon you're going to have to operate sitting down," Dr. Cook observed. "If I were your doctor, I'd have you on a diet."

"Am I ever glad that I'm family," Taekman returned.

"Who is your doctor?" Stanley asked.

"Don't have one. I'm healthy."

"That's the state I was in two days ago when Wayne turned a simple ear cleaning into a full physical."

"Heard about that," Dr. Chesney said. "I haven't done a physical on a man in so long I'd probably forget to do the important parts."

"Do you ever take male patients?" Stanley asked hopefully.

Alfredo walked in.

"Is this a private conversation?"

"Food!" several doctors exclaimed.

Alfredo handed out the boxes. There were extra.

"Leave them," Stanley said. "The hospital has taken me off the list for meals. And Aleta is planning to pick me up at seven or eight or nine or ten."

"She's very busy," Alfredo said. "She ate while she worked. So did your mother."

Stanley's hand stopped half way to his mouth.

"My mother is visiting the office?"

"She isn't visiting," Alfredo said. "Alice changed the daily meal order to include her."

"She's working for me?" Stanley gasped. "I can't have my mother working for me."

Herve chuckled.

"I can see Stanley needs an hour of therapy, and he has two pieces of chocolate cake."

"I don't pay in cake."

"We can work on that too," Herve said, smiling.

"Were you planning to go back to work this week?" Dr. Cook asked.

"No, but Mother shouldn't be working, should she, Dr. Hughes? I mean, isn't it too soon after her stroke?"

"I think it's a good idea."

"You're no help."

"Why don't you want her there?" Herve asked.

The doctors eyed Stanley curiously.

"O, for heaven's sake, I'm not a neurotic mess. It's just that she'll nose around. Mothers do that."

"I served forty five lunches at your office today," Alfredo said. "I got the feeling she was helping."

"Mother's a judge, not a lawyer."

"I'm a neurosurgeon," Dr. Taekman interjected. "But I still managed to deliver Lauren's baby at your party."

"I think she can struggle through a few small cases," Dr. Hughes said.

"Small?" Alfredo exclaimed. "She's representing the city."

"City?" Stanley gasped. "What city?"

"Willow Glen."

"She can't! I have interests all over town."

"Relax, Stanley," Dr. Cook said. "You'll break your stitches."

"Are you talking about the stitches behind my ear?"

"Unless you had something else fixed."

"Don't start with me!"

"Your mother hasn't forgotten what the term 'conflict of interest means'," Dr. Hughes said. "In fact, she's sharper than ever. Landing the city account is a plum."

"We're a child advocacy firm."

"Aleta is your partner," Wayne Cook said.

"Don't remind me, I brought this on myself. I told her she could take on every one of Stella's geriatric friends. How did she jump from the geriatric crowd to the politicos that live in city hall?"

"Jackson has a big case too," Alfredo went on.

"You know more about what goes on in my office than I do," Stanley muttered

Alfredo took this as encouragement and added more news.

"Cora Jo's on a diet. Tim told her my lunches were perfect for her diet because they were balanced, something about insulin making her hungry. She's lost ten pounds so far."

"Well, I agree with Tim," Dr. Cook said. "Your lunches are perfect, except that Stanley should give Herve that extra piece of cake so Herve can do the therapy he needs to get him back to being the pleasant chap we all know and love."

"You're talking to a man who spent twenty horrible minutes in a dumpster," Stanley declared. "I left my good humor buried under rancid barbecue sauce."

"That was two days ago," Cook declared. "I'm sure Aleta has already forgotten the incident."

"May I remind you that Aleta wasn't in the dumpster. I was."

"Stanley, cheer up," Dr. Cook said. "Geriatrics and politicos are safe clients. Politicians might talk you to death, but they don't shoot people."

"I won't remind you about the Oakwood mess."

"Your mother would never take a shady client," Dr. Cook assured him.

"You're right," Stanley agreed. "Herve, the cake is yours. Make me a happy men."

"I'll take the cake," Herve said, plucking it from the box. "And I can guarantee one of us will be a happy man."

"Better be me," Stanley grumbled.

Herve smiled and then he began what he referred to as his 'Praetzel therapy'.

"Your wife loves you. Your mother loves you. Your dogs love you. I'm not sure about your horse. She's hard to read. Your wife's stepmother loves you—always a plus. Your father-in-law loves you. Aleta's grandmother loves you. And I think her husband is fond of you. He's like the horse. The big ones are hard to read. And, if that's not enough, all of us came to your party and Aleta isn't even here. We like you too."

Herve paused for a moment before finishing.

"Oh, yes, your father is proud of you."

"He didn't see me covered in garbage," Stanley quipped.

"Wayne did, and he even gave you a physical."

"Don't remind me."

"You should be reminded. When you mentioned you hadn't had one, Wayne worried you might be hiding something. I know he made it seem like a joke, but you and Aleta have surprised him before. I'm surprised he didn't give you an MRI. It seems to be his favorite diagnostic too when it comes to either of you."

Stanley studied Dr. Cook's face for several minutes and then blurted out, "Don't stop being my doctor. I need you. I'm married to Aleta. And she tends to do things that get me shot."

The entire group laughed heartily.

That was in the past.

On the other side of Arborville, Tonia Morales looked out her kitchen window at Stella Woodbridge's empty house and thought about her neighbor.

Stella was braver then she was. Stuart Fonts had scared her into being silent about his attack. She wondered if Stella would have been so brave if she hadn't been rescued by the police.

Three times the week following that rape over a year ago, Stuart had showed up at her front door and returned her cat. The cat was unharmed, but Tonia got the message. She remained mute about what had happened, grateful that she had survived.

She locked her doors and windows securely every night. She suffered through the stifling summer heat not daring to let the cooler night breezes waft gently through the house restoring some coolness until the next day's sun beat down on it again. Her cat howled to be let out, but Tonia refused to open the door. Fluffy eventually resigned herself to being an indoor cat.

As Tonia looked out her kitchen window, she saw a car drive into Stella's driveway. Stella and a stout woman in her fifties emerged from the car.

Such pretty blond hair, Tonia thought, as she watched the stout woman open the door to the house. Stella was smiling.

I'm glad she's happy, Tonia thought as she watched them exit with armloads of clothes and a cardboard box.

I guess she's going to stay wherever she is for a while longer, Tonia thought. I don't blame her. Even though Stuart wasn't at his mother's house, he wasn't in jail either. No one knew where he was. That is, no one in the neighborhood knew.

She watched the car drive away and stared out the window for several minutes before returning to the chore of washing her lunch dishes. The cat meowed, but she didn't turn around.

"As soon as I'm done, I'll feed you," she said.

Tonia liked the daytime. She felt safe during the period before the lamps needed to be turned on and shadows hung in corners. Until she went to bed, she kept lights on in every room in the house, reasoning that criminals liked dark houses. She still had trouble thinking of Stuart as a criminal. Criminals were strangers with unshaven faces, scowling brows and furtive eyes. Stuart didn't quite fit the stereotype. He was overweight. His sloppiness was confined to his weight being distributed unattractively around his mid section. He was an innocuous appearing, taller than average, middle-aged man with thinning light brown hair.

Despite the fact that Stella Woodbridge had been attacked in the daylight hours, Tonia clung to her belief that with the sun came safety. She'd been attacked at night.

Stuart had said he would be watching her. Since the darkness held many hiding places, Tonia knew she wouldn't be able to tell, so she hadn't gone out, hadn't called for help, hadn't even moved from where he had left her for several hours, fearful that even the slightest movement might trigger another attack. She hadn't heard him leave.

It had been the longest, most terrifying night of her life.

She turned and put the dish with the fresh cat food on the floor and refilled the water dish. She threw the soft pouch in the garbage under the sink. She was surprised when she shut the cabinet door that Fluffy wasn't hunched over her food.

Odd, she thought. She was nearby a moment ago.

The bathroom, Stella thought. The cat went in to use the litter pan and closed the door accidentally again.

"Fluffy," she said as she climbed the stairs to the second floor. "You have got to stop rubbing your back on the door edge."

She heard the soft meowing as she approached the bathroom. The twinge of apprehension faded.

Just as she put her hand on the doorknob, a voice behind her said, "Leave the cat in there."

Tonia froze.

A hand grabbed her arm and propelled her into her bedroom.

She found her voice, "Please, Stuart. No! Please."

"Where is Stella Woodbridge?" he growled.

"I don't know," she said.

His hand came up. She winced expecting to be hit in the face, but the hand grabbed the front of her blouse and tore it from her body.

"No! Please. No!" she cried.

"Where is she?"

"I told you I don't know. No one does."

He pushed her down on the bed and tore off the rest of her clothes. Her fear forced her to reveal what little she did know. It wasn't much – just the hair color of the woman Stella had come home with and the fact that she'd arrived in a sedan. She didn't know what kind. She couldn't remember the color.

She begged him to leave, promising again not to tell anyone he was in the neighborhood.

He loosed his grip momentarily. She pulled away and raced down the stairs. He caught her pulled her over to where the knives where, grabbed one and then dragging her back upstairs, he planted the knife in the floorboard outside the bathroom door.

"That's for kitty," he threatened.

Where her next words came from, she didn't know. Perhaps a year of living in fear, assuring herself that her cooperation was keeping her safe, only to discover she had been clinging to a false belief, was what forced her to blurt out, "Kill her then and be done with it. I won't let you rape me again."

Stuart's laugh sent a shiver down her spine. She couldn't stem the trembling.

"I'm not going to kill her," Stuart informed her, his voice filled with hatred. "You won't get off that way. No, I'll tie you up, gag you, cut off her foot, then ..."

"No!" she screamed. "Oh God! No!"

The next two hours were a living hell. He wasn't interested in having sex. He wanted her terrified and compliant. He forced her to debase herself and ended each session by raping her. The rapes were violent. After the third rape, he got up and announced that he was borrowing her car.

"I'll be back," he said. "You stay right where you are until I return."

Tonia lay still, listening. She heard the car start up and back down the driveway. Still, she didn't move.

Quiet as the house was, she didn't hear him come in. When he appeared at her bedroom door, she jumped.

"Stay there," he ordered again.

She nodded mutely.

He will check one more time, she thought. If I'm wrong, I will have messed up my chance to escape.

She guessed correctly however.

He was back within minutes and threw that afternoon's Tri City Register on the bed.

"Just came," he said. "The newsboy almost caught me."

She stayed rigidly in place, trying to forget she was totally naked. Any movement on her part might reenergize him. She wanted him gone.

He came over to where she was lying and poked her injured breast. She yelped.

"Whoa," he said. "You bring out the animal in me."

And while she tried not to move, she blanched and her body began to tremble.

"How can I resist?" he sneered. "You can't get enough of me, can you?"

She couldn't believe he could manage to rape her again so soon. Her mind when blank as if the waves of pain were all it could handle. Her screams came automatically. She didn't know whether he told her to stop screaming or not. She barely felt the pillow jammed down on her face.

"Let me die," she prayed just before she lost consciousness.

When she came to, she felt an odd sensation from the breast not injured earlier. She glanced down. There was a note taped to her breast.

"Stay put," it read.

The house was quiet. How long had she been unconscious? How long had he been gone? How much time did she have?

She heard Fluffy meowing. She rose and stumbled toward the bathroom. She pulled the knife out of the floor and opened the door. Fluffy ran between her feet and scampered down the stairs toward her lunch.

Tonia sat down on the toilet and looked at the paper she'd picked up when she'd risen from the bed. There was a follow-up story to the one about the woman who was found in the dumpster. The paper identified her rescuer as Stanley Praetzel, an Arborville deputy, who had been involved in the rescue two weeks ago of Stella Woodbridge.

Tonia read the article to the end where it mentioned that the law offices of Praetzel, Locke and Praetzel were located on Main Street in Willow Glen.

As she rose from the toilet, Tonia saw that the bowl was filled with blood. The sight startled her. She dropped the newspaper and ran back to the bedroom.

There were spots of blood on the spread but none on the carpeting. Slowly, her mind grasped what she had seen. A few drops of blood had colored the water in the toilet. She wasn't bleeding to death.

She began to dress. She had to leave now. But Stuart had her car. And she didn't want him to know where she was.

And she had to take Fluffy.

She called a friend on her cell. "I need to take Fluffy to the vet and my car's in the shop. It's an emergency."

After, she finished dressing, she fetched the cardboard carrying case she used when she took Fluffy to the vet and searched the house for her cat.

Fluffy was in her favorite afternoon spot, the front window. Tonia plucked the cat from the sill and deposited her into the opened box, then folded the top down. Fluffy yowled her protest, but Tonia, seeing her friend drive up, grabbed the box and her purse and hurried from the house.

"Head for Main Street in Willow Glen," she said.

"Your vet moved?"

"Just drive me."

"This isn't and emergency?" the friend challenged.

"For me it is," Tonia said, deciding she would explain part of the problem. "Stuart Fouts is back in the neighborhood."

"You saw him."

"Yes. And he scares me."

"Surely, he wouldn't dare attack another women in the neighborhood."

Tonia decided to avoid responding to that statement so she said, "I have a friend. She's meeting me on Main Street."

"Why didn't she pick you up?"

"She's still working," Tonia said. "She said I could come there and wait."

"Where exactly are you going?"

"There's a law office on Main Street. She works there."

"I know where that is. I'll drop you at the back door."

CHAPTER 8

Tonia Morales took the elevator to the second floor. When the elevator doors opened, she saw a number of people waiting near the receptionist's desk.

Alice looked up and saw both the distressed look on the woman's face and the fact that she was carry in an animal in a temporary cardboard container. It was obviously a cat because it was yowling and scratching.

Not wanting a loose cat in the office, Alice ushered the woman past Tim and the next person in line.

"Emergency," she said to Tim.

He opened the door and Alice hastened to explain her abrupt entry to the younger woman seated behind the desk.

"Sorry, Mrs. Praetzel, but I believe this is an emergency. This woman just arrived and I'm afraid her cat is not going to stay in that box much longer and you being a lover of animals…"

"Thank you, Alice," Aleta said.

She handed the new client in front of her a slip and told him to see Mr. Chin. The man left and Alice closed the door.

"It's about Stella Woodbridge," Tonia said. "And that woman in the dumpster."

"I'm Aleta Praetzel and this is my mother-in-law, Judge Davis." Aleta said. "Who are you?"

"I can't talk in front of the judge!" Tonia said completely undone.

Lydia rose. "I can leave."

"If Robert's office is free, continue the interviews in there," Aleta said.

"Come, take my chair," Lydia said. "Relax, your secret is safe with Aleta."

After Lydia left, Tonia began. Her story was disjointed, but when Aleta didn't jump up to do anything or call anyone, Tonia settled down and told her everything.

When she finished, Aleta picked up her phone punched in Alice's number.

"I need Chief Milani on line one and Chief West on line two – a conference call. This is an emergency. And send Cora Jo in here."

"What are you going to do?"

"Protect you. Protect Stanley. Get your statement and get you to the hospital."

"I can't testify."

"Right now we need to catch him."

"That's the problem," Tonia said. "He was caught and the judge let him go."

"That won't happen this time," Aleta stated firmly. "He's now a serial rapist."

"I can't testify. I'm not brave like Stella," Tonia cried. "I can't do it. I know I can't."

"Let's not jump ahead," Aleta said, her tone warm and gentle. "I have to move fast because he needs to be caught before he hurts someone else. You just sit back and relax. I will ask for your approval before each step."

"You didn't ask for it before you called the police."

"I didn't need to for that."

"I thought lawyers kept things confidential."

"They do. But as an officer of the court, I must report a crime." Aleta explained. "The details are confidential except for his threats. I can't protect you or your cat without revealing those."

Cora Jo knocked softly and then entered.

"Mrs. Morales is going to make a statement and I need it typed and signed before she goes to the hospital," Aleta told her. "I'm expecting calls from Milani and West, so I'm putting you in charge of getting the statement. I already have the full story. I just need a bare bones statement so Stuart Fouts can be rearrested and charged again."

"Rape?" Cora Jo asked softly.

Tonia nodded.

"Multiple," Aleta added. "And other injuries. We'll let the medical report state the specifics."

"You poor dear," Cora Jo said sympathetically as she moved across the room.

"Let's just move over to the corner out of Mrs. Praetzel's way."

Tonia picked up the cat carrier and moved to the window.

"What's your cat's name?" Cora Jo asked as she pulled the dictation machine into position.

"Fluffy," Tonia responded. "He said he'd cut off her feet if I didn't do what he asked."

"Why don't you take her out and hold her?" Cora Jo suggested. "No one comes in here except by invitation, so we won't be disturbed."

Carefully Tonia opened the box.

"What a lovely long-hair," Cora Jo exclaimed. "Where ever did you get her?"

"From the rescue place outside Arborville."

"Let's get this over with," Cora Jo said.

After she recorded the essentials, she let Tonia talk and she recorded her words silently.

Meanwhile, Aleta was told both police chiefs were on the line. She was succinct.

"Stuart Fouts is in town. He raped another woman-- Tonia Morales. We're getting her statement now. He's looking for Stella and probably Stanley. Tonia said he was angry about that article in the paper about the woman Stanley rescued. Was she one of Stuart Fouts' victims? If she is, she needs a police guard," Aleta declared. "Stella and Eunice stopped by the house for more of Stella's clothes. Tonia told Fouts. They could be shopping in town."

"Is Tonia at your office?" Milani asked.

"Yes, she's here." Aleta replied. "As soon as you send a police unit to escort her, she'll be ready to go. She's been badly hurt. See if Dr. Chesney will do the rape exam."

"Are you dictating to us?" Lyle cut in.

"Of course, I am. That's my style and you know it so just listen and obey."

She heard both men chuckle. Her tone, however, remained somber.

"Tonia is not to be left unguarded for a second. He's threats were horrendous."

"I'll send a woman," Lyle said. "She can stay with her every minute."

"Standard division of forces otherwise?" Tom asked.

"What does that mean?" Aleta pushed in.

"It means I'll take care of Stanley and Tom's men will cover your house and office. Peets will guard Bessie's house."

"What about Stella Woodbridge? And Eunice? I'm sure that's who was with her," Aleta put in.

"Aleta, I have Stella's number," Lyle responded. "I'm calling her as we speak."

"Oh," Aleta said in a small voice. "By the way, Fouts stole Tonia's car."

She then read the license plate number and the description over the phone despite the mutterings about lawyers leaving out important facts.

"I'm representing the victim," Aleta said in conclusion. "She has rights."

"Hey, we're on your side," Tom burst out.

"Fouts' public defender is rough on rape victims, so I'm putting everyone on notice."

"Aleta, we're here to protect and serve," Lyle responded. "I think that's written in bold letters on all our police cars."

"We'll give you this one," Tom started, his tone slightly patronizing.

Aleta interrupted. "He raped her four times!" And he crushed her spirit. She's an old woman. There may not be enough years left in her life for her to heal from this wicked assault."

"We'll get him!" Tom asserted immediately.

"And we will protect her," Lyle added.

"Thanks," Aleta said and glanced over at the two in the corner. Cora Jo had just finished.

"What if I don't testify?" Tonia queried.

"You already have," Aleta said. "We're taking this one step at a time. After you've been examined, I'm going to suggest you stay in the hospital overnight. Tomorrow I will have a safe place for you to stay."

"What about Fluffy?"

"Do you have a neighbor?"

"Fluffy trusts Stuart." Tonia said apprehensively. "If he called her, she'd go to him."

Cora Jo spoke up. "I could watch her until you're settled. I like cats."

"You'd have to keep her inside. She will run home otherwise."

"All my cats have been inside cats," Cora Jo said.

"You have cats?" Tonia asked.

"I had three. My last one just died. Leukemia. He was only seven," Cora Jo said.

"Fluffy is five," Tonia said. "She was just about a year old when I got her."

"I'll remember she's your cat," Cora Jo promised.

"I won't want her back until Stuart is in jail for good," Tonia decided.

"I'll get another cat to keep her company, then when you come, I'll still have a cat."

Tonia brightened, "They had lots of nice cats at that rescue place out side Arborville. I think Fluffy would like a friend. Now I'm her friend because I'm home all day."

Cora Jo lifted Fluffy out of Tonia's lap. Fluffy began purring immediately.

"She likes you!" Tonia exclaimed.

"She knows I like her. Cats know things like that." Cora Jo said.

She glanced at her boss, gave Tonia back the cat and hurried off.

Stanley was half asleep when the police guard was positioned outside his hospital room. Shortly afterward, Chief Lyle West walked in.

"I'm sleeping," Stanley said, "because I don't want to know why I suddenly have a guard on my door."

"Stuart Fouts is in town. He raped another woman and made angry noises when he saw your picture in the paper."

"And we know this how?

"The victim went straight to your office," Lyle said. "And ..."

"And met Aleta and she told Aleta everything and now we've got a sociopath chasing us."

"I didn't label him. How come you did?"

"I'm taking lessons from Dr. Schwartzman. Herve described a sociopath as a person with no conscience and loaded with antisocial attitudes."

"I prefer the word criminal, meaning someone who's committed a crime," Lyle said.

"Of course a psychopath is also capable of violent social behavior," Stanley continued.

"Okay, I'll bite. What's the difference?"

"The psychopath is mentally deranged. The sociopath acts normally except he hasn't a conscience."

"You don't know anything about this case," Lyle put in.

"I know about the other one," Stanley countered. "He raped a ninety-year-old woman. If he had a shred of social conscience, he would have decided she was too old to be brutalized like that."

"Okay, you have a sociopath chasing you."

"Sociopaths aren't reasonable men."

"So?"

"He will escape because you are," Stanley predicted.

"I can't scramble my brain at will," Lyle protested.

"All you need to do is enlist the help of a sociopath."

"I thought you said they're antisocial," Lyle pressed. "How do I go about finding one first of all, assuming that is what I really want to do? Then how do I persuade him to help?"

"Sociopaths are very self-centered." Stanley prompted

"You're going somewhere with this," Lyle guessed.

"I can wait for your little brain to catch up to my big brain."

"You obviously have been watching old movies on TV. That's an Albert Brooks concept," Lyle shot back. "We're here. We aren't in the after-life state."

"I'm not sure I'm not," Stanley quipped. "Do you know how many commercials there are on in a one hour show? Half hour shows don't even exist. They consist of commercials broken apart by a bit of nonsense meant to ready you for the next string of commercials."

"You're just finding this out."

"I moved the TV into the guest room because Aleta kept getting visions on it and I really want her visions to happen somewhere else."

"Did it help?" Lyle smirked.

"God doesn't need a television set to broadcast. He doesn't even delete the commercials," Stanley muttered. "You have no idea how disconcerting it is to have Aleta get one of them when … never mind."

Lyle chuckled. "Claude complained about that too. He says he no longer worries about coming to soon. Harriet doesn't understand why pausing is not in a man's make-up."

"Do you talk to everyone about their sex life?" Stanley asked, irked.

"You brought it up," Lyle pointed out. "And I'm a good listener."

"Well, go listen to Stuart's mother," Stanley said.

"What do I say?" Lyle asked before presenting what he considered an outlandish approach. "Do you know where your son is? We have a warrant for his arrest. Your son's a sociopath and we think you are too."

"That's exactly where I would start," Stanley responded coolly. "But then, I'm a lawyer and I like to shake people up on a cross."

"I need some one like Herve to ask the questions," Lyle slipped in.

"Why not use Herve?"

"He's an old man. I don't want to give him a stroke."

"He's used to nuts."

"Enjoy your afternoon," Lyle responded. "You know the routine. No visitors. No food. And hide in the bathroom if someone comes in with a gun."

"That's lousy advice."

"I never give lousy advice," Lyle declared. "If you can think of better advice, follow it."

But Stanley couldn't. He figured that out in ten minutes. Then he began wishing Aleta were with him. He closed his eyes to better envision her. Without realizing it he fell asleep instantly.

He didn't hear the visitor come in, sit in the chair and watch him.

By the time the policewoman arrived at the law offices of Praetzel, Locke and Praetzel to escort Tonia Morales to the hospital, Cora Jo had finished typing the statement.

Tonia signed it and Cora Jo and Aleta signed as witnesses. It was almost three and the line of people waiting was still long.

Cora Jo took the cat back to the desk with her. Aleta followed her and told her to go to the pet store on the street below the offices and buy a sturdy cat carrier, one with an opening at one end that would enable Fluffy to watch people moving around. She was to also buy a collar with a tag with her address on it and whatever else she needed.

"Who'll watch her while I'm gone?"

"I will," Aleta said. "Take Tim with you to help you carry everything."

"We're still busy here," Cora Jo said.

"When I go to the hospital, I need to honestly assure Tonia we are taking care of her cat," Aleta explained. "Fluffy is terribly important to her."

Alice watched the two depart and pried Lydia out of the office she was using and told her Aleta was going to be in need of help. Lydia entered Stanley's office and found Aleta holding Tonia Morales's cat and crying.

She returned to the office she was using, made several calls, dispatched the petitioners waiting for her, instructed Alice to send all the seniors straight to Chin and rejoined Aleta to help her with the rest of the line.

Cora Jo returned. She and Tim were allowed to enter the office between clients and show Aleta what they'd purchased. Tim carried in a large box and set it down.

"Cat furniture," he announced. "Like a tree with branches to perch on. I told Cora Jo I'd come over to her place and assemble it.

"We can return it," Cora Jo said. "Tim thought you'd like it."

"Oh, I do!" Aleta said. "Fluffy will love it."

"It's expensive," Cora Jo put in.

"But you can use it with your other cat when Fluffy leaves," Aleta said.

"We need to get her other cat today, "Tim said. "I thought we'd go now."

Lydia gasped in surprise, but Aleta just laughed.

"Two cat lovers! What a kick! Of course, you may go."

"Aleta," Lydia stammered trying not to sound too motherly. "You're planning to leave too."

Aleta punched the intercom. "Alice, how many are still waiting."

"Only two from the first group, nine from the second. Tim passed on them all."

"Tell the last five, we'll see them first thing tomorrow. The others we'll see today."

"Yes, Mrs. Praetzel."

"Tim, take this stuff and Fluffy and drive Cora Jo over to get another cat. Make sure Fluffy likes the new cat. Have Alice give you a donation form petty cash."

"How much?" Tim asked.

"Twenty five to forty is the going rate," Cora Jo remarked. "I think."

"Tell her to give you two hundred. Donate it whether you find a cat or not." Aleta said. "Get a receipt. Stanley likes receipts."

Tim smiled, "Yes Ma'am."

Lydia frowned when they left. "There are clients waiting."

Aleta smiled at her. "Don't be concerned. Tim did his job. He's already screened the remaining petitioners. Karyn can take over ushering them in and out. Cora Jo was a terrific help with Tonia. She deserves a break. Alice can handle the secretarial end and I assume you can handle the remaining six since they'll all be your cases."

"Yes, but ..." Lydia started.

Aleta interrupted her.

"I can't handle anymore right now. I can't get Tonia out of my mind," she said. "I need to go to the hospital and see her."

Lydia's attitude changed radically as Aleta spoke. Her words reflected her newfound respect for her daughter-in-law. Aleta was thinking about her staff's needs as well as those of the strangers waiting all the while struggling with her own emotional upheaval. It wasn't that long ago that Aleta herself had been raped. It wasn't a trauma easily forgotten.

"You assessed the situation more accurately then I did, her mother-in-law said. "I can handle those remaining. I assume I, too, can send the contracts and wills to Stanley."

Aleta chuckled, "He'll love the irony."

Lydia smiled wryly. " Serves him right for getting his face fixed."

"I'm still worried too," Aleta said. " I hope it comes out alright. It's so swollen I can't tell."

"At least his nose is still there," Lydia said.

"I guess we should be glad he didn't lose it," Aleta agreed.

At that moment in the guarded Tri-City Hospital room, Stanley woke with a start.

"How'd you get in?" he asked. "How long have you been here? What time is it anyway? Is the guard still on the door? Has Fouts been caught?"

"You're all swollen," Harriet said.

"Talk about the obvious?" Stanley quipped.

"That's why I'm here."

"What's why you're here?"

"Aleta has been undone by one of today's cases. I don't have any details because Lydia didn't have any except that it's a rape case."

"I know. Lyle told me."

"What no one knows is how profoundly Aleta has been affected. Lydia says she's barely holding herself together. She found Aleta in her office holding Tonia's cat and crying."

"Aleta cries more readily then she used to. I think it's her pregnancy." Stanley said evenly.

"It's more," Harriet proclaimed. "I walked past the guard. I was all set to argue my way in here. I even brought my badge, but he never even saw me, so I'm suppose to be here."

"Back to my original question," Stanley snapped. "Why are you here?"

"You're wife has been mortally wounded. Whatever it is you did before your anniversary, do it again."

"I can't." Stanley said. "I can't explain why, but I can't."

"Why not?"

"I said I couldn't explain." Stanly reiterated tersely.

"Okay, I'm sorry I asked, but you need to understand that Aleta could be lost to all of us. I don't know what about this case pushed her to the edge, but something did. You're the only one she can talk to and not break a client's confidence."

"I can talk to her," Stanley said. "That I can do."

Harriet's head bowed and Stanley realized she was praying. Then her head came up. Her eyes locked onto his and held them.

"She needs the blindfold and all that goes with it." Harriet stated plainly.

Stanley gasped.

"What did you say?" he pressed, visibly upset.

Shocked, Harriet protested, "Me? I didn't say anything! You said you were going to talk to Aleta and I was praying."

"You stopped," Stanley proclaimed. "And you gave me specific advice."

"I did?"

"You know you did!" Stanley charged, anger coloring his tone. "What did Aleta tell you?"

"Stanley, I have no idea what you think she may have told me, but let me assure you, she hasn't told me anything that could be deemed private."

"But you said ..." Stanley started and then stopped.

"What did I say?"

"You really don't remember?"

"No, I don't."

"I guess I have my marching orders," Stanley said. "Don't worry. I know what to do. Can you make sure no one interrupts us tonight?"

"I can do that."

"And can you get her here to the hospital before eight?"

"She's here now," Harriet said.

"I need clothes."

"I can call Bertha."

"Never mind. There's no time. Get me some scrubs." Stanley said. "I'll call Bertha."

Harriet rushed out and Stanley picked up his phone and dialed his home number. "I'm bringing Aleta home in about twenty minutes. Can you put some supper in the oven and clear everyone out the house?"

"Aleta was planning to put up the dogs before you come home," Bertha said. "And bring you your clothes."

"I'm borrowing scrubs." Stanley said. "Don't worry about the dogs."

"Do you need me to stay the night?" Bertha asked.

"Can you take Gerard for the night?"

"Of course, I can."

Harriet walked in with hospital scrubs. Stanley finished his conversation with Bertha.

"Aleta's had a really bad day," he told Bertha. "Harriet came with a message. Aleta is here. My mother sent her. I need time alone with Aleta."

Dr. Chesney walked in as Stanley said his wife's name.

"You're taking her home I hope."

"Did you see her?"

"Yes. She's talking to Mrs. Morales about her cat. Mrs. Morales is doing okay, considering what she's been through. It's Aleta I'm worried about."

"So are my mother and her grandmother. God told me what to do, so I'm doing it," Stanley said taking the scrubs. "Harriet, at least turn around. I know you're invisible to the guard, but I can see you."

Dr. Chesney turned toward Harriet,

"Invisible?"

Harriet smiled and drew the curtain.

"Ask Chief West. It upsets him when I walk past his guards."

"But I saw you walk in before me," Dr. Chesney said.

Stanley shoved his feet into his hospital slippers and walked around the curtain.

"You're barely dressed," Dr. Chesney said.

"The police will be driving us home," Stanley replied calmly. "Now take me to Aleta."

"She's down one floor," Dr. Chesney said as they left the room.

Stanley followed the doctor and spoke to the guard.

"Come on, Vern, I'm going home."

"Hi Vern," Harriet said.

Vern did a double take.

"Where did you come from?" he asked. "How did you sneak past me? West will have my hide."

"Just tell him Harriet Locke got into the room somehow and he'll understand," Harriet told him. "I've done it before."

"But how ..." Vern stammered. "I know I didn't fall asleep."

"Keep your eyes open for Stuart Fouts," Stanley ordered. "Worry about Harriet later."

"Yes Sir!" Vern said.

He called West on his radio.

"Legal Beagle is heading for Beauty and then home."

Stanley laughed.

"When did West come up with code names?"

"Police bands can be monitored."

At the same time Stanley was entering the main elevator with his bodyguard, at the other end of the hall Stuart Fouts, dressed in scrubs, left the service elevator pushing a cart.

Vern, upon turning around in the elevator, caught sight of the orderly and reported his presence on the floor.

Stuart caught a glimpse of a uniform just as the main elevator doors were closing.

Good, he thought, the security guard is taking a break. Talk about luck.

Pushing the metal cart in front of him, Stuart Fouts headed for Stanley's room. When he entered the room, the curtain was drawn around the bed. He glanced around as he quickly withdrew the knife from under a folded cloth. Shoving the curtain aside with one hand, he raised the knife and held it aloft as he stared at the empty bed.

Angrily, he plunged the knife into the middle of the bed. He grabbed a bottle of betadine from the cart and made an outline of a man on the bed. The knife was plunged into what would have been his chest.

The sound of sirens started up in the distance while he was midway through his self-imposed task. It took a few seconds for him to realize the police where converging on the hospital.

He went to the window. It didn't totally surprise him that an officer was standing beside Tonia Morales' car speaking with his radio. The number of responses told him that either someone found her or she'd run to the cops.

Neither was a likely scenario, but he could think of no other.

"Whatever," he muttered, "I've got to get out of here now!"

He looked at the bed and grinned sardonically.

She'll hear about this and the heart will go right out of her, he thought. She'll never testify. Never!

He ran to the service elevator and took it to the basement. He heard a cop at one end of the basement. He was checking with another cop and Stuart realized he was caught between them.

He ducked into the morgue, yanked a tag off a toe, removed his shoes and tied the tag on his toe. He climbed into the drawer and lay down, his bare feet at the open end of the drawer, which he left partly open. No one knew he was dressed in scrubs and he counted on the cops not pulling the drawer out the rest of the way.

He didn't have long to wait. The cops lifted the sheets from the bodies on the gurneys and checked the supply closet. No one pulled his drawer out further.

CHAPTER 9

Chief Lyle West was one of the first to arrive at the hospital. He deployed his men as he checked on the location of his three charges and headed straight for them. He found Stanley and Harriet standing outside Tonia's room.

"I'm here to take Aleta home." Stanley said when Lyle appeared. "We need to be undisturbed the entire night. Harriet will explain."

"And why aren't you leaving?" Lyle said, noticing that no one was moving.

"Aleta won't come," Stanley said. "She chased us out of there. Lyle. She's like I've never seen her before. I have to get her home."

Lyle charged into the room. Aleta looked up and scowled. He could tell she was at the end of her tether so he spoke gently.

"I must move Mrs. Morales to a safer place. You must take Stanley home right now. They are both in grave danger."

Softly as the words were spoken, they chilled Aleta. She stood up at once.

"Is Stuart Fouts here?"

"He was. He left his calling card in Stanley's room."

Lyle radioed Tom in her presence. "I'm sending Stanley and Aleta home in a patrol car. Are your men at the house?... Yes, we're sweeping the hospital now. I'm moving Mrs. Morales to the prison ward... I agree. It was finished in the nick of time."

Peter French, Chief West's right hand man, took charge of Tonia Morales' transfer while Lyle escorted Stanley and Aleta to Vern's patrol car.

Lyle asked Vern if Harriet had slipped past him. He stammered out that she had.

"She does that," Lyle said.

"I wasn't planning to," Harriet said. "I even brought my deputy badge with me."

"If I amend my orders to allow you to pass anytime, will you stop scaring my men?"

"Don't do that," Harriet said. "I don't want someone pretending to be me to gain access."

"You're right." Lyle said. "Scratch that idea."

Stanley held Aleta in his arms as they were driven home. It wasn't a quiet ride as Vern was told to use his siren to cut through traffic. Lyle preceded him and Vern followed closely.

Lyle cut his siren when he hit the edge of the Praetzel property. Vern followed suit. He'd been told they weren't to scare the horses.

The sirens had made conversation impossible and Stanley was grateful for that. As soon as Aleta could speak and be heard, she worried about the dogs.

"Go into the house before me and stick Tank and Scooby in Gerard's room," Stanley suggested.

He walked over to Lyle who asked him quietly what was going on.

"Aleta is near to a mental breakdown," Stanley responded. "I've been told what to do, but I need not to be disturbed by anyone until morning."

"I'll take care of it," Lyle said, and then he told him what Fouts had done to his bed.

"Why is he angry with me personally?"

"I think he is galled because you rescued the woman in the dumpster," Lyle guessed.

"She was his?"

"Tonia said he flew into a rage when he saw the article in the Register."

"We're on our way," Bertha said as she and Robert came out the door

Robert was carrying Gerard.

"Paul took the girls home," Bertha continued. "I brought Hubbs his supper and fixed a thermos of coffee for the guards. Fortunately, Jamara was gone before they arrived."

"I'll be home all week," Stanley told her. "That should help some."

"The dogs are put away," Bertha told him. "Have a good night."

Stanley took Robert aside. "Ask your mother to explain what's going on."

Robert clapped his son-in-law on the shoulder.

"I'm trusting you in this. Aleta looks terrible."

"It's as bad as it looks," Stanley said. "I've been told what to do."

"By whom?" Robert asked skeptically.

"Ask your mother. She delivered the message," Stanley said. "I have to go in now. See you in the morning."

"Call us if you need us." Robert said.

"I will," Stanley promised.

He entered the house hastily and began to search for Aleta. He headed for the nursery by way of the master bedroom, opened his nightstand drawer and removed the silk scarf.

He opened the door gently and the dogs stayed where they were. He realized Aleta had put them on a down stay. She was standing staring at the empty crib.

He came up behind her and slipped the scarf over her eyes.

"Stanley, no!" she cried.

"Release the dogs," he ordered.

"Okay Tank! Okay Scooby!" she said.

Those were the last words she spoke. The blindfold was tied in back.

"Now, listen to me carefully," Stanley said evenly. "God sent Harriet to me. He told me what to do. You may choose to refuse to obey at any time. You may nod now and you won't bump my nose."

Aleta nodded ever so slightly.

He turned her around and drew her to him slowly. His hands positioned her head and slowly he bent and kissed her. It was a soft, sweet kiss. And Aleta felt tears threatening to spill from under her closed eyelids. She willed them to stay pushed back.

He led her to their bedroom and undressed her. She smiled as she envisioned him carefully folding every item. When she was fully unclothed he slipped her satin nightgown down her upraised hands and over her head.

"Now we eat," he announced. "And I talk."

Aleta nodded.

He took her hand and let her into the kitchen. Her thoughts of Tonia however, returned. Stanley sensed that she had gone away again, so he stopped and had her sit on the couch.

"I'm going to feed you in here," he said. She seemed more withdrawn than before. Desperately, he tried to think of someway to entice her mind away from the pull of the emotional trauma that was drawing her down into an abyss of despair.

The idea that hit him was bizarre. He could think of nothing else. He left her and went into the kitchen to prepare his little surprise.

When he returned, he laid her down with her head resting in his lap.

Vaguely, Aleta was aware she was lying as she did when he read to her.

"Open you mouth," he told her.

She did as she was told, her curiosity driving her.

"Now close and suck," Stanley ordered.

The order caught her by surprise but she did it. She almost laughed aloud. He was feeding her chocolate milk in a baby bottle.

"Keep sucking," he said. "And listen to me. I have the answer you're seeking. If you concentrate on everything I do with you tonight, tomorrow you will have the answer you need."

She paused. He could tell she'd heard him.

"Keep sucking," he said. "You need to finish before we can move to the next stage."

Aleta finished her bottle and Stanley led her to the kitchen. She heard the blender whirring. Surely, he wasn't …

The first spoonful told her he had pureed her supper. He'd not only pureed it, he'd put everything in the blender together. And he insisted she eat every mouthful and he wouldn't let her move her hands at all. She felt like such a baby.

He ate as he was feeding her and she longed to chew something. Then he set a plate in front of her.

"Finger food," he said.

Aleta knew she wasn't getting a utensil yet. He put her hand on the plate and she felt around. Her fingers touched a bit of biscuit and she eagerly popped it into her mouth. Her fingers searched for another, grateful he hadn't put liver on the plate.

She savored every bite of the biscuit. It was amazing how much she liked chewing.

She waited for dessert, but instead Stanley wiped off her fingers with a wet cloth and had her follow him into the living room. He gathered her in his arms as the music began. He placed her head on his shoulder and told her to keep it there. She understood.

Then they began to dance. Tonight all the music was slow and even. She relaxed in his arms. It's like being rocked to sleep, she thought. It was very pleasant.

Later she lay on the couch and he opened the book and began to read to her. She loved the sound of his voice. She listened to the words eager to find her answer. He felt her tense and knew what she was doing.

He left her briefly and when he returned he put a baby bottle in her hand.

"This is to help you relax," he said. "The answer isn't in this book. The answer is elsewhere."

He began to read again. Every time she began to tense he told her to suck. It was such a ludicrous situation that she began to stop trying to wring the answer from the words of a woman dead for over a century. Slowly she let herself relax and just let the words float down like snowflakes onto her mind. Slowly, they melted and were absorbed. The process was too gradual to be noticed.

A conclusion suggested by the reading pervaded her thoughts. Feelings not tempered by reason can betray one into acting irrationally. A child listens to his feelings and can be easily misled by them.

That idea prompted the unspoken question, "Am I being misled by mine?"

Stanley closed the book.

She was then led to the bathroom. Stanley gently removed her gown and helped her step into the shower. He placed her hands on the wall and began washing her. She wondered about his ears.

He told her he was wearing a shower cap and to stop worrying. She giggled and he knew she was coming back. She was imagining him in a shower cap. As he turned her he told her how to stand and she never once moved from the position he placed her in.

He toweled her dry. Again she didn't move even once to help. As he finished she could tell what was coming next.

She didn't know how to stop him. If she shook her head, she might bump his nose.

She would wait. There would be a moment. She had but to wait for it. His hands roamed her body lovingly and she didn't move. His kisses where light, like the brush of flower petal. They were sensuous, teasing, stimulating. Robbed of sight and frozen in place, all her senses were concentrated on his touch.

How does he do this, she thought and the answer to that question came immediately. He trusted her not to move. As long as she let him he is in control completely, he wouldn't be hurt.

She decided she wouldn't stop him. She wanted him as much as he wanted her. Would it always be thus, she wondered.

She had thought earlier that she would never feel joy again. She remembered her earlier despair as joy washed over her.

How she wished she could embrace her husband, but she restrained herself with the thought that he trusted her not to indulge herself and to let him bring her joy unaided.

All he wanted was for her to receive. And a few minutes later that's what she did.

He asked her first just as she knew he would, and she nodded. She wished she could shout her desires and her delight, but she let her body respond.

Afterward as she lay on her back, he took her hand and put it in its favorite place and whispered, "Please keep me from rolling on either ear. I need you to do that. Only that. You have your answer. I am so proud of you."

Aleta squeezed her fingers lightly to acknowledge his conclusion. How did he know?

All she knew is that she had asked herself a question. Maybe that's all she needed to do.

Sleep took over her body and spirit.

When the front door opened the next morning, Aleta woke up. She withdrew her hand, but didn't move. The next move was his.

To her surprise he dressed her. The clothes were casual. Evidently she wasn't going to the office.

She waited for him to remove the scarf, but he didn't. Instead he shaved and dressed himself.

Was he going to break precedent and not remove the scarf all day, she wondered.

And would that be so bad, she mused. She hadn't wanted for anything. She been fed, albeit strangely, bathed, dressed and loved with great tenderness.

No, she thought. It wouldn't be so bad.

When he lifted her to her feet, she smiled at him. He kissed her and untied the scarf. She opened her eyes, gazed into his and said simply, "I love you. Please protect me."

Guessing what she wanted, Stanley put the blindfold back over her eyes. "Is this what you want?"

She nodded almost imperceptibly. She didn't know how close his face was to her head.

"I was angry yesterday when your grandmother told me to use the blindfold."

Aleta couldn't stifle her gasp. It had come so quickly.

"That was my reaction," he commented. "But she didn't know what she'd said so I guess we're still the only three that know – you, me and God."

She patted his chest gently.

"That is a nice way to nod," he said. "Very safe."

She patted him again.

"I don't want to know what no is. I'll only ask yes questions."

Again she patted him.

"You do that any lower down and we'll wind up back in bed."

She giggled. He caught her hand.

"No, you don't!" he said. "I have a compromise. I will order you not to speak, but I will remove the blindfold until we are alone again. And you will help me work today and do anything I ask."

He paused.

"You're wondering what I could ask that you might refuse to do."

Her hand patted him gently.

"You've sent me all the wills and contracts to do," he responded. "You are going to suffer with me."

She giggled.

"I'm the head of the firm," he went on. "Even when I'm out on sick leave, I don't do wills and contracts."

He heard her chuckle.

"My underlings, one of whom is my wife, do those."

Her laughter burst out and he whipped off the scarf. Her eyes were merry.

"Not a word," he said, "until you know the rest of the answer you're seeking."

How did he know that she had only the question, she wondered. Still, the fact that he knew that pleased her.

She nodded and pointed to her mouth.

"You want it sealed with a kiss?"

She nodded.

"Careful!" he scolded. "I was about to comply."

She hung her head. He lifted it gently and held it in place while he lowered his lips to hers. As many times as they kissed, each time brought pleasure anew. He knew everyone didn't feel this way but, for him, at least, kissing his wife was sheer joy.

When they went into the living room, Lyle was in the new recliner nursing a mug of coffee, waiting.

He noticed immediately that Aleta was feeling better.

"Is Fouts in jail?" Stanley asked.

Lyle shook his head. "He got away. We figured out he hid in a drawer in the morgue. The cops saw a man in scrubs, feet end out, with a toe tag in a half-closed drawer, but while they looked under the sheets on the gurneys, they didn't pull out the drawer. Fouts stole clothes from one of the corpses and went out through the therapy wing on crutches."

"We're working from house today," Stanley said.

Aleta grinned. Both were dressed in jeans. Actually, hers were very short jeans-- Stanley's favorite.

"Good," he said. "Aleta, your client told Bobbie over and over she wasn't going to testify. She wants us to somehow tell Fouts that."

Aleta shook her head.

Lyle glared at Stanley.

"This is no time for her not to be speaking."

"You need to take us to see her," Stanley said.

"You're going to let Aleta speak to her?"

"I'm going to talk to our client." Stanley declared firmly.

"In your condition?" Lyle questioned.

"We're not working today." Stanley said purposely interpreting his question to be in reference to his apparel.

Aleta chuckled.

Again Stanley had chosen his own interpretation.

"Let me rephrase that. I'm not working. Aleta is working but at home. She is doing wills and contracts all day, after we visit Tonia Morales."

Aleta slapped her bare thigh.

Stanley responded at once, "You look fine."

Aleta patted her leg again.

"Yes, you are going out like that. It's summer. It's hot out. And you look great in shorts."

Lyle repressed a grin. Aleta did look good.

"After breakfast," Stanley said. "Aleta can't skip breakfast."

"I thought you'd never ask," Lyle remarked, heading for the table.

"Doesn't your wife feed you?" Stanley asked.

"Not if I don't go home," Lyle replied.

"You've been out all night?" Stanley burst out, shocked.

"You're lucky you're on sick leave."

"I'm also the intended victim," Stanley reminded him.

"I'm short-handed."

"You're always short-handed," Stanley retorted. "Why don't you hire more men?"

"Budget constraints," Lyle said tersely.

"I'm going to be owing you shifts forever, aren't I?"

"You're a great detective. You're a great shot. Why wouldn't I try to keep you?"

"Because I chose to be a lawyer. You understand choices, don't you?"

Lyle grinned.

"You're like a hooked fish struggling to get free. The more the fish struggles, the more determined the fisherman is to get him into his boat."

"And kill and eat him," Stanley quipped.

"We sportsmen throw the little ones back and sometimes the fighters as well."

"So which am I?"

"Does it matter? I won't call on you this week. And at the shows this weekend, we can go double or nothing," Lyle offered.

"I'm not showing with my face like this." Stanley asserted.

"If you decide to, it's double or nothing, Tank verses Morgan, you against me," Lyle said.

He could tell by Stanley's eyes that he wanted to win that bet.

"Either day?" Stanley asked.

"Either or both." Lyle said.

Aleta tugged on Stanley's arm.

"Aleta says 'no'," Stanley said. "She doesn't want me gambling away my time with her. I should listen to her. You're better in the ring than I am."

Aleta squeezed Stanley's arm.

Stanley winced. He glanced at her than readjusted his statement. " Aleta says we're an even match."

Aleta held up one finger.

"Saturday only," Stanley declared.

After breakfast Lyle drove Stanley and Aleta to the hospital to see Tonia Morales. The seventy-five year old was puzzled at the sight of Stanley. She looked at Aleta for an explanation. Stanley pulled up a chair and sat down.

"Aleta and I have taken the day off, but you were too important not to visit."

"I want to talk with Mrs. Praetzel alone," Tonia said.

Stanley cleared the room except for himself.

"You misunderstood me," Tonia said.

"Aleta can't speak today."

"She could yesterday," Tonia proclaimed.

"Yesterday she was well. Today she isn't," Stanley said matter-of-factly. "I know you don't want to repeat the horrors you experienced yesterday, and I don't intend to ask you about them. I am here to answer your questions"

Tonia relaxed. No questions. Just answers. Those she needed. She started right in.

"What will happen to me if I don't testify?" Tonia asked.

"The police will do nothing. The judge will do nothing. Stuart Fouts, however, will return and repeat what he did yesterday, only this time he will add to it because he will want to punish you."

"But Stella is going to testify. Won't that be enough to put him in prison?"

"Not if you testify for him."

"For him?" Tonia gasped, the color draining from her face. "That's crazy!"

"It's the next logical step," Stanley said with equanimity.

"Logical?" Tonia burst forth. "It's not logical. Why would I testify for the man who raped me?"

"Supposedly raped you. Your refusal to accuse him negates all the physical evidence," Stanley said. "In addition, it will make Stella's testimony suspect."

"Are you saying they won't believe her just because I won't testify?"

"That's exactly what I'm saying."

"Maybe if neither of us testifies, he'll leave us alone."

"So, he's a man of his word? An honorable man?"

Tonia sucked in her breath. "Honorable? He's pure evil! I want him out of my life!"

"After the first time a year ago, didn't he promise he wouldn't return?"

"Yes, but he said ... How did you know?"

"That's what such men always promise."

"Aleta said the lawyer Fouts has hired to defend him is nasty, I will be humiliated."

"That we plan to prevent," Stanley said. "We are your lawyers. We are committed to helping you."

"Can't you just get the police to keep protecting me?"

"Actually, it's you who are calling them off."

"Me? I never asked them to leave."

"They can't protect you against someone who hasn't hurt you."

"He raped me!"

"Which is why they are protecting you now."

"So why can't they keep doing it?"

"The next step is for them to jail him."

"I know that."

"But if you say you aren't going to testify, they have to let him go."

"Stella has accused him."

"If he's convicted on a single count of rape, he'll get four to six years and he'll be in jail for the rest of Stella's life, but not for the rest of yours."

"I'll take the six years. I don't have that much time left."

"You're ill?"

"Bad heart." Tonia said stoically.

"The choice is yours, but you don't have to make it now."

"But maybe if the police tell him I'm not going to testify, he will leave me alone."

"They can't do that."

"Maybe Aleta could."

"She won't call Stella a liar!" Stanley said harshly.

"I'm not doing that!"

"You're saying he's innocent. Stella is saying he's guilty. One of you is lying."

"You're being cruel."

"And you are not?" he charged, his anger breaking through.

"I did shameful things," she said defensively. "I won't be subjected to public humiliation."

"You have up until now done nothing shameful. Now you are betraying a true friend by choosing to side with your worst enemy."

"I'm choosing to be silent," Tonia said. "That's all. Everyone will understand."

"Not everyone," Stanley said, regaining his composure. "If I were you, I'd tell the police you're still thinking about what you're going to do. You can say that right now you're too scared to think straight. You are scared, aren't you?"

"Of course, I'm scared!" Tonia professed.

"Give Aleta a chance. She hasn't let you down yet, has she?"

"No."

"Just give her a little time. Rest and get well. Then decide."

"I have nightmares."

"So did Aleta," Stanley said.

"She was raped?"

"Didn't you know?"

"No, she didn't tell me that."

"Two men," Stanley explained succinctly. "She does understand what you are going through."

"Did they get away?"

"No, the didn't. The evidence was overwhelming. They pleaded guilty."

"So no trial?"

"That is a possibility," Stanley said. "Only you need to cooperate a little bit."

"How?"

"Do what I asked. Say you're too scared to think straight. Can you do that?"

"It's the truth." Tonia said.

"The truth is always good," Stanley said rising.

"Aleta said she wouldn't make me do anything I didn't want to."

"And she won't. Trust her."

"She found a good home for my cat. She's even got toys and a perch and another cat to play with. And Fluffy purred when the woman held her."

"What woman?"

"A lady in your office," Tonia said.

Stanley's face grew somber.

"Don't tell anyone where Fluffy is," he cautioned. "Tell no one – not a nurse or a cop or a neighbor,"

Tonia paled. "I didn't think."

"As long as you say nothing, Fluffy will be safe."

"Well?" Lyle asked when Stanley emerged from Tonia Morales' room.

"She's thinking about it."

The D.A. won't move on this without a commitment."

"She's as afraid of court as much as she is of Fouts." Stanley commented. "The future always looks more frightening than the past."

"But a woman's sexual history isn't considered relevant," Lyle put in. "Not anymore."

Stanley looked at Aleta who shook her head.

"She was under duress," Stanley said, "and that's all I can say because that's all I know."

"So we've accomplished nothing!" Lyle concluded.

"I wouldn't say that," Stanley said. "I found out she has a bad heart."

"Why didn't Dr. Chesney mention that?"

"It's probably in his medical report," Stanley replied. "Besides you weren't doing anything but trying to protect her which would help, not hurt her."

"No wonder he's been checking on her so much." Lyle said, taking his cell phone from his pocket and checking the text message.

Speechless, he gave his phone to Stanley to read.

"Mother!" Stanley exclaimed. "You can't leave her alone with a juicy case for one minute."

He looked at Aleta. "Did you give my mother carte blanche with the cases in the office."

Puzzled because she hadn't seen the message, Aleta nodded hesitantly

"Well, did you or didn't you?" Stanley pressed.

This time Aleta's nod was strongly affirmative.

"We need to go to the office right now!" Stanley announced.

Aleta patted her bare thigh.

"You're fine!" Stanley snapped. "I'm the one that's a mess!"

Aleta patted her thigh again.

"We are not going home to change. It's my face I didn't want to go out with." Stanley griped. "By now more people have seen it then I wanted to thanks to my best friend here."

Lyle swallowed his grin. Stanley's face was a mess. But even so, Aleta would have prevailed if she could talk. This he knew for sure.

Since he'd driven them to the hospital, Lyle knew he was going to get to see this drama to the end. He knew he could have ordered one of his men to drive the pair, but there weren't a lot of moments when his job presented a humorous situation in which no one was in any danger.

CHAPTER 10

When they arrived at his office, Lyle parked directly in front of the door to the lobby where cars weren't allowed to park.

Alice was busy at her desk when Lydia passed her.

"Stanley's here," she announced.

Alice looked up, startled.

Lydia smiled at her. "He's angry with me, not you. I'll be in his office."

Alice nodded and a moment later pointed to his office door when Stanley arrived. He hurried in. Aleta smiled and waved. Lyle followed, grinning.

His grin made Alice relax. She discretely called Robert and the two associates and informed them that Mr. Praetzel was in his office with his wife and mother and Chief West and they weren't to be disturbed. No one had planned to go into Stanley's office. Alice was just politely keeping them informed.

Lydia was sitting in a visitor's chair, waiting.

"Sit down while you scold me," Lydia said. "I hear better when we're on the same level."

Aleta sat in the other visitor's chair and Lyle took the third. All these chairs circled the desk. Stanley grumpily sat behind his desk.

"Why is Lyle here?" Lydia asked.

"You sent him the text message," Stanley said tartly. "Don't you remember?"

"What a neat question!" Lydia commented. "It means you know I didn't forget and you are holding me responsible for my actions. I think I will be able to return to the bench once you're done being beautified and you let Aleta talk again. I gather she can't or she would have talked you out of dragging her around in shorts."

Aleta laughed. His mother could handle Stanley without her help.

"What do you mean you've arranged to depose Tonia this afternoon?"

"I thought it was rather ingenious idea," Lydia said. "Mrs. Morales is in the hospital, which will make a nice setting. Judge Clancy is a softie at heart and he is free this afternoon. He understood the urgency. You can't do something like after weeks have passed. She is still upset and will be honest because she hasn't had time to think up any lies. And ..."

"Mother, we were proceeding in an orderly fashion," Stanley interjected.

"No, you weren't. You were taking care of Aleta and still are I gather. If she'd shown up this morning, I would have run all this by her, but she didn't, so I moved ahead. Now may I go on?"

"Can I stop you?"

"No."

"Then, please proceed." Stanley said graciously.

"Gray Zenon is still trying to impress you. The D.A. is willing to let us represent his office."

"Aleta ..." Stanley began.

"Is not speaking," his mother finished. "And it isn't my intention you let her even come, let alone participate. It will be good for Mrs. Morales to have to tell the whole story to someone who doesn't know anything more than that she's been raped multiple times. I've been doing research on her since early this morning. I can do this better than Aleta."

"Better?" Stanley questioned.

"Yes," his mother replied. "I was never raped. The images Mrs. Morales presents won't bring to mind any horrors in my past. I may not be as old as Mrs. Morales, but I'm a lot closer in age to her than Aleta. And I have experience with regard to what a judge will want to hear on a taped deposition. Finally, I told Aleta she could defang Mr. Zenon better than anyone else. That would have been true had this case not knifed her very soul."

Stanley looked at Aleta. She nodded her head vigorously.

"It's all yours, Mother," Stanley declared. "Run with it."

"What I need to know is what you said to her this morning," his mother said.

"Aleta, show Lyle the office," Stanley ordered. "Introduce him to Cora Jo. Mrs. Morales may have told someone that Cora Jo was watching Fluffy."

Lydia laughed. "And how is she suppose to do that?"

"She's clever. She'll figure out how."

Aleta grinned. She rose and Lyle opened the door.

"Now what was it you didn't want Aleta to hear?" his mother asked.

"I told Tonia Morales that Aleta was raped. She hadn't told her."

"What else?"

"I told her that if she refused to testify it was the same as calling Stella Woodbridge a liar."

"You were harsh, weren't you?"

"Yes."

"That's good to know. Thanks for telling me."

"She is more afraid of being humiliated in court than in being raped again and possibly killed by Fouts," Stanley finished.

"So I am on the right track," Lydia commented. "You've been a big help. I am so proud of you, Stanley. You and Aleta have developed a law firm that I would be proud to be a member of. But don't worry, I'm returning to the bench."

"Mother, you took a city case," Stanley said. "We're a child advocacy firm."

"Aleta may have to complete that one too," his mother said. "A man's dog bit a child that teased him inside the dog park where unsupervised children are not allowed.

"The dog had an injured ear. The child had been warned. The child was nipped not mauled. The mother is not only suing the dog owner, our client, but also the city. The city was going to settle. I couldn't allow that. I told the mayor we'd take the case on a contingency basis. They are out no money that way. The mayor liked that part."

"And we aren't committed to other cases?"

"Case by case basis," Lydia said. "It would be a good stepping stone toward Aleta becoming a judge some day."

"You are a good mother-in-law," Stanley said appreciatively.

"Tonia Morales' deposition is scheduled for two o'clock this afternoon. Will you be there?"

"With my face?"

"Were a coat and tie," Lydia said, then added casually, "Alice has a stack of folders with work that'll keep the two of you busy."

"We don't need busy work, Mother."

"Aleta took the cases and you either need to hire another associate or stop taking vacations any old time you feel like it."

"Do you have someone in mind?"

"The black associate in Hubert's firm who's doing the Tontine work. He's very sharp."

"Steal from my father?"

"Why not? He took Kay Rivers from you."

"Not directly," Stanley shot back. "She's on loan. Who will do the Tontine work?"

"That's not your worry, is it?"

"What's this man's name?"

Before Lydia could reply, Aleta entered the office.

Stanley turned and addressed his wife, "Aleta, do you have any objections to hiring a new associate?"

She held up her hand and disappeared.

"Wait?" he said to her disappearing figure. "Wait for what. It was a yes or no question."

Aleta returned dragging Chin. Jackson trailed behind the pair.

Aleta waited for Stanley to speak.

"Yes or no?" he asked.

She turned and indicated that he should ask Chin that question. Stanley realized what she was trying to tell him.

"Roland, did Aleta put you in charge of finding a new associate?"

Roland nodded.

Lydia chuckled. Stanley whirled around. "You knew!"

"Of course, I knew!" his mother said. "Roland, I've found you a prospect. He's working on Tontine cases in Hubert's firm. He's wasted there. Guess what his field of choice is?"

"Senior citizens?" Roland queried hopefully.

"He's also a whiz with contracts," Lydia said.

"Take him," Jackson urged. "We need someone junior."

Aleta laughed and everyone turned. She put two thumbs up.

"Give him the stuff on Alice's desk," Stanley said. "I assume he can start soon."

"He's waiting in the library," Lydia said. "Today soon enough."

"Nigel Oliver?" Chin asked.

"He's black!" Jackson blurted out.

"That's my line!" Chin quipped. "Don't worry, I'll be able to tell you two apart."

"How did you know we'd say yes?" Stanley asked his mother.

"Because he fits here better than where he is. He's been pigeonholed and he's better than that."

"How'd you get him so quickly?"

"Oh, Stanley, don't you think I have any pull with your father at all?"

"We haven't a desk or anything," Stanley contended. "This isn't how it's done – well, this is how Aleta does things."

"Exactly!" his mother exclaimed. "She started the ball rolling yesterday and I just happened to know someone."

"I hate to meet him looking like this," Stanley said.

"We'll apologize for you," Lydia said. "Mr. Chin, please show the gentleman in."

Nigel Oliver walked into the oddest assortment of people he'd ever seen. He recognized Jackson and Judge Davis but the other three surprised him. Behind the desk was a man in casual attire who looked as if he'd been socked in the nose with a baseball bat. Beside him stood a long-legged auburn haired beauty in the briefest shorts he'd seen. Next to her in full uniform stood a police chief.

Alice came in as Roland Chin was making introductions.

"Mrs. Praetzel isn't speaking today," Stanley said.

As Nigel shook her hand he asked, "Are you the Aleta Praetzel?"

She laughed and nodded.

"It is a pleasure to meet you. When you decide to talk again, I hope you'll talk with me a bit."

She grinned as she nodded again.

Alice looked at Aleta who made a slashing sign that told her Oliver's salary was to be even to the other two associates.

Stanley saw the exchange. "Even when she doesn't speak, Aleta outranks me."

Aleta and Alice both shook their heads.

"It's okay," Stanley said. "Welcome to the firm, Nigel. Use my office until Alice orders you a desk. Alice has paperwork for you to complete, lunch is provided. We don't work weekends unless we do. And Robert and I are child advocates and that's all I want to be. Aleta dips her brush just about every pail of paint she sees. You will be part of her group. We take no criminal or divorce cases. You will start on contracts and wills because I don't do contracts and wills even though my mother, Mr. Chin, Mr. Jackson and my wife all got together and gave me every single one that by accident landed on their desks. After your baptism in contracts and wills, you will be regular associate on par with Mr. Chin and Mr. Jackson. Does this sound satisfactory?"

"Say yes," Jackson hissed.

Nigel smiled. "Thank you. You are an engaging group of people. It is my pleasure to accept your offer of employment since it does have the one thing I value most – a free lunch."

The entire group laughed and Stanley and Aleta left.

Interestingly, it was Stanley, not Aleta who walked into the house exhausted. Aleta led him to the bedroom, pulled back the covers, indicated he should lie down and helped him off with his jeans and shirt. The cool clean sheets felt good as he lay back on them. She massaged his leg that still knotted up when he sat too long, even though in his estimation the pain had come a bit sooner than usual. He nevertheless closed his eyes. He didn't know when he fell asleep. Aleta did, but she kept massaging his leg until it was again loose.

She left him sleeping, signaled Bertha that he was asleep and retired to the office when she opened the first of the folders she had brought home. Stanley was right. Even when he had time, contracts and wills were not what he should be doing. It had been wrong of her to spend his talent that way. She had assumed that he would have nothing to do.

How presumptuous of me, she thought. Well, I accepted the cases, so I guess I'd better help do them. It is my area of expertise, after all.

Bertha served her lunch in the study. She didn't understand what was going on, but Aleta busy was one step better than the Aleta she'd seen walk through the door the night before.

At one o'clock Stanley's alarm went off. He woke to find Aleta sitting in the chair watching him. His clothes were neatly laid out at the end of the bed. The shower was running. She held out his shower cap.

He rose took her head in his hands and kissed her gently.

"Thanks," he murmured. "You know why you aren't going, don't you?"

She nodded. She had guessed that she wasn't. If she couldn't speak, there would be no purpose to her being there. In addition, Lydia needed to command the situation totally.

They didn't need her.

Stanley looked into her eyes and read the reawakening of the despair that he'd battled furiously the night before.

"You've been working, haven't you?" he asked. It was a totally irrelevant query but he didn't know how to explain that he had to hear Tonia Morales' story. He had to come up with some clue as to what had triggered her reaction the night before.

When she didn't respond, he got back on the track she was on.

"You do know God sent you this case--you, not me, not Mother, not anyone else – you."

The nod was almost imperceptible but the despair suddenly deepened. He had hit a nerve.

"You are to go to bed and nap while I'm gone. Do you understand?"

She nodded and lay down on her side of the bed fully clothed. Stanley went in and took a brief shower, shaved again and dressed, all the while noting that she was staring at the ceiling, her body tense.

He felt he had to go.

"Think about the lesson I was trying to teach you last night. If you find the answer, you will find comfort."

She nodded and waved at him to go.

"Close your eyes," he said

She obeyed. He mustn't stay. He must go. The woman in the hospital bed was in despair as well as she, but Tonia Morales was alone.

Stanley left the room and Aleta almost cried out 'Don't leave me', but she didn't, not verbally anyway. Her heart wept.

Someone entered the room and sat down. She knew it wasn't Stanley. She heard the sound of a baby nursing and realized Jamara had been sent in to watch her.

Well, she could wait.

Her mind had pushed out Stanley's admonition to think about the answer to the question she had posed.

The question, however, lingered in the back corner of her mind.

Was she letting her feelings dictate her actions without listening to reason? Was that what Stanley had been telling her—that she was acting like a baby?

Stanley had no idea what fear she was hiding in that closet she had in her mind. Even she didn't know. She didn't want to know. Her guilt was already more than she could bear.

She kept her eyes closed. She didn't want to be watched. She didn't want to be stopped. One act of bravery and the anguish that gripped her and held her would be defeated.

She heard the phone ring. She opened her eyes. She was alone.

Jamara was gone.

She heard Bertha talking on the phone. Slowly she rose from the bed.

She glanced outside and saw Hubbs walking Shadow toward the house. What was he doing? Was something wrong with Shadow?

She hesitated, puzzled.

The horse seemed to be walking okay. No limp. He didn't appear to be in any distress. Yet here Hubbs was bringing the horse to her. She took a step toward the window.

And then Hubbs turned and walked the horse back toward the barn. He was just giving him a bit of exercise or maybe he'd seen something when he was checking on the horses in the pasture and was checking it out.

Whatever it was, Hubbs was taking care of it.

She turned, her bare feet aware of the carpet's softness. She smiled. Stanley had insisted that the bedroom carpet be soft. She'd asked him how he'd chosen it.

She remembered him telling her he liked the feel of it and it didn't come in too many colors so he'd chosen brown because that seemed like a reasonable color.

Reasonable, she thought. Only you would choose a reasonable color. Everyone else chooses a color they like.

She remembered telling him that and his answer had surprised her.

"But I don't have a favorite color," he had said. "I like all the colors."

After a few more conversations, she'd discovered he did indeed like all colors, but he felt strongly that each color had its place and should stay there. Red, for example, didn't belong on his body. On hers it was fine.

She heard the door open and spun around and headed for the bathroom.

"It's an emergency!" Bertha said holding out the phone.

Aleta raised and eyebrow.

"It's Martha Cook." Bertha said. "I told her you can't speak, but she insisted. Here."

Aleta took the phone.

The crackly voice of the ancient matriarch came over the phone. "If you can hear me, tap the receiver once with your fingernail."

Aleta did so.

"Okay, send everyone out of the room," Martha ordered. "I need to talk with you privately."

Aleta motioned for Bertha to leave although it seemed a bit ridiculous since there would be no verbal responses at her end to clue anyone in to their conversation.

"Are you alone?" Martha asked.

Aleta tapped once.

"Sitting down, I hope," crackled the ancient voice.

Aleta sat in the chair by the window and tapped once.

"The guilt that weighs you down is unforgivable," Martha stated flatly. "Do you want to know why?"

Aleta tapped once.

"Because it is based on a lie," Martha answered. "Do you want to know what lie?"

Again Aleta tapped once.

"That you are omnipotent."

Angrily, Aleta tapped twice.

"Omniscient?" Martha asked.

Two taps told her no.

"The truth will set you free, Aleta," Martha said. "Forget your feelings. Do not act on them. Go to bed, lie down, close your eyes and wait for love to wake you."

Suddenly, Martha giggled and added, "Not Stanley."

Aleta tapped once and hung up. She put the phone on the table and climbed into bed. She was suddenly very tired. She closed her eyes and thought, I'm too upset to sleep.

Bertha came in and retrieved the phone. Aleta didn't stir.

Jamara asked if she should sit with Aleta.

"Martha took care of it. She's really asleep this time."

"Best to leave the door open," Jamara said as Bertha was closing it.

Bertha opened it and Scooby and Tank rushed in. Scooby climbed on the bed and plunked down bedside Aleta. She didn't stir. Tank settled alongside the bed on her side.

"If she gets up, they'll us," Bertha said.

"I be watching all the same," Jamara declared, settling into the recliner from which she had a clear view into the bedroom.

CHAPTER 11

Stanley and his mother met Judge Clancy in the hospital hallway outside the prison section. Chief West escorted the TV cameraman through the security check personally. The others waited for their turn.

"Hello Dennis," Lydia said. "May I introduce Cora Jo Hayes who will be our recorder this afternoon.

"I was told we were videotaping the deposition," Judge Clancy questioned.

"I don't trust video equipment not to break down," Lydia responded. "Miss Hayes is reliable."

"I've missed you, Miss Hayes," Judge Clancy remarked.

"I'm working for Praetzel, Locke and Praetzel now," Cora Jo said with a modicum of pride.

"They are fortunate to have you," Judge Clancy said kindly.

He turned to Lydia.

"I was expecting the younger Mrs. Praetzel."

"She's ill," Lydia said. "Her husband is here as Mrs. Morales attorney."

"Is he familiar with the case?"

"He knows what she wants," Stanley's mother replied. "He's very good with frightened children."

"For whom are we waiting?" Judge Clancy asked.

"The public defender," Lydia said. "Mr. Gray Zenon."

"Are you here as amicus curiae again?"

"I'm representing the District Attorney's office. He wants this deposition."

"Why?"

"Because Tonia Morales is not committed to testifying."

Judge Clancy eyed his fellow jurist shrewdly.

"Are you wasting my time?"

"I believe the setting is conducive to getting the whole truth out of her."

"But if she won't testify…" Judge Clancy said.

"She has a heart condition, Dennis. Let's do this so the criminal who raped her doesn't get off if she dies before the trial," Lydia said. "That's our main purpose today."

Gray Zenon walked up.

"I'm sorry I kept you waiting."

Chief West then escorted the group through the security check and into Tonia Morales' room. While Cora Jo was setting up her recording equipment, Stanley took a chair and set it next to Mrs. Morales."

"Where's Mrs. Praetzel?" Tonia asked.

"She couldn't come," Stanley said and made no attempt to explain further. "Anyway, since you're going to be televised, wouldn't you rather have this homely face next to yours?"

"I guess no one could look worse," Tonia said. "I don't understand."

"We aren't in court," Stanley said. "But this is serious. If you answer every question honestly, you may never have to go to court."

"Suppose some are too personal?" Tonia asked.

"Then whisper that to me and I'll see what I can do."

"You could do something?"

Stanley leaned over and whispered in a conspiratorial fashion. "I would rather not interrupt my mother, but I'll interrupt any man you want me to."

Tonia smiled.

Chairs were arranged in a semi circle around the bed. The cameraman set up so that he had a full-face view of Tonia. He was on Lydia's side of the semicircle. Cora Jo sat on the far end next to Gray Zenon.

Just after the preliminaries were taken care of, Dr. Chesney slipped into the room. He introduced himself to the judge and told him that Stanley Praetzel had requested the presence of a doctor.

"Are you a cardiologist?" Judge Clancy asked.

"I'm a gynecologist. I did the rape exam."

The judge entered his name as a witness to the proceedings.

Lydia asked the first question.

"Mrs. Morales, you were married for forty-seven years, correct?""

Gray Zenon smiled. She was taking the same path as before. He'd counted on this.

"Yes." Mrs. Morales said.

"Did you and your husband make love regularly?"

"Yes.

"And was he pleased with your offerings?"

Tonia smiled.

"Oh, yes."

"So giving a husband sexual pleasure is something you believe a good wife should do?"

"Yes," Tonia said firmly.

"And you believe sexual acts belong exclusively in the marital bed between a husband and his wife."

"Yes."

"Did you ever stray into an affair?"

"Heavens no!"

"Did a man other than your husband every make sexual advances to you?"

"Yes."

"What did you do?"

"Mostly I told them to take a hike."

"I notice that you still wear your wedding band. Why is that?"

"I still feel married," Tonia said. "I mean, he's gone and all that, but I didn't bury my love for him with his body. I even talk to him sometimes when I'm lonely. I believe he hears me."

"Did you tell him about being raped?"

"Oh no, I couldn't!" she cried.

Her heart monitor beeped wildly. Lydia decided to venture one more question."

"Don't you think he would understand?"

Gray Zenon cleared his throat. Judge Clancy glared at him. He settled back in his seat.

"I don't know," Tonia stammered, her heart still beating wildly.

"Do you have a pet, Mrs. Morales?" Lydia asked.

Her heartbeat began to slow.

"Yes. A cat named Fluffy."

"Did you get the cat after your husband died?"

"Yes," Tonia said, relaxing completely. "The house was so empty."

"You love your cat, true?"

"Yes."

"You would protect her from harm if you could, wouldn't you?"

"Yes."

"Would you husband approve of you caring for a cat?"

"Objection!" Gray Zenon said, petulantly. "Enough about her dead husband and her fantasies about having conversations with him. This is a legal proceeding and we deal in facts here."

Lydia spoke quietly, but with determination.

"The fact that Mr. Zenon is overlooking is one of the most important in a criminal case—motive. Mrs. Morales acted under duress during the incident and did things that she would not normally have done."

"Proceed," Judge Clancy ruled.

Lydia had Cora Jo read back the question.

"He liked animals too. We'd had cats and dogs over the years, but as we got older we worried about not outliving our pets so we didn't have any when he died. I talked to him about my getting a cat and I felt like he approved."

"So he would want you to protect Fluffy, right?"

"Yes."

"If he had been you, would he have tried to save Fluffy?"

"He wouldn't have let anyone kill her."

"So he would have fought to save her."

"Yes."

"Isn't that what you were doing--fighting to save Fluffy?"

The heartbeat quickened.

"I didn't fight," Tonia said. "I caved in."

"You caved in and did things that you feel were shameful acts, correct?"

"Yes."

Her heartbeat became erratic.

"I'm not going to ask you to describe those actions," Lydia said.

The heartbeat settled down.

"I'm going to ask questions that only require a yes or no response. Can you handle that?"

"I think so," Tonia replied.

"Did Mr. Fouts threaten your cat?"

"Yes.

"Did he threaten to kill it or maim it?"

"First he was going to kill her. I don't know why he changed his mind, but he did. He said he'd cut off her foot."

Tonia began to cry at the memory and then elaborated, "Fluffy trusted him. She didn't know how evil he was. She would have let him catch her. And he would have betrayed her trust. And he planned to make me watch. He was going to tie me up so I couldn't help her. And leave me helpless watching my cat die in agony. He is a horrible, hateful man."

"Yet you made love to him," Lydia challenged abruptly.

The heart monitor's beep accelerated, but Tonia Morales's voice soon overcame its drumbeat.

"I didn't make love to him. I did sexual stuff to save my cat, but I didn't make love to him. He was a foul-smelling, fat, ugly man and I almost threw up when I touched him, but I did what he asked because Fluffy was locked in the bathroom and he'd put a knife outside the door and after how much he hurt me and, seeing the pleasure he got from that, I knew he'd hurt Fluffy. I couldn't fight him. He was too big, too strong. So I tried to please him only I didn't. He didn't want sex. He wanted to hurt me. And he did—in every way possible.

"It sounds to me, Mrs. Morales, as if you fought him with the only weapon you had," Lydia stated strongly. "Your compliance."

"What I did was horrible," Tonia retorted. "I can't speak about it. Not ever."

"Then don't," Lydia said. "It's your choice; however, I need to ask one more question and then we will move on. Did you use both your hands and mouth to bring sexual pleasure to your rapist in order to save your cat from injury?"

Stanley leaned over and whispered, "If it's all true, just answer yes and I will guarantee this will be the last question on this subject. If it is not, tell me now."

"Yes," Tonia said firmly. "It's all true."

Her heartbeat began to even out.

"Now, Mrs. Morales, tell us the order of events, starting with where you were when you first became aware of Stuart Fouts presence in your house."

Tonia Morales began with standing in the kitchen looking out the window and Fluffy meowing for her lunch.

When she finished, Stanley patted her hand gently.

Gray Zenon began his questioning.

"You were not bound in any way at any time, were you?"

Stanley leaned over and whispered. "He will ask some questions to clarify what you said. He needs to do this. Keep your answers simple."

"No, I wasn't." she replied.

"Still, you only tried to escape once, correct?"

"Yes."

"Why didn't you try again?"

"He reminded me Fluffy had four paws."

"Did he ask you to perform specific sexual acts?"

"No."

"So it was your choice."

"Asked and answered," Stanley said.

"Which of the sexual acts was the most loathsome?"

Stanley spoke up.

"This query has no purpose other than to further traumatize the witness. She is not guilty of a crime and should not be so treated."

Judge Clancy eyed the public defender.

"Keep you questions to the point."

Gray Zenon frowned, but complied.

"Mrs. Morales, Mr. Fouts visited you occasionally, did he not?"

"After he raped me the first time, he regularly would show up at the door to return Fluffy."

"What did you do when that happened?"

"I made Fluffy an inside cat and plugged up all the exits she'd gone through."

"I mean, when Mr. Fouts returned your cat, did you invite him in?"

"Not exactly. He walked in with Fluffy and set her down after he closed the door."

"Then what?"

"I thanked him and told him I was too busy to talk."

"Then what?'

"He left."

"Hardly the actions of a rapist, wouldn't you agree?" Gray Zenon pressed.

Stanley whispered in Mrs. Morales' ear and she said, "I don't know."

Gray Zenon appealed to the judge.

"Your Honor, instruct Mr. Praetzel not to coach the witness. This is her deposition. We want her replies."

"Mrs. Morales, what did Mr. Praetzel say to you?" Judge Clancy asked.

Worried, Tonia looked at Stanley who nodded at her and smiled.

"He said not to say what I didn't know."

"I'll allow it," Judge Clancy said. "Continue."

Zenon continued. "I suggest you were being make love to, albeit violently, and that you felt guilty, so when he left, you carefully dressed, called a friend, put your cat in a carrier, and went, not to a hospital or the police as a normal rape victim would do, but to a lawyer's office, isn't that true?"

Tonia put her hand over her heart, which was beating wildly.

Stanley leaned over quickly and whispered, "Tell me your answer."

"He's an asshole!" she hissed, her heartbeat still wildly erotic.

"You can't say that in court," Stanley cautioned softly.

"Even if it's true?"

Cora Jo caught the conversation and was recording it."

"Can he get away with so many lies?" Tonia charged.

Stanley's attitude remained calm. Tonia's heartbeat began to quiet. Judge Clancy, aware that her doctor had been frowning, allowed Stanley a bit of latitude. Gray Zenon was not happy about that.

"Your Honor," he complained. "He's doing it again."

He knew Stanley didn't want the deposition to stop. He had some clout at this juncture.

"I want an answer to the question," Zenon insisted.

"Answer it honestly," Stanley said.

"Can I ask the lady to read it again slowly, so I can answer each part?" Mrs. Morales asked.

Judge Clancy ordered Cora Jo to do just that.

"I suggest you were being made love to..." Cora Jo read and paused.

"I was raped," Tonia said.

". . .albeit violently..."

"That part is true," Tonia said.

"...and felt guilty..."

"Yes, I did because I'd done things I knew were wrong. My reason was good, but my actions weren't."

Cora Jo continued, ". . .so when he left. . ."

"I was unconscious for I don't know how long," Tonia reiterated.

". . . you carefully dressed. . ."

"You better believe it! My breast hurt like hell! I didn't even want to put on clothes. I cried the whole time."

When she stopped, Cora Jo continued. ". . . called a friend. . ."

"Yes, I did that," Tonia said.

Stanley swallowed a smirk. Gray Zenon was getting his question answered but in a way he hadn't envisioned.

". . . put your cat in a carrier. . ."

"Yes, I did that. I couldn't hold her. My breast was killing me."

". . . and went, not to a hospital or the police as a normal rape victim would do but to a lawyer's office. . ."

"I don't know what normal rape victims do," Tonia said. "But I think a lot of them go to a friend or relative first.

I couldn't think of any and I remembered that Mr. Praetzel had rescued Stella and I thought he would believe me, so I went there. It made sense at the time."

Lydia Davis had pulled all but one of the snake's teeth. That one the scared, reluctant witness had managed to pull out all by herself.

Stanley patted her hand gently. Her decision to answer the question in pieces had been brilliant.

Gray Zenon had one last query. Defanged, he struck toothless.

"Did Mrs. Praetzel prep you for this deposition?"

"She didn't know about this deposition when we talked," Tonia said. "In fact, when we talked, she didn't talk at all. She didn't even tell me that she had been raped. I think most people would have said, 'It happened to me, so I understand.' but not her. She just listened to me. Sure she prepped me. She believed me. That gave me the courage I needed today."

Stanley patted her hand again. And then it was over.

Stanley stayed by Tonia's side while the equipment and chairs were folded up and one by one everyone left. Both judge Clancy and Lydia came over and told Tonia that she had handled a difficult situation well.

When they all left, Tonia looked to Stanley for more assurance.

"Your husband was proud of you today," Stanley said.

"Men don't understand," Tonia said.

"Stanley patted her hand. "Some men don't. But you wouldn't have loved that kind of man for forty six years."

Her eyes brightened. "He was a good man."

"He would be glad you saved the cat."

"Would you?"

"Now that I have animals I love, the answer is yes," Stanley said. "Let me tell you a little story just to give you something to laugh about when I'm gone. You saw the huge aquariums in my office."

She nodded.

"When I first met Aleta, we were working on a case together. She was a practicing attorney from California and I had a one-man office with one secretary and two big fish tanks. The case had some danger involved, but I was so smitten with her I could barely think. We had to do some rather involved legal word and we were in the office of the bank manager and I said I could work better if I could watch my fish."

"And she bought that line?" Tonia chuckled. "It is original, I'll admit."

"I wanted her to see my office, small as it was," Stanley admitted. "And I guess I wanted to impress her just a little bit."

"So was she impressed?"

"We were watching my fish and I was naming them for her. That impressed her. I had fish named for just about everyone I liked including my mother."

"And she remembered which one that was, didn't she?"

"Yes, she did. While we were standing there, a sniper shot at us. The first bullet grazed her scalp and shattered the glass in the fish tank. The second caught my ear. Suddenly we were drenched in water, and there were flopping fish everywhere. Even thought she was bleeding, Aleta began picking up fish and handing them to me. She was sitting on the floor, which I knew was a safe place for her to be. We got all the fish but one safely into the other tank. When the cop assigned to guard us made it up the stairs, Aleta was holding the dead fish in her lap, crying. The cop rounded the corner into the office just as she said, "I killed your mother.""

Tonia chuckled. "And the cop looked for the body?"

"He couldn't believe she was crying over a fish," Stanley finished. "The bullet that grazed my ear killed the fish. Aleta blamed herself."

"But she didn't shoot the gun!" Tonia protested.

"And you didn't break into a house and rape anyone. Just keep in mind who is at fault," Stanley said. "So what is happening with my wife is not your fault."

"Why are you telling me this?" Tonia asked, puzzled.

"Because you are a smart lady and that idea will occur to you," Stanley said. "She is very sick right now."

Tonia nodded solemnly.

"You want me to remember that I didn't kill the fish either," the older woman said.

"Yes," Stanley said. "And I want you to know that neither of us is angry with you. I am very pleased with you. And what you did will make Aleta happy."

"So one never gets well again?"

"One gets better. Some traumas are never forgotten, but they fade in the memory."

"Like the death of a husband."

"Like that."

CHAPTER 12

Stanley checked with Bertha when he was preparing to leave the hospital. She told him about Martha's phone call and that Martha had evidently told Aleta to sleep because she went right to sleep after that call.

"I need to finish up a few things at the office," he told her, and then said goodbye quickly as a nurse was hurrying toward him, calling his name.

He turned and waited for her.

"Mrs. Betty Smith wants to see you," the nurse said between breaths.

"I don't know anyone by that name," Stanley said.

"Smith isn't her real name," the nurse said. "No one knows what her real name is. She hasn't said a word until this afternoon when she heard a couple of us talking about you being in the hospital taking a deposition from Mrs. Morales."

"I'm a children's advocate," Stanley said. "I don't represent adults."

"Please come and tell her that," the nurse begged. "We need information."

"I'm in no condition to see anyone," Stanley said.

"Your face?" the nurse said.

"Yes,"

"Hers is just as bad," the nurse said. "I think that's why she asked for you. We were talking about that and that's when she asked me to fetch you."

Stanley sighed. "Lead the way."

Stanley noticed the guard on the door and realized that he was visiting the woman he had rescued from the dumpster.

He entered the room behind the nurse who said, "I brought him. He says he's a children's lawyer."

"That's what I need," the woman said. "Please leave us alone until we're done."

"When the door closed," the woman asked. "How come the guard let you though?"

"I'm well-known children's attorney," Stanley said.

"He greeted you by your first name."

"You said I was the type of attorney you needed," Stanley said. "You were attacked, thrown in a dumpster and left for dead."

"You left out raped. Stuart Fouts raped me too."

"Are you willing to testify to that?"

"As long as no one knows who I am, I'm safe."

"You have a guard on the door," Stanley said.

"So much for that theory," the woman smiled. "My names Olivia Qucher. You saved me from death. You owe me."

"I owe you?" Stanley gasped.

"If I were dead, I wouldn't have to live with what happened to me, hence, you owe me."

"I guess from your perspective that could seem to be true."

"So I need you to keep me alive," Olivia said. "No person should have to die twice, especially the way I died. And you know that Stuart Fouts will come after me again."

Stanley sat down.

"What would you have me do?"

"Shoot him."

"I don't go around shooting people," Stanley said evenly. "But with your testimony and Tonia Morales' testimony, Stuart Fouts will be convicted and sent to prison."

"Can you call back that judge and court reporter? I don't want to be videotaped."

"Let me use your phone."

"Please protect me as you would a child," Olivia said. "That's why I said you were the lawyer I wanted."

"But you don't know how I protected Mrs. Morales," Stanley protested.

"The nurses were laying odds on whether she would be able to do a deposition at all, and I heard their disbelief when she completed the task. You made it possible for her to do that. I want you to make it possible for me to do it too."

"When?"

"Now," Olivia said. "Judge Clancy owes me."

"Like I owe you?"

"When I retired he said, 'If ever I can do a favor, call me.' So I'm calling in that favor."

"Let me use your phone," Stanley said.

He called the front desk and within minutes both Judge Clancy and Cora Jo entered Olivia Qucher's room. Gray Zenon arrived five minutes later.

"I have not heard Mrs. Qucher's testimony in detail," Stanley said. "However, the doctors consider her condition serious, and Mrs. Qucher doesn't think she will live much longer, so I am suggesting that we take the deposition now."

"We don't have a doctor present," Judge Clancy noted.

"Listen to my testimony, Dennis, simply because you promised me a favor and this is it."

"She doesn't have a heart condition like Mrs. Morales," Stanley said. "We could ask a nurse to be present and call a doctor if one is needed."

"Do it," the judge ordered.

"Olivia, do you like the nurse that fetched me?"

"Yes, she's really nice. She listens," Olivia said. "Her names Vivian."

A couple minutes later, Vivian joined the group around Olivia Qucher's bed and the deposition began. Following Stanley's suggestion, Olivia was allowed to tell her story in her own words without interruption. Her account was lucid and telling. Stuart Fouts had visited her twice. The first time her dog had bitten him on the ankle and stopped that rape session after she'd been raped only once. She had reported him; she had no idea who he was. A rape exam was done and the results had been lost. The prosecutor refused to prosecute without any forensic evidence and no positive ID.

Stanley patted her hand and asked if she needed a break. She smiled at him and shook her head.

"The second time was the worst," she said. "I recognized him and my fear showed in my face and excited him. He told me to lock my dog in the closet or he'd cut him into little pieces. He pulled out a knife and pushed the door open. I grabbed Tiny and shoved him into the hall closet and shut the door."

Olivia took a deep breath and described the first beating which Stuart Fouts had told her was he due because her dog had bitten him. Then he raped her. She remembered fighting him, but he only laughed as hit her back and she gave up. The blows to her face hurt as much as the rape.
He raped her a second time and she cried. That excited him and he raped her a third time. That one was extremely painful and she remembered screaming. She had no idea what else he might have done. The next thing she remembered was being in some place that smelled bad, but she couldn't bring herself to wake up. She had only a vague recollection of a man grabbing her and lifting her and then she heard a siren blaring. She woke up in the hospital. The doctor gave her a shot for the pain and she refused to give her name. She thought her silence would protect her. She didn't know whom to trust until Mr. Praetzel took Mrs. Morales' deposition.

"So no rape exam?" Gray Zenon asked.

"I'll have Dr. Chesney do one," Stanley said.

"There won't be any semen," Gray Zenon said.

"There will be massive tearing and bruising," Stanley said. "She testified that she cried the second time and she screamed the third time. Each rape was worse than the prior one. I think we will find severe trauma to the vagina."

"But right now we have no forensic evidence that she was raped."

"We have evidence she was beaten," Stanley said. "We have evidence that will support the charges of assault, kidnapping and attempted murder. We will go with those charges for now. We'll add rape later."

"Kidnapping?"

"She didn't consent to being dropped in a dumpster and covered with garbage," Stanley said evenly.

"You've been a kid's attorney too long," Gray Zenon said. "You don't even know what to charge a person with."

"She was taken from her home by force," Stanley answered. "That's what kidnapping is. Just because a child is sleeping when he is taken from his home doesn't mean that he hasn't been kidnapped. I believe the same definition is applicable here."

Olivia laughed. "Oh, Mr. Praetzel, you did it! Thank you!"

Gray Zenon looked confused.

"What did he do?"

"He saw the charge I wanted proven above all else. No one is going to care that my little dog is dead, but he is. If Stuart Fouts had left me in my home, whoever found me would have found my dog and called Animal Control."

"Any questions, Mr. Zenon," Judge Clancy asked.

Gray Zenon was about to decline to question Mrs. Qucher when Stanley's mother entered the room.

"Sorry I'm late," she breathed. "Where are we?

"Done," Gray Zenon said.

"Mr. Zenon hasn't questioned the witness," Stanley said. "The deposition will be tossed out unless he does."

"That's why I'm here. Hello, Olivia. It's good to see you again. I'm sorry I need to ask the hard questions for this deposition to be accepted by a judge," Lydia said. "But first I need ten minutes to be brought up to speed. Stanley, you're elected."

Then minutes later, Lydia plowed in, "Mrs. Qucher, let's start at the beginning."

Olivia smiled. "Ask away."

"I am only going to deal with the second rape," Lydia said. "But the fact that you said you had been raped once will be the basis for my first question. Why did you remove the dead bolt and let Stuart Fouts into your house?"

"I had just gotten home from the store and I was juggling two bags of groceries and Tiny's leash. I still had my key in my hand and when I went to slam the door with my rear, I didn't throw the dead bolt. My hands were full. It was a bad mistake."

"Did Stuart Fouts knock on the door?"

"Yes."

"Why not throw the deadbolt before opening it to see who it was?"

"All I thought about was setting my bags down so I could deal with keeping Tiny from running off down the street."

"So why not slam the door shut the minute you saw who it was?"

"I did."

"How did Stuart get in?"

"He stuck his foot in the door and then he waved that knife around and told me to lock Tiny up. All I could think about was that Tiny had his harness on and the leash was fastened to it which meant that Stuart could grab him and cut him like he said he planned to do. I have a pretty vivid imagination and it took over. All I saw was how much danger Tiny was in. When I put him in the closet, I unsnapped the leash."

"He still had his harness on," Lydia said. "Why not take it off?"

"Stuart grabbed me from behind and pulled me back before I could do that. He is a very strong man."

"Why didn't you cry the first time he raped you?" Lydia asked.

"I thought if I did, he'd hurt Tiny."

"Did you cry the second time because he told you that you could?"

"I wasn't trying to please him," Olivia shot back.

"Wasn't he more excited when you screamed?"

"Yes."

"In your experience, don't men like women who make noise during intercourse?"

"Yes."

"So each time, you gave him more of what he wanted. Isn't that true?"

"Yes."

"Have you had violent lovers?"

"Yes."

"Was he more violent than your other lovers?"

"He wasn't a lover. He was a rapist," Olivia stated. "And he hurt me. And I didn't consent to a single action that he took. He's a fat pig and I hated every second."

"Did you call him a pig?"

"As a matter of fact I did," Olivia said. "My physical blows weren't stopping him, so I thought verbal blows might. I was wrong. He enjoyed those as well."

"Enjoyed?"

"I was hit every time I spat out one. But he wasn't mad. He liked being able to hit me when I insulted him. I think he was hitting his mother."

"So you think he was acting crazy?"

"No. I think he was pretending I was his mother."

"That sounds a bit crazy to me."

"It was a fantasy. He enjoyed it. But he knew it was a fantasy. That's why I say he wasn't crazy. He knew I wasn't actually his mother. But his hatred of his mother spilled out in that room. He couldn't rape his mother, so he raped me. People do it all the time. It's called displaced anger. It doesn't mean you're crazy. It means that the person you are angry at is too powerful to confront directly."

"Do you fancy yourself a psychologist?" Lydia asked.

"No."

"You spouted a log of psychological reasoning."

"I took a couple psych classes eons ago. The stuff stuck in my memory. It came in handy over the years."

"So you're a layman, aren't you?"

"An educated layman," Olivia said.

"Stuart Fouts is going to claim that the sex was consensual, that you invited him in because you knew he liked having sex with older women, that you weren't finding too many men eager to have sex with a woman of your age and that you still had sexual needs."

"He's right about most of that. I am older. I like sex. I haven't found any men willing to supply that. And I did know he liked older woman."

"So you invited him in and. . ."

Olivia cut in. "That's the part that's wrong. I didn't invite him in. I definitely did not want to have sex with him. I found him repulsive. I was raped and I was beaten. I didn't invite either type of assault. I said 'no' loud and clear."

"Thank you, Olivia," Lydia said. "I have no more questions. Perhaps Mr. Zenon would care to weigh in now."

"Mr. Zenon, have you any questions that you thought of while Judge Davis was questioning Mrs. Qucher?" Judge Clancy asked.

"No, Your Honor."

"Mr. Zenon, do you believe that this deposition is complete enough to be accepted as testimony in a court of law?"

"No," Gray Zenon said.

"Then obviously you have unanswered questions," Judge Clancy said. "I suggest you ask them now."

"Mrs. Qucher, do you have numerous lovers?"

"Objection," Stanley said. "Mrs. Qucher's sex life is irrelevant."

"Sustained."

"Exception."

"Noted."

"Mrs. Qucher, did you enjoy being raped the first time?"

"No."

"But according to you testimony, you like violent sex. Is that true?"

"Yes."

"So what was different this time?"

"I said no."

"Did Stuart Fouts believe you?"

"Yes."

"How can you be so sure?"

"I socked him in the nose."

"Wouldn't that just have encouraged him to continue?"

"He likes to inflict pain, not receive it."

"Strike as unresponsive," Zenon asked.

"Strike the question and the response," the judge ordered.

"Did he hit you because you hit him?"

"No."

Surprised at her response, Zenon asked, "He let you hit him and didn't retaliate?"

"Yes."

"But you were hit?" Zenon charged, now completely off script.

"Stuart couldn't be goaded into hitting by any physical action on my part," Olivia stated. "He hit me when I said something nasty and only then."

"That doesn't make any sense," Gray Zenon exclaimed.

"My blows weren't strong enough to really hurt him, so he brushed them off. It was very disconcerting. I felt so helpless," Olivia explained. "But my words angered him enough to hit me."

"Still, you kept on insulting him. So, you were responsible for your own beating, isn't that so?"

"No."

"You said he only hit you when you said something nasty to him. Why didn't you stop?"

"He wouldn't let me," Olivia said.

"What did he do?" Zenon said sarcastically. "Hit you?"

"Yes."

"He hit you when you said something nasty and then he hit you when you stopped? Is that what you are saying?"

"Yes."

"That's not reasonable," Zenon observed.

"It is to a man who wants to hit someone and feels that he can only do that when that person says something nasty. It makes perfect sense."

"Did this happen the first time he raped you?"

"No."

"Didn't you call him names the first time?"

"No. I just told him to stop."

"Didn't he beat you the first time he raped you?"

"Not like this time," Olivia said. "I think I hit a nerve."

"I suggest that you liked the first time you had sex and this time he took it to another level and you heard that Mrs. Morales was going to testify and you hopped on her bandwagon."

"Mostly that is true."

Without thinking, Gray Zenon asked, "What isn't true?"

"That I liked it the first time. I never liked him raping me."

"Then what's true?"

"He took it to another level. He didn't stop like he did the first time. Of course, Tiny bit him, so it wasn't as if he didn't plan to rape me a second time. But I didn't think he could do it a second time so soon. This last time I found out that he could," Olivia said. "And yes I jumped on Mrs. Morales' bandwagon. You have no idea how great it is to have someone in the same boat as me."

"I suggest that you belong in separate boats," Gray Zenon said. "I suggest that this time it was another man who raped you and you are angry about the time he did rape you and you are pinning this rape on him because you want revenge for the time he got away with it. Isn't that true?"

"No."

"He has an alibi."

"His mother?"

"Yes."

"So she helped him dump my body."

"They were at home together."

"He thought I was dead." Olivia said. "That's why she helped him dump my body. But first they went into the barbecue place and ate. And then he lost the receipt for the meal and so they decided to say they were at home."

"That's a fanciful bit of reasoning," Gray Zenon said.

"I heard them arguing."

"You didn't mention it before."

"Because it didn't make any sense. But I heard her scolding him because he lost the receipt."

"I'm done, Your Honor," Zenon said abruptly.

Stanley stayed with Olivia as the others packed up and left.

"I don't dare go home," she whispered.

"Let me call Animal Control and tell them about your dog. I'll make sure he's taken to a vet. I'll make sure they know he has an owner who loves him."

"I don't dare hope."

"They might not be able to save him, but I will let you know if they are trying," Stanley said. "Give me a day to come up with a place you'll be safe when you leave the hospital."

Later, when Stanley Praetzel entered his house, the smell of cooking greeted him, as did the gurgle of a happy baby being held by his buxom black wet nurse whose chair was facing the open door to the master bedroom. It was the first time since they'd been married that that particular opening was truly beneficial. When he was a bachelor, he'd only planned two rooms in his remodeled farmhouse—a bedroom suite and a living room-kitchen combination. He now had a large family room on the other side of the kitchen, which Aleta's Uncle Paul, a former California architect, was using, as his studio. Paul Locke said the light was just right in that room and Stanley and Aleta had turned it over to him.

He addressed Bertha immediately upon entering the house.

"I hate to impose . . ." Stanley began.

"We will be glad to watch Gerard tonight," Bertha volunteered.

"I think this will be the last time I will need to ask that."

"She was much better this morning," Bertha reported. "And then she relapsed this afternoon. Martha called and after that she went to sleep."

"The dogs be in there," Jamara commented. "They be there all afternoon."

"I guess I'll have to walk them," Stanley said.

He then thanked the two women and bade them good night. After they left, he entered the bedroom and closed the door. Scooby bounced into a stand and wagged his tail.

As he was hanging up his suit coat, Stanley saw Scooby step on Aleta. Aleta grunted. Immediately Scooby stepped back and apologized by licking her face.

She woke laughing.

"You're unpillowed," Stanley said immediately.

"Martha said love would wake me," she murmured. "I wasn't expecting a face wash."

"The deposition is done," Stanley reported, sitting beside her on the bed. "Tonia Morales was brilliant. She said you gave her the strength by believing her."

"I wasn't good . . ." Aleta began.

"On the contrary," Stanley cut in. "You obeyed Martha and slept. Your actions were one hundred percent good."

"It's late," Aleta noted glancing at the clock. "Surely the deposition didn't take that long?"

"I arranged for another deposition. Stuart Fouts raped our dumpster lady. Since everyone was still around, more or less, we took her deposition as well."

"It couldn't wait?"

"She was up for it at that moment, but her prognosis isn't good."

"What made you rush the deposition?"

"I considered it a death-bed confession and persuaded Judge Clancy to go with that interpretation. Gray Zenon wasn't too happy. He refused to ask any questions, and then my mother showed up and took over his job. Judge Clancy put him on the spot when he asked him if he would declare the deposition satisfactory as testimony. When he said that he wouldn't, Judge Clancy made him ask the questions he was preparing to ask in trial."

"Clancy will accept the deposition if the case lands in his court."

Stanley took his wife's hand in his and asked, "Do you have the answer to your question yet?"

She shook her head and her countenance showed her despair.

"Do you want to talk?"

She nodded her head.

"Begin with what Martha said."

"She said my sin was unforgivable," Aleta spat out.

"That's what you heard," Stanley said evenly. "Tell me exactly what she said."

"I don't remember," Aleta grumbled sullenly.

"What was the last word she said that you objected to the most?"

"Omniscient,"

"That God is omniscient or that you think you are?"

"I don't think that!" Aleta objected. "And I don't think I'm omnipotent either!"

"So she didn't explain?"

"No," Aleta sputtered. "She just spit out the words."

"In reference to you or God?"

"Me, of course! Everyone knows those words describe God."

"What else did she say?" Stanley asked gently.

"That the truth would set me free," Aleta repeated. "As if I don't believe that."

"What lie are you embracing?" Stanley questioned softly.

"None! I don't embrace lies," Aleta insisted.

"I told Tonia the story about the fish that was shot," Stanley said.

"Why did you do that?"

"So she wouldn't believe she was responsible for Stella being raped."

"Why would she think that?"

"She didn't report Stuart Fouts the first time he raped her."

"She was frightened," Aleta shot back. "Besides she didn't know he would rape Stella."

"Did you?"

"Did I what?"

"Know that Stuart Fouts was going to rape Tonia Morales?"

"No, of course not!" Aleta protested.

"So why are you feeling guilty?"

"I knew he was dangerous and the judge didn't believe me."

"And why should he have believed you?"

"Because Stuart Fouts had raped an old lady."

"Which hadn't been proven in a court of law yet."

"But we had a solid case," Aleta insisted.

"Which he didn't know."

"He's a serial rapist."

"Which none of us knew."

"We know that now," Aleta stated.

"There's a warrant out for his arrest on the new charge," Stanley said. "And after Olivia Qucher gave her deposition, Judge Clancy issued an arrest warrant on those charges."

"That proves that I wasn't persuasive enough," Aleta insisted.

"You didn't know. I just found out."

"I knew about Stella Woodbridge. I simply wasn't persuasive enough."

"Even Jesus couldn't persuade a man whose mind was set to take another path. God Himself couldn't persuade you to consider thoughts that were opposite to your feelings."

"That's not true," Aleta denied vehemently. "My reason never takes a back seat to my feelings."

"Doesn't it?" Stanley questioned softly.

"No, it does not," she retorted. "Definitely, absolutely does not!"

"I can prove that your feelings sit on your reason and, like a jackass, absolutely refuse to budge," Stanley asserted.

"I dare you!" Aleta charged.

Stanley smiled.

"When you saw Hubbs leading Shadow toward the house before Martha called, what thought did you have?"

"How do you know about that?"

"He told me. Answer the question. What did you think?"

"That something was wrong and he wanted to talk with me about it."

"And when he turned to return to the barn?"

"That Shadow was okay."

"Did you think that Shadow was in good hands?"

"Yes."

"And that he would be well looked after should you die?"

"Yes, I thought that."

"What message did you refuse to accept?

"No message."

"Aleta, be honest," Stanley urged. "It was only a whisper, but you heard it. What was it?"

"That their hearts would be broken," Aleta murmured.

"Your reason told you this, didn't it?" Stanley queried. "Your feelings, however, were so overwhelming that there was no room for reason. You feelings were the jackass sitting on the carrot that he wanted to eat."

"I guess."

"You're hedging."

"Okay, so I'm a jackass."

"False feelings," Stanley said.

"Not false," Aleta protested. "They were real."

"Okay, not false feelings," Stanley conceded. "But irrational ones. Martha was right. You feel guilty because you didn't try to contact your sister. If you had, her suffering at the hands of your mother might have been shorter. This case where a cat was threatened reminded you how much Jocelyn suffered in an effort to protect her horse."

"Shouldn't I feel guilty?" Aleta charged. "I knew my mother was cruel. I never checked on my sister."

"Did no one check on her?'

"Andrea and Lettie tried."

"And Andrea is your mother's friend," Stanley said. "So didn't you believe she was the best one to stay in contact with Jocelyn?"

"But I was wrong. My mother fooled Aunt Andrea."

"So Andrea should feel guilty?" Stanley posed.

"No, of course not. She trusted Marian. And she took Lettie to the stables where Yudi was so she could leave messages for Jocelyn. They couldn't believe that Jocelyn wouldn't ride her horse regularly. She tried."

"But she never told you that she was unable to contact Jocelyn."

"She was busy getting ready to move," Aleta jumped in. "And she trusted Marian."

"Do you remember why you didn't call?

"I thought if I did, I would upset my mother and she'd take her anger out on Jocelyn."

"Didn't you agree with Jocelyn before she left that she should call you?"

"Yes."

"So, why the guilt?"

"I should have known something was wrong."

"You did," Stanley said. "You just didn't' know what."

"I should have acted."

"You did. You chose not to interfere."

"I was wrong."

"So were a lot of people," Stanley surmised. "It's the human condition. We are neither omniscient nor omnipotent. We can only act on what we know."

"Well, I knew Stuart Fouts was dangerous. I failed to persuade the judge and. . ."

"There's a passage in Romans that holds the answer to some of the inexplicable reasons certain happenings occur."

"The answer is I failed."

"No, it's not. You are not omnipotent either. The passage in Romans reminds us of Pharaoh's response to the repeated visits of plagues. Moses didn't fail. God hardened Pharaoh's heart."

"What does it say in Romans?" Aleta pressed more as a challenge than because she wanted an answer.

"That God will have mercy on whom He wills and He hardens the heart of whom He wills."

"Did you memorize the whole Bible?" Aleta accused.

Stanley grinned.

"Just the passage that I would need when a judgment goes against me in court. It also reminds me that it may not be my brilliance that results in a win. God may have opened the judge's heart to my words."

"Don't mix my food tonight," Aleta said as she closed her eyes and waited for the blindfold.

CHAPTER 13

The next morning Stanley and Aleta sat down at the breakfast table and Stanley announced, "We aren't going to work today."

The casual attire of the two Praetzels at the table had already told those eating breakfast that they weren't.

"Stanley's not going to work," Aleta said. "I am."

"Not dressed like that!" Stanley exclaimed.

Aleta was wearing the short shorts he liked. Until yesterday she'd never left the grounds wearing them.

"You took me to the hospital and the office dressed like this yesterday, so I figured you considered this proper attire."

"Well, it isn't."

"I'm not changing," Aleta said.

"Why are you going in?"

"I need to see your mother."

"Then you definitely need to change."

"That's why I need to be in shorts. That'll tell her I'm not back."

"You could wear slacks."

"You said I had great legs," Aleta teased. "Did something happen last night that made you change your mind?"

"You have great legs, but I want them to stay here."

"You mean go in legless?" she chuckled.

"You know what I mean."

"Go off and talk to Dad while I eat."

"How did you know?" Stanley asked. "Nevermind. Robert, bring your breakfast into the study. I need to talk with you for a few minutes."

Bertha followed them and set down a plate of food in front of Stanley.

"Thank you," Bertha said as Stanley settled in the chair behind the desk.

Stanley looked at her quizzically.

"You restored her soul," Bertha said.

Robert nodded.

"She's shaken off whatever brought her down."

"For now," Stanley said. "I need your help now."

"Anything."

Stanley looked at Bertha who was standing hesitantly in the doorway.

"Would you close the door as you leave, please," he requested.

After the door closed, Stanley said. "I need to know more about Marian."

"What has she got to do with this?" Robert asked. "I thought it was a rape case that triggered what happened."

"So did I until I remembered how deeply we had dealt with that. Then Bertha said something about Jocelyn and I looked at this case from that perspective. It wasn't the rape but the threat to the cat that was the trigger."

Robert chewed thoughtfully for a few minutes, took a sip of coffee and then said, "What do you need to know?"

"Just tell me everything. I'll talk to Herve Schwartzman and get a professional's take."

"Should she see a psychiatrist?"

"I'll ask Herve. I trust his professional judgment. Aleta is clever. If she wants to hide something, she can, but I don't think that's what's going on. I think there's something in her background driving her that she's unaware of."

"What do you see that you don't like?"

"Nothing. I like everything about her."

"Then what is it?"

"She doesn't have the same good feeling about herself that I do."

"She's a heck of a trial lawyer," Robert countered. "One can't be that good without self confidence.

"I think when she's in the courtroom, she's using the part of her personality shaped by you," Stanley explained. "But she's carrying around her mother's influence as well."

"I don't see much of her mother in Aleta," Robert confessed. "She reminds me more of my mother. For one thing, Marian didn't like animals and Aleta and Jocelyn love them. Marian was a perfectionist and very dependent on what other people thought."

"Most of that I already know," Stanley said.

"What on earth are you hoping to gain?"

"A bit of insight that might help her when self-doubts plague her."

"We all have self-doubts."

"For some reason, Aleta's devastate her," Stanley said. "When you go to the office, take the contracts Aleta has finished, will you?"

"Sure."

Stanley searched through the folders on the desk.

"Where are they?"

"Maybe Aleta moved them," Robert suggested.

Suddenly, Stanley jumped up.

"She left while we were in here."

"Surely she ate breakfast," Robert said as he followed Stanley into the kitchen.

"She left, didn't she?" Stanley stormed.

Bertha turned and scowled.

"She said to tell you to calm down and trust her. She is supposed to be there this morning."

"Why did she put on shorts then?"

Bertha shrugged.

"She be happy," Jamara put in. "She say there be a new man in the office what likes her legs."

"Nigel?' Robert laughed.

Stanley scowled.

"I think she be teasing you," Jamara suggested.

"I know she is," Stanley said. "I teased her this morning and she's one for payback."

At the Willow Glen office of Praetzel, Locke and Praetzel, Aleta Praetzel made her way up the stairs past the people lined up waiting for an appointment. Her lively step and dress made her look years younger than she was. When she got to the head of the line, she kept the illusion intact.

"I want to see my mother," she said to Alice and then walked into Stanley's office.

A very young girl stepped out of line and followed her.

"I'm with her," she said to the secretary as she hurried into Stanley's office after Aleta.

Aleta turned as the child shut the door to keep the secretary out.

"Who are you?" Aleta asked.

"Kim Conner," the girl said.

Aleta guessed the young blonde child was eleven or twelve. She hadn't yet lost the boyish look of the pre-teen. Her hair was short and purposely jagged which, on her, was attractive.

"Please tell your mother to be my lawyer," Kim begged the young woman in shorts.

"You need a lawyer?' Aleta asked.

Kim fished a dollar out of her pocket.

"I saw this movie on television and the boy got a lawyer for a dollar. I will pay more, but I heard that Aleta Praetzel will take monthly payments."

"She never takes monthly payments," Aleta said, taking the dollar. "But I'll tell my mother you paid the fee."

"But you took the money."

"It was for Aleta Praetzel, wasn't it?"

"Yes."

"I'll give it to her," Aleta said. "Now tell me why you need a lawyer,"

"I saw a crime, only my mother said it wasn't because it happened to an animal, but I want a lawyer to tell me if killing a cat and cutting off its feet is a crime."

Aleta felt a chill run down her spine.

She sank into a chair and told the girl to do the same.

"Tell me what you saw," she said.

"It's pretty horrible," Kim said. "Maybe I should wait."

"My name is Aleta Praetzel," Aleta said. "I'm here to see my mother-in-law, Judge Davis. She's been helping out at our office this week while my husband and I are on leave."

"Do all those people in line know that?" Kim asked.

"I guess they don't," Aleta said.

She went over to the intercom pressed Alice's number.

"Tell Lydia I'm busy. And what's being done about the people in the line outside the door?"

"Judge Davis said that she'd see the first ten," Alice reported. "I was just going to send Tim down the stairs to tell everyone."

"Change the order," Aleta charged. "Send all seniors to Chin. Have Tim take down the particulars of all those wanting wills and give that to me. Then give Lydia ten to interview. And bring me client number eleven."

"Yes, Mrs. Praetzel," Alice said. "Your husband said that you were to come right home."

"Alice, if he calls again, put him through to me," Aleta said. "Meanwhile, follow my directions."

"Yes, Ma'am."

Aleta turned around and focused her attention on Kim.

"Now let's hear your story—all of it."

The child was brief. She'd seen old lady Fouts out in her yard with a net. She'd been sitting in her brother's tree house. She'd snuck up there while he was at Little League. She was supposed to be at a girlfriend's house.

Old lady Fouts had been acting strangely at night and Kim wanted to see what the old lady was doing out in back by the bushes. The bushes were tall and made the Fouts' backyard very private.

Kim had heard some noises coming from that yard that sounded strange.

She saw the old woman put out some chicken on a plate and leave it. A couple of stray cats pounced on the offering.

"I thought she was being kind," Kim said. "But then the cats started acting funny and after a few minutes they all keeled over. Mrs. Fouts came out of the house with this big fat knife and she hacked away at the cats. I saw her cut off the feet of one. Then I saw one crawl away and I climbed down out of the tree house and caught it. I carried it back up into the tree house with me. I barely got up there before that crazy old witch burst through the bushes looking for the cat.

"Just then the cat threw up the chicken and everything else it had eaten. And I thought sure the witch would hear it but she didn't. It was a mess. I didn't dare go into the house to get stuff to clean up the mess because she might see me.

"The cat just lay there after it vomited and I left it. It was a pretty orange cat with long hair like Mrs. Morales' cat Fluffy. It had white paws so I called it Boots. It was dirty. Fluffy was always clean.

"Pretty soon the old hag gave up looking for Boots and went back to the dead ones. She stuffed the bodies into paper sacks along with their feet and tails. Only a witch would have done that. I almost threw up on top of poor Boots. Mrs. Fouts snuck over to Mrs. Morales' house. She went in through the door to the basement.

"I was too scared to climb down out of the tree house. You can see the tree house really good from Mrs. Morales'

window. So I stayed and watched. After a while, old lady
Fouts came out with the bags all folded up and threw them in
her trashcan.

"When did all this happen?" Aleta asked.

"Yesterday afternoon," Kim said. "Didn't she commit
a crime?"

"Yes, she did," Aleta said. "Where's Boots?"

"In my brother's tree house. I took Boots some milk,
but he couldn't eat it, so I fetched my dolly's baby bottle and
filled it and fed Boots that way. He looked so weak. I was
so afraid he would die."

"He still might."

"When I found out Boots couldn't stand," Kim
continued. "I made him a bed in the tree house."

Aleta flipped open the intercom.

"Alice, get me Chief West."

As she waited, Aleta said to Kim, "'I'm going to send a
police chief for Boots. Is that alright?"

"To kill him?" Kim asked alarmed.

"To take Boots to my vet," Aleta responded gently.

Aleta told Lyle what the child had seen. He told her
he'd take care of it without involving the child. When she
hung up, Aleta punched the intercom.

"Alice, Kim needs a note for school. She's late
because she had an appointment with me."

"I'm sorry your mother won't let you keep Boots,"
Aleta told Kim.

"How'd you know?"

"Boots is still in the tree house."

"Will you find a good home for him?"

"I have a great home already picked out. I'll see that
you get pictures, okay?"

After Kim left, Alice ushered in an elderly gentleman
who had thinning light brown hair, rimless bifocals, scraggly
brows, penetrating blue eyes and a crooked smile that
revealed even straight teeth, obviously not his own.

Aleta raised an eyebrow, but before Alice could explain, the old man extended a gnarled hand and said, "Zachary Triggs. I'm a friend of Herve Schwartzman's. I recognize you by your legs. Herve said they were the finest pair he'd ever seen."

Aleta laughed.

"Well, Mr. Triggs, what can I do for you that my associate Mr. Chin can't?"

"You can come out from behind that desk," Zachary Triggs stated bluntly.

"Alice, you may leave," Aleta said. "It's alright."

Zachary Triggs looked at Aleta.

"Are you afraid to come out?"

Aleta grinned at him.

"Alice is calling my husband."

"Doesn't he know how you came to work today?"

"I'm not supposed to be working."

"He wants the legs to be viewed by him alone, is that it?"

"Pretty much," Aleta agreed.

The light on her phone flashed. She picked up the receiver.

"Hello, Stanley."

"Alice is worried."

"The question is, are you?"

"Why are you still there?"

"A new development in the Morales case," Aleta said. "And the case God wants me to take just entered the office."

"The lech?"

"The same," Aleta said. "I'll come home right afterward. I'll bring you work to do if you're bored."

"Do not bring me any contracts or wills."

"I could bring you Mr. Triggs. Come to think of it, you aren't a Mr., are you?" Aleta said addressing the gentleman standing on the opposite side of the desk. "You're a doctor, aren't you?"

"Do I get to see the legs if I am?" Dr. Triggs asked.

"Stanley, I'm bringing home a case. Have Bertha make coffee."

She hung up.

"Okay, Dr. Triggs, follow the legs."

She passed Alice and asked, "Where's Nigel?"

"In with your mother-in-law, Judge Davis," Alice said.

Behind her she heard Dr. Triggs chuckle.

"Would you have him step out a minute? I'm leaving."

A tall, black man emerged from Lydia's temporary office. Aleta introduced the men.

"Dr. Triggs, meet Mr. Nigel Oliver. You didn't want a specialist in senior citizen affairs, but I have a feeling you will wind up working with him nonetheless."

Nigel shook hands with the old man who noticed that while firm, his grip was gentle.

"Don't worry, Nigel. He didn't pick me out for my superior brain. Dr. Schwartzman recommended me on the basis of my legs, which, of course, is why I'm in shorts today. That, and I told Stanley I'd let you have another look at my legs."

"I. . .I'm. . ." Nigel stammered.

Dr. Triggs broke in with a chuckle.

"They do take one's breath away, don't they?"

"Er. . . yes, Sir."

"Just keep on appreciating the finer things in life and encourage your boss to institute a 'casual Friday' when women can wear shorts to work," Dr. Triggs suggested.

"That would be inappropriate, Sir."

"So, he's already scared you."

"Please Sir, don't blow it for me. This is a good place to work and I don't know yet how much levity is allowed."

"Ah, Mrs. Praetzel, you did pick a winner in this one," Dr. Triggs said.

"I thought you'd like him," Aleta said. "Now, Mr. Oliver, would you kindly grab about half the folders on your desk and give them to me."

"Why, may I ask?" he uttered, regretting his query immediately.

"Because you're overloaded."

"Mr. Praetzel said I was to work them in."

"Mr. Praetzel doesn't know his mother took ten new cases this morning and that Mr. Chin got another half dozen," Aleta said. "Send Tim out, will you?"

Before Nigel was back with the folders, Tim appeared.

"Did you understand my instructions?"

"I think so," Tim responded. "I took down the particulars from all those wanting wills."

"Draft up the wills. Bring me the wills and your notes tomorrow afternoon. We'll go over them together. Two o'clock. Call first."

"Yes, Ma'am."

Nigel brought an armload of folders and Aleta took them. She turned to Alice.

"No new clients for a week."

Alice nodded.

"Except for child advocacy cases," Aleta added. "Stanley will be back on Monday."

Alice smiled.

"He is so pleased with you, Alice," Aleta commented. "You do know that, don't you? He couldn't get along without you."

Alice blushed.

"I'm taking Dr. Triggs home with me," Aleta said. "Don't fret. We're riding in a patrol car."

This time it was Dr. Triggs who was surprised.

"My husband would never let me out with these legs without a police escort."

"Herve was right about you," Dr. Triggs chuckled. "Who do I pay?"

"Alice will bill you," Aleta said. "You do know I'm the most expensive lawyer here, don't you?"

"Doctors always go that route. It's called ego."

"You not only a doctor," Aleta decided. "You're a psychiatrist, aren't you?"

"Yes, I am."

"Stanley is going to love you."

"I'm not too sure about that," Dr. Triggs said warily.

When the patrol car rolled up the long driveway from the road to the house, Stanley came outside to meet it.

"Are you okay?" he asked Aleta, obviously concerned. "You said there was a new development in the Fouts case."

"Didn't Lyle call you and tell you what he found?"

"No. What did he find?" Stanley asked.

"I don't know," Aleta said. "Stanley, may I present our newest client Dr. Zachary Triggs. He's a psychiatrist. He's paying full rate and he doesn't give free advice either."

"What's that mean?" Stanley probed.

"You were holed up with my father all morning . . ."

Stanley interrupted, "Ten minutes."

"The only thing you had on your mind was me, so you had to be asking my father about Marian."

"Who's Marian?" Dr. Triggs asked.

"My biological mother," Aleta replied, turning back to Stanley. "You shooed Mom out."

"Who's Mom?" Dr. Triggs questioned.

"My housekeeper and cook, Bertha. She's married to my father."

"I figured that was part of it," Dr. Triggs chuckled.

"Jamara isn't related," Aleta said. "But the baby she's breast feeding is my son."

"Our son," Stanley corrected. "Even though he looks like you, I know he has some of my genes in him."

"About fifty percent," Triggs put in. "A child is definitely a joint venture."

"May we go in now?" Aleta asked.

"Dr. Triggs, please go on in. Bertha has fresh rolls and coffee ready. I need to talk to my wife for a minute.

Dr. Triggs entered the house and was greeted by the huge Irish Wolfhound.

"Oh, my!" he exclaimed.

"Just leave the door open a minute," Stanley called and then whistled.

Three dogs came bounding out and began running toward the barn. Stanley and Aleta fell in step behind them.

"Is he going to scold her for bringing me home?" Dr. Triggs asked the chunky, smiling housekeeper as he watched the pair walking toward the barn through the giant window at the far end of the living room.

"The scolding will last until he puts his arm around her waist," Bertha said as she set a mug of coffee on the table along with a plate and a knife. The fresh rolls were already there.

"He did that right away."

"He probably said something like 'don't bring our clients home' and she said she wouldn't do it again unless God asked her to and he lost his anger."

"That's got to be the fastest argument on record," Dr. Triggs said.

"Oh, there was one faster," Bertha said. "He said something. She just looked at him and he said, 'You win'. Remember that one Jamara?"

The black woman nursing the redheaded baby nodded.

"He had every argument lined up in his head, like a chess master," Jamara explained. "And he told us what they were. It's as if she said 'checkmate in five moves'."

Bertha's jaw dropped.

"Why don't you talk like that all the time?"

"Cause I chooses not to."

"They're coming back," Dr. Triggs said. "They look happy.

Bertha and Jamara looked out the huge window on the far side of the room.

"Now the kiss," Jamara said.

"No," Bertha corrected. "He's got to hold her head."

"Why?" Dr. Triggs asked.

"So she doesn't accidentally bump his nose," Bertha explained. "He just had surgery and he's hoping no one will notice."

"He's black and blue," Dr. Triggs pointed out.

"That's why he's hanging out at home," Bertha said. "And he wants Aleta here."

"So he likes to keep a tight rein on her?"

Bertha laughed.

"She doesn't even have a bit in her mouth."

"So she's the boss?"

"Except when he is," Bertha said.

"You mean she pretends to let him have his way? He seems too smart for that ploy."

"She be in charge until he is," Jamara said.

"Doesn't that make it hard to work here?" Dr. Triggs asked. "Not knowing whom to obey?"

"On the contrary, you never get into trouble obeying either one, but if Aleta gives an order, it must be obeyed instantly."

"But only if it be an order," Jamara put in.

"Look. They're turning around."

"They're waiting for the dogs."

Outside, Stanley whistled and Tank and Scooby came bounding out of the tall grass. Auggie followed them and was panting heavily by the time he caught up to the bigger dogs.

"Tank was chasing a rabbit is my guess," Stanley said.

Aleta laughed as she picked up the Pug.

"Auggie, you aren't a Wolfhound. When will you learn?"

As she held him, she suddenly sobered.

Stanley started toward the house. After a few steps he realized Aleta hadn't moved.

He hurried back.

"A vision?" he asked.

"A warning, I think," Aleta said. "All I know is that you are to say 'pillow' when I say 'Mother'. That's all I know."

"Any idea why?"

"It's important, but I don't know why."

Suddenly, she cried. "Oh, Stanley! It could be forever!"

Stanley's mouth dropped open.

"Forever?"

Her tears began to flow freely.

"I don't understand at all."

"Ask God if it's His command," Stanley urged.

Aleta bowed her head.

"He says we're in danger," she reported a moment later.

"What do we do?"

"We obey," Aleta said. "Oh Stanley, I don't want to live without you."

"What if you need to prophesy?" Stanley asked. "That was always an exception to the 'pillow' rule."

"God will protect us," Aleta said. "The pillow rule allows me to write, doesn't it?"

"Yes, it does," Stanley said.

He took her into his arms.

"I'm not sure I'm strong enough to do this."

"You must," Aleta declared. "The minute you release me, I die."

"Then nothing will move me," Stanley affirmed.

"Let me say once more," Aleta said. "I love you with all my heart."

"What are you doing?" Stanley asked looking at her moving hands.

Aleta followed his gaze.

"I'm signing. When did I learn to sign?"

"We are in for the long haul," Stanley predicted, sighing. "I love the sound of your voice.

Aleta giggled.

"Fortunately, that's not all you love."

"Well, I do like our quiet evenings."

"You like the sound of your own voice."

"Is that the last thing you want to say to me?" he quipped.

"I love the sound of your voice," Aleta said. "I can still hear. We can still dance."

"Tell me I'm handsome," Stanley said. "I like it when you say it."

"Stanley, you are the best looking man in the world," Aleta said. "You define the word handsome in the most complete sense."

"Are we ready for this?" Stanley said, holding her close.

"We need to live," Aleta said. "I don't need to talk. But to answer your question, no, I am not ready for this."

"Suppose you're wrong?" Stanley asked, releasing her and turning toward the house.

"Stanley, I can sign," Aleta proclaimed.

"You're right," Stanley said. "We need to go in."

"Yes, we do," Aleta said. "Yea, though I walk through the valley of the shadow of death, I will fear no evil, for Thou art with me."

"Thy rod and Thy staff, they comfort me," Stanley added.

"Thou preparest a table before me in the presence of my enemies," Aleta went on. "Thou annointest my head with oil. My cup overflows."

"Surely goodness and mercy shall follow me all the days of my life," Stanley finished. "And I will dwell in the house of the Lord forever."

"We have been truly blessed," Aleta said as she reached for the doorknob.

"I love you, Aleta," he whispered as she turned the knob.

"I'll be able to hear, you know," Aleta reminded him.

"I'm taking no chances."

She opened the door and they entered the house. Aleta noticed Paul was in the kitchen waiting. Her stomach knotted up.

"You got a phone call from your mother," Bertha said.

Aleta gasped.

"My mother?" she coughed.

The word came out garbled, but Stanley recognized it. He didn't hesitate.

"Pillow," he said quietly.

Despite the softness of his command, in the silence that followed her gasp, the word rang as loudly as the clarion cry of a trumpet.

Aleta's shock at the suddenness with which her freedom to speak had been snatched from her left her wordless. Without thinking she signed, "So soon?"

Dr. Triggs asked. "What's so soon?"

As he spoke, he signed.

"I can hear," Aleta signed. "I have been forbidden to speak."

"Who forbade you?" Dr. Triggs asked without translating what Aleta had just signed.

She signed her answer.

"I don't believe you," Dr. Triggs stated flatly.

"God did it?" Bertha asked, shocked.

Aleta nodded.

"Why?" Bertha asked.

Aleta signed a single word.

"Danger?" Dr. Triggs exclaimed. "From where?"

Stanley entered into the conversation.

"All we know is that Aleta must not speak."

"You be thinking God be telling you this?" Jamara asked, her skepticism blatant.

Aleta doesn't know how to sign," Stanley commented. "Although she seems to be able to understand and speak whatever language she needs to. We've always considered that ability a gift from God."

"It be so," Jamara said, still skeptical.

"How long is this going to last?" Paul asked.

"Aleta told me it could be forever," Stanley answered.

"You can't do that!" Paul exploded. "That's inhumane!"

"What part of the word 'danger' didn't you hear?" Stanley shot back. "Aleta has never had an incorrect vision. She's never sensed danger when there was none. And she senses danger."

"Is that true, Aleta?" Paul asked.

Aleta nodded.

"You go along with obeying this order as long as it takes?"

Again Aleta nodded.

"And you're happy about it?"

Aleta shook her head.

"Well, that I believe," Paul said.

Aleta chuckled and the two women joined her.

Aleta signed. "Paul knows me too well for me to lie."

Dr. Triggs translated for her.

"Are we to expect a lightning bolt from heaven as a sign the danger is past?" Paul joshed.

Aleta shrugged and Stanley intervened.

"If it comes, it better not strike me because only I can release her."

Bertha inhaled sharply.

"Do you mean if you die without releasing her, she can never speak again?"

Aleta nodded.

"Oh my God!" Bertha exclaimed.

"Amen." Stanley said reading Aleta's sign.

A flurry of hand signals followed.

"No," Stanley hastened to explain. "I can't read signs, but that's what you would have said.

Aleta threw her hands around him and kissed him soundly. He stood flabbergasted. When she finished, she giggled.

"Have you forgotten my nose?" he asked.

She signed, "I love it."

"Yes, but we don't want an extra bump on it, do we?"

"I didn't bump it," Aleta signed.

Dr. Triggs translated what she signed.

"You could have. You weren't inches away. You were touching it," Stanley scolded.

"I'll take the blame."

"I don't want you to feel guilty every time you look at me. No more kissing. . . by you."

Smiling demurely, she nodded her acquiescence.

Then she signed at Dr. Triggs who said, "Mrs. Praetzel suggests we go to her office and complete our business."

Stanley glanced at Aleta who nodded. He turned to Bertha.

"Call Chief West. Tell him we need him. You can tell him what you know."

Bertha picked up the phone on the kitchen wall as the study door closed. Chief West answered at once.

Bertha explained the situation and added, "She needs Lauren."

"I can sign," Lyle said.

"She needs her best friend right now," Bertha said.

"Stanley has done this before," Lyle reminded her.

"This is apt to be long term and she's suffering the loss. Neither she nor Stanley are in control."

"We'll be right there," Lyle said. "I'll call Tom. If he arrives before I do, feed him."

Bertha chuckled. "Yes, Sir."

Meanwhile, in the study down the hall past the laundry room and the nursery, Aleta sat behind the desk and Dr. Triggs swallowed a knowing smirk.

"I'm too old to do anything," he signed.

"Speak when you sign," Aleta signed, her face grim. "And translate everything I say accurately or you will pay my fee and I will refuse to take your case."

"Mr. Praetzel," Dr. Triggs said.   "I owe you an apology. I made a suggestive and inappropriate remark to your wife. I thought I could use my age as a shield, but she has properly called me to task."

"She does have great legs," Stanley said calmly. "But she is married to me. If you will remember that, we will get along."

Dr. Triggs nodded.

"I really do need your help. Hear me out, please."

"Go ahead," Stanley said.

"Am I paying for both your services?"

"Yes you are, only I'm taking my payment in kind. I want an hour of your time in return."

Dr. Triggs assented with a nod.

"My sister, Matilda Trent, is involved with a men who, as far as I am concerned, is after her money. Our parents left us each sizeable trusts. One of her children, Russell, is deaf which is why I learned to sign, as did she. I know Matilda had planned to leave the bulk of her estate to her deaf son. Her hearing children, Morris and Ruth, didn't understand this and they squabbled until Dixon Mager entered the picture. He smoothed things over and promised he'd straighten everything out. He encouraged Matilda to make out a new will leaving everything to her children in equal shares. Morris and Ruth backed off. They are happy with him.

"Russell thinks equal shares are actually fair. He's making a decent living, is married, and has two children, one hearing and one congenitally deaf. He is a computer programmer.   His wife teaches fifth grade. They live modestly. Russell is not the problem.

"Matilda's eldest, Morris, is a chronic gambler. He's mortgaged to the hilt. He would have hit on his younger brother were Russell not handicapped.

"Ruth has loaned Morris too much already and she has cut him off. Ruth is hoping to pay of her debts with her share of the inheritance. Matilda hasn't long to live."

"I'm sorry," Stanley said. "But I don't see a problem."

"Here's where it gets weird," Dr. Triggs went on. "Dixon Mager, with the backing of Morris got Matilda to sign over the management of her bank account into which the earnings from her trust investments are deposited. When she was able, she used to reinvest these monies after taking a small stipend to cover her living expenses. Now none of it is reinvested. The boyfriend and Morris pocket it all.

"The reason I'm here is because Matilda is being pressured to begin selling off the assets of the trust. She understands some of what is happening. She doesn't want either Dixon or Morris to go to jail, but she wants the carnage to stop."

"You want me to do for your sister what I did for Dr. Schwartzman, right?" Aleta signed.

Dr. Triggs translated her words and then affirmed them.

"The situation is not the same," Aleta pointed out, signing. "First of all, your sister isn't asking me. Second, she can cancel the power of attorney any time. If her boyfriend and eldest son continue to be a force in her life, this would only be a temporary solution. They will persuade her to revoke the power of attorney."

"So there's nothing that can be done?" Dr. Triggs asked.

"Have your sister and her deaf son here at one o'clock this afternoon. You will, of course, come as well. This is non-negotiable," Aleta signed with Dr. Triggs translating for Stanley's benefit. "Bring them in a limousine."

"A limousine?" Dr. Triggs questioned.

"A cab won't be allowed past the front gate," Aleta signed. "And don't tell me you can't afford it."

After Triggs translated her words, he asked Stanley, "Does she always spend other people's money so freely?"

"Usually it's just mine, but considering she senses danger, let's do it her way. You do want to come out of this alive, don't you?"

"Any idea what she has in mind?" Dr. Triggs asked Stanley as the pair walked to the front door.

"I just remembered," Stanley said. "Your car is at my office."

He turned and addressed the woman at the sink loading the dishwasher.

"Bertha, Dr. Triggs needs a lift to the office."

"Yes, Sir." Bertha said, pulling off her apron and giving Jamara a few instructions.

"Alice will have papers I need. Please pick them up," Stanley added, and then he went back to his study and made phone calls in the order that Aleta had written them down.

CHAPTER 14

By the time Stanley was finished making phone calls, Willow Glen Police Chief Tom Milani was on his second sweet roll and Arborville Chief Lyle West was driving up the driveway with his wife in the front seat of his official car. Their baby was in her lap.

Stanley ushered them into the house and explained what had happened that morning and added, "While I could have told Tom all this, getting information out of Aleta will be easier with direct communication."

Aleta signed and both Lyle and Lauren laughed.

"Private joke," Lyle said.

"Let's communicate everything, shall we," Stanley said tersely.

"Okay, Stanley, let's start with a few basics," Lyle said. "No admonition on your speaking?"

"No."

"And the key word was 'mother', but she didn't say it distinctly before you shut her off."

Aleta's signing was fast.

"I'm not a water faucet. Words don't pour out of my mouth non-stop."

Lauren translated for Aleta.

Lyle grinned.

"Don't they?"

"Not always," Aleta signed.

"The point is that the word 'mother' isn't the trigger."

"Interesting that that was not only the first word she uttered upon coming into the house, but that she choked on it," Stanley elaborated pensively. "We are talking about a voice activated explosive device, aren't we?"

"It would seem so," Tom said. "You've had all sorts of noise in here all morning, so it has to be keyed into her voice pattern.

"Do we assume that the devices were planted this morning while she was gone?" Stanley asked.

"Probably," Tom said.

"But I was here," Stanley pointed out.

"The guard went to the office with Aleta," Lyle said. "Didn't you leave the house?"

"The horses got out," Stanley said. "And Bertha helped Hubbs and me round them up."

"I takes Gerard outside," Jamara said. "Paul, he be with me. But no one come."

"They were already here," Lyle said. "They set the horses loose. This place is crawling with workmen working on your new addition."

"We'll do a search," Chief Tom Milani said. "I'm guessing there's more than one."

"I agree," Lyle said. "If we find one, we'll know what we're looking for, so the next one will be easier."

"We'll impound the cars," Chief Milani said. "I'm sure they're wired. My men will transport you. You can talk in the patrol car."

Aleta shook her head and then signed. "I will talk nowhere. I will take no chance with my life nor the lives of those around me."

"As soon as you find the first one," Stanley commented. "We'll have some idea of the man's cleverness."

Aleta's grandmother and her new husband, Claude, entered the house.

Aleta signed.

"When did you learn sign language?" her grandmother asked.

"About an hour ago," Aleta signed.

This time Stanley interpreted for Aleta.

"You know sign language too?" Harriet questioned.

"No, Grams, he doesn't," Aleta signed. "He just knows what I'm going to say."

Lauren translated her explanation and Aleta continued, "Evidently, there's a voice-activated bomb—well, more than one, we're guessing—that my voice activates."

"Let's go outside and talk," Harriet suggested.

"God was clear," Aleta signed. "I'm not to speak at all."

"That always gets you in all sorts of trouble," Harriet observed.

"This time I can sign. People will think I'm deaf."

"You may not like that any better," Lyle observed.

Aleta smiled and signed. "I haven't a choice."

Then she sighed. "I will miss my verbal exchanges with Stanley though."

Lauren started to translate, but Stanly took over.

Aleta signed her query excitedly, "Can you sign?"

Stanley shook his head as he replied, "No. However, I can now understand you."

A new voice broke in.

"I was planning to hand in my resignation," Jamara said, dropping her lingo. "So I asked the Lord for a sign that would tell me I was to stay and that I would be safe. And then, Mr. Praetzel, you began to understand your wife. That's a miracle. I saw the puzzled look on your face when Mrs. Praetzel made a joke with her hands and only Chief West and his wife laughed. You were angry. You couldn't read her hands then. You can read them now. So I'm here for the duration."

Aleta went over and kissed Jamara on the cheek.

"Just don't you be saying, 'you're welcome' if I say thank you."

Aleta laughed and shook her head.

"We came for Auggie," her grandmother said.

"So soon?" Aleta signed.

"Claude and I are going up early," Harriet said. "We want to enjoy the lodge before everyone else gets there. And I want to try traveling with Auggie before we go on the circuit."

Aleta nodded and signed.

"His collar and leads are in the RV. I'll get them."

Harriet followed Aleta out. Stanley watched them through the window. He saw Harriet embrace her granddaughter and he could tell that Aleta was crying.

Harriet sat Aleta down in the RV and grasped her granddaughter's hands lovingly as she spoke.

"I was sent over with a message. It made no sense to me at the time, but now it makes a bit of sense. It's almost the very last verse in Ecclesiastes. 'Fear God, and keep his commandments, for this is the whole duty of man.'"

Aleta eyed her grandmother questioningly.

"I think it means that God expects absolute obedience to this commandment that He has given you. He gave you a sign that it was from Him and He gave Jamara a sign. As for me, those two signs tell me that you have interpreted His will correctly."

Aleta agreed by nodding.

"Assume no place is safe," Harriet said. "Fortunately, there will be three people with you this coming weekend who can sign."

Aleta raised an eyebrow.

"I repeat. God expects absolute obedience," her grandmother reiterated. "This must be important or He would not have given you so many signs that this is His will."

Lauren knocked on the door and called out, "May I help?"

"Do come in," Harriet said. "I think Aleta would like to say something right now."

Aleta signed and Lauren translated.

"You don't think that all these signs are because the request is strange?"

"No," Harriet replied. "You've managed not to speak for several days in the past. I think this is bigger."

"Longer?" Aleta signed, her brow showing her concern.

"Maybe forever," Harriet said.

Aleta signed. "That's what I foresaw too."

Lauren paled as she translated those words.

Then she burst out, "You can't mean it?"

Aleta signed and Lauren translated, not realizing it was a message to her.

"You already do all the planning and sorting of people at our parties. All you need to do is be sure I have someone at the table who signs."

"Let's see. That would be Lyle or me or his parents or Stanley. I guess I can manage that," Lauren said. "When's our next party?"

Aleta signed. "We have to celebrate Stanley's new ears."

Harriet laughed. "You can't do that. He'd hate it."

"Will your new addition be done?" Lauren asked.

Aleta nodded.'

"Then we'll celebrate that and take a tour." Lauren said. "A week from Friday."

Aleta nodded.

"I am sorry," Lauren said. "I know that Lyle and Tom's men will work hard to find the bombs."

"Stanley says having a silent wife has its compensations," Aleta signed.

Lauren laughed. "That's a man for you. They all want us barefoot and pregnant, preferably silent with legs like yours."

Aleta blushed. She looked at her shorts and signed, "Stanley likes me to wear these."

"Claude bought me a pair just like those," Harriet said. "I told him I'd wear them on the trip where I wouldn't know anyone."

"Like at the lodge?" Aleta signed.

Lauren chuckled as she translated.

"Of course," Harriet said. "With no one else there, I should look pretty good. In a few years I'll be more wrinkled, but his eyes will be worse and I will look all blurry, so I should be able to keep his interest alive."

"For heavens sake, Grams," Aleta signed. "He's not just interested in your legs."

"True, he does like other parts of my body," Harriet admitted slyly.

Aleta signed furiously.

"I meant your mind."

"You are so naïve, my dear," Harriet responded, smiling. ""Men like the bodies wrapped around the mind, even old men."

"And old women?" Aleta challenged.

"If it walks, it's handsome enough. If it has parts that work, that's a plus."

"And Claude's parts work?" Aleta signed.

"They work very well, I'll have you know. I'm surprised you'd ask me about my sex life."

"Remember you did make all the newscasts on your honeymoon when Claude was shot," Aleta signed, chuckling.

"I may never live that down," Harriet sighed. "Families have the longest memories in the world."

"If I may ask," Lauren said. "Why didn't you grab a robe?"

"It wasn't handy."

"And the gun was?"

"It was under the couch."

"You were naked on the couch?" Lauren gasped."

"Where's Locke?" Harriet asked. "I thought Lyle had a rule against holding him when he's in uniform."

"Jamara is holding him."

Harriet noticed a change in Aleta's demeanor. She guessed rightly that the gravity of the situation was beginning to weigh on her.

"Let me take Auggie's stuff to my car and talk to Stanley for a few minutes. You two stay here and finish this conversation without me chaperoning."

Harriet took Auggie's leads and collar, brushes, treats and traveling crate. After she placed them inside her car, she went inside the house. She took Stanley aside.

"God sent me with a message. I think I should tell you too. He wants her not to break her silence even for a prophecy"

"She was worrying about that," Stanley said.

"I don't understand why some places aren't safe. I would think all the bombs would be here, but God wants her not to break her silence anywhere."

"You are worried. Why?"

"I think the idea of this being a long term situation is taking her down again," Harriet said. "I wanted to tell you that Claude and I will cancel any and all of our plans if you need us to."

"Don't do so yet," Stanley said.

"We can be home from anywhere in a few hours," Harriet said. "I feel terrible that I delivered such a depressing message."

"It will be easier now," Stanley said. "We know what we need to do."

"This isn't going to be easy. She's had her heart set on being a trial lawyer."

"I know," Stanley sighed.

At one that afternoon, Dr. Triggs stepped out of his rented limousine. His sister, Matilda Trent, and her son, Russell Trent, followed him.

Bertha led them to the study and Aleta rose to greet them. She was dressed in a business suit, as was her husband. Bertha served coffee and small freshly baked apple tarts and then closed the door

Aleta began with background information.

"Mrs. Trent, you gave your friend Dixon Mager access to the bank account where the interest and dividends from your holdings are deposited," Aleta signed.

Matilda nodded her head in affirmation.

"Mr. Mager and your eldest son, Morris, have been withdrawing from this account regularly."

Again the elderly woman nodded.

"They have depleted the account," Aleta signed. "There is not enough to cover your current bills."

"They said I needed to sell stock," Matilda said.

"Let's take this one step at a time," Aleta signed. "Do you want to leave your children equal shares of your estate?"

"Yes."

"Then we need to stop Morris from taking money now and still demanding and equal share. Do you understand this?"

"Morris is not suppose to be taking any money for himself," Matilda said.

"Mrs. Trent," Aleta signed and nodded at Stanley to interpret verbally. "Your son is addicted to gambling. He can't help himself. He is not able to handle your money."

"He knows it's not his yet," Matilda repeated.

"You need to give your son Russell power of attorney to handle your financial affairs."

"Morris was supposed to pay my bills," Matilda said. "I can't believe he didn't."

Aleta pulled out a single sheet of paper and put it in front of Matilda Trent. "Here is a list of your current debts," she signed and Stanley translated.

Aleta gave Russell and Dr. Triggs each a copy.

Matilda studied the list.

"I've been getting calls.   I told these people that my son had paid them."

"No checks have been written on your account," Aleta informed her. "Only cash withdrawals have been made. We had our investigator check the cash withdrawals against the cash deposits in Mr. Mager's account in another bank. Every time a withdrawal is made from your account, he deposits money in his account."

"Dixon is taking my money too?" Matilda asked.   "I suspected Morris might be taking some because I knew he liked to gamble, but I had no idea Dixon was taking any."

Russell tapped his uncle on the arm and signed, "Are these the lawyers Herve Schwartzman has?"

Dr. Triggs nodded.

Russell tapped his mother on the arm and signed, "Mom, these are the lawyers Dr. Schwartzman has.   His investments are growing."

Matilda turned to her brother.

"It's true," Dr. Triggs said.   "They have a terrific financial advisor."

Russell tapped her on the arm again and signed. "Mom, you need to give them your financial power of attorney.   Morris can't fight them. Ruth and I will forgive him what he's taken only please stop him now."

"Morris won't go to jail or anything, will he?" Matilda asked.

"That's not our goal," Aleta signed. "We don't even want to deprive him of his inheritance.   And we won't prosecute him if you don't want to."

"I don't," Matilda stated firmly. "Now can you get me out of this mess?"

"Yes, we can."

"Dixon says I need to sell Trust assets," Matilda said. "Is there no way around that?"

"There is," Aleta signed. "We will take out a loan."

"I don't want to borrow money," Matilda declared. I think it's wrong."

"You are already borrowing money," Aleta responded. "When you don't pay a debt, you are actually borrowing another man's income."

"Wouldn't it be better to just take some of my assets and pay my creditors?"

"You mean rob your children of part of their inheritance?" Aleta signed. "A few years ago you decided to take your dividends and interest and leave the trust intact for them. Many of the investments are appreciating and the Trust is growing. It was a wise monetary decision."

Matilda nodded. She knew it was.

"You made a small mistake. You trusted the wrong people."

"I don't think Dixon knew what Morris was doing," Matilda said.

"Isn't Dixon encouraging you to sell your assets?" Aleta questioned.

"Yes, he is. Dixon says we'll pay the bills and go on a cruise. I've always wanted to do that. He's booked one. We leave Friday."

"How did he pay for this?" Aleta probed.

"He used my credit card."

Aleta turned to Stanley and signed, "What do you think?"

Stanley responded and Aleta signed his words so Russell could understand what he was saying.

"Dixon Mager will have Mrs. Trent sign the power of attorney before she leaves. He will not be on the ship when it sails. He will clean her out while she is gone."

"He won't! You're wrong," Matilda declared vehemently.

"Are you willing to bet your entire Trust on that belief?" Stanley charged.

"I don't bet!" she trumpeted proudly.

"You just did," Aleta signed.

"I trust him," Matilda affirmed staunchly.

"We need an expert," Aleta signed.

"I'll call her. You people go on with your discussion," Stanley said.

Aleta left the room with him, closing the door although the three had immediately reverted to signing.

Harriet was at their door in ten minutes. She was in shorts.

Aleta signed her anger to Stanley. He translated her words to her grandmother.

"I'm to meet clients?" she gasped.

"I've never seen you in shorts," Stanley added.

"Claude picked up that idea from you!" she quipped. "I thought it was an emergency."

"It was. It is," Stanley stumbled. "You do have great looking legs. I see where Aleta gets hers."

"Flattery is going to assuage my annoyance a tad, but not enough for you to feel comfortable."

Aleta chuckled and the sound relaxed Harriet a bit more.

"Thanks for the compliment," Harriet managed to say.

Aleta signed something to Stanley who didn't translate it.

"Tell me what she said," Harriet demanded. "If you want my help, you need to keep me totally informed."

Stanley glared at his wife.

"From now on keep your jests to yourself."

"What did she say?" Harriet insisted.

"She said that Dr. Triggs is going to love meeting you."

"Explain that," Harriet pushed.

Dr. Triggs was terribly taken with Aleta in shorts."

"He's a leg man?" Harriet asked.

Aleta giggled as she nodded.

"Let's go meet everyone," Harriet said. "Stanley, I expect you to give me a proper introduction and apologize for my appearance."

Stanley did that, but not before Dr. Triggs uttered an appreciative, "Wow!"

Harriet began to speak and her rough voice soon commanded the attention of all but Russell. He, however, sensed that this woman was exuding powerful vibes.

"I understand, Mrs. Trent, that a gentleman friend has designs on your money, but despite the evidence presented to you, you prefer to deny it."

"They are mistaken," Matilda declared.

"Facts are facts," Harriet said. "He has no money. You have lots of money. He has already taken some of your money without telling you."

"I'm sure there's an explanation," Matilda contended.

"Oh, there's an explanation. He wants a piece of your pie.

"He's not like that," Matilda insisted. "He is kind and pleasant and he treats me well."

"And he is being well-paid for his graciousness," Harriet said. "Why don't you just give him all your money now and be done with it?"

"Because I want to leave some to my children."

"He will see that you leave them nothing but debts to pay."

"I don't want to lose him," Matilda said. "He makes me happy. You people are being cruel."

"He's abusing your children," Harriet declared.

"He is not!"

"He's blackmailing Morris."

"He isn't!" she denied.

"Yes, he is," Russell signed. "That's why Morris is paying him, so he won't tell you what Morris is doing with your money."

"Maybe that's true, but he's not hurting you or Ruthie," Matilda insisted.

Again Russell began to sign and Stanley translated for Harriet.

"Ruthie is in debt because Morris borrowed from her and she couldn't say no. He promised to pay her back out of his part of the inheritance. Ruthie can barely make ends meet because she's paying so much interest on the money Morris owes her. And Dixon is going to take Ruthie's last chance to get back on her feet. Morris wants her to declare bankruptcy. Did you know that Mother? He wants Ruthie to do that so he won't have to pay her back. And Dixon Mager has persuaded her that that's what she should do.'

"I didn't know that," Matilda said.

Russell continued to sign.

"You don't want to hear the truth anymore. This man has taken away the mother I once had. You used to care about me. If you die in debt, I will pay off every bit of it to preserve your honor, but I will suffer as a result. Mr. Luther is correct. He is abusing all of us."

Matilda let the tears come. Through them she could see more clearly than she had in a long time.

Harriet began to speak.

"This is what you need to do immediately. You need to set up a new checking account and notify the bank handling your investments of the change."

Matilda nodded and then said, "I want a new will. Morris will only waste the money."

"Leave him something," Stanley advised. "Otherwise, he'll contest it and your trust will be tied up in probate for a long time."

"Not a specific amount," Aleta advised. "A percentage."

"Forty percent to Russell; forty percent to Ruthie; twenty percent to Morris, only he has to pay Ruthie back," Matilda said. "I will take out the loan as you suggested. Russell, can you get Ruthie to tell me how much of her debt is her brother's?"

"All of it," Russell responded. "Two hundred thousand."

"We need the loan to cover that as well as all my creditors," Matilda said. "The interest must be killing her."

"Don't give up your cruise," Aleta advised. "There was a widow who was attacked. She is in the hospital under police guard because she is in danger. I need to hide her. I will pay if you will allow her to share your accommodations."

Matilda's eyes lit up. "If we like each other, she can stay with me when we get back."

"Mrs. Trent, did you sign any papers giving either Morris or Mr. Mager power of attorney?" Stanley asked.

"My brother insisted I not sign anything until this meeting."

"Dixon Mager is too clever not to have foreseen this move," Stanley predicted.

"I agree," Harriet said, "We must go to the bank at once."

"To Chicago?" Mrs. Trent asked.

"No," Harriet said. "To Signet Bank here in Willow Glen. I can co-sign a loan, if necessary, to expedite matters, but only here where I am known. You can close your checking account and arrange a wire transfer of the money in that account to your new account at the same time. Mr. Stevens will expedite the changes."

"Who is he?"

"A friend. President of the Bank."

"Do you have a printout of the holdings in your investment account?"

"I have," her brother said.

Harriet scanned the financial readout quickly.

"Oh my!" she exclaimed. "You'll take a bath if you don't get rid of a few of these stocks at once."

"So I should sell? Dixon was right?" Matilda asked.

"Sell and buy," Harriet said. "I can suggest four stocks that will rise in the coming year."

"Mother, take her advice," Russell urged.

"I need to borrow some clothes, Aleta," her grandmother said. "We'll talk on the way to the bank."

Dr. Triggs said to Stanley, "Do you want your hour now? Mrs. Luther can guide my sister in the financial decisions she needs to make. Mrs. Praetzel can keep Russell informed.

"Not your sister?" Stanley asked.

"Matilda may not tell Russell everything."

"I'll take my hour now," Stanley said.

CHAPTER 15

After the group left, Stanley and Dr. Triggs sat down in the study with fresh coffee and newly baked sweet rolls.

"My wife lacks self-esteem," Stanley began.

She has tremendous self-esteem," Dr. Triggs countered.

"She shines as a lawyer. She is assertive, confident and powerful when functioning as one."

"I can't believe she fails as a wife. I watched you two walking together when we first got here. She appears responsive and even a bit forthright."

"She doesn't fail me," Stanley said. "But yesterday she was under a suicide watch by the two nurses that you know as my cook and my son's nanny."

"Are you certain she was suicidal?"

"That's why I mentioned that Jamara and Bertha were nurses. Both have dealt with suicidal patients. So the answer to your question is yes."

"Suicides don't recover so quickly."

"I have devised a therapy, but there is a problem so deeply buried that I can't get to it without a bit of help."

"Do you know what the problem is?"

"Her mother."

"The one she was shocked called her. The one no one suggested she call back."

"She's in jail. Aleta put her there. The victim was Aleta's younger sister. It was a nasty affair involving serious deprivation of all sorts, imprisonment and finally sexual abuse."

"And she witnessed this?"

"No. We flew out to California to rescue her sister. Aleta represented her sister in court and, in essence, was the prosecutor. She got her mother to confess on the stand. Aleta is a superior trial lawyer. I'm not certain how to handle that loss either."

"Treat it like grief over a death because that's what it is," Dr. Triggs said. "Are you sure she won't be safe in a courtroom?"

"Yes."

"Explain."

Stanley told him about Aleta's grandmother being a prophet as well as Aleta. He finished by telling him that the two women separately came up with the same constrictions which Aleta must live under."

"Let's go back to her mother," Dr. Triggs said when Stanley finished. "Aside from being shocked that her mother called and a bit dismayed, your wife showed no abnormal behavior."

She has dealt with the guilt over her past in that drama although it does crop up now and then," Stanley said. "There's something else."

"Tell me about your first meeting with her mother," Dr. Triggs said.

And Stanley began talking.

While Dr. Triggs listened, he was impressed with the insight Stanley had into the problems his wife had faced and was facing. The young husband was already light years ahead of where a good therapist would be after years of treatment. His radical therapy was both outrageous and brilliant.

When he finished, Dr. Triggs said. "I can only give you a few ideas."

"That'll be enough," Stanley said.

"First, motherhood has reminded Aleta of her relationship with her own mother," he began. "Unfortunately, no one knows what expectations Aleta's mother may have had for her first born. But somehow Aleta didn't meet them. Her rejection of Aleta at two is the basis for her shaky self-esteem. The result is that you have more than one problem," Dr. Triggs said. "Aleta may be trying to be the exact opposite of her mother. That's one. The second is that Marian herself grew up in a dysfunctional family, which is why she embraced society's perfectionist norms. Most families recognize societal norms as guidelines, not absolutes. Marian saw them as the means to acceptance and happiness. Aleta couldn't help but pick up achievement as essential to being a worthwhile person."

"How did she ever break out of her mother's hold to marry me? I don't fit at all."

"Was she close to her grandmother early on?"

"Very."

"That may have been what saved her," Dr. Triggs concluded. "Her grandmother is a powerful woman. My guess is that hers was a loving home."

"Her two sons attest to the fact that it was," Stanley affirmed.

"Get Aleta to talk about her grandmother. . .wait. . . you can't. Okay, here's what you need to do."

As Stanley listened, Dr. Triggs outlined a plan of action that made sense to him. It was one he would not have thought up on his own.

When the limousine returned with the group that had gone to the bank, Harriet ran inside to change back into her own clothes and Stanley followed her.

"I need something from you," he said before she closed the bedroom door to change. "Dr. Triggs suggested it."

Harriet nodded as he explained what he wanted.

That night just after six, Aleta sat down at her place at the table and unfolded her napkin.

Stanley moved behind her and slipped the scarf over her eyes.

Oh, no, she thought, not baby food again.

"Relax," Stanley said softly. "Just go with the flow while I explain. And open your mouth."

She felt the round bottom of the spoon and reluctantly took the food. It was mashed potatoes, all by itself. The next spoon held a piece of a lamb chop. Then came the peas, her favorite.

He put a roll in her hand and she heard him cutting his meat and hers. She took a bite of the buttered roll and searched the area around her plate for her fork.

She heard him laugh.

"You are so independent!"

She nodded.

"You're wondering why the blindfold, right?"

She nodded and began to sign. He put his hand on hers and stopped her.

"This is the time of night when you are silent and blind because I order it. This is when we slip away from the burdens of the pillow command and we go back to our quiet evening where you can only nod. This is our private time."

She nodded hesitantly.

"Come morning, you will see what this does for you," Stanley said. "If you like it, we will do it regularly. If you don't, this will be the last time."

She nodded. That she could handle. Besides it was pleasant to be the sole focus of Stanley's attention. She smiled and Stanley began again to feed her. The meal was a pleasant one.

He chatted about how well she had handled the Trent case and asked her if she thought Mrs. Trent was on board with dumping Dixon Mager.

She nodded and frowned a little. She was frustrated because there was more to the story. Then he surprised her by asking the questions she wanted to ask and then answering them thereby drawing out the rest of the story including the fact that Harriet had called Lyle and told him about Mrs. Morales and the cruise that would keep her safe for the next seven days. Then he told her that Lyle told Mrs. Morales that he would send a policewoman to her house to pack for her. Then he asked her if she remembered Olivia Qucher and Aleta nodded a bit nettled. Her memory was fine.

Stanley kissed her lightly and smiled. It hadn't been a dig. It had been an opening to a new topic.

"She was worried about where she could go when she was discharged from the hospital," Stanley began. "I told her about Tonia Morales going on a cruise with Mrs. Trent and she asked me if I could make reservations for her too."

He paused and Aleta raised an eyebrow in query.

"I reminded her that she was sicker than Mrs. Morales and wouldn't be discharged as soon as Tonia would."

He read the disappointment on Aleta's face. She cared about these women.

"When I checked back with her to tell her that her dog was at the vet and would be there at least a couple more days. Olivia asked me if the vet would board Tiny for at least a week and I told her yes. Then she told me that she had asked the nurse she liked, Vivian, to accompany her on the cruise as her nurse and friend. I made the reservations for them and they will leave when Tonia does. Lyle will see that a policewoman packs for Olivia and guards her until she's settled in her stateroom."

Aleta indicated she wanted more.

"I told Lyle that I would underwrite the cost. Olivia is not a rich woman."

Aleta's smile showed her surprise and delight. It was followed by a worried frown.

"We can afford to treat them. Lyle can't charge the city for Olivia since they need to put her into some safe place until Stuart Fouts is caught. And no, I don't know why not. And yes, it could be because Tonia was only paying half and Olivia would need to pay double. But Olivia needs this as much as Tonia does."

By the time he finished, Aleta was nodding her head vigorously.

That wasn't the end of the evening's surprises. When Stanley dressed her for their evening activities after dinner, she found the clothing strange. It was flimsy and she guessed it was sheer. There were several layers, but she had the feeling she was not covered at all.

"I borrowed these from your grandmother," he said. "You may feel them while I dress. They are quite sexy."

Aleta was surprised at the cut. The lingerie was extremely sexy.

"I thought I'd give myself a glimpse of what you're going to look like in forty years," he said.

She could tell he was smiling.

"You are still beautiful," he said.

Aleta wanted to protest that she hadn't aged forty years in the last forty seconds but she didn't.

He kissed her—warmly, passionately, fervently—and she forgot she was wearing her grandmothers' lingerie and responded.

They danced and then she lay on the couch, her head on his lap, while he read to her. First he read from the book he was in the middle of reading to her, and then he read a Psalm, and finally, an old letter. The letter was about her father. Stanley read it again as Aleta fed Gerard his evening bottle.

Gerard played with the ends of her scarf as he nursed and Stanley talked to her about his conversation with Dr. Triggs.

She couldn't ask questions, but Stanley was careful not to draw any conclusions and she soon relaxed and listened as she had when he read the pages of the novel.

After he finished telling her Dr. Triggs had concluded that her grandmother had been the influence that marked Aleta the most, Aleta felt a new joy rise from deep inside her.

"As a child, you identified with her," Stanley postulated. "You learned to do the things she liked—shoot, hunt, show dogs, hate shopping, steer clear of parties and excel in whatever you chose to do. It is your grandmother you take after. You see people as your father and grandmother do. Perhaps when you ruminate about whom you take after, you might recall that as a child, she, not your mother, was your role model."

Later, when they made love, her responses were more vibrant than ever.

The following morning, after he removed the blindfold, Aleta found that being able to see again was an unexpected rush. Then Stanley asked a question and she responded by signing, she realized that having two abilities restored was revitalizing.

"How did you know?" she queried, signing.

"I hoped," he said.

"Please repeat that regularly. I need it,"

"It was so nice to have a quiet wife."

"I'm quiet now," she signed, protesting.

"Your hands are talking," he rebutted. "They are as demanding as your voice."

"My voice is not demanding."

"I am already looking forward to tonight."

"You said arguing with me sharpened your thinking," she signed.

"Are you going to throw everything I say back in my face?" he grouched.

Aleta laughed and signed. "Pretty much. I remember you told me I was beautiful."

"And you were and are. Do you want to see what you were wearing last night?"

Aleta nodded.

"Stand in front of the mirror and I'll find the pieces if I can remember where I threw them."

Aleta giggled at the thought of Stanley throwing anything on the floor."

"Oh, here they are, all neatly folded. I wonder who did that?"

This time Aleta laughed.

He dressed her again and she had to admit the three-piece outfit was stunning. She couldn't imagine her grandmother in such an outfit.

"I asked Claude to pick out some for you," Stanley remarked.

Aleta blushed.

"I can cancel my request, but I don't have the eye he does."

"Can't you just borrow?" she signed.

"Okay," Stanley said. "I'd just as soon he think about his wife when he's buying them. Or I could just ask him to buy two of everything."

Aleta nodded.

He embraced her from behind.

"You are truly mine. I love that about you," he murmured.

Aleta turned and raised a brow. When he nodded, almost sheepishly, she smiled and slowly untied the ribbon that held the filmy peignoir closed

The following morning when Bertha arrived, she heard the shower running so she figured she had twenty minutes. She went into the nursery, changed Gerard and brought him into the kitchen.

Aleta and Stanley were sitting at the table.

"You're still wet!" she exclaimed, setting Gerard in his infant seat.

Aleta signed something and Stanley laughed. Bertha looked at him hard, but he just shook his head.

"I don't know if I like you two being on vacation," she complained. "You are so unscheduled when left to your own devices."

"Aleta wants a big breakfast," Stanley announced. "I do too. We have a lot of work ahead of us."

"Work?"

"Aleta brought home half of Nigel Oliver's work yesterday," Stanley explained.

Bertha was silent for a minute and then she said, "I thought after Jamara gets here, we might go riding. I need to talk to both of you."

"Nine o'clock?" Stanley asked. "We could take the dogs for a fifteen minute walk now and tell Hubbs."

"Yes, do that," Bertha said crisply.

Aleta popped up and went to the front door. Tank, Scooby and King raced to be the first ones out.

"She's worried about something," Stanley said when he caught up to his wife. "Don't worry. We'll take care of whatever is bothering her."

As they approached the barn, Stanley said, "Hubbs doesn't know about the silence thing yet."

Aleta signed. "Jack Turner is still here."

"I'll let Hubbs explain it. We need to let Tank chase a rabbit."

Aleta put her whistle in her mouth and blew it. The three dogs came running. She waved her arm toward the back field and all three took off.

Stanley briefly told Hubbs that he, Aleta and Bertha were going out at nine. He added casually that Aleta was not speaking and asked him to explain it to Jack.

The young boy stopped his work and looked at Stanley who told him Hubbs knew what that meant.

"That means she's mad," Jack put forth.

"When Aleta is angry, she either cries or argues. She doesn't stop talking," Stanley said, turning to follow his wife. "Tell him, Hubbs."

"He done told her not to," Hubbs said.

"So, what's the big deal?"

"She won't talk 'til he tells her she can."

"You're pulling my leg."

"Nope. They done it before."

"He punishes her like that?"

"It's something else. According to Bertha, he's saved her life doing it."

"How?"

"Dunno."

At nine o'clock the three left the house to go riding. Stanley had finally given up trying to hide his face until the swelling and discoloration had disappeared. The ear that had been torn apart by the bullet had already healed. In the repair process, the surgeon had moved it closer to his head and when the bandages finally came off, Stanley realized that one ear stuck out further than the other. The unevenness was noticeable and it bothered him. He asked the plastic surgeon to realign the other ear so the two would be even. The surgeon had proposed a slight change to his nose to balance the change he was making to his ears. To leave it untouched would make him uglier. To reduce the size of his nose slightly would leave him looking like himself.

Jamara changed the bandage on his ear each morning and checked for infection. She said he was healing faster than normal, but every day when he looked in the mirror, his nose looked the same.

"Maybe ears heal faster," he told Aleta as they walked. Bertha was uncharacteristically silent.

Stanley watched her trying to be polite to Hubbs. The old man wasn't fooled.

"She's upset," Hubbs whispered to Stanley.

"I know," Stanley replied. "She's going to tell us about it on the ride."

After Aleta mounted Shadow, Hubbs said. "You two ladies sure sit on a horse nice."

Both women smiled at Hubbs and the old man told them to have a nice go.

It wasn't until they crossed the back field and exited the gate in the far corner that led to the horse path that Bertha spoke. She was riding between her two companions so each heard her clearly.

"It's your mother, Aleta," she began and then stopped.

"Go on," Stanley urged. "We know you are not blaming us. What did she say to you?"

"She called me that fat pig Robert married just so he could have a whore willing to be poked for fun," Bertha replied. "She sprinkled swear words in as well."

"Go on," Stanley prompted.

"I got upset and hung up. I'm sorry, Stanley. That was unprofessional of me."

"No one has the right to swear at you or say a derogatory comment while you're doing your job," Stanley declared. "You acted appropriately."

Aleta nodded.

"She called back," Bertha said. "She demanded to talk with Aleta. I told her Aleta was not at home and she accused me of lying. Then she said she'd be calling every day until Aleta talked to her. I told her Aleta would probably not take her calls."

"Perfect!" Stanley exclaimed.

"She said I'd married Robert for his money, but she was going to see she got hers first. She said Robert had given her a mere pittance and she was going to get the rest."

Bertha's voice broke.

"Relax," Stanley said. "She hasn't a case. My father is a very careful lawyer. What you and Robert have now is safe."

"Robert gave me a pre-nup when we got married, so my house would always be safe he said."

Aleta signed and Stanley translated for her. "He knows my mother. She's very vindictive."

She paused and then signed, "Stanley, am I like that?"

Stanley translated her question.

Shocked, Bertha burst out, "You are not at all like your mother. Neither is Jocelyn. You're both your father's daughters. If you take after anyone, it's your grandmother."

"I told you," Stanley put in with a smug smile.

Aleta signed again and Stanley translated.

"Bertha, you aren't a whore. You're a wife. And Dad didn't marry you just to have sex."

Bertha let a tiny smile appear at the corners of her mouth. "I'm not too sure about that."

"I think Bertha is right. Robert, like me, was desperately in love when he got married," Stanley put in.

"I didn't get a pre-nup." Aleta complained, signing.

"You did too," Stanley said, translating her query before answering her verbally.

"Did I sign one?"

"No, you didn't."

"That makes no sense. You had all the money. You still do. That reminds me, am I in your will?"

Stanley laughed. Aleta's mind took strange twists sometimes.

"I'm sure you're in there somewhere," he managed to say between chuckles.

"Did you leave me more than a dollar?"

Bertha laughed.

"I'm so glad God didn't rob you two of your ability to spar."

"God didn't rob us of anything," Aleta signed. "He's protecting my life."

"I'm sorry," Bertha said. "I misspoke."

"You're still upset about that phone call," Stanley observed.

"She said she'd keep calling. I thought she was in jail."

"She's bribing a guard for phone privileges." Stanley guessed. "She wants to make Aleta's life miserable, if not directly, then through you. She knows her two daughters love you. That must gall her."

Aleta signed. "Did you tell Dad?"

"Heavens no!" Bertha exclaimed. "I can't repeat those ugly words to him."

"I'll take care of it," Stanley promised. "But until I say it's okay, let the answering machine pick up all calls."

"Suppose your family wants to get hold of you?"

"They have my cell number," Stanley replied.

"You're sure she's not out on appeal?"

"She pled guilty to half the charges," Stanley responded. "If she's appealing, she's appealing from jail."

"What about parole?"

"Too soon."

"Maybe I'm worrying over nothing," Bertha said. "I just want Jocelyn to have a good senior year."

"Robert got word from one of his colleagues in California that Jayline's husband is suing for divorce," Stanley said. "That may have been what prompted Marian's sudden desire to get hold of Aleta."

"I'll make those phone switches as soon as we get back," Bertha determined.

"She'll start calling the office," Aleta signed.

"I'll alert Alice," Stanley said. "She'll handle it."

"Aleta, you aren't like your mother at all," Bertha said. "Robert told me Marian threw her hands up in defeat when you were barely two."

"She bought all my clothes." Aleta signed.

"Robert said she never took you shopping. She simply put your new clothes in your drawer and you wore them."

"I got dumped on Grams a lot. Gramps was alive then. He was fun too."

"I thought your grandmother worked." Bertha said.

"Banker's hours," Aleta signed. "I went to her house after school. Dad would pick me up on his way home from work."

The three riders had stopped so Aleta could sign. She finished with Jocelyn tagging along as she got older and how she didn't like that.

"Now don't go beating yourself up over that," Bertha said. "You were a child. Jocelyn says you were a wonderful sister. You never teased her. You taught her to ride. You helped her with her math. And you stood up to your mother. She moved out here because you were her role model. You had Grams. She had you."

"I wasn't that nice," Aleta protested.

"Jayline was mean to her. You never were," Bertha said. "And when you were her lawyer, you protected her and loved her. Aleta, you healed her."

Aleta's hands fluttered and Stanley said, "Bertha, you've rendered her speechless."

Bertha grinned.

"It's about time," she declared. "Let's ride. I have these two demanding employers who will expect everything to get done whether I'm there or not."

"Lead on," Stanley said as Bertha chose a new path. It led to a wide expanse of land and Bertha let Yudi gallop down the horse trail that bisected the grassy field and led into a grove of trees and back out again.

Stanley and Aleta followed, their horses racing down the long winding track, taking different forks each go around.

When they again slowed to a walk, Stanley addressed Bertha, "You do know that this is private property, don't you?"

"It belongs to Hubbs' former employer, Claudine Babcock," Bertha said. "His lawyer won him the right to use it anytime he wanted to."

"I know," Stanley said.

"He told me his lawyer told him that any horse that he was in charge of could use it."

"I read the contract," Stanley said. "It seems that Claudine Babcock considered that an inconsequential request as he and his horse were so old."

"These horses are in his care," Bertha said.

"Technically, you're right."

"Hubbs used that phone you gave him and called the lady. She said he could use it between nine and eleven weekdays and she wouldn't be upset. He wanted me to use the privilege."

"Weekends too?" Aleta signed. "The girls would love to ride here."

"Just Saturdays."

"Let's the three of us do this again tomorrow," Aleta signed. "This is wonderful!"

"While we're on the subject," Bertha said. "I'm going to need another washer and dryer in the new wing."

Aleta and Stanley laughed.

"We were on the subject of laundry?"

"We were getting to it," Bertha said; "I just skipped all the preliminaries."

"I guess you did," Stanley said. "We don't have six children yet."

"We have two on the way."

"I'll see to it," Stanley said. "And while we're on the subject of washing machines, did you hire a permanent housekeeper to help you?"

"My service will take care of major cleaning once a week."

"Three times a week," Stanley said.

"What will I do?"

"Remember that you're pregnant and take long walks with the dogs. Ride Yudi. Play with Gerard. Talk to Hubbs. Bake. Talk to Jamara. And be there for all of us."

Aleta signed, "Lauren and I are throwing a party a week from tomorrow."

"Not to celebrate my ears, I hope," Stanley charged.

"Why would anyone want to celebrate them?" Aleta signed.

"Good."

"Now your nose is another matter," Aleta signed.

As soon as he translated her words, Stanley admonished his wife, "Aleta, there will be no mention of my nose."

"We could always have a tour of our new addition," Aleta signed.

"As long as no one mentions my nose."

He looked at his wife as he said that and saw her smile.

I'm going to be sorry I said that, he thought.

When they returned to the barn, Stanley said, "We took advantage of your privilege to ride on Claudine Babcock's land. We three will be going out at nine tomorrow for another go at it."

Hubbs chuckled.

CHAPTER 16

When Aleta and Stanley walked back into the house after helping Hubbs with the horses, Chief Tom Milani was waiting for them. He had a cup of coffee and half a sweet roll in front of him, so both knew he hadn't minded waiting.

"Hawk found the first one," he announced. "It's a voice activated bomb alright. Hawk's lifted prints from all over the car and the lab is processing them now."

"That's a relief," Aleta signed. "At least we know we're on the right track."

"Bertha, what are you doing?" Stanley asked.

Bertha pulled her head out of a lower cabinet. "They didn't put anything back where it belongs."

Bertha, get out of there," Stanley ordered. "Get one of your women over here."

"They're all busy," Bertha said. "For heaven's sake, I'm pregnant, not injured."

"Interview a new one and do it now!" Stanley said sternly.

"Yes, Sir!" Bertha snapped.

Tom raised an eyebrow. Stanley spotted it.

"Don't say a word."

Aleta giggled.

Stanley whipped around. "And you neither."

Aleta hurried back to the study, giggling all the way.

Bertha pulled a slip of paper from her pocket and made a call.

"Come dressed to work," she said. "That's how I interview. I will pay for the work you do whether or not I hire you."

"She'll be here in fifteen minutes, Mr. Praetzel," Bertha reported.

"Good," Stanley said. "Remember, you are now a supervisor, not a day laborer."

"Yes, Sir," Bertha said. There was a lilt in her voice.

Tom relaxed. She was still employed. He'd come to like visiting this house. Bertha always sent him back to the station with a few goodies.

"Almost gut punched you, eh, Tom?" Stanley quipped. "I'll go back to making Aleta's life miserable."

"How will you do that exactly?" Tom asked.

"She brought home half the contracts and wills she took on. She expects me to help her. I don't do contracts and wills."

"Wasn't the Tontine work all contracts?" Bertha asked.

"I had to do that work. I was courting Aleta. But I'm the Senior Partner. Senior Partners don't do contracts and wills," Stanley said walking out of the kitchen.

"Why is he so bugged?" Tom asked.

"Aleta took on a load of cases. He's been spending a lot of time helping Aleta with her cases. I guess he just drew the line," Bertha answered.

"Aleta seems cheerful, considering," Tom observed.

"She's beginning to realize this could last a long time."

"Maybe there was only one," Tom suggested.

Bertha shook her head.

"Remember what you told me about the bomb in the car. The man's clever."

"Hawk almost didn't find it and we were sure there was one or else he never would have gone over the car until he found it."

"And why did he find it?"

"There were no prints on the steering wheel."

Hubbs walked in the back door.

"Gotta see Mrs. Praetzel."

"She's in the study," Bertha said.

Hubbs knocked softly and Stanley opened the door for him. He held out Shadow's bridle.

"Someone's been fussing with it," he said.

"Fussing with it?" Stanley questioned. "How?"

"Don't know."

"Why do you say someone's been fussing with it?"

"Don't feel right."

Stanley called to Tom. He showed him the bridle. "Hubbs says it doesn't feel right."

Tom took it and turned it over in his hand. "Looks okay to me."

"Maybe you can have Hawk look at it," Stanley suggested.

"Yeh, okay," Tom said hesitantly.

"It's probably nothing," Stanley went on. "But I'd appreciate his checking it out."

"I'm not sure when he can get to it."

"Just tell him about it. Let him decide."

"Sure. I can do that," Tom said.

Bertha handed Tom a bag of homemade cookies and when he got back to his office, he shoved the cookies in the bottom drawer in his desk and stuck the bridle in there as well. He decided not to waste Hawk's time with it.

At that moment, Harriet removed Auggie's collar and threw it into the drawer with the other collars and leashes. She put a new collar around his neck, one with her cell phone number on it.

A little before five, Harriet came over to borrow a suitcase.

"Paige needs it," she said. "She's been carrying her clothes around in paper bags. I told her Aleta had extra."

Since Aleta was still busy going over Tim Jordan's first drafts of wills for clients, Stanley led the way to the bedroom and pulled out the yellow case in the front of the closet.

"This is a good case," Harriet commented. "It's one she uses all the time."

"Her mother gave it to her," Stanley said. "This is the wrong time for her to be reminded of her mother."

Harriet studied the still discolored, slightly swollen face of her granddaughter's husband.

"Tell me what's going on," she demanded.

Stanley told her.

"Robert knows his ex-wife all too well," Harriet observed. "I gave him the house and he immediately put it in Bertha's name. Then he had Bertha write a will leaving everything to her children.

"He prepared for this?" Stanley asked.

"I questioned him about the wisdom of those moves at the time. Now I see he may have been wiser than I thought."

Stanley snickered.

"Marian's new lawyer will investigate his financial status and find he owns a truck which was a gift from his mother and the clothes on his back."

Harriet continued the explanation of her son's decisions.

"They're putting any extra money into a trust for Jocelyn and the baby, of course, and into those flying lessons of his."

"No retirement?"

"He says he and Bertha plan to mooch off us," Harriet revealed.

Stanley laughed.

"He has a plan. I wonder what it is."

"I told you," Harriet insisted. "He plans to depend on my largess."

"Bertha won't let him."

"That's what I'm counting on," Harriet remarked. She picked up the yellow suitcase and left.

Tim Jordan left at the same time with Aleta's briefcase full of documents to be typed.

Bertha found Stanley in the bedroom.

"There's a call from Judge Clancy's law clerk for you."

Puzzled, Stanley asked, "You answered the phone?"

"I recognized the courthouse number when it came up on the caller ID."

"Law clerks don't call lawyers at home," Stanley stated.

"It wasn't Marian," Bertha said defensively.

Stanley opened his cell and called his secretary.

"Alice, has Judge Clancy been trying to reach me?"

"No, Sir," Alice replied. "If you're expecting a call, I can wait for it."

"I'm not expecting a call," Stanley said. "Someone from the courthouse called my home phone."

"I've been here all afternoon." Alice said.

"It's someone new, I expect," Stanley said. "Don't worry. I'll take care of it."

Stanley picked up the bedroom extension.

"Stanley Praetzel here,"

"What took you so long?" said a voice Stanley had heard before.

"How may I help you?" Stanley said politely.

"I don't like to be kept waiting," the man barked. "I want to give you a tip on where one of them bombs is, but it'll cost you."

"How much?"

"Fifty grand."

"I'll wait for the police to find it," Stanley said coolly.

"Twenty-five," the man said. "And it's not the only one."

"How many are there?" Stanley asked. "Two? You didn't have time to plant more."

"That's what you think! There are twelve," the voice shot back, hesitated and then added, "Maybe more."

"Ten thousand is all I'm willing to give."

"That ain't enough," the voice said. "Think it over. I'll call back at seven. You pick up right away."

The caller disconnected.

Stanley dialed Tom Milani.

"I heard from the bomber. He wants money. He's calling back at seven."

"West and I will be right over."

In a run-down farmhouse straight north of Catalpa Grove, Doyle Conan's mother was stirring a pot of stew on the stove. Cousins she didn't mind feeding, but she wished they hadn't invited such big friends.

Lennie Archer was an average-sized man, a bit on the small side and lightweight, like her own son, Doyle. Lennie was her sister's son. Stuart Fouts, her late husband's nephew, was large like his father, but the one she objected to the most was Lukas Kvidahl who was over six feet and weighed close to three hundred pounds.

He wasn't anybody's friend. He was a mere acquaintance of Stuart Fouts and she couldn't see why he was here at all. He was a big complainer and an even bigger eater. He went on about some lawyer who messed with his business with his mother.

Butch Lennert was a big man too, but he was Lennie's traveling companion so she didn't mind him so much. He wasn't as big as Stuart and he wasn't mean at all. He treated her nicer than the rest.

Lennie and Butch were the first to land on her doorstep and they spent the first day in the basement with Doyle. The second day Lennie went to Chicago and returned with a huge smile. He had made a sale he said. He brought back enough liquor to keep all three soused until Stuart showed up with his friend Lukas Kvidahl.

After that the drinking stopped and the five got busy with a project that Doyle told her was going to get Stuart out of a jam.

Now as she cooked, she listened to their conversation.

"Did he agree?" Butch asked.

"We're negotiating," Lennie replied.

"What's negating?" Butch asked.

"Negotiating, Dummy," Lennie snapped. "It means bargaining."

"But you set the price," Butch pushed on.

"And he set a lower price," Lennie said. "So I told him I'd call him back at seven. He'll come around."

Doyle butted in.

"Which one are we going to tell him about?"

"Not mine," Lukas Kvidahl said. "I almost got bit changing that stupid hound's collar."

"He's right," Stuart spoke up, his voice carrying his authority as a leader. "If we tell him about one collar, they'll check the others."

Butch burst in. "Not mine neither. It was a helluva job getting them two under the roof. I had to stay up there half the day before the coast was clear so I could get down."

"We aren't giving those up either," Stuart Fouts decided.

Butch grinned happily.

"We only go one in the barn and the RV," Lennie said. "No back-up. I say we leave them."

If I point to the one in the suitcase, then they'll look in the briefcase," Stuart observed. "They don't get two for one."

"That leaves the bridle," Doyle said. "Or the coat rack or the toy over the baby's crib. Those were my best work."

"Yeh. They were the best ones," Butch agreed.

"Which is why we'll use one of them," Stuart decided. "We want them to know how clever we are."

Doyle smiled at the idea.

"The bird over the baby's crib," he said. "That'll really scare them."

"Yeh," Lucas Kvidahl laughed. "I watched them cops crawling all over the room and all the time it was whirling above their dumb ass heads."

"The crib is like the car," Lennie put in. "It won't lead them to any of the others."

"Okay, Lennie. We give them the bird," Stuart decided.

Lennie laughed.

Back at the Praetzel farm in Willow Glen, Chief West arrived only minutes after Chief Milani. Chief Milani was already settled at the table with a fresh cup of coffee when Lyle West walked in.

"I recognized the voice," Stanley announced at once. "It was the man who robbed us in Iowa."

Aleta signed and Lyle nodded.

"That was the impression I got too," Lyle said.

"What impression?" Tom asked. "I didn't get any gift from heaven. I don't understand sign language."

"Aleta said that he didn't seem smart enough to have pulled off this job. He was a clumsy grab-and-run kind of thief." Lyle responded.

"So he joined someone else?"

"He said there were twelve bombs," Stanley reported.

"Twelve!" the two chiefs chorused.

Aleta signed her query first.

"How come he told you that?"

"I told him I was willing to wait for the police to find the other one."

"And he burst out with how many?" Aleta signed.

"No. He said there was more than one and I said he didn't have time to set more than two," Stanley reported. "He had to brag."

"Twelve?" Tom considered aloud. "We only found the one in the car. Maybe he's just trying to scare you into thinking there's more when there isn't, so you'll fork over the cash."

"There are more," Aleta signed. "How much does he want?"

"Fifty thousand," Stanley said.

"He'll want that for each of them," Aleta said.

"That's over half a million," Tom remarked.

"The price could go up," Stanley said. "In fact, I can guarantee it. I offered him ten and he said that twenty-five was as low as he would go."

"That would seem like a fortune to the two who robbed us," Aleta signed. "But I think the man behind this won't settle for twenty-five."

"You aren't suggesting I pay fifty," Stanley asked.

Aleta looked at Lyle when she signed.

"If Hawk had another bomb to work with, would that help him at all?"

"Hawk said he'd begin to get an idea how the man thinks if he had one more."

"We're going to be gone for five days," Aleta signed. "There's the dog show and the annual meeting of the Tontine following the show. Hawk and Paige will only be there for the two weekend days of the show. We will be staying at least through Tuesday. Hawk may not be in his lab, but his mind will be working. He'll be ready when he goes back to search some new places. So pay the fifty. Get us the clues he needs."

"It's a lot of money to pay a criminal," Lyle said. "You can bet they will have a drop off spot we can't monitor."

"I say pay him nothing," Tom interjected. "Give us five days and we'll find another one."

"Tom," Aleta signed and Lyle translated. "Hawk found the only obvious one and he almost didn't find it. Your men looked hard. There are eleven other bombs. They are well hidden or one of your men would have found one. Let's pay for the clue. Then on Monday, we will let Hawk direct the new search."

"Well, okay," Tom agreed grudgingly. "But not fifty."

"How much do you have in the house?" Lyle asked.

"Enough," Stanley replied.

"Sequential?"

"I have no idea."

While Tom's men are setting up, we'll take down the serial numbers," Lyle said. "Aleta can help us."

"Bertha, you don't have to stay," Stanley said.

"And who exactly do you think is going to feed everyone?"

We won't be eating. We'll be working."

"Aleta will be eating," Bertha announced. "Tom will be eating. Gerard will be eating. Lyle has worked a full day. He's looking at a long night. He eats too. So do you."

"Yes, Ma'am," Stanley said. "Just tell us when."

Lyle and Tom exchanged glances. Bertha was evidently not going to be denied. They assumed she was caring for Aleta who would never eat unless everyone else did, and so Stanley's wishes took a back seat.

At exactly seven o'clock, Stanley's cell phone rang. He answered it in order to tell the person that he'd call him back. The voice was new.

"You offered my partner ten. That's not enough," said the new voice, one Stanley didn't recognize.

Aleta began signing. "Fifty. Don't play around."

"You win!" Stanley said. "Fifty."

"He heard the man whisper. "He said fifty. Now what do I say?"

"Where do you want it?" Stanley asked.

"You got it all?" the man asked, surprised.

"Yes," Stanley said.

He heard a hissing in the background and a new voice came on.

"From your safe at home?" the new voice inquired.

The voice was muffled. Stanley assumed that a handkerchief had been put across the mouthpiece. The leader was someone he knew.

"I have it," Stanley said coldly. "Do you want it?"

"You mark the bills?"

"No."

"Put that purple stuff on them?"

"No."

"Take down the serial numbers?"

"Yes."

"An honest lawyer," the voice exclaimed. "Switch them."

"I don't have enough to do that," Stanley said. "I can give you half and half."

"Put the list in with the money. I want it in a green garbage bag. You've got one minute. Put the phone on speaker so I can hear what you say."

Stanley gave the order. Lyle and Aleta complied

"Start walking," the man said. "And tell that police chief you work with that he's driving."

"Suddenly, Stanley knew who it was.

"Chief West, you're the driver," Stanley announced. "He'll give us directions as we go."

The original unfamiliar voice gave the first turn and Stanley knew that he would be guiding them from that moment on. They were back on the leader's initial plan.

They left Willow Glen and entered Arborville. The voice told them to park next to the row of patrol cars and switch to car number 207.

"The keys are in the car," the voice said.

Now he had surprised them. Lyle and Stanley got in and drove east toward a main highway from Chicago.

Suddenly, the voice said, "Slow down to thirty, lower both windows in the front. When I tell you, throw the bag out the window on the side I will tell you."

"We're ready," Stanley said.

"After you throw it, stop at the first gas station on the right. That's where you will get the envelope. You will have three minutes. No radio contact. Keep your cell phone open. You'll need your siren to make it."

"Understood," Stanley said.

A few minutes later, the order came for Stanley to throw out the bag. As soon as Stanley heaved it, Lyle hit the siren and sped away.

Stanley looked back.

Three minutes later, Lyle roared into the first gas station on the right and stopped.

"Now what?" he said.

"Look in the glove compartment," The voice said just before the phone went dead.

Stanley pulled out an envelope and showed it to Lyle.

"Shouldn't Hawk see it in place?" Stanley asked after he showed Lyle what was written on the paper".

"We can see where he would have looked, "Lyle said, flipping on the siren and telling dispatch to send Hawk to the Praetzel residence.

After a few moments, Lyle said. "I saw Aleta tell you not to play around. I assume she meant I shouldn't either."

"I'm sure she did." Stanley said. "I wasn't happy when they told us to open both windows. I think they meant to give us a warning shot."

"That was my interpretation as well."

"We accomplished our goal," Stanley said. "One of the voices was Stuart Fouts. He's diabolical."

"You don't know how right you are," Lyle commented.

"You found a dismembered cat in Tonia Morales' house," Stanley guessed.

"They were prepared for that. But I sent Bobbie over to pack for Mrs. Morales and she picked out Mrs. Morales' nicest suitcase, opened it and promptly lost breakfast and lunch."

At the Praetzel house, when Hawkins Monroe arrived, Bertha hurried ahead of him to pick up Gerard. Bending over to pick him up, Bertha cooed at him.

"Come on, you precious little one, let's have an early night bottle. I'm already warming it."

"The birds over the crib," Hawk said. "Did anyone look at them?"

Everyone exchanged glances.

"Why did you zero in on them?" Lyle asked.

"It's the most logical place," Hawk said. "I assume Aleta would normally talk to the baby as Bertha did. The blast would hit her full in the face."

Stanley caught Aleta as she fell. He carried her to the living room and laid her on the couch.

"Will she speak when she wakes up?" Tom worried.

"I'll make sure she doesn't."

A few minutes later, Aleta stirred. Stanley put his lips on hers and kissed her until he felt her waken completely.

She smiled at him, a trifle groggy. Her mouth opened to comment and Stanley kissed her again. This time her arms encircled his neck, and when he tried to pull away, she rose with him.

When they parted, he scolded her, "We have company, Aleta."

She signed and Lyle translated. "You kissed me."

"You were going to say something," Stanley charged.

"You thought I was going to say something," she countered, signing.

"I had to act," he professed.

"I applaud your choice of actions," she signed, smiling. "I just thought you ended it too soon."

Stanley heaved a huge sigh.

"You are the hardest woman in the world to please."

"No, I'm not," she signed frowning. "Take that back."

"We have company, Aleta."

"Tom and Lyle and Hawk and Bertha aren't company," she signed.

"Tom has a whole contingent of men here," Stanley said.

Then he stopped suddenly and took his wife in his arms.

"It was a terrible thing to envision," he said softly. "It was as unnerving for me as for you. Go ahead and cry. I'm sorry I snapped at you."

"She put her head on his shoulder and he held her while she cried.

"I think Aleta just never envisioned someone dying with her," Stanley said.

Hawk appeared in the doorway with the apparatus in a large bag.

"I'm taking the whole thing. It's only one bird, but I'd like to see if the other ones yield any clues as to our perp."

Stanley nodded.

Aleta pushed herself away from her husband and signed, "Hawk, may I have a tiny amount of the explosive. I want to see if I can teach Scooby to find some other bombs for us."

"The steering wheel has more than this has. I'll bring some over tomorrow." Hawk said. "But you do know Emma is already trained."

"To sniff out drugs," Aleta signed. "A dog has to be trained for each item separately."

"Did you train your dogs on all the birds separately?"

"We just have to train them on a few. Then they get the idea what a game bird is."

"I'll get you a sample," Hawk said.

"Is it safe to handle?" Stanley asked.

"Soldiers carry it in their packs," Hawk told him.

"Suppose they get shot?"

"Bullets don't set it off. It has to be triggered by something like an electrical charge."

"So, if a dog sinks his teeth into it?" Stanley posed.

"It's like clay. It'll stick to his teeth but it won't explode. I would suggest that you bury it inside something too big to swallow though."

"Any idea about the rest of the house?" Tom asked Hawk.

"The nursery was easy. I think that's why he gave you that one," Hawk responded. "Don't worry, Aleta, we'll figure it out."

Aleta nodded, but she was sobered by the fact that Hawk was the only one of the group to think of the birds swinging on the wire above her baby's head. And Hawk said that that was the obvious one.

CHAPTER 17

That night after everyone left, Aleta signed her thoughts to Stanley.

"I'm a bit disheartened too," he replied. "But your idea of using Scooby is a good one. I'll help."

"The Lord giveth and the Lord taketh away. Blessed be the name of the Lord," Aleta signed.

"Are you telling me someone is going to die?"

She shook her head and tears began to roll down her cheeks.

"You can't sign anymore?" Stanley asked.

She nodded.

"Can you write?"

Aleta shrugged.

Stanley fetched pencil and paper. Aleta took both eagerly.

She wrote, "The signing was an interim aid. A transition. I am about to lose the ability to write. Please don't think I've lost my ability to think. Ask me questions so I can show you my brain is alive. I love you."

After those last three words, the pen made undulating wavy lines.

"Aleta, do you know why this is happening?"

She nodded.

"Forgive me if I ask preposterous questions."

This time she smiled when she nodded.

"Were you told that your ability to communicate would anger your enemies?"

Aleta nodded vigorously.

"I can guess the rest," Stanley said. "We don't want their efforts to kill you to increase. And, Aleta, I will listen to you."

Aleta smiled through her tears. She didn't dare form any words silently lest she forget and let her breath take them from her mouth.

Stanley left for a moment.

I'm not in hell, she thought. I'm living my worse nightmare.

She couldn't speak, sign or write. But there were still things she could do. "She could see, hear, touch and taste. She could walk and ride, hold her baby and kiss her husband.

She smelled something coming from the kitchen. It smelled like brownies, but Stanley didn't bake. She heard him fussing around in the kitchen.

He was preparing a surprise for her, she realized.

The thought warmed her. Stanley's surprises were always fun.

Her wait wasn't too long. He appeared with a plate on which was a brownie topped with ice cream. There were two lighted candles sticking out of the ice cream.

"We'll celebrate each time we find a bomb," he said. "By the time we reach twelve, you'll have to eat a whole cake."

He held the plate in front of her.

"Make a wish and blow out the candles."

She thought for a minute and then blew. Stanley had brought two spoons. He handed her one. It was a pleasant interlude.

Afterward Stanley carried her to bed. Their lovemaking was tender and reciprocal.

Afterward Stanley whispered, "You made me feel loved tonight."

She touched his nose gently.

"It doesn't hurt," he said. "Wouldn't it be great if the swelling went away?"

Her hand left his face and patted his chest before sliding down to its usual position.

She fell asleep almost at once and Stanley prayed for guidance. He hadn't actually done that deliberately before.

Her hand squeezed him lightly. The pressure brought him comfort. She was still alive and still his.

In the morning, they showered together with Gerard who gurgled delightedly the whole time. When they entered the living room, both were smiling radiantly.

Stanley handed the baby to Jamara and told Bertha to fix Aleta a big breakfast.

"We're leaving for the lodge right after our morning ride," Stanley announced, and then added casually, "By the way, Aleta can no longer sign."

"How is she going to communicate?" Jamara asked.

"She can write notes," Bertha said.

"She can't write either."

Bertha gasped.

"Why would God do this?"

"We think it's a safety measure to keep her enemies from changing their method of attack," Stanley replied. "We think they want her dead to silence her. They want her not to be able to communicate at all. What I can't figure out is how they found out she could sign."

"I told my children," Jamara said.

"Both Lettie and Jocelyn knew," Bertha added.

"Teenagers," Stanley sighed. "Do let them know the latest."

"How is she going to communicate?" Jamara asked.

"Evidently, she's not," Stanley said. "That's the reason we're leaving early for the lodge."

"Because you can talk there," Jamara concluded.

Aleta shook her head vigorously.

"We're leaving because Aleta can't do any more work. We may as well swim and lay in the sun and play with the dogs," Stanley said.

"We'll keep things humming here," Bertha commented. "Do you want me to pack for you?"

"You feed Aleta. She's already loaded my suitcase with shorts and swim trunks as if I'm going to live in them."

Aleta nodded vigorously.

"Just feed her while I pack for her," Stanley said.

Aleta signaled that Bertha would pack for her.

"I'll start your case," Stanley said. "If I'm wearing shorts, you're wearing shorts."

Aleta chuckled and blew her husband a kiss.

"Tell Robert I need to see him as soon as he gets here."

"He's driving in now," Bertha said.

"We'll take our breakfasts in the study," Stanley said, changing the direction of his movement.

When Robert entered the study, Stanley hung up the phone. Robert had no sooner settled than Bertha entered with two plates of food. Aleta came right behind her with coffee and juice on a tray.

"We'll need more coffee," Stanley said. "I'm expecting my parents."

Aleta raised an eyebrow as a query.

"Bring them in when they get here," Stanley said. "Aleta, you can stay if you like. Give me five minutes with your dad."

Stanley shut the door and began immediately.

"Aleta lost the ability to sign last night. She also can't write. This changes things."

"How is she taking it?"

"Hard, but she's trying not to show it. That's why I'm leaving for the lodge this morning. Yesterday she could work. She sent the contracts with Tim to be typed. She helped him with about six wills. He'd done a first draft. You can maybe continue to use him that way. She said that he's quite good. Mother can check the final product. That's her area of expertise."

He paused, took a breath and then pushed on.

"I'm afraid I'm leaving you with all the child advocacy work. We will be busy with Tontine business Monday and Tuesday. I'm rushing through this. Are you following me?"

"Basically, you're telling me you're putting Aleta first and I'm to run the office," Aleta's father said.

"You've got it."

"I'm not sure I can do it without help. Aleta took on a pile of cases and all our associates are still pretty green."

"That's where I'm hoping my parents will step in," Stanley said.

"Your father has a practice and your mother is planning to return to the bench," Robert pointed out.

"I know. But maybe . . .Here they are," Stanley said as the door opened.

As soon as everyone was settled, Stanley explained to his parents what had happened to Aleta that morning. No one spoke until he finished.

"This latest change has pretty much knocked us for a loop. Aleta and I aren't sure quite what to do. The expectations of our clients under contract must be considered. We have a good staff, but we need more top level experience."

"I can stay as long as you need me," Lydia offered. "I'm enjoying the work immensely. Working with talented young attorneys is exciting."

"Chin has too heavy a case load," Stanley observed.

"Everyone does," his mother said. "With Robert taking your child advocacy cases as well as his own, there will be only me to handle the cases Aleta took on when she figured that there would be two of us."

"On top of that, when we come back, there will be more Tontine work," Stanley said.

"You need another full-time associate," Hubert said. "I know one who's available. I know for a fact that he'd love to be part of your group."

"What's his area of expertise?"

"He's a criminal attorney."

"We don't handle criminal cases."

"You don't handle tax work either," Hubert said, nodding in Robert's direction.

"Robert came in at the bottom," Stanley said. "Is your man willing to do that?"

"Yes."

"Dad, that makes no sense," Stanley said. "Robert was looking to start over after his divorce. Is this man getting a divorce?"

Hubert laughed. "My wife would kill me!"

"You?"

"Why not me? My practice isn't any fun anymore. I'm getting tired of defending criminals. I liked working with you and Aleta. I'll even bring my secretary with me. She's a mild-mannered sort and Alice will love her. I don't want to be a partner. I've been there, done that. You can stay small if you can rein Aleta in. I'd like to be a member of your firm. And I can start tomorrow."

"Tomorrow is Saturday," Stanley said, unable to come up with any response he deemed reasonable.

"Lydia tells me the case load is enormous."

"We haven't discussed salary," Stanley said. "I'm not sure we can afford you."

Aleta got up, walked over to the desk and took a small calculator of the drawer. She punched in a number and handed it to Stanley.

"I can't ask him to work for that!" Stanley exclaimed.

Hubert sprang to his feet, reached across the desk and turned the calculator around.

"Deal!" he said, holding out his hand.

Aleta shook it. Robert rose and shook Hubert's hand.

"Welcome to the firm," Robert said. "You do know that Aleta and I can outvote Stanley, don't you?"

"I do now," Hubert said, clapping his hand on his son's shoulder. "Don't worry, Son. I'll make you proud."

Startled, Stanley blurted out, "I'm proud of you already. I just don't know how to handle having you work for me."

"It'll be a new experience for me too," Hubert said. "My partners will never understand."

"Count me in their group," Stanley quipped.

"Stanley, you and Aleta have called on me to help several times and I loved those times. I'm not as creative as you or Aleta, but I am a good attorney and I will sit second chair to you or Aleta anytime and be glad to do it."

"And me too?" Lydia asked, a twinkle in her eye.

"My dear, I've been second chair to you all my life. Why should I change now?"

"We need to rearrange the load," Stanley said. "Aleta, I'll suggest and you tell me yes or no."

Aleta nodded.

"Hubert to help Lydia with the other cases you assigned her."

Aleta nodded.

"Andrew Jackson stays on the discrimination case."

Aleta nodded. She then rose and left the room.

Before anyone could speculate as to what Aleta was up to, Lydia spoke up.

"Aleta promised Chin that he would get the next big case, but he's too overwhelmed with Senior Citizen cases to take one if it came along. Nigel Oliver is interested in that area of law. Maybe now would be a good time for Nigel to pick up Chin's load, only then who would pick up all the contracts, pre-nups and wills?"

Aleta returned to the study holding their Scrabble game. She motioned to Stanley to vacate his chair. He immediately guessed what she had in mind, as did the others in the group.

She pulled out the L tile and pointed to Lydia. Soon everyone's initials were on the desk, including Tim's and Maya's. Nigel's tile was removed from the group and put in the holder. Aleta spelled out "old" and thus Nigel became the litigator of the seniors.

Next she divided the casework between Chin, Lydia and Hubert.

"I guess she's reorganized us," Stanley said.

Everyone nodded.

"What about Tim?" Stanley asked.

"Wills," Aleta spelled out, and then added, "L check."

The last tile placed on the holder was an A. Aleta spelled out 'research'.

"You?" Stanley asked.

Aleta nodded, then grabbed various tiles from everywhere and made a sentence.

"I do all interviews of prospective clients."

"How can you interview them?

Aleta spelled out, "Flash cards."

"It could work," Lydia affirmed smiling. "We can make up the questions. She can have cards with everyone's name and cards with the fee levels too. That's what she gives Alice now."

"Where are we going to put everyone?" Stanley asked.

Aleta spelled out, "Tontine offices."

"While you're gone," Lydia said. "I'll use your office and Hubert can use whatever desk he can find."

"I was hoping for fish," Hubert said.

Aleta chuckled and nodded.

"I should have bargained," Hubert grumbled.

Aleta spelled out, "New office with fish."

"Yes," Hubert said. "I want my own fish."

"Deal," Aleta spelled out.

"Who does all the contracts?"

Aleta spelled out, "Lydia."

"Ugh!" came the automatic response from her mother-in-law.

Aleta added two more words, "in charge".

"That's better," Lydia said.

"Not all to Hubert. We love him."

Lydia chuckled. "Actually, so do I."

Aleta spelled out one more sentences.

"No interviews until Wednesday."

Hubert looked at Stanley.

"Are you going to rein her in?"

Stanley saw the light in his wife's eyes and shook his head.

"She won't overload us," he said.

Lydia shook her head.

"Stanley, your wife works at twice the speed of normal folk."

"You aren't normal folk. You three are at the top of our profession. Our associates are the cream of the crop," Stanley proclaimed. "Aleta knows what she's doing. She may take small cases, but she never takes foolish ones."

"That's true, Lydia agreed. "She reads people extremely well."

"I just want to do a good job." Hubert said.

"Dad, you always do a good job," Stanley said. "I wouldn't have hired you at such a ridiculously low salary if I didn't trust you to do a good job; but, if you ever hope for a raise, you'd better do better than good."

The whole group laughed and parted on that note.

Stanley took Robert aside.

"Get Cook Construction to look over the office changes we need today. They'll move on it because they want the Second Street work."

"What about the Tontine?"

"There's a suite of offices across the street that is now available. I just finished painting them and laying new carpet. They are move-in ready. Harriet has first dibs."

"Any other instructions?" Robert asked.

"Be sure to give Hubert an aquarium," Stanley said. "Do you want one?"

"Yes, I do," Robert said. "If we put aquariums in the rear offices and the front offices have windows facing the street, our clients will feel good about whichever lawyer they are assigned."

"And our younger associates won't feel Hubert pushed them aside," Stanley said. "That's good thinking. See what everyone wants. Remember, Aleta will want the whole staff to be happy."

"Might I suggest that Aleta share one wall of fish with you?

"You mean take out the wall between our offices?"

"Yes."

"Do it."

"We are working this weekend, aren't we?"

"I hate to ask it, but I don't see any way around it. Make Saturday the day you all get to tour the new area. That'll brighten the day a lot."

"And you'll be back in the office on Wednesday?"

"Aleta pretty much decided that, didn't she?"

"I can change the first day of interviews to Thursday," Robert suggested.

"Do it," Stanley said.

"Do you expect trouble?"

"I never expect it," Stanley remarked. "But it does seem to visit us a lot."

CHAPTER 18

Stanley had no sooner parked the RV in the large parking area next to the Minnesota lodge than Aleta opened the door and released the dogs. She ran straight toward the water's edge where her grandmother and Claude were lying on lounge chairs sunning themselves.

Scooby rushed past them straight into the water. Two Chessies rose and followed. Keeper, who was pregnant, was tethered in the shade under a nearby oak. Auggie was snuggled next to her. He had a harness on.

"Where's Stanley?" Claude asked as he fended off Tank's effusive greeting.

Aleta pointed at the RV. Then she pantomimed Stanley picking up her clothes, folding them and putting them in a drawer.

"Neat bugger, isn't he?" Claude commented.

Aleta laughed and took her grandmother's hand to urge her to swim with her. Harriet rose and Tank led them to the water. He waded out a few feet and then stopped.

The two Chessies and Scooby swam toward them and greeted them before either woman was more than ankle deep in the cool water. Each dog shook the water from his coat. Laughing, both women ran the rest of the way and dove into the water. The dogs ran up onto the shore, approached Claude and shook again.

The cold water was a shock. Claude realized that he had probably been in the sun too long. He raced the dogs back into the water. He swam out to warn Harriet and Aleta about being careful not to get sunburned. Harriet was swimming between her two Chessies, one hand on the shoulder of each, so Claude approached Aleta first. He treaded water while he warned Aleta about the sun.

Aleta nodded and pointed toward Harriet. Claude glanced over and then turned back.

"You can talk out here," he said.

Aleta shook her head. As she did so, Tank, who had waded up to his neck, took one more step and found he could no longer stand on all fours and keep his nose above water. He began to paddle with his front feet in an effort to keep his head aloft. His back feet were still anchored on the bottom of the lake. The paddling, however, moved him forward into deeper water. The first thing he did was turn around.

Aleta clapped sharply, holding her hands above her head as she tread water. Tank turned back and swam awkwardly toward her.

"There are no bombs out here," Claude proclaimed. "And your dog needs you. Talk to him. Calm him down."

Tank had indeed begun to panic. His front legs rose out of the water as his rear sank.

Aleta swam a few strokes toward her dog, took a deep breath and dove under him. She placed her hand beneath his belly and lifted his rear from underneath. As he leveled out, Tank began to paddle effectively. Aleta emerged from under the water and gasped for air. She rolled over on her back and swam toward shore. Tank followed. When he could stand, she stood, threw her arms around his neck and hugged him. She stroked his neck with both hands and Tank wagged his tail, sending water everywhere.

Stanley, who had emerged from the RV just in time to see Aleta dive under a thrashing dog, had yelled for someone to help her.

Only Scooby heard Stanley. He turned instantly and swam toward him. He could hear the panic in Stanley's voice, but he had no idea it was Aleta in trouble. He swam as fast as he could. When his feet touched bottom, he bounced through the water and raced up to Stanley and jumped on him, sending him backwards on the grass. Stanley struggled to rise. Scooby licked his face.

By the time Stanley was on his feet again, Aleta was on her back swimming leisurely toward shore. Stanley saw her stop and hug Tank. He yelled at her. She came out at once, puzzled over his obvious anger.

"You tried to rescue a drowning dog?" he charged. "Where's your common sense?"

Tank greeted Stanley effusively, shaking twice before Stanley could stop him.

Aleta pointed at her bathing suit and then at his shorts and shirt.

"I won't swim with this ear," Stanley explained. "Don't change the subject. Tank is a large dog. He could have drowned you."

Aleta showed him what she'd done and indicated that now Tank could swim. Before Stanley said another word, she grabbed Tank's collar and ran back into the water with him. Scooby followed the two and Aleta waved at Stanley to join her.

He shook his head. Tempting as it was, he chose not to. Not only was he not dressed for swimming, he had his ear to consider.

Then, suddenly, she dropped out of sight.

She's got a cramp, he thought.

He waited about thirty seconds before he kicked off both shoes, ran through the shallow water and then took a flying leap into the deeper water and swam toward where he had last seen her. He held his head up and watched for her to reappear, but she didn't. He stroked faster.

A strong swimmer, Stanley was soon at the spot where Aleta had disappeared. He was about to dive when she popped up beside him.'

She raised her eyebrows.

"You weren't in trouble?" he asked.

She shook her head.

You weren't trying to get me out here?"

Another headshake told him she'd gone under for another reason. She took his hand and placed a smooth white stone in it.

"You went down for this?" he asked, aghast. "You scared me half to death."

Harriet was close enough to hear him.

"Aleta likes to dive for stones," Harriet said. "So does Jocelyn. They both have great lung power."

"I need a manual that tells me when not to worry," Stanley grumbled.

Aleta shook her head and Stanley said, "I guess she's telling me not to worry."

"I guess she can't sign in the water," Harriet said. "Let's go where she can."

"She could speak," Claude interjected. "We are in the middle of the lake. How could there possibly be any danger out here?"

"What about it, Aleta?" Stanley asked.

Aleta shook her head.

"I guess it's not safe," Stanley said.

"How can it not be safe?" Claude argued. "We're a zillion miles from your RV and we're in swimming suits."

"She's not to speak anywhere," Harriet said. "That's what I told her. So don't give her any grief. Just be grateful she can communicate. It could be worse,"

"It is worse," Stanley cut in. "She can't sign anymore."

"Now we have to go ashore," Harriet charged.

Stanley followed Harriet in, as did Claude. Aleta, however, stayed in the water with the dogs, choosing to swim in wide circles with Tank.

"Why isn't she coming in?" Claude asked.

"It's hard for her to be around people who can talk when she can't," Stanley explained.

"Leave her be," Harriet agreed. "She's having fun."

The three settled in lounge chairs under the huge oak and watched Aleta as they talked.

"The gift went in an instant," Stanley related. "It shook her to the core. But that's not all of it."

Harriet frowned in consternation.

"She can't speak," Harriet said. "She can't sign. What else is there?"

"She can't write either," Stanley answered.

"Oh, my Lord!"

"When you told her not to speak anywhere, weren't you talking about at home?" Claude inquired. "Surely you didn't mean at a place like this?"

"I meant everywhere," Harriet reiterated. "Until this is over, she is not to speak. But if she can't sign or write, how's she going to communicate. She won't be able to do anything. She'll be miserable."

"She plans to keep working," Stanley said.

"How can she?" her grandmother asked.

"We had a partner's meeting this morning after her gift to sign was taken away. At that time, she was told she couldn't write. Then we met. You wouldn't believe what Aleta managed to do. She reassigned the work, hired a new attorney, setting his salary on the spot and decided we needed more office space."

"That sounds like Aleta," Harriet said proudly."

Stanley thought this the perfect time to bring up a matter that would affect Harriet.

"You know there's a clause in your contract that allows me to take over your offices."

"Aleta pointed it out to me before I signed," Harriet said. "I just never saw your little firm growing so fast."

"She's agreed to slow down," Stanley said.

"Maybe it's a good thing she can't speak. That should slow the client flow."

"She's taking over the intake process."

"She's going to interview?" Harriet sputtered.

"She and Mother worked that out in about two minutes."

"But with Aleta sidelined, you need a seasoned trial lawyer to handle the cases she'll take on."

"That's what we hired."

"Can you afford him?"

"I didn't think so," Stanley expounded. "But he took Aleta's first offer and asked for a perk afterward, which she gave him."

"What did she give him?"

"An aquarium with fish in it."

"And she did all this without speaking?"

"She was very creative."

Suddenly Harriet got the full picture.

"What's your father going to do with his firm?" she asked.

"I have no idea. The deal was made without a lot of talk. I didn't even vote. Robert and Aleta voted we hire him."

"You're worried he'll want to take over," Harriet guessed.

"He won't mean to, but he's used to being in charge."

"He doesn't want to run your firm," Harriet proclaimed. "He wants to be a member of a firm of lawyers who are breaking new ground with every major case they try."

"That's Aleta," Stanley said. "Not me."

"Don't be ridiculous! It's the two of you. She was a caged bird before you set her free."

"I thought I was setting a canary free, not an eagle."

Harriet laughed. "Life is full of surprises, isn't it?"

Stanley began to put on his shoes.

"I need to change," he announced. "Aleta wants to teach Scooby to sniff out the C-4 in our house. Will you help?"

"Do you have some?"

"A small packet, thanks to Hawk," Stanley said.

He called to Aleta and signaled her to join them. Aleta came running in.

"Your grandmother is going to help us train Scooby," Stanley said. "I thought you'd want in on this."

Aleta nodded as she grabbed a towel.

"I think we'll put the C-4 in a canvas bumper," Harriet began. "We don't want him to swallow our only sample."

"But he's been fetching bumpers," Stanley said.

"Then we'll put out two or three bumpers and he only gets a reward if he picks up the one with the C-4," Harriet said. "Then we'll put the C-4 into something else and set it in the middle of a pile of bumpers. He'll soon catch on to what we want. Then we'll start to really hide it, like in a shoe under the bed or inside a cabinet."

Aleta nodded her approval of every suggestion.

"I'll kennel my dogs so they won't join in the game," Harriet said. "And Auggie can sit in our RV for a spell."

"And Tank?" Stanley asked.

"He hasn't been taught to fetch," Harriet said. "So while he may run along with Scooby, he won't fight him for the bumper. He may be a sight hound, but his nose is a good as a retrievers if not better, so there's always the off-chance he could catch on to what we're doing."

"A small off-chance," Stanley predicted. "He's a clown."

"We'll put him up if we have to," Harriet decided. "But we give him a chance first."

While Claude checked the outdoor barbecue grill and started the fire, the other three began to train Scooby on the large tree-studded grounds between the lodge and the lake.

Aleta stood with a pocket full of treats and waved Scooby toward the bumper with C-4 imbedded in it.

Harriet had forgotten that Aleta couldn't speak. She looked at Stanley and asked him if Scooby would obey him.

"Yes," Stanley replied. "But he's fetching the bumper for Aleta just fine."

"That's what I thought we wanted. The fact that Aleta can't speak made me rethink this whole thing."

"Why?" Stanley asked. "Don't we want him to fetch?"

"He couldn't have fetched the steering wheel in the car," Harriet said. "We want him to point. Labs can be taught to do that. And he needs to be rewarded verbally as well as with cookies."

Aleta shook her head.

Harriet argued her point.

"In the field, the reward is completing an act that a retriever is bred to do, so we never feed them. This is different. This is not a natural act. This is a man-made situation. It takes different tactics."

While she was speaking, Harriet heard a clicking noise. Scooby came over and was immediately given a bit of the bacon biscuit Aleta had chosen as a reward.

"When did you start using a clicker with Scooby?" Harriet asked.

Aleta laughed.

"Just now?" Harriet guessed.

Aleta nodded.

"Okay. Show me your plan."

Harriet dropped the bumper ten yards away while Scooby was sitting beside Aleta. She waved toward it. Scooby took off like a shot. Tank, who had been standing, watching, beat the chocolate Labrador Retriever to the bumper by a stride. Aleta clicked once when Tank reached it and a second time when Scooby joined Tank.

"You can't do that," Harriet called. "You'll confuse Scooby. Let me put Tank up."

Aleta shook her head and held up three fingers.

"You want me to put out three bumpers?"

Aleta nodded. Then she took Tank and had Stanley hold him.

This time when Scooby went out, he saw three bumpers. Confused, he nosed each of them. Aleta clicked when his nose was on the right one. He picked it up and was rewarded when he brought it in.

The lesson was repeated four more times. Then Stanley held Scooby and Aleta repeated the lesson with Tank, only this time she followed him to the bumpers and clicked when he nosed the right one, rewarding him each time. Eventually, he zeroed in on the bumper with the C-4 and ignored the others.

"I think that's enough for one session," Harriet said. "A dog needs a couple hours to let the lesson sink in."

"So that's it?" Stanley asked.

"We can repeat this lesson at dusk when their noses will have to do the work. If they do well, we can move on. This is the basic lesson. We can't consider it learned until they can repeat it nine times without error."

Aleta held out the bumper.

"You want me to keep it in my RV?" Harriet asked.

Aleta nodded.

"Good thinking," Harriet commented.

"Why?" Stanley asked.

"They won't turn off trying to get you to reward them for finding it," Harriet explained. "Stick them in your RV. They need to think."

"They'll sleep," Stanley predicted.

"The point is they won't be out here begging for food and forgetting their lesson."

Stanley grabbed Tank's collar.

"Come on Tank. You heard the boss. You have to think."

Scooby trotted along behind Tank. The Lab entered behind the hound, and once inside the RV, he went into his crate automatically. Tank flopped down in front of Scooby's crate, closing the door as he did so. It didn't latch.

Stanley's mind went immediately to Aleta's inability to communicate. He remembered he had his laptop with him. He went into the bedroom and fetched it. On his way out, he glanced at the crate and saw that the door was closed and Scooby was inside. He tucked the laptop under his arm and left.

"Aleta, can you use this?" he asked putting the laptop on the table. He opened it and turned it on.

She put her fingers on the keyboard and thy remained there motionless for several seconds. Tears flowed down her cheeks.

"You can't remember how to type?" Stanley asked.

She nodded. Stanley reached for the laptop, but her sobbing increased, so he took hold of her instead and wrapped his arms around her.

"I'm sorry. I didn't know."

She clung to him as sobs wracked her whole body.

Claude stood stock still, staring, his spatula raised.

"Don't burn the steaks!" Harriet cried.

He turned back to the grill and flipped the remaining two steaks. Then he turned back.

"Aleta, I'm so sorry I gave you a hard time."

Harriet closed the laptop and set it on the end of the table. By the time the steaks were done, Aleta's crying had stopped and she was again calm. Her boisterousness had, however, disappeared.

At the end of the meal, Claude who was facing the RV parking area, announced. "Here comes Tank."

Stanley turned around.

"How did he get out?"

Scooby came trotting in his wake, a round ring clamped between his teeth.

Scooby came straight to Aleta and sat down in front of her, ears perked, tail wagging. Aleta reached into her pocket. Her hand clicked the clicker as she fumbled around searching for a piece of biscuit.

Tank sat next to Scooby and wagged his tail too.

"Scooby's got Tank's collar," Stanley exclaimed.

Aleta took the collar from Scooby's mouth and gave each dog a biscuit.

"What did you do that for?" Harriet asked.

Aleta shrugged as she hugged both dogs.

"You rewarded them for an action you don't want repeated."

Aleta laughed and shook her head. Then she slipped Tanks collar over his head.

"What kind of collar is than anyway?" Claude asked.

"A break-away collar," Harriet said. "It's what all my dog's wear. If the collar gets snagged by a branch, the dog can pull his head out."

Aleta laughed and all turned in time to see Scooby pulling the collar over Tank's head. He trotted over and sat in front of Aleta. Tank joined him.

Again both got biscuits.

"You're teaching them a new trick, aren't you?" Harriet said.

Aleta nodded.

"It's not a desired behavior, you know," Harriet scolded lightly.

Aleta bowed her head, as a chastised child would do.

"But, it is a cute one," Harriet admitted. "And if Tank gets lost, Scooby will be right there holding his collar."

Aleta laughed at the thought and her spirit was renewed.

"Let's get to the real training while there's still room in their stomachs," Harriet said. "People are starting to arrive. Claude will feed them"

The growing dusk didn't hamper either dog not did putting the C-4 inside Claude's wallet or Harriet's small hand calculator case or even a tin of band aids.

"Tomorrow we teach them to point," Harriet said as she called an end to the night's lesson.

"Tomorrow's the show," Stanley reminded her.

Harriet waved her hand at the group that had been watching them.

"Claude told them what we've been doing," Harriet said. "They'll give us the time after the show."

Aleta let Tank go and Stanley released Scooby. The chocolate Lab chased the Irish Wolfhound around the area and then both stopped. Tank lowered his head and Scooby grabbed the collar and pulled it off.

Only a few people saw it. They laughed when the two approached Aleta and sat, tails wagging, ready for their biscuit reward.

"Can you get them to do it again?" Molly shouted. "I didn't see the trick."

Aleta slipped the collar back on Tank and stepped back. Scooby promptly approached Tank why lowered his head obligingly. Scooby took hold of the collar and held on while Tank pulled his head out.

Both dogs came up to Aleta who laughed at their creative twist. Each got a biscuit, a hug and heard lots of clapping from the onlookers.

You're creating a pair of hams," Harriet commented. There was no scold in her tone. Aleta was enjoying their antics.

When they reentered their RV, Stanley took off Tank's collar and placed it on top of the kitchen cabinet near the vent. Both dogs put their front paws on the counter and pointed their noses at the vent.

"I know it's up there," Stanley said. "Leave it."

Scooby knew the command and dropped his feet onto the floor. Tank followed suit. Then, since his masters were preparing for bed, Tank squeezed past them and settled himself in the middle of the bed.

"I thought you'd prefer the privacy of our RV tonight," Stanley explained. "Your grandmother will bring our friends up-to-date on what happened today."

Aleta turned and waited for Stanley to embrace and kiss her. She didn't have to wonder whether he would or not. She'd undressed. Her nightclothes were all neatly folded in her drawer.

It was an open invitation and he accepted. Tank was shoved out into the hallway and the door was closed.

The big dog grumped and that made Aleta giggle. Stanley filled in the words.

"I'm glad he doesn't talk."

CHAPTER 19

The next morning when Stanley drove the RV into the reserved parking space assigned to them, two of the country's top-ranked professional handlers, Tom Wilson and Chuck Rigden, were at his door before he was out of his seat.

They loved to have Aleta fill in when they had conflicts. She always energized their dogs when she showed them and she never failed to impress the judges.

"You're late," Tom said. "You're never late."

Stanley stepped out of the RV and closed the door.

"What's up?" Chuck asked.

"Aleta can't speak. Before yesterday she could sign and she thought she could show. Now she's not sure."

" Has she got laryngitis?" Chuck asked.

"An enemy planted twelve voice-activated bombs at our place. The police only found two," Stanley said. "She's vowed not to speak until all twelve are found."

"Surely she's safe here," Chuck argued.

"We aren't sure. The bomber is exceedingly clever in placing the ones we found," Aleta is taking no chances."

"I still want her to show the Saint," Chuck Rigden said. "She perks him up. And the family likes her. I'll take care of talking to them."

Stanley opened the door and called in, "You have the Saint."

Tom Wilson shouted before the door closed, "And Maggie."

Aleta emerged a bit sheepishly.

Tom went on, "George Sciretta is here. He will want you on Maggie whether you can talk or not, but Stanley, please tell him what's going on so he won't assume Aleta's angry with him."

Stanley nodded.

The talk went on.

Harriet joined the group and found out they were discussing Auggie.

"Aleta, take him in," her grandmother urged.

"What about Maggie?" Stanley asked for Aleta.

"I'll take him in," Tom Wilson said. "My assistant can cover the Frenchie if Harriet will take in my Dane."

"Me?" Harriet uttered, astonished.

"Why not?" Tom said. "The Dane's a pup. Six-to-Nine class. Very nice. I'd like a reserve."

"Not the points?"

"You sound like Aleta," Tom chuckled. "Now I see where that attitude came from."

Stanley winked at Aleta and she smiled. So she was like her grandmother in more ways than she thought.

"George is coming over," Stanley said.

"I'm taking Maggie into Breed," Tom said. "Aleta will handle him the rest of the way, if that's alright with you."

"So she's taking in the Pug?" George asked.

Aleta nodded. The little man had learned a lot since he first started.

Stanley stepped in and explained the reason Aleta wasn't speaking. George Sciretta's eyes narrowed and he asked a number of pointed questions.

"I like that necklace that you wore at the last show," George said. "I'm surprised you aren't wearing it today."

"It was stolen as we were leaving the show," Stanley explained. "The thief is in our area. He's one of the men involved in this bombing plot."

"You think he sold it to a fence in Chicago?" George pressed.

"Yes," Stanley said. "They know their way around Chicago."

"Anything special about it?"

"I had the jeweler spell her name in the silver filigree that held the stone."

Aleta's surprise was obvious.

"I thought you'd like that," Stanley said simply.

"You don't mind if I look, do you?" George said. "I know a number of jewelers in Chicago."

"Aleta would love to have it back," Stanley said. "I could replace it, but she doesn't want a replacement."

"It's okay for Tom to take Maggie in this morning," George said abruptly. "Maggie will be surprised in Group. That'll pump her up. Don't let her see you before then."

Aleta nodded and the two faded back into their RV and closed the door.

Stanley took her in his arms.

"I know you're aching to talk."

Then he kissed her. His passion delighted her.

A voice interrupted them.

"I this is going to lead somewhere, I'll come back."

The two broke apart abruptly.

"Don't act guilty," Dr. Chesney chuckled as he opened the screen door and stepped into the RV. "You two do know you're married, don't you?"

Both blushed.

"I can't believe one and a half babies later and you still act like you got caught with your hands in the cookie jar."

"My ear," Stanley said. "It feels pretty good. I'm sure it's not infected."

"You do hate this procedure, don't you?" Dr. Chesney said. "I heard you went swimming in the lake yesterday."

"But I didn't get it wet."

"If you had, you would have seen me last night," Dr. Chesney said cheerfully. "Come on. If it's really healed, this will be painless."

Stanley sighed and sat on a stool. Dr. Chesney opened his bag and pulled out an instrument. Stanley looked away. He felt a tug behind his ear."

"What are you doing?"

"Taking out the stitches."

"Can you do that?" he asked as he felt another tug.

"I'm a doctor."

"I mean, aren't they supposed to stay in for ten days?"

"They're supposed to stay in until they need to come out."

"How do you know they're supposed to come out?"

"Jamara told me," he stated as he removed another one.

"Jamara?" Stanley blurted out. "She's a nurse!"

"Well, my telling you I was a doctor didn't seem to carry any weight."

Stanley glanced at his wife.

"Aleta, stop smiling. This isn't funny!"

"There! Done!" Dr. Chesney exclaimed. " Now that your ear is full of holes, I'll dab a bit of antiseptic on it. It'll sting and the holes will disappear like magic."

"That's not how it works," Stanley contended.

"Sure it does," Dr. Chesney said, dabbing the holes with a wet cotton ball.

"Ow!" Stanley yelped.

"One of the holes is a bit infected I think," Dr. Chesney noted. "I'll check it again later."

"I have an infected hole behind my ear and you aren't going to give me a shot or anything?"

"Dr. Cook did say you had a tendency for overkill," Dr. Chesney said solemnly.

"Do I get a shot or not?"

"If you want, I can give you one," Dr. Chesney said. "But you don't need one. Of course, that's just my opinion as a doctor."

"You're toying with me," Stanley groused. "And I don't want to have any part of this surgery redone."

"Stanley," Dr. Chesney said soberly. "I am a doctor. I am particularly well versed in stitches and infections. You've healed faster than normal. If we left the stitches in until Wednesday, you'd have permanent scars. And while they won't be seen behind the ear, we don't like leaving scars anywhere. As for the infection, it's just beginning. I hate to interfere with a strong immune system doing its job. The antiseptic should be enough. If it isn't, I'll give you a shot this evening."

Aleta presented Stanley with a mirror.

"I saw my nose this morning," he grumbled.

She pointed at her ear.

He reluctantly took the mirror.

"They look the same," he said surprised.

Aleta laughed.

"They are the same," Dr. Chesney said. "Your surgeon didn't replace them."

"I mean they aren't flat."

"Did you want them flat?" Dr. Chesney asked.

"I expected some change."

"The change is subtle," the doctor said.

Aleta nodded.

"He did a good job," the doctor added. "Your face appears untouched."

Stanley looked at Aleta's smiling face.

"You approve?"

She nodded vigorously.

"I'll leave you two to carry on," Dr. Chesney said opening the door. "Hi Harriet. Ears don't need a bandage. He looks almost normal again."

The showing went well. The surprise of the morning was Harriet taking Best of Winners for the Great Dane puppy's first point.

"I have to use you more often," Tom responded when he heard about the win."

"I'll be available for the next two months," Harriet said. " I want to move Stoney up in the rankings."

"Win the Chessie National," Tom said.

"I hope to," Harriet said.

Stanley won the Breed in Irish Wolfhounds with Tank and Lyle took the Breed in Labrador Retrievers with Morgan. The bet was on. The winner would be whoever was given the highest placing at the Group level.

No one noticed Lennie and Butch wandering around on the show grounds. Lennie had bought a catalog and they went from ring to ring and watched Aleta Praetzel show various dogs while Stanley Praetzel only showed one, the huge Irish Wolfhound. The Praetzels were running back and forth between the rings and their RV all morning and Lennie absolutely didn't want to be inside the RV with Aleta. He decided to wait for the competition at the end of the day when the dogs were divided into Groups.

Lennie didn't understand all the divisions. He did understand that the littlest dogs were in the Toy Group. There was a group for just the hounds, big and small. And the terriers had their own group. All those groups made sense. So did grouping the field dogs like retrievers and pointers and setters and calling them the Sporting Group. That's as much as Lennie could explain to Butch who when he got done, asked why there wasn't a group just for pointers because they pointed and one for retrievers because they swam and those two things weren't the same at all.

That's when Lennie stopped explaining and told Butch that the important thing was to find out which of Aleta Praetzel's dogs got purple and gold ribbons because later she would show those dogs again and then it would be safe to go into her RV.

"What about Mr. Praetzel?" Butch asked.

"He'll be watching her," Lennie replied, grateful to be back on a topic that Butch could understand.

It was almost noon when Aleta was passing by the Golden Retriever ring when Evelyn came out after winning the Breed. It was sheer happenstance that Lennie was standing close by studying the catalog trying to find out what ring Aleta was going to with the Saint Bernard at the end of her leash. Lennie didn't want to be seen following Aleta. He had seen Chuck Rigden's assistant deliver the big Saint named Rolex to Aleta at ringside. What he hadn't seen was the assistant handing Aleta the armband as well. He waited to see which ringside table she would approach to sign in. When she walked away from the nearest rings, Lennie was confused. He didn't know that she was simply taking Rolex for a little walk so his family could settle in on the other side of the ring and Rolex's attention would be focused on her

He had no idea that Aleta was three rings away from where the Saints were showing when she encountered Evelyn. All he knew is that she had stopped to talk and he was too close to her. Evelyn's first words, however, made him freeze in place.

"Would you take Topaz into Group for me?" Evelyn asked a bit timidly.

Aleta looked surprised at the request.

Evelyn rushed on, "I know you're showing Maggie all the way, but I can't beat Lyle in Group. The Best in Show judge breeds Goldens. I have a real chance."

As it happened, Lennie understood just enough to know that Evelyn was holding on to a Golden Retriever, so the reference to Goldens made sense to him. He also gathered that this older woman wanted Aleta specifically to show this Golden Retriever in the Group competition. He was happy when he saw Aleta nod her head.

"I know that you can't take him into Best in Show because you're committed to taking Maggie in," Evelyn continued. "But all I want is to walk into the Best in Show ring with Topaz under a breeder judge."

Aleta smiled and nodded again.

That was twice that Lennie had heard the older woman refer to Maggie. He needed to find out what kind of dog Maggie was and whether Aleta was going to show her in Group as well.

As luck would have it, Evelyn was concerned about the fact that that Non-Sporting followed Sporting.

"Will you be too tired to show Maggie," Evelyn asked Aleta as Lennie began to move away. He glanced back and saw Aleta smile and shake he head in answer to that query. Lennie hesitated just long enough to hear Evelyn give a verbal explanation for the head shake.

"Of course, Maggie is a Bulldog and they don't run very fast."

Lennie walked away with the answers he needed. Aleta was going to be in two groups one after the other. They would have more than enough time to search the RV.

Lennie reasoned that the best time to sneak into the RV would be when Aleta was showing in the ring. He was certain her husband would be watching her. The RV would be empty.

His study of the front pages of the catalog brought him to a bold-faced line that announced that the Groups would start at one-thirty in Ring 5 and then listed the order. Lennie looked at the order and found that the Sporting Group was fourth, followed by Non-Sporting. Hounds were last. Lennie figured that he'd time the first group and then he'd know how long they had to search the RV.

What Lennie didn't realize is that he was looking at Sunday's schedule for the Group showing order, not Saturday's and the order wasn't the same on both days. On Saturday, the Sporting Group was first and the Non-Sporting second.

It was when he and Butch were standing outside the Saint Bernard ring, that Lennie got another answer. He heard one spectator ask another how long each Group took.

"I want to see the Working Group and it's the third group."

"Figure 15 to 20 minutes. It depends on how large the group is and how fast the judge is."

Lennie moved away then and Butch went with him. Butch was puzzled.

"Why ain't we staying to the end?"

"It is the end, Dummy." Lennie said. "The judge pointed to her and said, "Breed."

"Yeh, but we didn't see what kind of ribbon she got."

"Nevermind that. I found out what we need to know another way."

"When are we gonna eat?" Butch asked. "I'm hungry and those hamburgers smell mighty good."

"We're going to eat right now," Lennie said. "And you can even go back for seconds."

"Really?"

"And maybe even thirds."

"Wow!"

At one thirty when Aleta was lining up to enter the Sporting Group, Butch was standing in line for his third burger. Lennie was sitting at the table recalculating how much time they had before it would be safe for them to enter the RV.

Aleta entered the ring and assessed the competition. Her grandmother had been right. It would take a miracle to pull a first against the Irish Setter whose long dark red coat shimmered in the sun. Lyle and Morgan, both impeccably clean and well groomed were also a team it would be hard to beat.

To Aleta's utter delight, the Flatcoat in front of her was a bitch in season and according to Topaz, she was ready to be bred.

Morgan, who was behind Topaz caught a whiff of the Flattie and he too reacted. His reaction, however, was less noticeable as he was already excited about being there. Topaz, being older, needed a giant incentive to rise to the occasion.

When the Flatcoat wagged her black, feathered tail, she fanned her scent directly into Topaz's nose. As the judge walked down the line, he saw Aleta standing in front of the Golden, but slightly off to one side. He immediately guessed the reason.

He took a long look at the aging Golden. Not many wins left in this one, he thought. He moved on. The Labrador's resplendence made him hesitate again. A rich red Irish, a magnificent Golden and now a Lab who made black a color richer than the brightest hue. Those three made the cut along with the Clumber and Stoney.

As Aleta stood in line between the Irish and the Lab, she wished she had a soccer ball. Topaz was an inveterate soccer fan.

She wondered later if she had asked God for a soccer ball and He'd sent what He did for fun. What Aleta was the recipient of was a pair of flies determined to mate on her forehead, moist with sweat from the afternoon sun. A quick brush with her hand didn't dissuade the persistent flies. She then did what a horse does. She shook her mane. Her light auburn hair flew out. The action sparked in Topaz a dormant memory of flying hair glistening in the hot sun followed by the appearance of a soccer ball in the ring. He'd gotten to chase it. It had only happened once, but he had not forgotten.

Topaz's body tensed in anticipation. He looked around for the ball. He pranced lightly, his hopes high. His tail wagged excitedly. The judge was captivated by his antics. Topaz beat Morgan and took first. Harriet took fourth behind the Irish. It was a heyday for the retrievers.

"It was close," the judge told Lyle. "But I've never seen a dog so excited stay in place. Quite a feat."

"Aleta has a magical quality," Lyle said warmly.

Aleta left the ring glowing. Stanley met her. Harriet repeated the conversation during the awarding of the ribbons.

"You were great!" Stanley exclaimed. "Evelyn is overjoyed."

Tom Wilson handed Aleta a bottle of water and said. "Non-Sporting is next. You look hot."

"Take off your jacket," Harriet said.

Aleta pointed at Tom's jacket.

"I don't care if he's hot," Harriet quipped, taking hold of Aleta's jacket and pulling it off.

Aleta pointed at her blouse.

"So it's sheer," Harriet observed. "It's tasteful."

She replaced Aleta's arm band as Tom chuckled and asked, "You do know who's judging Non-Sporting, don't you?"

Aleta shook her head.

"Jott's going to love you!" Tom exclaimed as he took his Frenchie from his assistant.

Another assistant shoved Maggie's lead into Aleta's hand and she had no time to change her mind.

She'd selected the blouse because it was lightweight and she knew the coat would make her hot. The blouse was pale beige and had long full sleeves. The sleeves billowed out below the three-quarter sleeve of the jacket and added a pleasant feminine touch to the ensemble. She had worn the coat closed.

Stanley thought the blouse was sexy and he'd bought the sapphire for her to wear with it. Now without the pendant, she felt exposed.

At that very moment Butch was finishing up his third burger and wondering if he could ask Lennie if he could buy a little apple pie. He felt like dessert. To his surprise, Lennie suggested it. There was no line at the food truck any more. Lennie got his pie right away.

Back in Ring 5, the group ran around the ring. Aleta's flowing skirt and the billowing sleeves of her blouse captured

Judge Jott's eye instantly.   He scarcely saw the tubby Bulldog striding alongside her.

When Jott went down the line, Aleta stood in front of Maggie, who wagged her stub of a tail to tell Aleta again how glad she was to see her.

After the judge passed, Aleta crouched down and ruffled Maggie's ears to let her know she was glad to see her too. Usually she talked to the squat little Bulldog but today that option was denied her.

Jott caught the uncharacteristic movement and wondered what she was doing. By the time he'd looked at the last dog, Aleta was standing again. Jott liked the fact that she was discreet. She was a beauty. He hoped the Bulldog was a good one.

When she presented her dog, she spoke not a word. Her silence Jott chalked up to discretion. She didn't flirt. All she did was wear the most provocative, yet tasteful, outfit imaginable.

Jott knew dogs, however, and the handler's beauty only tipped the scales if the dogs being presented were of equal quality. In the Group ring, half the dogs were outstanding representatives of their breed. If the bulldog were good, Jott would give her a place.

On Maggie's first run, Jott had focused on Aleta to such an extent that he barely noticed the dog until they were halfway back. By the time they reached him, Maggie was panting heavily. It was the hottest part of the afternoon and the ring was bigger than usual and Jott had forgotten to tell Aleta to go half way and so she had run the full length of the ring, as had the bigger, lighter weight dogs. It had been a long run for the Bulldog.

Jott asked her to go down and back again. This time he was determined to watch the dog. To his amazement, she shook her head, twirled around and made a short arc to the end of the line. Jott saw Wilson's assistant hand her a cool coat and a spray bottle.

At that moment, Lennie, with Butch in tow, checked Ring 5. He surveyed the dogs lined up inside the ring and missed seeing Aleta squatting down next to Maggie near the ring ropes. He saw Stanley sitting at ringside with a woman between him and a tubby man that looked familiar. He looked away quickly, hastily backed away from the crowd around the ring and headed away from the ring.

George Sciretta turned to Harriet.

"She didn't do what the judge asked, did she?"

"No, she didn't," Harriet said. "Your dog was too hot."

"What'll he do?"

"It depends," Harriet said. "He did see her put Maggie in a cool coat and spray her face, so she was looking out for the dog. That was a plus. On the other hand, she refused to obey outright. Only we know she couldn't explain. He doesn't know that."

"Couldn't she have gone half-way?"

"I'll ask her later and tell you her answer. This much I know, Aleta always puts the dogs first, even over winning."

"There's always tomorrow," George said, disheartened.

Aleta pulled the cool coat off Maggie and took her place in the line.

"He's making his final cut," Harriet said.

George watched silently, his hopes dashed.

Judge Jott moved the Poodle up and back and pointed to a spot in the center of the ring. He moved two more dogs. Only the Keeshonden was asked to join the Poodle in the center of the ring. He moved Tom and his Frenchie next, and then skipping over Aleta and Maggie, he sent Tom and his Frenchie into third position. Then he walked back to Aleta and asked politely if she would move her dog up and back.

Aleta coaxed Maggie into a nice even gait. Jott thanked her and asked if Maggie could manage to circle the ring behind the three in the center. It was an odd query. Aleta nodded solemnly.

She took her place at the end of the line and bent over and ruffled Maggie's ears. Tom spotted the change and told Aleta to give him room. Even though Aleta did as he asked, Maggie caught up to Tom's French Bulldog half way around the ring. The judge signaled Aleta to move inside the line of gaiting dogs. And then he pointed to Maggie and said, "One!"

Aleta moved directly to the sign designating first place and the other filed into the places behind her.

George Sciretta was unable to refrain from shouting, "Holy Mary, Mother of God! She won!"

Judge Jott handed the blue rosette to a smiling Aleta and said warmly, "Nice handling, but I could have used an explanation."

Tom left his place among those who placed and said. "Aleta can't speak, but she does apologize."

Aleta nodded.

Jott looked at Aleta and said, "You were wise. That last run was magnificent."

Tom interjected. "I told her to give me room. Next time I'll tell her to give me half the ring."

CHAPTER 20

While Aleta was having her photo taken, Lennie was heading back to his car in the lot. Butch was protesting leaving the grounds. Lennie began talking to him as they were walking.

"We know he carries a lot of cash," Lennie told Butch.

"So why are we walking away?" Butch asked.

"We gotta move the car closer."

"There won't be no necklace," Butch said. "We took it last time."

"Cash is better," Lennie insisted.

"Not fake cash," Butch grumbled.

Lennie swore silently.

Butch had never seen a bill larger than a twenty, so Lennie had told him the others were probably fake. He'd then divided the twenties evenly and given Butch all the smaller bills.

"All the bills last time were real," Lennie told Butch, adding. "I had them checked out."

Butch scowled.

"Where's my share?"

"How much is your share?" Lennie asked.

"There were lots of bills," Butch said, frowning as he tried to figure out how much to ask for.

"Mostly fifties," Lennie said. "Five fifties and one hundred."

"How much is that?"

"About two hundred dollars."

Butch smiled when he heard the two. He was back to a figure he could handle.

"I want a hundred."

Lennie took a single one hundred dollar bill from this pocket and handed it to Butch.

"You guessed right," Lennie said.

"This is real?"

"Yes."

"One hundred dollars?"

"Yes."

"How many twenties is that?"

"Five."

"How much do you think we'll find this time?"

"More than last time."

"Why?"

"Because they was robbed once."

"Yeh, sure," Butch said as if he understood.

After they moved the car, Lennie had them take a more circuitous route through the vendors in order to enter the RV area from a less traveled route. Earlier when they'd taken a direct route, they'd been stopped.

Meanwhile, Aleta, using a series of gestures, told Stanley she wanted to return to the RV and nap.

"I'll wake you when I come for Tank," he said.

Aleta nodded.

"Where is she going?" Harriet asked.

"To catch a short nap."

"Will she be alright?" Harriet worried.

"I have to treat her normally," Stanley said. "Besides Scooby and Tank are there."

"Suppose she puts them outside in their pens?"

"They'll bark," Stanley responded. "She has a phone. Mine is set on vibrate. She only has to call and I'll see her number and go."

Harriet relaxed.

"I wish she could text."

"We're down to basics," Stanley explained. "She punches 'contact' and I'm the first on the list. We practiced it this morning."

"Isn't the list alphabetical?"

"I programmed myself in as Abba Stanley Praetzel. She laughed."

Less than five minutes later, Aleta opened the door to the RV. The two dogs greeted her enthusiastically.

She turned up the air conditioner and Tank immediately plopped in the center of the bed and rolled over on his back so the cool air could caress his tummy.

Scooby whined to go out. Aleta put him in the pen outside. It was warm but shaded.

Then she considered whether she was tired or just hot. She decided to cool down quickly. A shower would do it. It wouldn't even need to be a long one, just a cool one.

As Aleta stepped into the shower, Lennie and Butch approached the RV parking lot.

Butch was getting nervous about their planned caper.

"We don't have masks nor nothing."

"We're going into an empty RV, Dummy."

"Suppose it ain't empty?"

"We saw him sitting watching the show."

"There could be dogs."

"And you're worried they'll identify us?" Lennie scoffed.

"Dogs is smart," Butch declared.

"But people ain't learned to talk dog yet," Lennie barked. "Now stop jabbering. You're getting on my nerves."

Inside the tiny shower, Aleta turned on the water. It was cold, but not icy. She gritted her teeth and let it work its cooling magic.

While the shower was on, Scooby barked. From inside the shower, Aleta didn't know it was Scooby. As soon as the water stopped, she recognized the bark. She opened the door and had one foot outside the shower when she felt the RV shake.

Too late, she realized.

She reached over and locked the bathroom door. Then she ducked back into the shower stall.

She heard male voices.

They were inside the RV. She stood in the tiny shower naked, shivering and wondering if they knew she was inside the RV.

"See!" a voice exclaimed. "I told you we'd strike it rich!"

Tanks deep growl reverberated through the RV.

"Lennie, let's go," a second familiar voice said.

"We were gonna look around. Remember. You're the one who wants to steal another necklace."

"I told you we got the only one." Butch reiterated. "There ain't no more. Come on, Lennie. Let's go. I changed my mind."

"Go," Aleta urged silently.

"We're not leaving without looking for other stuff," Lennie snapped. "Take the clip."

Aleta's heart sank. She wrapped her arms around her body. How could one get so cold so fast?

"Is it gold?" Butch asked.

"Yeh, sure," Lennie affirmed. "He's rich. It's gotta be."

Aleta moved a foot and made a sound. She held her breath. Had they heard it?

"There's a dog in the bedroom," Butch said.

"Then, Dummy, I guess you don't look in the bedroom," Lennie snarled.

Aleta had scarcely noticed Tank was growling so involved was she with her own predicament.

"He don't like us being here, Lennie."

Tank's growl had become more threatening and he began scratching at the door.

"That door ain't gonna hold him. I'm outta here."

"Butch Lennert, you do what I say. You hear me!"

Two seconds later the knob to the bathroom door was rattled. Aleta's heart leaped into her throat. She clamped her hand over her mouth and stood stock-still.

"It's locked," Butch called out. "Do you think someone is in there?"

Aleta held her breath.

Lennie answered, "They lock the toilets so people don't come in and use them."

"Like gas stations?"

Aleta sensed that Butch had moved away from the door. She heard a drawer open.

"Yeh, like that," Lennie answered. "You find anything?'

"Yeh. They got a game. Can we take it, Lennie?"

Inside the shower, Aleta almost cried out in protest. Without it she wouldn't be able to tell anyone what happened.

She scolded herself silently, "Don't be silly. You'll find a way."

Stanley was good at figuring out how to help her communicate.

Then her mind latched onto a new worry. Stanley was due to come wake her. Suppose he came early. She couldn't warn him.

"Hey, Lennie," Butch called. "You did the RV. Where did you put it?"

Aleta strained to hear.

The next sound she heard was a loud guffaw, which caused Tank to renew his effort to get out of the bedroom.

So noisy was he that Aleta barely heard the words that followed.

"They ain't never gonna look there."

Suddenly, she heard a shout.

"What did you find?" Butch asked.

"Another necklace! And she's a beaut!"

Another necklace? Aleta puzzled. Stanley was going to give her another one. He'd told George he wasn't going to replace it.

Then she smiled. Not a replacement. He'd bought her a new one--unlike the other.

"Didn't I tell you that we'd hit it big," Lennie bragged.

"Yeh, Lennie, you're right. Can we go now?"

Aleta heard the panic rising in Butch's voice.

"That dog's gonna come through that door any minute."

"I got a gun," Lennie said.

Aleta shivered.

"Tank," she almost whispered. "Don't break down the door."

"We gotta go," Butch insisted.

"Stop worrying about the damn dog."

"Lennie, someone's gonna hear him," Butch cried, his panic now full blown. "We're gonna get caught. That would be really dumb."

Lennie caved.

"Yeh. Okay. Let's go. Say what's that you got?"

"The game. You said I could have it."

"It's Scrabble, Dummy. It's a spelling game."

"You can teach me," Butch said plaintively.

"Take the damn game," Lennie grumbled.

Aleta felt the RV shake as the two tramped down the steps. She hurried into the bedroom and opened the closet and with trembling hands, dug her cell phone from her jacket pocket.

She opened it and pressed 'contact'. She stared at the name that was lit.

Not Stanley, she noticed. Her finger must have tapped on the screen accidentally. The light showed 'Arborville Police Chief Lyle West'

She had memorized pressing twice so that's what she did. She pressed the center button and Lyle's number came up. The rest was easy. She pressed 'send' and listened for the ring.

Then she put the phone down and dried herself off. Hastily, she began to dress. Her mind said hurry, so she put on the blouse she had decided wasn't going to wear again. She was too flustered to make choices. She had to concentrate on remaining mute. There was a bomb in their RV.

Tank had calmed down but she didn't dare open the door. There could be clues.

Lyle's knock was light. Aleta slipped out of the bedroom and opened the outside door.

She held up two fingers.

"Two," he guessed. "Two what? Are you sure you wanted me?"

She nodded and pointed at Scooby.

"Dogs? Two dogs are loose?"

Aleta shook her head. In the opened kitchen drawer, she spotted a pack of cards. She took it out, extracted two jacks and set them on the counter.

"A pair of jacks," Lyle said. "Two men?"

She nodded. Then she pointed at the open drawers.

"You were robbed?"

Again she nodded.

"Where were you?"

She put her hands over her eyes.

"Hiding? Where?"

She pointed at the bathroom. Lyle noticed her hair was still wet.

"You were taking a shower?"

Aleta nodded. Then she cupped her hand behind one ear.

"They talked and you heard them?"

She nodded her head vigorously.

"Did they use names?"

Another nod told him that they had.

Back at ringside, Stanley had seen Lyle look at his cell phone and then leave Lauren's side. He leaned back to speak to Lauren who was sitting on the right side in back of him and asked, "Anything wrong?"

"He just said he had to check something back at camp," Lauren responded, annoyed. "He never lets go of that job of his."

Stanley settled back and thought about what would pull Lyle away from his wife. He pulled out his cell to see if he'd missed a message from Aleta. He hadn't.

Then he remembered that Aleta hadn't been able to handle scrolling down the list of contacts and he relaxed. She hadn't called Lyle. Ed and Beatrice moved into seats behind Stanley as the Terrier Group was ending. They always stood or sat behind someone so Belle wouldn't see them and be distracted. Stanley didn't dare move.

Tom Wilson took a first with Belle and Stanley turned around and congratulated Ed and Beatrice.

"I need to get Tank," he said and rushed off.

When he arrived at the RV parking area, he saw Scooby in the pen outside his RV. When he saw Lyle come out of his R, he broke into a run. Lyle spotted him. So did Aleta. She ran to him.

"She's fine," Lyle told him. "You were robbed. Stay out of your RV."

Aleta touched her neck with her free hand and he knew the robbers had found the necklace.

"I was going to surprise you tonight," Stanley said. "A gift to remember something special."

Aleta raised a brow in query.

"You always do something special," he said. "It was an emerald. Not quite as lovely as you are. Thank heaven they missed my real jewel. Where were you by the way?"

She fluttered her fingers as she raised and lowered her hand.

"In the shower?"

Lyle joined them.

"She heard them talking so we need to get that information from her, but right now I need to process your RV, so if you'll go show Tank and let me work, I'd appreciate it."

"Should I fetch Hawk?" Stanley asked.

"It's his day off," Lyle said tersely. "Now go. No talk of this until after the show. I won't have the local cops disrupting the final events."

"But shouldn't we start a search right away?" Stanley asked.

Aleta shook her head.

She heard them," Lyle said. "Your RV was their target. They're long gone."

Stanley looked at Tank standing inside the exercise pen.

"He looks all tuckered out."

Aleta pointed toward the rear of the RV.

"He was in the bedroom?" Stanley asked.

Aleta pantomimed the dog pawing at the door. She lifted her lip and Stanley got the picture.

"Poor guy," he said. "Tired and frustrated."

Stanley stroked his head, telling him what a good dog he was. Slowly, Tank responded.

Aleta picked up his front paw and checked his nails. One was bleeding.

Aleta went into her grandmother's RV and fetched the styptic pen and grabbed Stoney's show collar and lead.

"Where do I put this?" Stanley asked holding up Tank's breakaway collar.

"On the counter," Aleta responded. "Stoney won't touch it."

Stanley opened the door and threw the collar on the counter. He didn't see it slide off, but Stoney did. Anything on the floor was fair game.

Stanley and Tank made it in time for the Hound Group. Stanley could tell that Tank was flagging.

When he circled the ring after the individual examination and wound up behind Tom Wilson and Rufus, Tom mentioned that Tank seemed a bit off.

"He is," Stanley said. "Tell you about it later."

The final cut of six included both Tank and Rufus. Even on an off day, Tank was prepossessing in appearance.

Tank looked around for Aleta. Stanley recognized that his dog was still worried about her. He talked to him softly.

"She's okay now. You did your job. You're a good boy."

The last words brought Tank's head around just as the judge surveyed those that had made the cut. He had them circle the ring once.

Rufus who was last in line took the Group. The giant Irish Wolfhound took a fourth beating out a Bloodhound and a Saluki.

Aleta met him outside the ring and hugged Tank.

"It's quite a dog you chose for me. Have I thanked you enough?" Stanley asked.

Aleta grinned impishly and shook her head lightly.

The Toy Group moved into the ring and Aleta went back to her seat to watch her grandmother show Auggie. The Pug was keyed up and took first hands down.

Stanley sat down to watch the Best in Show competition. Tank lay at his feet. Exhausted, the big dog put his head on Stanley's shoe and fell asleep. He didn't stir when Aleta rose and lined up with Maggie for the final competition of the day.

As the dogs filed into the ring, Stanley rubbed his aching thigh. Would that old bullet wound never heal, he wondered.

He noticed that Lyle had returned to the empty seat beside his wife. George Sciretta moved into Aleta's seat because he wanted to be next to someone who would root for his dog.

Stanley's loyalties were divided. Aleta's grandmother was showing Auggie beautifully. He stood out in Stanley's mind. He wondered if he stood out in anyone else's.

Claude leaned over.

"Harriet looks good, doesn't she?"

Stanley nodded.

George Sciretta whispered in his other ear. "Does Maggie have a good chance?"

"She's one of the best in the ring," Stanley said honestly.

George nodded.

In the ring, Judge Melvin Roberts surveyed the group gathered for the biggest prize of the day. He recognized three top handlers and two long-time breeders he's seen many times. He wondered briefly if this was the Golden that had won two Best in Shows out of the Veteran class.

There were two women in the ring that were new to him. They could be sisters were it not for the age difference. He crossed them both off the list.

After examining the Saint, Judge Roberts felt he had his winner. He smiled at Chuck Rigden who then knew he was in contention.

Judge Roberts gave Topaz a good look. He was a beauty. It helped that he had won twice. Evelyn could tell that the judge liked Topaz and this fact energized her. Topaz sensed that he was pleasing her. He began to sparkle and the judge knew then he was going to have tough decision to make.

When Aleta brought Maggie up for her individual examination, she moved in front of her without checking her stack. An amateur, Judge Roberts thought until he found that the dog was in perfect stack. She either lucked out or she knew her business. The Bulldog's movement was free flowing and Roberts realized that he couldn't dismiss her either.

Tom Wilson waited for the table and set his Scottie on it using his foot to steady it.

Another really deserving dog, Roberts thought. He couldn't find a fault in the alert, little black terrier. Her movement was as good as her structure.

Rufus was next. Madge had seen Tom steady the table with his foot and she did the same. Rufus was enjoying the limelight and he was as sparkly as Belle had been.

This is going to be tough, Robert concluded. He now had five that were equal in his eyes. Only the herding dog hadn't impressed him.

At least it won't be six Roberts thought as the gray-haired woman approached. Instead of putting the dog on the table, she put her hand on it and then reached down and actually adjusted the leg. She tested it again before setting her Pug on it. Auggie stood like a rock while he was being examined. The judge finished and stepped back. He found that the woman had waited for his signal to move the dog. She had given him time to study her Pug. She was no amateur. He's a winner, Judge Roberts thought.

When all had been judged, Roberts walked down the line. He paused at the Saint and then at the Golden whose sparkle was still evident. The Bulldog had begun to flag a bit. The heat was taking her down. The Scottie got a long look, as did the Dachshund. The Pug jumped out of line, demanding attention. The judge walked back and looked at the Golden. He was a splendid old chap, one he would have been proud to own. Then he walked back to the Pug. There was no denying such quality. His eye roamed back up the line to the Saint and he remembered that he was another almost perfect dog. It was a short distance from there to the Golden.

There he stood, the sun glistening on his rich golden coat, every inch of him striving to please the elderly woman at the other end of the lead. The judge knew that this particular Golden had won two Best in Shows. He kept track of such things. A win today from a breeder-judge would put a final stamp of approval not only on a superb Golden, but also on the woman who bred him. Today was the day to honor a lifetime of achievement.

Topaz won.

As the group neared the RV parking area, Stanley mentioned to Harriet that Tank's collar was inside her RV.

"Tank's wearing Stoney's," he explained.

Then he told her about the robbery and Lyle commandeering his RV.

When they arrived at the RV parking area, Stanley put Tank in the pen with Scooby without removing Stoney's collar from Tank's neck. Harriet entered her RV to fetch Tank's collar so they could switch.

She came out a few minutes later and shrugged, "I can't find Tank's collar.

Aleta went in to look. She also emerged empty-handed.

Hawk, who entered the area with Paige, heard the two women discussing what Stoney could have done with the collar.

"Send Scooby in to find it," Hawk suggested. "He seems to have a liking for Tank's collar."

"He likes taking it off Tank's neck," Harriet noted.

"He and Tank are in the same pen and he hasn't taken the new collar off," Hawk pointed out.

"He smells Stoney's smell on it," Harriet explained.

"I don't think that's what's going on," Hawk said. "Aleta, so you have any of those training biscuits?"

Aleta entered her grandmother's RV while Harriet was taking Stoney outside and putting him in his pen. Stanley took Scooby out of his pen and walked him over to Aleta who took him to the door of her grandmother's RV, opened it and waved at him to enter. He bounded up the stairs and disappeared inside the RV. The gathering crowd conversed in quiet murmurs. Scooby's scratching could be heard.

"Aleta, is he tearing up my RV?" Harriet asked.

Aleta shrugged.

"I don't want it torn up," Harriet complained.

Aleta blew her a kiss.

Her grandmother frowned.

"That doesn't work any more."

Aleta eyed her grandmother skeptically.

"Alright. All right. Stoney didn't put it where we could find it. I guess he buried it."

A minute later, Scooby bounced out of the RV and hurried toward Aleta, the torn collar hanging from his mouth.

"I guess Stoney chewed on it a bit too," Harriet admitted.

Scooby sat in front of Aleta who took the collar from him and gave him a biscuit.

"May I have it?" Hawk asked.

Aleta handed it to him.

"Since it's been chewed on, may I take it apart to examine it?"

Aleta nodded.

The local police arrived. Chief West went to greet them. Stanley snuck into his RV for his badge and gun. The gun was gone. He opened the drawer where the Scrabble game was kept. It was gone too.

He approached Chief West without thinking.

"It's gone," he blurted out, interrupting Sergeant Mopes' tirade. "The Scrabble game. It's gone."

Aleta nodded and Stanley saw her response.

"They took it?" Stanley asked, shocked.

She nodded sadly.

"That's stupid!" Mopes blurted out. "No one steals a Scrabble game."

Aleta pointed to a child.

"A child?" Stanley asked.

Aleta pointed to her head.

"A child in the head," Stanley said. "A retarded man."

Aleta nodded.

"Dummy and Lennie?" Stanley guessed. "Of course. They're keeping track of us. They figured we were easy enough marks before."

Aleta was nodding vigorously. She made a stretching mark with her hands as one does in the game of Charades.

"You know Dummy's name?" Stanley asked.

Aleta nodded.

"Why worry about the Scrabble game being gone?" Mopes questioned. "She can type out the letters."

"She can't," Stanley responded. "I can't explain why but something's wrong with her visual transmission of information. The Scrabble tiles have letters that can be felt so she can spell using them.

Hawk came trotting over and burst into the conversation as usual.

"Boy, am I glad you didn't talk just. . ."

"You mean she can speak?" Mopes charged.

"Be glad she didn't," Hawk said. "There wasn't much C-4 left, but there was enough to blow us all to kingdom come."

"Where?" Mopes challenged.

Hawk held up the collar.

"Put it down," Mopes shouted. "And call the bomb squad."

"Here's the trigger," Hawk said, holding up a plastic bag.

"So the dogs are trained," Stanley commented.

"At least partly," Hawk said.

Aleta tugged Stanley's sleeve. She pointed to the RV.

"They talked about the bomb in the RV?" Stanley guessed.

Aleta nodded vigorously and then put her hands over her eyes.

"Hidden," Stanley interpreted.

Aleta nodded and again asked him to expand on the word.

"Well-hidden."

Aleta asked for more.

"So well-hidden no one would ever find it?" he guessed.

Aleta clapped her hands excitedly. She turned to Hawk and pointed to her RV.

"You want me to look?" he asked.

She nodded.

"Hey, wait a minute," Mopes said. "Forensics hasn't done a workup yet."

"What do you need?" Hawk asked.

"Who are you?" Mopes grumped.

"A forensic expert," Hawk said. "I will get whatever you need."

"I lifted prints off the drawers and knobs," West said. "Aleta knows the names of the robbers. We need a Scrabble game so she can spell them out."

"The Chesneys have one in their RV," Hawk said. "Don't play against Paige. She's a whiz."

"She beats you?" Lyle asked.

"She beats everyone," Hawk exclaimed, his pride in this ability of his wife obvious.

After a moment's pause, Hawk sobered and asked the local police officer if he could enter the RV since West had already printed it.

"If there's a bomb, we need to call real experts," Mopes said, eager to put down someone in the Illinois group.

"Voice-activated," Hawk said. "As long as Aleta doesn't speak, we're safe."

"That's dumb!" Mopes protested. "There are safe places."

Claude broke it. "That's what I said this morning. We were swimming in the middle of the lake. Who knew. . ."

"Knew what?"

"The dog that was swimming alongside us was wearing that collar with the bomb," Claude finished. "I'm alive because she didn't take a chance."

Hawk spoke up. "May I take the dogs into your RV with me, one at a time. They may be able to show me where to look."

Aleta nodded.

Stanley took Aleta aside. "I'll take care of the dogs. You go into the Chesney's RV with Lyle and spell out the names."

Aleta nodded.

Stanley turned to Sergeant Mopes. "She'll give you the names of the robbers if you'll follow her.'"

"Okay, Hawk," Stanley said. "Lets see if we can find number four."

Once inside with Scooby, Stanley shut the door and let Scooby off lead. Scooby immediately put two paws on the counter and looked up at the top of the cabinet.

"We put the collar up there last night," Stanley mentioned.

Hawk nodded. Stanley didn't say anything more. He stood on the bottom step of the RV and leaned against the door. He rubbed his thigh where he'd been shot.

Hawk sat in the passenger's seat, which he swiveled around to face the interior.

Neither man moved or spoke for several minutes. Scooby never moved.

Finally Hawk broke the silence.

"Reward the dog," he said.

"He didn't do anything."

"Yes, he did," Hawk said quietly.

Stanley pulled a bacon biscuit from the tin and, petting Scooby, said, "Good dog."

He offered him the biscuit and Scooby went back down on all fours and gulped it down with only a couple of quick chews.

Tank was next.

Once released from his pen, Tank headed straight for the open RV door.

Stanley closed the door. Tank immediately went to Hawk and sniffed him.

"Find it," Stanley said.

It was the order he gave during training. He wasn't even sure Tank would respond. With Scooby who had been sent into Harriet's RV to find Tank's collar and then been rewarded, hunting in a second RV would seem like another exercise. Tank had been brought in cold.

"Find it," Stanley said one more time.

This time Tank left their visitor and meandered over to the kitchen counter in front of the window. He stood on his hind legs and stretched his neck trying to reach what was obviously just above him.

Hawk studied Tank for several minutes and then ordered Stanley to reward him.

Stanley did as he was told without argument.

After Stanley put up Tank, he returned and stood quietly on the bottom step, back against the door.

"I need a ladder and a tool kit," Hawk said.

Stanley returned a couple minutes later with a small stepladder and a tool kit. Lyle slipped in the door and closed it behind him.

"You got the names?" Stanley asked.

Lyle nodded.

"Mopes is gone."

"Stanley, tell him what the dogs did and see if he can figure it out," Hawk suggested.

Stanley stared at Hawk.

"You mean you know where it is?"

Hawk nodded.

Stanley told Lyle where both dogs had stood and where their noses pointed. The two men guessed several places and discarded them all.

"They were specific," Hawk said. "That's why I had them point for so long."

"I thought you just wanted to see if they were serious," Stanley remarked.

"Serious?" Lyle snickered.

Stanley shot an annoyed glance at his best friend and snapped, "Don't snicker. You haven't figured it out either."

"Obviously you've bested us, Hawk," West conceded.

"That wasn't what I meant to do."

"Of course you did," Lyle said.

Hawk smiled.

"I don't want you to think I'm not valuable."

"For Pete's sake, Hawk, where is it?"

Hawk came over and took the same position Tank took.

"I'm looking at it," he said.

"You're looking at the corner between the cabinet and the wall," Lyle said.

"I told you," Stanley said. "It's on top of the cabinet."

"Lying in plain view?" Lyle scoffed.

"Disguised somehow?"

"What else is up there?" Hawk prompted.

"The top edge of the blind," Lyle said.

"Nothing else?"

"There's the light," Lyle mentioned off-handedly.

"Finally!" Hawk exclaimed.

"The light?" Lyle questioned, flipping the switch. "But it works and I don't see any dark glob of anything."

"That's what the dogs were pointing at," Hawk affirmed.

"Then the dogs were wrong," Lyle avowed strongly.

"Take down the light," Stanley said. "I would never have believed Tank's collar could have been wired."

"The C-4 was stuck under the closed buckle," Hawk said. "Because you slipped the collar on and off without unbuckling it, even I didn't think to look there at first."

Lyle scrambled up the ladder and called for a screwdriver. He removed the long florescent bulb and handed it down. Then he unscrewed the fixture and carried it down.

The C-4 had been pressed flat against one end of the fixture and the wire that would carry the charge was almost unnoticeable. The wire stretched from a small metal object attached to the backside of one of the ends of the bulb holder.

"My word!" Stanley exclaimed. "This guy is clever,"

"I'll go over your house on Monday," Hawk said. "I know you and Aleta will be here taking care of Tontine business, but I could use a dog."

"I guess we could send one home with you," Stanley said.

"Come to think of it, scratch that idea. We haven't room in our car and Paige needs Topper if I'm called away at night, " Hawk said. "But Topper is a smart dog. Could you and Harriet train him as you trained Tank?"

"When?"

"Maybe tonight Topper and I could join you."

Stanley agreed quickly and then suggested that Paige handle Topper so Hawk would be free to consider the places Topper pointed out when they searched his house.

"Paige would enjoy that," Hawk declared.

CHAPTER 21

After the barbecue at the RV area that evening, Harriet took her four students with their three dogs to a section of the fairgrounds where the stables were located. The smell of manure and hay mingled to remind everyone that horses lived there when races were held. For Tank and Scooby the smell was familiar. Topper found it excitingly new.

Harriet had Paige take him around to process the myriad of new smells while she set up an advanced training exercise for the other two dogs.

After she ran Tank and Scooby through their exercises, Paige was eager to try Topper.

Harriet put the C-4 back in the sock and put the sock on top of the bucket and Paige walked Topper to it. Harriet picked it up and tossed it.

"Go get it," Paige yelled. Topper ran out to it and stood over the sock, staring at it, puzzled.

"Quick!" Harriet said. "Run out and reward him."

To Harriet's delight, Paige obeyed instantly.

Topper was praised and fed a piece of a dog biscuit while he was standing over the sock."

"Now pick it up and tell him 'good boy' again," Harriet instructed.

"We're rewarding the behavior incrementally, aren't we?" Paige asked.

"You are a quick study, Paige. Just remember that Topper doesn't have your background."

"Can we do it again?"

"We'll vary it each time until he'll search for the sock without seeing me toss it."

A short time later, after Topper seemed to have mastered the lesson, Harriet said, "Stanley, we need Topper to know which smell he's searching for. Take off your socks."

"What?"

"It'll smell like you, not me." Harriet said matter-of-factly. I'll have you put it out where Topper's been finding the other items."

"I can go back to the RV and get a fresh pair," Stanley said.

"I want the ones you're wearing."

"Both of them?"

"One will have the C-4. The other will be a decoy."

"Why not use Hawk's"

"We're not trying to teach Topper to fetch Hawk's sock," Harriet snapped. "Come on. Surely, you've put your shoes on without socks before?"

"Never." Stanley said.

Aleta giggled, but Harriet didn't stop.

"Enjoy the experience."

Grumbling, Stanley kicked off his shoes and removed his socks. He held them out to her.

She refused to take them. She had Stanley fish out the packet of C-4 and drop it into one of his socks and then tie a knot above it. Then she told him to tie a knot in the other sock, and drop both socks in the area where the others had been.

"I'm barefoot," he complained.

Aleta sat down, took is foot, rubbed it on her jeans and stuck it in his shoe.

"You never do any thing in a conventional manner, do you?" he griped.

She tied his shoelace and grabbed his other foot. He was silent until she finished.

"Now that you've thoroughly embarrassed me, are you happy?"

The training session continued. By the end, Topper seemed to have gotten the idea that presenting something containing C-4 earned one a treat.

"Stay overnight tomorrow night," Stanley suggested. "We can give Topper another lesson tomorrow after the show on the lawn in front of the lodge. You already have a room there tonight."

"We have to leave for home as soon as the show is over tomorrow," Hawk said. "I have to be at work at eight."

"Harriet is going on a circuit from here. She won't be available to give Topper another lesson at home," Stanley said. "Your Newf is doing so well."

"We could leave early Monday morning," Paige suggested.

"Aren't you scheduled to spend the day at my house?" Stanley asked.

"Yes, but that doesn't mean I can be late."

"You already spent hours on the case this weekend. Log in those hours. I'd appreciate it if you began the search of my place with a better trained dog."

"It's true I have put in a couple of hours," Hawk agreed.

"Include dog training time."

"I can't do that. I'm taking a flyer."

"It's not an untested theory. Because our dogs were partly trained, you found two more bombs. Training your own dog is tantamount to buying a piece of complicated equipment that you need for your job and then taking the time to learn how to use it."

"I can see why you're considered a top-flight lawyer," Hawk remarked. "You argue well."

"So, you're leaving after breakfast on Monday?"

"I'll pass it by Lyle."

Paige squealed delightedly and ran off.

"Where is she going?" Stanley asked.

"Pretend she's your wife."

"Do you need Lyle's permission?" Stanley asked. "I thought you were autonomous."

"I am."

"So why ask Lyle?"

"To see if he agrees with you."

"And if he doesn't?"

"Paige will persuade him."

That evening Paige and Hawk found themselves alone at the lodge. Everyone else were in their RV's parked on the show grounds.

The young couple sat on the porch swing and gazed at the moonlight sparkling on the glass-like smoothness of the water. The breeze was slight and the coolness of the night was creeping in at a snail's pace.

"Nice night for a swim," Paige said. "I'm still hot."

"What about Topper?" Hawk said. "I imagine he's hot too."

"He can come with us."

"Wasn't he bathed just for the show?"

"He worked hard tonight. He deserves a reward."

"They have a tub for dog's here," Hawk said. "In fact they have a whole room."

"All the members of the Tontine show dogs," Paige said. "We can wash him after we swim. They'll have stuff we need."

"Let's change," Hawk said.

"Ever gone skinny dipping?" Paige said, pulling off her tee shirt.

"No. And I don't want to."

"I think it'd be fun," Paige said, stepping out of her jeans. "Go get your suit on. Topper and I will be in the water waiting for you."

"You can't go alone. You're not that good a swimmer yet."

"I'll have Topper with me," Paige said. "He can rescue me."

Hawk hurried after her, peeling off his shirt as he went.

The lodge had no close neighbors. There was no one watching them. He's always thought it would be fun. He guessed part of the fun was doing it on a whim.

By the time Hawk had reached the shore, Paige was already in the water. He joined her minutes later. With strong strokes, he caught her quickly. He grabbed her and his touch stopped her.

"You want to play out here?' she asked.

"Why not?" Hawk joshed. "We're dressed for it."

Topper's head came between them.

Paige laughed. "This is going to be fun."

The three stayed in the water for a long time. Topper had a variety of moves that kept the two apart to Hawk's dismay and Paige's delight.

When they finally emerged, spent and cool, they lay naked on the grass and stared at the cloudless sky. Topper shook himself several times and then lay down beside them, content with himself. They all fell asleep.

When they woke, they found each other. Quietly they joined while Topper slept on.

Afterward, he followed them into the lodge. Then to the big Newfoundland's amazement, they washed him, giggling and laughing as they did so. They toweled him dry and then used the blower.

They went upstairs together. Hawk set the alarm and checked it twice. All three slept soundly straight through the alarm.

When they finally woke up, Paige hurried outside to air Topper while Hawk showered and shaved. When she returned, Paige headed straight for the shower. Topper followed her into the bathroom dragging the opened yellow suitcase by its handle.

"What's with the suitcase?" Hawk said, wiping the last bit of shaving cream from his face.

"Oh, Topper," Paige sighed. "Not the suitcase."

Topper let go of the handle and sat beside the case, wagging his tail.

Paige ruffled his ears.

"I know you were trying to be helpful, but I can find my own clothes."

"That won't be hard to do," Hawk noted. "They're all on the floor. Has he done that before?"

"I used to carry everything in paper bags," Paige said. "But we didn't reward him for fetching yesterday, just pointing."

"I wonder," Hawk murmured.

"Wonder what?"

"Who gave you the suitcase?"

"I told you that Harriet did. It's one of Aleta's cases that Stanley said she wouldn't use anymore because it would remind her of her mother."

"You didn't tell me all that."

"You think that Topper could smell Stanley's scent on it?"

"Something like that," Hawk said cagily.

Paige, busy picking up her clothes, replied as if her supposition were true. "We need another lesson for sure."

"We're staying until after breakfast tomorrow," Hawk answered.

"When were you going to tell me?"

"So Lyle told you it was up to me," Hawk smiled.

"Yes, he did. He said you were your own boss."

"I think I told you that."

"Well, yes, you did. But I though you meant that you ran the lab. I didn't know you ran yourself too."

"Now you do."

"Does that mean we can . . ." Paige started and then stopped. "Is our honeymoon over?"

"Why?"

"Well, after the honeymoon, you can't do it more than once a day."

"Our honeymoon isn't over then," Hawk said.

Topper whined. He was still holding the suitcase handle in his mouth.

"Give him a biscuit," Paige said. "There a box on the dresser."

Hawk went to the dresser and took a biscuit out of the box.

He took the suitcase, saying "Good boy."

Then he handed Topper the biscuit and shoved him out of the room.

The two heard Topper flop on the floor outside their door.

"We may be locked in here for all eternity," Hawk quipped.

"Or until I say the word 'biscuit'," Paige whispered.

They made love quietly, but Topper whined outside the door.

Paige laughed when they had finished.

"I guess we better take him to the dog show."

"He's got to not do that." Hawk said.

"I'll find out what others did."

"You can't ask anyone."

"Of course, I can. Most of the people we know have dogs and enjoy sex. I'm not the only pregnant one in our group. I'll be circumspect."

"How late are we?"

"If we hurry, we'll be in time for the Chessies, the Newfs and the Showmanship classes.

"We won't have missed a thing."

"Nothing as important as what we did," Paige commented.

"You, my dear Paige, are every man's dream."

Paige blushed prettily.

CHAPTER 22

Sunday morning began for Aleta when Tom Wilson, Chuck Rigden and George Sciretta knocked on the door to the Praetzel RV.

Aleta and Stanley were lying on their backs in bed wondering if they should get up at all. They were both enjoying the afterglow of a most satisfactory coupling and neither wanted to move.

"Did we oversleep?" Stanley asked.

Aleta flipped her hand over.

"They under slept, is that it?"

She poked him.

"I'm not going. They want to see you."

She rose and gestured. Stanley knew she was asking, "Like this?"

"Better you than me." Stanley quipped.

She started for the door.

He yelled, "Aleta, put on your robe."

The three outside laughingly shouted. "Aleta, don't!"

Aleta stormed back into the bedroom and threw Stanley's robe at him.

"Okay," he said. "I'll go with you."

When Aleta opened the door, Tom came up the steps. Chuck and George crowded in behind him.

"We're glad you're not dressed," Tom said. "George has a surprise for you."

George held out a jewelry box and handed it to Aleta.

Aleta opened it slowly. Her eyes widened when she saw what was inside. Tears came to her eyes as she touched her sapphire necklace.

Stanley lifted it from the box and put it around her neck. Aleta patted it as if unable to believe it was real.

"Thank you," Stanley said, his voice choked with emotion.

"It's back where it belongs," Tom observed.

"You aren't afraid to wear it?" Chuck asked.

"It wasn't show people," Stanley observed.

A short time later, Claude told Stanley that the weatherman predicted a big storm moving in.

"Before the barbecue?" Stanley asked, knowing that was what Claude was worried about.

"I've got my fingers crossed."

Many of the dogs attached to the Illinois contingent did as well on Sunday and they had the day before. But this day was not going to be a repeat.

The major change was born in the Newfoundland ring when Paige presented Topper for his individual examination. Judge Downing had assessed the young dog on the first go-around as a well-balanced dog.

When Paige presented Topper for his individual examination, Judge Downing felt the coat and said, "Feels natural."

"We went skinny dipping last night," Paige blurted out. "And Topper refused to take off his coat, so it got wet."

"Hmm," Judge Downing smiled. "A Newf in the water. Imagine that?"

"They are water dogs," Paige said politely.

Judge Downing kept smiling.

"Is he a good swimmer?"

"We stayed in the water a long time and he never left us," Paige rushed on. "I think he was hoping one of us would drown so he could rescue someone."

"He feels clean."

"We rinsed him off," Paige said giggling. "He was so surprised. I think he thought we were nuts."

"I'll bet he did," Judge Downing said. "Move him up and back please."

Paige took the class and then the points.

"I like the feel of a natural coat," the judge told her when he handed her the purple ribbon.

"We were afraid that we'd ruined his chances," Paige returned. "But we couldn't go swimming in a lake without him. It wouldn't be right."

All four of the Newf specials were good dogs and when the class puppy beat them for the Breed win, there were murmurs of surprise from the gallery and grumblings from the owners of the losers.

The handlers congratulated Paige warmly. They recognized how big a win this was for a neophyte.

"What did I do right?" Paige asked the judge bluntly.

"You let your dog go swimming with you. You renewed his spirit."

The handlers overheard the comment.

Paige's win was the hot topic at lunch. A puppy taking the Breed over four professionally handled Specials surprised them all.

When Tom joined the group, they plied him with questions. Instead of answering, he asked Paige, "What did you say when the judge asked you about his coat?"

"Just that we let him swim with us."

"You made a joke," Tom pressed.

"It wasn't proper," Paige demurred.

Now everyone was listening.

"Go on Paige, tell them," Hawk urged. "It's actually funny."

Paige hesitated and then said. "I told him we'd gone skinny dipping and Topper refused to take of his coat so he got it wet."

The whole group laughed.

"Was that what did it?" Evelyn asked, unsatisfied. She had scolded Paige when she first saw Topper that morning.

"He said he liked the feel of a natural coat," Paige said.

"They all say that," Evelyn said. "But this would be the first time I've known a judge to act on it."

"I think Paige has her hands on a superior dog," Tom Wilson pronounced soberly. "And she showed him well. He was in high spirits this morning and I think Downing was saying he gives spirit higher marks than coat sheen. Topper, however, does have a great natural coat."

"We can fix the coat before Group," Evelyn said.

"I wouldn't," Tom said. "If Downing told Paige's story to Jott, Jott will be expecting an untouched coat."

Paige nodded solemnly. She understood.

Evelyn, however, didn't.

"I know what Tom is saying," Evelyn told Paige later. "But judges don't remember jokes told over lunch. However, they do mark off for every little fault in the Group ring. All Jott will see is that Topper's coat isn't as brilliant as it could be."

"I think I will take Tom's advice," Paige said firmly. "But just this one time. Otherwise I will do as you say."

Mollified by the last remark, Evelyn hugged her.

"Don't let me spoil the fact that you won. Tom said you're a good handler. You beat four pros which proves you did a lot of things right and Topper seems in such high spirits."

"We had so much fun in the lake last night," Paige said. "It was like we were on our honeymoon still."

The first drops of rain fell as the afternoon competition began. The show committee announced the delay so the rings could be set up indoors.

Hawk left Paige with the clean up and knocked on Lyle's door. The rain had begun to come down hard so Hawk stepped into the tiny living room and the two men sat down.

"I think we have a problem," Hawk started.

"Lyle smiled. "In what area?"

Hawk looked surprised.

Lyle knew Hawk's mind was on work, but he thought he'd tease him a bit.

"When they move indoors, sometimes the Group rings are smaller," Lyle said. "But I think Topper will still be able to run more than two paces."

Hawk frowned slightly as he mentally brushed West's comment aside.

"I think the bombs are scattered."

Lyle sat bolt upright.

"Scattered?"

"I'm almost positive one was planted in the suitcase Aleta loaned to Paige. Topper brought it to us last night and he expected a reward. It could be that he was watching Scooby being rewarded for fetching and was trying that trick, but the bomber is clever. Why not put some in items Aleta might take with her?"

"I assume you had planned to test your theory tonight," Lyle said.

"If it's pouring outside, we would have to do it inside," Hawk said. "I don't want to panic everyone."

"Trust your dog," Lyle said.

"You're okay with that?" Hawk asked.

"Absolutely."

"Other items might have been taken from the house," Hawk said. "I can ask Stanley, but I hate to tell Aleta she won't be safe until we track them all down."

"She knows that."

"It might take weeks or months."

"Stanley has told me that she has already figured that out," Lyle responded.

"I'll talk to them tonight," Hawk said.

At that moment, several hundred miles south, beyond the edge of the current storm that was assailing the fairgrounds in Minnesota, Lennie Archer and Butch Lennert entered a pawnshop on the southwest side of Chicago and showed the proprietor their newest acquisition.

Rather than being either surprised or delighted on being offered such a fine piece, Sid Kachman blew.

"You guys know who you're stealing from?" he lashed out.

Taken aback, Lennie shoved the emerald necklace under the metal grid that separated the proprietor from his irate customers.

"Why do you care?" Lennie spat out. "The necklace is good."

"I should've known better than to deal with a couple of hicks," Kachman growled, starting to shove the necklace back and then changing his mind.

"Don't you go calling us no names," Butch threatened.

"It's only because I told them you were a couple of dumb hicks that nobody is gunning for you."

"Lennie, he called us dumb. You gonna let him do that?" Butch blustered.

He wanted Lennie to show him the gun. People respected guns.

But Lennie was hearing a warning.

"Why does anyone want to kill us? All we did was heist a couple of pieces from some rich guys."

"The ones you robbed," Kachman spat out. "They're connected."

"Naw," Lennie protested. "That can't be. We didn't rob a member of no family."

"They aren't family. They're special," Kachman said. "I had to let go the damn necklace. I'm out the six bills I gave you."

"That was dumb. It was worth twice what you gave me," Lennie argued.

"You don't get it, do you?" Kachman snapped. "You're pissing off some guys nobody pisses off that wants to live."

"I think you're trying to scare us so we'll take less for this necklace," Lennie charged.

"Yeh," Butch joined in. "We don't scare. Show him the gun, Lennie."

Kachman paled.

"You got a gun?"

"Yeh. He's got a gun. Took it off that guy we robbed."

"Look, Boys, there's no reason to come at me. I protected you."

"So, how much for this piece?" Lennie asked with as much cool as he could muster.

"I'll take it off your hands and tell Vannella you saw the light and want to return it."

"What light?" Butch asked. "Lennie, what's he saying. Isn't he gonna pay us?"

"He don't want to, but he is," Lennie said.

He pulled out the gun.

Kachman grabbed the emerald necklace and ducked down underneath his counter. He opened his cell and punched in a number and said two words, "They're here."

"Get the hell up and give us the damned necklace," Lennie demanded.

Butch rattled the metal grid separating them from Kachman.

"If you're smart, you'll leave," Kachman shouted from his niche under the counter.

"Not without my necklace," Lennie growled.

"I called them. They're coming," Kachman shot back. "Leave while you can."

"You're bluffing. You didn't call nobody," Lennie barked. "Now give me the necklace."

"I can't. They'll kill me."

"Shoot him, Lennie," Butch yelled.

"Hand it up," Lennie demanded. "Or I'll put some bullets right through that counter you think is bulletproof."

"It is," Kachman said. "And if you shoot, you'll bring the cops. Just get the hell out of here while you can."

"I'm not leaving without my necklace," Lennie declared.

Butch rattled the metal grating.

"We want our necklace."

"You can't sell it. The word's out," Kachman said.

"You're lying, you sonofabitch. You give it up or we'll come back when you ain't hiding and get it and more besides."

"No, you won't," said a voice from behind.

Lennie and Butch spun around. The two big men facing them had guns. Kachman's head came up as Lennie gave up his piece.

"These the ones you called about?" Maloney asked.

"Yeh," Kachman said. "They tried to hock another necklace. And they took that gun from the guy too."

Maloney pocketed the gun and held out his hand.

"I'll take the necklace."

Kachman slipped it under the grid.

"Don't do anything in here. You'll bring the cops," Kachman said.

"We ain't going to kill them. The boss wants some information. We only aim to get them ready to cooperate."

By the time Vannella arrived at one of his empty offices, both Butch and Lennie had received numerous kidney punches to let them know that they had screwed up royally.

When Sergio Vannella arrived, Maloney handed over the emerald necklace and Stanley's gun and told his boss that he had heard Lennie threaten Kachman because he wouldn't hand over the necklace.

"Did Kachman explain that these are special people?" Vannella asked.

"He said something like that," Lennie grunted.

Vannella nodded.

"Let's move on. Word has it you're involved in the bomb threat against Aleta Praetzel. Is that true?"

Vannella's eyes moved from Lennie to Butch. The latter caved in under the glare and begged not to be hit no more.

"Butch, shut the hell up!" Lennie yelled.

The fist that plowed into Lennie's face broke two front teeth. It had been fitted with brass knuckles. Lennie sank to the floor, blood gushing from his mouth.

Vannella turned to Lennie's partner.

"Okay, Butch, tell me who is behind this bombing plot."

"He'll kill me," Butch declared.

"And you don't think I will?" Vannella charged.

"He's crazy. You ain't," Butch stated with a clarity that shocked Lennie.

Vannella nodded and Maloney hit Lennie in the face again.

"What did you do that for?" Butch protested.

"I want the name."

Butch gave in.

"Stu."

"Stu what?"

"Just Stu," Butch said.

"Who else?"

"Lukas and Doyle and Lennie and me," Butch rattled, and then added, "Doyle's mom was there but she mostly fed us. She don't know anything."

"Where are the bombs?"

"I dunno," Butch said.

Lennie was punched again. This time he cried out. "He don't know. None of us knows."

"You personally planted the one in the RV," Vannella snarled.

Lennie paled. How the hell did he know that?

"Yeh, I did that one," Lennie mumbled.

"Prove it," Vannella growled. "Where?"

"In the light above the sink."

"That's where they found it." Vannella said. "Go on."

"I put the one in the steering wheel. Those were my two," Lennie said. "Butch put one in the big dog's collar."

Butch was about to protest that Lukas did that one, when he got a feeling that if he did, Maloney would hit Lennie again for lying. He decided to keep quiet.

"They found that one too," Vannella said. "Go on."

"Doyle put one in the bird above the baby's crib," Lennie said.

"You gave them that one," Vannella grumped.

Lennie saw Maloney about to strike.

"Butch's second one was the big one. It's in the rafters above where the kitchen table sits. It'll take out half the house. Stu put one in a suitcase. That's all I know."

Vannella turned to Butch. "Is he telling the truth?"

"I didn't know about the suitcase," Butch said. "But he showed me the one in the RV. He said they'd never find it. And they did. They got someone smart on their side. Stu and Doyle got this plan going to hold them up a couple more times."

"You put the one in the attic above the kitchen?"

"Yeh. That was scary. I thought it maybe would go off with me still there. Oh, and Lukas, he did stuff in the barn, but he wasn't scared. He told me they couldn't go off without her speaking. That don't make no sense to me. But that's what everyone said."

Vannella looked Lennie in the eye that wasn't puffed shut.

"I'm letting you go. You tell this Stu character to call in the location of all the bombs."

Lennie nodded.

"Aleta Praetzel and her family are special. They aren't to be harmed. You got that?"

Again Lennie nodded.

The two were taken back to their car just as the storm spread southward and rain began to pour down. Lennie directed Butch to the nearest supermarket and told him to get him a couple of steaks and a bottle of aspirin.

"You should maybe go to the hospital," Butch suggested.

"I need the steaks now, Butch."

"Okay. I'll get them, but then I take you a hospital."

"Yeh, Butch, sure." Lennie mumbled.

He could barely see out of one eye, but he could sense they were being followed.

He watched as a car parked half way across the empty lot. A man got out and went into the store after Butch.

Lennie was glad he hadn't told Butch what his plans were. When Butch came out, the man exited right after him.

"We got anything to drink?" Lennie asked as he tore the plastic packaging off the meat.

"You want I should get something?"

"Naw. There's a gas station up ahead. You can get me a bottle of water when you fill up."

"We got half a tank," Butch said.'

"Just do it," Lennie snapped, slapping a steak on each eye.

"That lip looks real bad," Butch observed.

After you fill up, head for Arborville. They got a Free Clinic that don't ask questions."

"That's over an hour away."

"Don't argue."

"You sure you don't want to stop somewhere closer?"

"You do like I say."

"When we gonna tell Stu what the man said?"

"We aren't going back."

"Where we gonna go?"

"Someplace far away where nobody can find us."

"Stu is gonna get more money from that Praetzel guy. We got a share coming."

"Not no more we ain't. When Stu finds out what we told Vannella, he'll kill us."

"We didn't tell that Vannella guy about all the bombs," Butch said.

"You did good, Butch," Lennie said. "But I ain't taking another beating."

"Yeh, okay. We'll go wherever you want soon as you get fixed up."

"That blue case," Lennie said. "You don't let anybody take it."

"What's in it?"

"That's not important," Lennie mumbled drowsily. "You make sure nothing happens to that case."

"Yeh, Lennie. Sure."

Butch drove in silence. Lennie had said he did a good not telling Vannella about more of the bombs. Lennie hadn't ever praised him like that before. It made him feel good.

Back at the dog show, the Groups had begun. The Illinois exhibitors were seated at ringside. They had a number of their friends in the Groups. The Working Dog Group was the first. Big dogs all of them. Chuck Rigden had kindly guided Paige into falling in behind him.

"Just do what I do," he said.

She nodded gratefully.

"My word!" Hawk breathed. "I thought Topper was big."

"He's only a pup, isn't he?" Claude chuckled.

"I think he's full grown." Hawk responded.

"You hope he's full grown."

"Isn't that what I said?"

"That's what you meant to say," Chuck finished. "Paige is doing a fine job."

Hawk settled down to watch his wife. She did look as if she belonged in the Group. She gaited Topper around behind the Saint Bernard and then stacked him quickly. Topper's tail was wagging gently, his eyes on Paige.

The judge walked down the line. He gave no indication that any dog had caught his eye.

The truth, however, was that Judge Jott had noticed the young girl on the Newf when the group circled the ring. The Newf was keeping up with the Saint who had made it to Best in Show the day before. He had also noticed one of Chuck's young female assistants on the Bullmastiff. The Boxer had a handler he owed. The Samoyed caught his eye as the group stopped and stacked their dogs.

Jott's walk was almost perfunctory. He had selected his five finalists on the first go-around. As he walked the line, he added the Great Dane and the Mastiff. He kept them both after the individual examination.

Chuck's Saint impressed him. Jott understood why he's won the day before. Mentally, he put him at the top of the list.

Paige smiled at him as she presented her dog. The dog's tail wagged gracefully as Jott studied him. The first word that came to mind was 'nice'. He took time going over the young Newf. Judge Roberts had been impressed with him. Jott had laughed at the story and thus remembered that this dog was worth a good look. The Newf was young but nearly full-grown. He was heavily boned and his coat was thick and full with a decent undercoat considering it was the end of summer. He liked the feel of him. He was as good as the Saint already.

When Paige moved him, Jott noticed the forelegs and hind legs moved straight forward. He'd noticed the reach when the dog had circled. This was a good mover. He moved him up next to the Saint in his mind.

He watched Paige circle to the end of the line and stop with the dog in profile. That reminded him that the Newf had a good topline and carried his head high.

Smart handling, he thought. She's a winner too.

After he finished the individual exams, he pulled the out the Dane, the Mastiff, the Saint, the Newf, the Boxer and the Sammie. He had the six circle the ring. He noticed the young girl hesitated before following the Saint, widening the gap between them. Her Newf caught up by the time she'd completed her circle. She had adjusted so as not to run up on the back of the Saint.

He reassembled his line putting the Newfoundland first, the Saint second, the Sammie third and the Mastiff fourth.

The crowd was quiet. Jott knew he could switch the young girl on the Newf with the Saint being handled by Chuck Rigden. Paige smiled at Topper and the tail wagged faster.

"One!" Jott said, pointing at the Newfoundland.

The crowd went wild.

Two hours later, seven dogs and their handlers lined up for Best in Show. Paige looked around at her competition and Lyle West could tell she was terrified.

Lyle told her to get in line behind him and do what he did. Relief flooded her face.

"Just give me a bit of room," he whispered.

She nodded gratefully.

Lyle moved behind the Poodle and Paige slipped in behind him, inserting herself in front of a Belgian Tervuren whose handler objected. Lyle scowled at him and he backed off grumbling.

Judge Jacobus Ferre had the group circle as they entered. Paige hesitated as Lyle had asked her to do.

The Terv handler behind her growled, "Go on, Girlie."

Paige turned and scowled as she'd seen Lyle do.
That's when she saw him tighten his lead. He meant to go
around her. Her reaction was immediate. Paige took off.
Judge Ferre who had been watching Lyle caught two dogs
starting off together. He knew the Newf was next. He had
wondered why the Lab handler chose to precede the larger
dog.

The Terv handler took the line closest to the judge
blocking the judge's view of the young girl on the Newf.
Paige circled wide behind the Terv. Her Newf outdistanced
the Terv. Paige pulled up behind the Lab first. The Terv
handler crowded in behind her leaving her too little room to
properly stack her dog.

Even though Judge Ferre turned back to watch the
smaller dogs, he kept and eye on the young girl. He saw the
Lab handler move the girl into his place in line. He took the
position behind her. The Terv handler backed up.

Interesting, Judge Ferre mused.

Ferre began the individual examinations. He spent
time going over the Newf. He couldn't remember when he'd
seen a puppy from one of the larger breeds in the Best in
Show ring. He'd seen some fast-maturing small dogs in the
final competition, but the big guys took longer to develop.
This one already had substance and bone. The problem with
a big dog developing fast was that he often wound up
overdone. Still as a judge, his responsibility was to judge the
dog on the day presented which is evidently what Judge Jott
had done.

When Judge Ferre moved the Newf, he saw what Jott
had seen. This pup was a true mover. The young woman
had her hands on an exceptional young Newfoundland.

He watched the Newfoundland finish the circle and
come to a halt behind the Poodle. The young handler drew
him into a perfect stack.

Ferre turned back to judge the Lab. He was taken with
the beauty of the black dog. Even inside the huge building,

this dog, bred for the ruggedness of the untamed lakes where ducks flocked to nest, looked good. He was well muscled with a firmness that bespoke of continual conditioning.

"Who hunts over him? Ferre asked.

"I do." Lyle said simply.

"He work well?"

"He brings in all I shoot."

"Miss many?"

"I don't dare. He counts shots."

Morgan cocked his head and his brows did a dance during what he considered an obvious inquisition.

The judge chuckled. "I see what you mean."

"He has rules for every activity," Lyle commented.

"Down and back."

Judge Ferre was pleased to see how clean the Lab's movement was. When Lyle pulled up, Morgan was in a perfect stack.

Two other dogs were outstanding. Chuck Rigden had a Westie and Tom Wilson had a Dachshund and both were top handlers. Judge Ferre had four worthy dogs to choose from. He eliminated the Newf. He was simply too young. That left the Lab and the two little ones.

He stepped back and looked at the line. Suddenly, he remembered what the Lab handler had said about his dog knowing the rules. And he remembered the Lab handler had broken a rule by switching places with the young girl.

He went to the table and marked his winner and picked up the large red, white and blue rosette… He walked to the center of the ring.

He turned and said, "The Lab."

Paige threw her arms around Lyle and kissed him.

"I'm so glad!"

Flustered, he accepted the congratulations of the other handlers in a perfunctory manner until Tom and Chuck approached and teased him.

"If I'd known I'd get a kiss, I would have tried harder, "Chuck Rigden quipped.

"I don't think he's fully recovered," Tom said and he's worrying about it.

"I can see that," Chuck retorted. "Do you think he knows he's won more that a kiss?"

Lyle grinned suddenly. "Oh, believe me, I know. I beat you two reprobates!"

"That you did," Tom said. "It's getting to be a habit."

CHAPTER 23

Later, Chief West told the small circle of people involved in the bomb threat that Peter French had called and told him that both Butch Lennert and Lennie Archer were in custody.

"I don't want this to go any further, but it appears, Stanley, that Lennie threatened a fence with your gun. A couple of Vannella's men intervened, took the gun and the emerald necklace, and worked over Butch and Lennie. Lennie got the worst of it. The two gave up the location of some of the bombs."

"Only some?" Stanley asked.

"It seems that five men planted them," Lyle said. "Butch says he doesn't know where they all are. French thinks he's lying, but he's clammed up, saying he won't say anything more until Lennie is okay again. Lennie is in surgery right now. Hematoma. Taekman is doing him."

"So all Butch gave us were what he told Vannella?" Hawk asked.

"That's about it. Lennie was clever when talking to Vannella. He mostly gave up the ones we know about already—the car, the bird, and the dog collar. He did say there was one in a suitcase, so, Hawk, your guess is confirmed. He also said that there was one in the rafters above the kitchen and two in the barn."

Hawk turned to Aleta and Stanley.

"How do you feel about cheesy walls?"

Aleta nodded, chuckling.

The next day Paige and Hawk pulled into the Praetzel drive a few minutes after twelve. Bertha met them at the door.

"I thought you might like lunch outside because once Topper comes in, you'll wind up working," she said. "I'll walk him around while you wash up. Your lunch is on the counter. Just bring it out."

When they were alone, Hawk hissed at Paige, "Why is it you had me wear jeans?"

"So you wouldn't tear your good pants crawling around in the attic and barn."

"I do this kind of stuff all the time."

"No you don't. You kneel over corpses and take fingerprints and think."

"Who told you that?"

"Natsumi."

"I do more."

"Well today you will do more in jeans," she finished.

A few minutes later, carrying their plates out to the picnic table, Hawk worried about whether Topper was ready.

"He had a good lesson last night," Paige said. "And it was inside the house."

"The barn is the big problem. I don't know where to begin."

"We could start there," Paige said. "Has he ever seen a horse?"

"He is a horse," Hawk quipped. "I was told he's going to get bigger."

"You're the one who wanted a big dog," Paige reminded him. "Besides I feel safe with him around.

Hawk spotted the lines of worry crinkling Paige's brow.

He took her hand.

"Paige, I love him too."

"He's a quick learner. We can teach him things."

"You mean like not to whine when we lock him out of the bedroom."

"Evelyn says they play music. Topaz whines too."

"You asked?"

"She guessed," Paige replied. "She said Harriet suggested it. Stoney whines too."

"And their dogs stopped whining?"

"I don't think so."

Hawk leaned over and kissed his wife on the cheek.

"If Harriet can't train Stoney not to do it, then I don't expect us to train Topper not to. And I don't know that I want to. It's his way of saying he wants to be with us. That's not a bad thing."

Paige brightened.

"I do so want to please you."

"Paige, everything you do pleases me." Hawk said. "Even making me wear jeans."

"Really."

"Look at where we are," Hawk said. "We're dressed properly for being on a farm."

Bertha approached the pair with Topper.

"Your dog got excited with the smells in the barn. Now that the blacksmith is done, all the horses have been put in the pasture, so the barn is empty."

"We thought we'd start there," Hawk said.

Bertha nodded.

"The girls will be here after school and they'll want to saddle their horses."

"We'd better start. Come on, Paige."

"Let me take the dishes back to the house," Paige said.

"That's my job, Mrs. Monroe," Bertha said politely.

"Thank you for a lovely lunch," Paige responded warmly.

Hubbs greeted them as they approached the barn.

"Kin I watch?" he asked.

"Sure," Hawk said. "We'll all stand out here and let Topper tell us where to look."

"He knows?" Hubbs asked.

"He did last night," Hawk said, stopping at the entrance. "Send him, Paige."

"Go find it," Paige ordered.

Topper took off and went straight to a beam and raced around it and then tried to climb it. Finally he sat down staring at the rafters above.

"There ain't nothing on that there beam," Hubbs said.

"Is there a way to get to the rafters?"

"There's a ladder, but I don't think he can climb it."

Hawk told Paige to reward Topper and stay with him.

"Tell me when I'm at the spot Topper's nose is pointing at."

He found the bomb in five minutes. When he came down the ladder holding it, Hubbs jaw dropped.

"Them bombs is big outfits, huh?"

"This one is," Hawk said. "It would have taken out the whole barn."

"Will her go off?"

"Shouldn't," Hawk said. "But I'm going to remove the trigger."

"Guess you thought I was foolish sending that bridle to you," Hubbs remarked. "Ain't no way one of these could've fit on it without me seeing it."

Hawk was concentrating too hard on his task to note what Hubbs was saying. Paige, however, heard the old man worry about being foolish.

"Not so foolish, Hubbs," she responded. "We found a small one of these in Tank's collar when we were at the show."

"In his collar?"

"Under the buckle," Paige went on. "It would have killed him and whoever was standing next to him. C-4 is powerful stuff."

"In a dog's collar," Hubbs ruminated. "Don't that beat all."

"It's defused," Hawk announced. "Paige, see if he can find another."

Paige sent the dog several times. Each time he came back and sat in front of the dismantled bomb. Finally, he laid in front of her and whined.

"You're mixing him up," the ancient horseman remarked. "He's done his job. He don't understand."

Paige looked at her dog. His eyes were sad.

She bent down and patted him and said, "You're such a good dog."

He sat up and wagged his tail.

"Maybe we should try again later," Paige suggested. "After you clear this stuff out of the barn."

"We could give him a shot at the house," Hawk said. "At least I already know where one is there."

"Why are you so sure there is one more of them out here?" Hubbs asked.

"It's a matter of numbers," Paige said. "Five men did the planting and each planted more than one."

When they got to the front door, Paige unclipped Topper's leash and said, "Go find."

Topper immediately pawed at the standing coat rack and toppled it over. It fell with a crash that brought Bertha running from the kitchen.

Topper grabbed it in the center of its long post, and, holding it in his mouth, sat in front of Paige, tail wagging.

"You don't suppose?" Paige queried."

Hawk removed the rack from the dog's mouth and examined it.

Paige absently patted him. Topper could sense her worry. He leaned against her and nudged her arm. She crouched down and hugged him.

"You are a good boy," she said, giving him a biscuit.

He sensed her misgivings. Still he took the biscuit.

He took her arm and pulled on it. She followed him into the kitchen. He let go and put both paws on the kitchen table and looked upward.

"Hawk," Paige said. "Look at Topper."

Hawk looked up.

Topper scrambled from the chair onto the large oak table. He sat in the center as if trying to figure out how to reach the light that swung above his head.

"He found it!" Hawk exclaimed. "Reward him, Paige."

He set the coat rack back where it belonged and asked Bertha if there was an access to the space above the ceiling. She showed him the pull down staircase in the laundry room and handed him a flashlight.

Ten minutes later he brought down the bomb.

Paul emerged from the family room to stare at it. He had the same question Hubbs had.

"Is it safe?"

Paige quickly set two chairs next to the table. Topper saw them and hopped onto then and then to the floor.

Hawk set the bomb on the table and was working on dismantling it when the noise of a crash startled all those intent on what Hawk was doing. They turned to see Topper carrying the hall tree toward them.

Paige rushed toward him and praised him enthusiastically.

"I looked at it," Hawk said, refusing to take his eyes of the task of dismantling the ceiling bomb.

"Look again," Paige insisted.

"Put it back," Hawk ordered.

Reluctantly, Paige took the coat tree and set it by the front door. Topper followed her tail wagging. That was the way the game was played at the house the previous night.

"Come on, Topper," she said cheerfully. "Let's look in the bedroom."

He trotted after her and she waited until she was in the bedroom before she issued the order to find it. Topper went straight toward the smell that brought rewards. He jumped up on the bed and pawed at the wall above the headboard.

"We found another one!" Paige shouted excitedly, rushing over and praising Topper. She fed him a biscuit and hugged him.

Topper was no longer confused. He wagged his tail and licked her face.

Hawk came in.

"Where?" he asked.

"Where the paw marks are on the wall," Paige told him.

"Take him for a walk," Hawk said. "I don't want him attacking the hall tree again."

"Should I take him to the barn?"

Hawk dismissed her, saying, "Fine. Whatever."

"Come on, Topper. When he gets engrossed, he doesn't know we're here."

When she left the bedroom, Hawk was moving the bed away from the wall. As she walked across the living room, on a whim, Paige whispered, "Go find it."

Topper headed straight for the hall tree. He pushed it with his paw, only this time Paige was there to catch it. She gave him a biscuit and told him he was a good boy. She put the tree back and took Topper for his walk.

"Come back for another go?" Hubbs asked.

"He found three in the house," Paige said happily, and then sobered. "Only Hawk says that one isn't a find."

"How come?"

"It's the coat rack in the hall," Paige said. "Topper brought it to us first thing. Hawk couldn't find anything so I think he thinks Topper was still confused."

"Could be."

"But then Topper found the one in the ceiling in the kitchen and then he brought me the coat rack again."

"Maybe he just likes it because he can carry it."

"Topper doesn't carry sticks and stuff," Paige said.

Hubbs picked up a short rake.

"Try this."

Paige put it in Topper's mouth and Topper spat it out. She tried with several other items. Topper shoved them all out of his mouth.

"Guess he don't fetch," Hubbs said.

"Not sticks anyway," Paige said. "He'll fetch people out of the water."

"Do he now?"

"That's how we played with him when we went swimming in the big lake up at the lodge," Paige said. "We had such a good vacation."

"Mister seems a bit out of sorts."

"He is so worried about not being able to find all the bombs," Paige said.

"How many did he find?"

"The dogs found most," Paige said. "But he was the first one to pay attention to them. That's why I can't understand the coat rack. He believed Topper when he dragged over my suitcase."

"That's weird. In your suitcase?"

"It was Aleta's suitcase. I was borrowing it," Paige said. "Anyway, I don't understand why he doesn't believe Topper all the time."

"He said he knew where one was," Hubbs said.

"They caught a couple of the men. One said there was one above the kitchen light."

"Expecting sometimes blinds people."

"You mean he was so set on Topper finding the one in the kitchen that he couldn't consider one anywhere else? But that's not true. He did examine he coat rack."

"Maybe it's hid good,"

"He told me he had to examine the car several times before he found that one," Paige reflected.

"S'cuse me Miss," Hubbs said. "You just let that dog hunt the barn. I'll be back."

"Sure. Okay," Paige said.

As Hubbs hurried away, Paige unclipped Toppers leash and said, "Topper, go find it."

Topper poked his nose in every stall and roamed around the entire barn. He sniffed under the door to Hubbs' room and then came back to Paige, head hanging, tail drooping.

She knelt down and stroked the fur on Topper's neck.

"You're a good boy," she said. "You can't find what's not there."

She clipped his leash on and walked over to the fence, leaned on it and gazed at the horses in the pasture.

"Those are horses, Topper. That's what Hawk said you are going to grow as big as. But you aren't, are you? But you can grow. He says he loves you. And I'll love you no matter what."

Hubbs voice came from behind.

"Okay, Miss, send him into the barn now."

"He's already looked," Paige said.

"I planted something."

Paige turned and walked Topper back.

"Go find it," she said, a bit hesitantly.

Topper took off. His nose took him straight to the rear of the barn. He dug under a pile of straw and emerged carrying the coat rack.

"Topper!" Paige squealed with delight. "You wonderful dog! I believe you!"

She took the rack from his mouth, set it down and hugged her dog.

As she set it down, Hubbs studied it.

"What's that doing there?"

Paige looked at the coat rack.

"What?'

"That top. Nobody put a brass top on one of these back then."

He shook his head. "Everybody always gotta fancy stuff up nowadays."

"That top's not original?" Paige asked.

"Nope."

"Oh, Hubbs, thank you." Paige gushed. "Come on, Topper, let's go tell Hawk."

She trotted off toward the house with Topper trotting happily beside her.

She burst into the house and yelled, "Hawk, where are you?"

"I'm here, Paige. We've got number eight," Hawk shouted from the bedroom.

Paige and Topper appeared in the doorway.

"So there was one in the wall?"

Hawk smiled at her from the floor.

"Yes, there was."

She held out the coat rack.

"Here's number nine. I had Topper hunt all over the barn and he came up empty and then Hubbs hid this under some straw and he found it right off."

"He likes it," Hawk said, brushing her off.

"Ohhh! Sometimes you can be so obstinate!" Paige snapped. "It's the top, Hawk. Hubbs says it doesn't belong."

Hawk unfolded his long legs and rose slowly. Paige handed the rack to him. He sat on the edge of the bed and looked at the top.

"It's screwed on," he noted churlishly. "Nobody screws a bomb on top of a coat rack. That's ludicrous."

"You just don't trust Topper," Paige charged, her voice cracking slightly.

Hawk sighed.

"Get me a screwdriver."

Paige ran into the kitchen asking Bertha for a screwdriver.

While she was doing that, Hawk scolded Topper, "You see what you've done. She can't think straight. I meant for her to get me one from my case by the door."

Topper hung his head.

"You just better be right," Hawk grumbled.

The tip of Topper's tail wagged hopefully.

Hawk softened.

"Come here, you big mutt. It's okay. I don't think I gave you proper credit for finding the one in this wall. That was a big find. We never would have looked there."

Paige reappeared with several screwdrivers.

"Bertha wanted to know what size and what kind."

Hawk picked one, unscrewed the screws and removed the top. He turned it over so Paige could see. Inside was what even she recognized as a miniature bomb.

"Number nine," he announced officially.

"Good boy, Topper," Paige said. "You were persistent. I'm so proud of you."

While Hawk dismantled the bomb, Paige returned the screwdrivers and told Bertha that they now had found nine."

"One was in the coat rack?" Bertha asked.

"False top," Paige said and then added, "We found one in the suitcase Aleta loaned me. Did anything else go out of the house after the bombs were planted?"

After a brief pause, Bertha said, "Harriet came over and got Auggie."

"We tested his collar and Scooby's," Paige said.

"Stanley gave Chief Milani a bridle to give Hawk to test but that was last week," Bertha recalled, her brow furrowed in concentration.

"Oh, yes. Aleta's assistant was here. He left with a briefcase. Jamara took the baby's diaper bag home with her. That's all I remember."

"The briefcase and diaper bag are real possibilities," Paige said. "I'll tell Hawk after we finish here. He doesn't like me to rush ahead of him."

"Typical man," Bertha commented.

There were in the guest room when Chief Milani arrived.

"How many?" Milani asked.

"Total of nine so far," Hawk replied. "Three to go."

"Any my men should have nailed?"

"Maybe the suitcase unless Harriet picked it up before your men started their search."

"I'll check on that one," Milani said gruffly.

"I expected to find one in the study," Hawk went on. "But I didn't. Paige was told that Aleta's assistant took a briefcase out of here."

"We checked out all the briefcases," Milani said. "There was an edge in his tone."

"I thought I'd take Topper to their office," Hawk said calmly. "His nose finds things our eyes can't."

"A waste of time," Milani commented dourly.

Tom wasn't happy his men had missed so many. Until now he had believed that there weren't any more. It upset him to be so wrong, especially as he had been so vocal."

"I'm going over there," Hawk declared. "I think some bombs were carried off the property."

"Suit yourself," Milani grumped. "Personally, I think they fudged on the number."

"I disagree," Hawk said evenly.

Half and hour after that conversation, Topper found the briefcase that had traveled from the house to the office.

Hawk called Tom with the news.

"I knew there had to be one in the study," Hawk said. "Paige and I have a couple more leads to follow."

"I called Lyle," Tom reported. "Everyone is impressed."

"I'll call if I find anymore," Hawk promised.

"That call wasn't made that night or the next. The well had run dry.

CHAPTER 24

On Wednesday, Stanley and Aleta returned to their home, bringing Harriet's two female Chessies with them. Tank and Scooby thought Keeper was very attractive, but she soon let them know she was in no mood for any tomfoolery. Keeper took up residence in the family room with Paul and Tank learned he had been replaced.

That evening to Aleta's surprise, Stanley pulled out the silk scarf and covered her eyes.

"I remember you telling me that it felt good to wake up and be able to see again. It helped you adjust to not being able to speak," he explained.

She tapped his chest. It was true.

Once she was blindfolded and settled into his arms, he began to read to her. She hadn't seen him put the book on the table by the couch. Had she noticed it, she would not have been surprised.

He'd been reading scarcely twenty minutes when the phone rang. He kept on reading, letting the answering machine screen the call.

She put her hand on his and pointed to the phone. He set the book in her lap and placed her hand on the open page.

"Be my bookmark," he said and then was gone.

He lowered the volume and heard the voice he was hoping he'd never hear again. It told him to pick up when he called in ten minutes. He spent a few minutes attaching the tape recorder and then returned to the couch where Aleta sat unmoving.

"It wasn't your mother," he said.

He saw her relax slightly, so he went on. "It was our bomber. He wants more money."

"Why not?" he asked as if Aleta had told him no."

Quickly he withdrew the query and said he'd give her what reasons he could think up and hoped they were hers.

She nodded. She could tell by his voice he was standing in front of the fireplace facing her.

"He could give us one we already have."

She nodded.

"He might ask for an outrageous amount of money."

She nodded again.

"He could lie."

She nodded and spread her hands apart, thus telling him to expand on that.

"Lie and then demand I bet on his telling the truth the next time?"

She nodded vigorously.

"I could be hurt in the delivery."

She nodded.

"You are willing to wait for Hawk."

She nodded. Then she held up her fingers, first two, then three, then four. She shrugged.

"We don't believe there are more?"

She wiggled her hand.

"We want proof there are more?" Stanley asked. "We want a free one."

She nodded.

"He won't do it," Stanley said. "But I'll put him on speaker when he calls back. I will let you guide me. I want you to know that I will pay anything you agree to."

She smiled.

"Do you want the scarf removed?"

She shook her head. She held up her finger.

"One more thing?" he asked and received an affirmation.

She held up two fingers, then four.

Stanley thought for a minute.

"He may only know about the two he knows we found or he may know about those two and the four Lennie and Butch gave up to Vannella and to the police, but not about all those Hawk found using the dogs."

Aleta nodded, and then made a face.

And that would infuriate him."

She nodded.

I'll keep that in mind. Let's move you where you can hear."

The phone rang as they were walking toward the kitchen. Aleta released her hold on Stanley and he hurried to answer it.

Marian's strident voice shouted, "Let me talk to that nig. . ."

Stanley cut her off in the middle of the word.

He went to his wife and led her to a chair.

"We must answer. You know that, don't you?"

Aleta nodded.

The phone rang again. Stanley picked it up at once.

Marian's bitterness coated her first words.

"You goddamn. . ."

Again Stanley hung up.

The third time the voice was that of Stuart Fouts.

"Why was your line busy?" he demanded.

"I was called," Stanley said. "What do you want?"

"It ain't what I want. It's what you want. I'm willing to sell you the location of another bomb."

"We were told there were two in the barn. I'll pay only for those two," Stanley said.

"Two will cost you double," Stuart Fouts said.

"It has to be tonight. Right now. One hundred thousand. You and me."

"I'm listening."

"You know where the entrance to the Preserve is?"

"Yes."

"A horse trail leads to it from my back gate. I'll come on horseback. I need five minutes to saddle up and ten minutes to reach that spot. You meet me there in fifteen minutes and you'll be one hundred thousand dollars richer."

Stanley then hung up. He grabbed Aleta by the hand and pulled her into the bedroom. He opened his cell.

"Hubbs, I'm going out on Minx. Get her ready."

He ripped off Aleta's blindfold.

"Get one hundred thousand dollars from the safe. Put it in an envelope while I change pants.

Aleta smiled as she twisted the dial. Only her husband would change before making a mad dash to deliver ransom money. She took out ten marked packets and ran to the study for a large brown envelope. The dogs followed her. She shut Tank and Scooby in the nursery. Keeper she put in Paul's studio.

She met Stanley at the front door.

"I'll be careful," he said. "I'm counting on the fact that this is too fast for them to plan anything. You stay here and take care of Gerard."

He flew out the door without waiting for an answer.

Aleta went to the gun cabinet and opened it. She took out a rifle and loaded it. Then she fastened the strap on the gun and slung it across her back.

When she got to the barn, Hubbs was half way to the gate that Stanley had opened. Hubbs planned to close it.

Quickly Aleta opened Shadow's stall, slipped the bridle over his head and led him over to a bale of hay. She hopped up on the bale and from there onto his back. She'd ridden bareback frequently as a teenager. If she didn't have to jump, she'd be all right.

She cantered the horse to the gate and Hubbs heard her and held it open. He saw the rifle on her back.

Something was amiss. He pulled out his cell phone and called Chief Milani. He had a direct line.

"He's gonna meet with the bomber guy," Hubbs said.

"Where? Who?"

"He's on his horse. Don't go spooking the horses with sirens and lights. You hear me. Aleta, she's bareback. She's got her rifle."

"Where is he going?"

"They took the trail to the Preserves."

"When did they leave?"

"Called you soon as Mrs. Praetzel went past."

"They aren't together?"

"He doesn't know she's there."

"Thanks, Hubbs."

Milani called his dispatcher and started setting up roadblocks.

Stanley meanwhile had urged Minx into a trot. As the trail was familiar, he felt safe given the brightness of the moon in the cloudless sky.

Behind him Aleta was catching up. Shadow was faster than Minx. She stopped Shadow short of the rendezvous point and walked him off the path behind a hillock. She wrapped Shadow's reins around a small tree and climbed up to the top of the small hill.

She flattened herself before the crest of the rise and crept the rest of the way.

She slid her rifle off her back quickly. The meeting was already taking place. She positioned her gun, sighted down the barrel and zeroed in on the driver of the car as Stanley approached him.

The car door opened and the driver emerged. Stanley and he exchanged envelopes.

Suddenly a second man emerged from the car. The driver grabbed Minx's reins. Aleta's bullet hit the hand gripping the reins.

The crack of the rifle reverberated in the stillness of the night. Behind her, Shadow snorted and reared, yanking his reins. The tree was yanked from the ground when Shadow turned and raced back to the safety of the barn.

Alerted to her presence, the two men turned toward her.

The driver immediately sought shelter in the car, gripping his bleeding hand as he squeezed his fat body behind the wheel.

The second man pointed his gun at Stanley.

"You drop your gun or he dies," he shouted.

The man was huge and his voice roared across the space between them. A third man emerged from the back of the car and pointed his gun in Aleta's direction. If she fired at the man holding the gun pointed at Stanley, the man behind the car would take her down.

Then she heard Stanley say, "That officer is the best marksman on the Arborville force. Which of you wants to die. Cops don't put down their guns. Why not just drive off with the money?"

She saw the third man duck back inside the car.

"He comes with us," the big man shouted, his gun pointing at Stanley.

Suddenly a gun was fired from inside the car. The bullet skimmed across Minx's rear and whizzed past Aleta's ear. She felt a slight sting as it burned the top of her ear. Her reflexes were as fast as the horse's.

Minx reared. Aleta squeezed the trigger.

The bullet hit the big man in the left temple. He dropped instantly. His falling body brushed the mare's rear leg as she dropped back to the ground.

Minx leaped forward and raced down the road. Stanley leaned forward and urged his horse to run.

The car took off after the man and the horse.

He's leading them away from me, Aleta thought. She watched the man on the road for any signs of movement. She didn't dare approach him.

Headlights caught his body in their beam in time for the car to stop. It was a county sheriff's car running without a siren or flashing lights. That frightened her. She stayed hidden.

As she lay in the grass, peering through the sparse blades, she thought about her predicament. She had no way to communicate. She couldn't talk, sign or write. She had been in similar situations before. They had always turned out badly.

She decided to wait it out. If no one found her, she'd go home and turn herself in.

She heard the deputy on the radio.

"Dead," he was saying. "Shot in the temple. It looks like the shot came from the Forest Preserves. I'm not going in there in the dark alone. Send back-up."

Aleta was shocked. How could he be facing so it would look like the shooter was in the forest? Did she miss? Did the man in the car shoot him? No, that couldn't be. That man shot at her. Her ear confirmed that.

She closed her eyes and saw Minx rear as the man went down. The horse must have spun him around.

A second car joined the first. This one had flashing lights.

She scrunched down as far as she could and still see.

Another deputy got out. He swung his flashlight in a circular motion. Aleta withdrew her head completely.

She heard the newest officer announce that they were going into the woods.

That's a foolish move, she thought

Then she heard him report on the radio.

"There were two shots. There's only one body with only one bullet in it. The other shooter could be wounded."

She thought about getting up, but realized they might shoot her accidentally. She couldn't explain.

As soon as they entered the woods, she scrambled backward down the small hill and ran back toward home and safety. She was met halfway by Hubbs who was leading Shadow. She hugged him. Then she climbed on a nearby rock and mounted her horse.

"I kin walk," Hubbs said when she offered to share the ride. "You got a baby what needs you."

Aleta rode home. Hubbs would be all right. It was Stanley she was worried about.

She heard Gerard fussing when she entered the house. She put her rifle in the cabinet, took the empty shells from her pocket and put them in the ammunition drawer and then locked the cabinet.

Ten minutes later she was sitting in the new recliner with her freshly diapered baby in her lap sucking on a warm bottle of breast milk. She was staring out the picture window through which she hoped to get the first glimpse of Stanley returning astride Minx.

She didn't realize she had fallen asleep until Stanley lifted Gerard from her arms and said, "Your mother did it again, didn't she? She always falls asleep feeding you."

He kissed her before she could utter a word.

When he finished, he said, "I understand you've been lying on hillsides shooting people."

She hugged him.

"Thank you," he said.

She pointed at the phone.

"I told Tom that we'd be there first thing in the morning and you'd make a statement. I have a surprise for him."

She raised one brow questioningly.

"Don't worry. I was there. I know what happened."

She nodded.

They fell asleep in each other's arms. Stanley was simultaneously grateful that Aleta had successfully prevented his being kidnapped but angry because she had followed him in the first place. Aleta was grateful that Stanley had survived but angry over his having concocted such a foolhardy scheme in the first place.

Their emotions were too mixed to even communicate. Both were exhausted from the ordeal. Sleep was the most reasonable course of action. But their overwhelming relief that they were both safe pulled them into an embrace that lasted the whole night.

The following morning, Stanley called his secretary and told her that Aleta and he had an eight o'clock appointment with Chief Milani. They would be in as soon as they were done.

When Chief Lyle West entered Willow Glen Police Chief Tom Milani's office, he knew at once that he had been called because each of the three men already sitting in that office had a beef.

Since it was Chief Milani's office, Lyle nodded at Tom to begin.

"You made Stanley and Aleta deputies and they took matters into their own hands and a man is dead."

Stanley dove into the fray.

"I could have followed procedure—as a matter of fact, I did follow procedure and I trusted the Willow Glen Chief of Police to do his job and he didn't, and it cost me one hundred thousand dollars to find out that he didn't."

Hawk plowed in. "I don't know what these two are talking about, but Chief Milani kept telling me there weren't any more bombs and he's sitting on one and he knows it. We are supposed to be cooperating here."

"Who died?" West asked calmly.

"Lukas Kvidahl," Milani answered.

"Who is he?" Hawk asked.

"One of the bombers," Chief West said. "Who shot him?"

"Aleta did," Chief Milani said.

"I assume she's here to give a statement," West said.

Aleta nodded.

"Let's delay all other matters until that's done."

Stanley and Hawk nodded.

Chief Tom Milani shoved a tape recorder toward Aleta.

Stanley said. "I'm going to make her statement verbally. I'll do it in simple sentences and we will either agree totally or we will scratch my last statement and redo it until we get it right."

"She can speak," Chief Milani said. "She's not going to be treated as if she can't."

"If she talks, someone could die," Stanley declared.

"Let's do it Stanley's way," Lyle decided.

 Stanley began.

"I heard a phone conversation between my husband and Stuart Fouts."

Aleta nodded.

Bit by bit, Stanley recounted the events of the prior evening and all went smoothly until he came to the shooting.

Chief Milani objected, "You're telling her what her motive was."

"I'll skip that part," Stanley said.

Frowning, Chief Milani signaled him to continue.

Stanley went on. "I saw the driver of the car take hold of Stanley's horse."

Aleta nodded.

"I shot him in the hand."

Aleta nodded.

Milani jumped in. "I want to know why. The man wasn't accosting your husband. He only grabbed the horse's reins and you shot him. Suppose he was just trying to steady the . . .what's that wave mean?"

"It means no," Stanley said.

"Tell her to shake her head," Milani barked.

"You tell her. She's not deaf," Stanley thundered.

"What's the finger mean?" Milani growled.

"It means she wants you to ask one question at a time. It has to be one that can be answered yes of no."

"Okay," Milani agreed. "Did the man assault your husband?"

Aleta shook her head.

"Did he threaten him verbally?"

Aleta shook her head.

"All he did was grab the reins?"

Aleta nodded.

"And you consider that a hostile act?" Milani asked, expecting a head shake.

Aleta nodded vigorously.

Stanley interjected, "To grab the reins of a horse being ridden is to take control away from the rider."

"How is that hostile?"

"To a horseman it is."

"Did either of you tell him to let go?" Milani asked.

"I didn't," Stanley said. "I was too surprised by his move. I had paid him. I didn't expect such an action."

"That's a little naïve for a so-called deputy," Milani scoffed.

"There's an old adage that one doesn't kill the goose that lays the golden egg," Stanley proclaimed. "I overlooked the possibility that one might kidnap the goose."

"That's why you needed to involve the police," Tom said.

To Tom's surprise, Aleta was nodding her head vigorously.

"That was a mistake," Stanley admitted. "Shall I go on?"

Chief Tom Milani nodded.

Stanley continued to verbalize Aleta's statement for her.

"I shot the hand of the man holding the reins and he got back into his car."

Aleta nodded.

"How come he was lying in the road dead shot in the head?" Milani charged.

"I shot the driver in the hand," Stanley said, still speaking for Aleta.

She nodded her agreement.

Stanley then chose to stop speaking for Aleta and to dictate his statement in which he detailed every action of every man and himself at the time of the shooting. Then he described the pursuit, which stopped when he turned Minx onto a trail too narrow for the car carrying the bombers to navigate.

Chief Milani gave the tape recording to the typist and turned to Stanley.

"So, did they give you what you paid for?"

"I think Hawk should be heard next," Stanley said. "I should have trusted him to complete the job assigned in a timely fashion. I was too impatient."

Hawk plunged right in. That he had held back was surprisingly uncharacteristic.

"Paige told me that Hubbs handed Mr. Praetzel a bridle that he said felt funny, and if what I just heard is correct, Stanley gave it to you with the request that I look at it and everyone assumed that you did. But you didn't. So where is it?"

"The bridle?" Tom asked. "Yeh, he gave it to me. He said Hubbs said it felt funny, but I looked at it. I'm sorry I didn't return it right away, but I got distracted and forgot about it."

"So where is it?" Hawk pressed. "In the evidence room?"

"No, I didn't log it in."

He opened the bottom right hand drawer of his desk and dug it out from under his package of cookies.

"Here it is, Aleta. Sorry I kept it so long."

Stanley snatched it from Tom's hand and slammed it on the desktop. He took an envelope from his pocket and handed it to Tom.

"These are the two places in the barn containing bombs with C-4 and triggers to set them off."

Tom opened the folded piece of paper and read, "Rafter above Shadow's stall and Shadow's bridle."

Tom held up the bridle.

"They're pulling your leg," he proclaimed. "This isn't big enough."

"It's bigger than Tank's collar," Hawk said taking it. "Thank you, Aleta for not blowing us all to kingdom come."

Hawk saw Aleta pale. It was then he realized that she hadn't known the bridle was in the office.

"Didn't you know about the bridle?" he asked and then added quickly, "Don't speak for God's sake and Paige's."

Aleta managed a wry smile with her headshake.

"I will be forever grateful that you didn't cave in today," Hawk said. "Now if you will all excuse me, I'll get this out of here. Please remember there is still one out there."

Having said that Hawk left immediately and headed for his lab.

"Number eleven," Stanley said. "Only one to go."

Aleta put a finger to her lips.

"Oh, yes," Stanley said. "If the two who are still at large don't know that we've found all but one, they won't plant more and they will still try to contact me."

"Surely they know better," Tom said cautiously.

"Greedy men are obsessive," Stanley argued. "They can't help themselves. They are going to come back. And I am going to tell you."

"I'm putting a couple men at your house," Milani decided. "And each of you gets a police guard. That was an attempted kidnapping. I think that's what they'll try again. They have a bait that tempts you to grab at it."

Stanley got up.

"Thanks, Tom. For what it's worth, I never dreamed a dog collar or a bridle would hold a bomb either."

Stanley and Aleta sat in the car for several minutes before Stanley turned the ignition key and the motor hummed alive.

"Talk to me," he urged her. "One pat on my leg for yes and two for no."

Aleta patted his leg once.

"Did I get too angry with Tom?"

Two pats told him Aleta didn't think so.

"It wasn't the hundred thousand, you know," he went on.

A single pat told him she understood.

Next time I'll follow through."

A double pat told him not to.

"Trust him?"

A single pat affirmed that choice.

"He thought his men should have found some on their own," Stanley went on. "What he doesn't realize is that Hawk didn't find any without either the help of the dogs or a hint from the bomb makers."

Aleta patted his leg three times.

"You just gave me a yes and a no," Stanley noted. "So now the guessing begins. Hawk had help."

Aleta patted his leg once.

"The dogs helped with some."

Another yes.

"Hints from the bomb makers?"

Two pats meant no.

"Not from bomb makers"

"A single pat told him yes."

He could see Aleta nodding vigorously out of the corner of his eye.

"Butch isn't a bomb maker."

A yes pat told him he had guessed right.

"Lennie isn't either." Stanley said and then added. And neither is the man you killed-- Lukas Kvidahl. He has a record of assaults, but no bomb making."

Aleta held up two fingers.

"Our bomb makers are still out there," Stanley concluded. "But Aleta, we have two men in jail who know what Doyle's name is and where the farm is. He and Stuart Fouts won't leave the area. I'm a goose that can be persuaded to lay golden eggs."

"One bomb left? Is that what worries you?"

A single pat told him yes.

"They don't know that," Stanley said. "And I will pay for information on others even if I get ones we have already discovered."

A double pat told him that she objected to that.

"Aleta, I won't run out of money," Stanley said. "Our only chance to catch them is if they stay in the area."

Her hand lay still.

"I don't like paying out so much money," Stanley told her. "I'm hoping that Stuart Fouts' greed will trip him up. But I promise you that I will never hand deliver another payment."

She squeezed his leg.

"We knew you were going to be in this state for a long time," Stanley said. "And I have more ideas that I'm working on. I know Lyle and Tom are giving this their full attention. I think Tom has a new appreciation for your staunchness in remaining silent."

Aleta squeezed his leg.

"We're going to make it, Aleta. And it's not going to be forever."

Aleta patted his leg three times.

"Peets has Butch in his jail," Stanley told her. "He's planning on training others in his method so he won't be the only interrogator the other chiefs call upon."

Three pats told him she wanted more information.

"Both Milani and French have to send him a trainee," Stanley said. "One gets Butch. The other one gets Lennie when he regains consciousness."

Aleta squeezed his leg.

That's their plan," Stanley said. "That's not my plan. And yes, I think they may not know where more bombs are, but they do know who Doyle is and where the group holes up between hits."

Stanley pulled into his parking space in the lot behind the office.

"Are you ready?" he asked. "We need you, you know. You read people better than anyone else in the office. And your idea of doing research on cases means you will have real input on the cases you accept."

Aleta's hand lay still.

"You don't think there will be any more lines of people waiting to hire us, do you?"

He felt the light pat.

"If we don't have a line, you win two extra consummations of our marriage vows and if I win, I get three extra consummations of our marriage vows."

Aleta was still laughing as they entered the lobby through the rear door and saw the line snaking down the stairs and out the front door,

The joy stayed in her eyes as the two of them entered the elevator, rode up one floor, and exited a few moments later to be greeted warmly by Stanley's secretary

"We're all set up for you, Mrs. Praetzel," Alice said. "I'm so glad you're here."

Those simple words made everything all right with Aleta. She was still wanted, needed and loved.

What more was there?

The Prophet Series